FRIGHT NIGHT

HELLBOUND

MICHAEL HARBRON

WITH

TOM HOLLAND

ABOUT THE AUTHOR

Michael Harbron is an American fiction writer who brings a unique, yet traditional approach to the horror and supernatural genres. His debut novel, "Interview with the Devil," exemplified the blurred lines between reality and the unimaginable. Harbron's storytelling resurrects dormant fears, proving that true horror lies not in what is seen, but in what is felt.

Tom Holland is an American filmmaker. He is best known for his work in the horror film genre, penning the 1983 sequel to the classic Alfred Hitchcock film Psycho, directing and co-writing the first entry in the long-running Child's Play franchise, and writing and directing the cult vampire film Fright Night.

FOREWORD

When I first wrote Fright Night back in the mid-eighties, I never imagined it would live this long. The film was meant to be a love letter to the monsters I grew up with — a story about what happens when the darkness of old horror creeps into the modern world.

Time has a way of reshaping legends, and it's rare to find someone who understands that balance — who can honor what came before while making it new again. Michael Harbron has done exactly that. He hasn't just revisited Fright Night; he's expanded it, weaving a mythology that feels both ancient and immediate. The vampires here aren't only predators — they're history, grief, and the reflection of everything we try to bury.

Working on this book, I recognized the world I created — but through a darker, more human lens.

I couldn't be prouder to see Jerry Dandrige and Billy Cole reborn in these pages, stalking new streets, haunting new souls. Every generation deserves its own monster, and every monster deserves a storyteller who treats them with awe and a little fear.

I'm ecstatic to herald Harbron as the writer and creative voice leading the next stories in this universe. He's taking the mythology forward in ways that are both bold and true to its roots.

Welcome back to Fright Night.

— Tom Holland

For Debbie and Josh

CONTENTS

PROLOGUE

The Vampire is no passing tale, no shadow born of superstition. It is an heir to mankind, a darker child of creation, drawn forth by the Devil himself.

Where man turns upon beast, the Vampire turns upon man. This is the order, a cycle sealed in blood. Humanity slaughters with appetite; the Vampire slaughters with necessity.

Yet the creature is not without remembrance. Within its hollow heart lingers the echo of breath, the sorrow of love, the weight of what it once was. It may walk among men with grace and humility, speaking as friend, as lover, as kin.

For a season it may seem human still. But the hunger is eternal. In time, all roads lead back to the darkness that sustains it.

The Vampire endures not as brute, nor sorcerer, but as a paradox: human and inhuman, bound by recollection, driven by thirst.

It is this duality that makes it the most perilous of myths, for within its struggle lies the reflection of our own.

CHAPTER I

SOMETHING EVIL

1950

The very air of New York City invited calamity just as much as it did culture.

Merely five years out of the war, the city simmered with jazz, rationed ambition, and the cracked dreams of returning soldiers who found their neighborhoods changed.

In Harlem, the aftershock of the Renaissance still echoed through smoky nightclubs and borrowed bedrooms, while the boroughs bristled under the weight of overcrowded buildings and the tightening noose of red-baiting politics.

While the newspapers splashed headlines about the Soviet menace and Senator McCarthy's crusade against imaginary communists, real violence still played out in the streets—quietly, but with consequence. Black men were still being arrested without cause and Puerto Rican families were arriving by the shipload only to be corralled into crumbling buildings and underpaid jobs.

Culture clashed with repression. The Village had its poets, young and drunk on existentialism and Dostoevsky. But uptown, the rhythm section hit harder where bebop roared, horns cried, and pedestrians cursed the traffic in their thick accent.

It was amidst the swelter of July, amidst all this violence and uproar, that the Moreno family came to New York from Puerto Rico. Maria could not walk properly still after the unbearable and quite consequential labor she'd gone through two weeks ago. Doctor Ortiz had told her that she might never walk as she once did; the injection in her spinal cord had been a botched job during a tropical storm that caused power outages every hour. Maria did not care about walking straight. She cared that her daughter, Lucia, was alive, well, and had her whole life ahead of her. A life that, unbeknownst to both mother and daughter, was going to emulate the city's pattern. Culture and calamity, hand in hand.

The polluted, smog-hued, orange sky with billowing fumes from building-tops and factories was not quite the backdrop that the Moreno family had expected, given that the tales told to them from mainland Americans had been only grandiose and nothing else. The tallest building in the world, the Empire State Building, the biggest park that you could ever imagine. Lakes in that park with geese swimming in them. Old money royalty walking their pedigree dogs on the sidewalks. Castles upon castles built by the sea, the Hudson idyllically swimming alongside the greatest city in the world.

This was not much better than the city they'd left behind. That was Maria Moreno's first thought as she saw a giant rat gnaw its way into a black garbage bag bulging out of a corrugated trash can.

"Mind your business!" the woman in her pink mini dress that only went past half her thighs yelled at the Morenos as they paid the cabbie and stood in front of a nondescript apartment building.

"Come along, Maricita," Walter Moreno, a stiff-mustached, tan-skinned man with drooping eyes and age lines marking the territories of his cheeks, said as he put his arm around his wife. In his hand, he held one of the few bags they'd brought with them, a bag containing some recently converted currency, dried herbs, two books, and a journal filled with stories that the Church refused to accept.

Maria looked up at her husband, her eyes squinting every time a loud noise issued in the background: a gunshot, a modified car's exhaust roaring as it drove by, the skittering of the rodents toppling over a trash can, the drunken couple's fighting devolving into fists and curse words. Her eyes filled with tears, a drop of which fell upon the forehead of her two-week-old daughter.

The husband hugged his wife firmly, planting a kiss on her temple, and giving her back the support she needed to walk up the dilapidated stairs, nudging her to watch out for the second step, where a brick was missing and the concrete was crumbling. Bracketing both sides of this brief stairway were wrought iron grills, and beyond the grills was a flowerbed with all its flowers wilted or dead, no shrubbery, and only the odd patch of grass. Walter couldn't help but grin, knowing that Maria, the moment she settled down in her new home, would remedy the barrenness in less than a heartbeat. Just as he, part-time mason that he was back in Puerto Rico, would make this place livable ever so slowly, beginning with the missing brick in the stairs.

"This is no place for a child to grow," Maria whispered as she studied the landing of the shoddy Brook Avenue building. Bulbs in dirty sconces buzzed and flickered, making the walk-up seem more ominous than it probably was. Once upon a time, someone had put up cheap wallpaper on the walls, dark green with golden flowers. The wallpaper had been ripped off in places, revealing red brick, and in the corners, where it was not peeled off, it was a deep black, indicating mold.

"And yet they grow," Walter commented, pointing his index finger upward. For a second, Maria stood still, looking at her baby, then looking up at the stairwell and focusing to hear the sound of dozens upon dozens of children speaking different languages, laughing, screaming, crying, their parents scolding them, lulling them, kissing them. She did not feel all that alone anymore. There were immigrants in this building. Yes, the building was weighed down by so many of them packed in it, but the building was also alive, its bent and warped stairwell looking like the spinal column of a sea beast.

As they climbed the creaking stairs, Maria and her husband were bombarded with a plethora of contrasting smells. Plantains, spices, rice, potatoes, dishes from their homeland, dishes from other homelands—their odors carried from underneath the spaces of doorways and, in some cases, ajar doors that allowed them a brief glimpse into the life of the Lithuanians, the Greeks, the Irish, the Indians, the Mexicans, the blacks.

"I hear the Indians like spices as much as we do," Maria chuckled, her nostrils assaulted by turmeric and cumin.

"We'll have to swap dishes and see for ourselves, *mi dulce esposa*,"

"*Ay, ay, ya basta, papacito.*"

"I still can't believe that I'm *papacito* in a real capacity."

"Don't worry. To Lucia, you'll always be Papa. Papacito you are for me only."

"*Mi amor.*" Walter kissed his wife on the lips this time, especially now that it felt earned. They were on the top floor of the six-story building now, and the air coming through the hallway's open window was somehow much cooler than it was down on the street. Less noise too, thank the gods.

Walter unlocked the door to their apartment, the two of them walking inside just as soon as Lucia woke up from her cab-induced nap and started to cry in her sweet, high-pitched voice.

Maria inserted a finger in the back of the diaper, pulled it, and peeked inside, grinning, saying, "*La princesita ya hizo su popi.*"

"Are you sure it's her and not the apartment that smells this way?"

"You ought to know, you got it for us."

"I got it because if you go to the roof, it's got a view of the city," Walter said. "And it was the only affordable two-bedroom thing available on short notice."

"I can see why," Maria said, studying the water damage on the yellow wallpaper. The water damage had dried quickly on account of the ample sunlight teeming in through the windows. The place was certainly cramped, with little room to move, especially after Walter had insisted on having his way and arranging the furniture a whole week before Maria had arrived. It was all in the right place—the sofa by the windows, the coffee table in front of the sofa, the old clunky TV placed on the shelf that joined the kitchen to the living room— and yet all of it was wrong. No energy flow. Maria would spend the next week and a half rearranging everything until it was all well. Until the spirits spoke.

In the kitchen, Maria was inspecting the cabinets, the small stove that stood ready to serve. She pulled open one of the boxes that were lined on the kitchen shelf, and took out her prized kettle, a cream-colored thing of beauty adorned with dandelions, the bottom of it burned from overuse. She washed it once with the tap water, and then filled it, knowing that for a travel-tired man and wife, strong tea was the first order of business.

Walter sat carefully in the living room, holding his daughter like the fragile thing she was. She squirmed in his arms, making her displeasure known at the presence of poop in her diaper.

"Why don't you change her for a change?"

"Me?" Walter asked, his eyes widening, losing all their droopiness.

"You're only her father, after all."

Before they could discuss the matter further, a closet slammed shut in one of the two bedrooms, alerting

Walter so suddenly that he stood up, nearly losing his daughter.

Maria poked her head out of the kitchen, her senses assessing what had just happened.

"Probably just the wind," Walter said, putting his daughter in the crib. The crib was placed right by the sofa, making it very difficult to cross over to the other side where the bathroom was. Lucia cooed as she felt the familiar comfort of the crib's mattress against her back. Walter proceeded to walk into the room from where the noise had issued.

Strange. He didn't recall leaving the window open. There was no fire escape out this window, so it didn't make much sense that someone would pry it open from the outside. Outside the window was a drop all the way down to the sidewalk.

Another gust of wind blew, and the bang followed soon after.

The closet door swung open and clanged shut. And then swung open again.

"*Ay, Dios mio*," Walter sighed and then walked over to the empty closet, peering inside out of habit. There was nothing but darkness within, and a dead smell, as if a small animal had curled up and croaked. He pushed the closet door shut and then went to the window, pulling it down too.

Behind him, the closet door creaked slowly as it opened again. Only this time, it didn't clang shut. It just stayed open.

While he was still standing, having a staring contest with the abyss inside the closet, Maria swooped in, whispering something quite fast, a small glass bottle in her hand. She dripped the liquid on her fingers and consecrated the closet. Then she placed her fingers on the hinges and rubbed the liquid there.

"I guess it's decided which room is ours and which room is Lucia's," Maria said, closing the closet door and pushing it so it'd stay closed.

"I guess," Walter said. "Holy water?"

"Annatto oil, dummy."

"You blessed annatto oil?"

"What did you expect me to do? We were all out of olive oil."

The kettle whistled from the kitchen, making the husband and wife both jump at the same time.

"Tea," Walter said, his voice a little shaky.

"Yes. Tea," Maria said as she produced a diaper and wet wipes seemingly out of thin air and pushed them against Walter's chest.

The man watched his wife with love and longing as she disappeared into the kitchen. And then he extended the same affectionate gaze toward his daughter. A sigh of relief escaped his up-till-now tightened chest.

They would make it work.

Somehow, they would make it work.

1951

Baby Lucia, a year old now, could babble as coherently as she could. The TV was on, playing an episode of *The Lone Ranger*, but what did that matter to a kid? It was just babble to her, the black and white cowboy hero and Tonto moving in and out of focus, the static fuzzing as the signal weakened, then disappearing as the antenna swayed and strengthened it.

She wore a pink romper and had a hand stuffed down her mouth, four fingers touching all the places where her sprouting teeth gave her pain. Sweat beads on her forehead and saliva dripping down her elbow, she stood with her weight against the crib's wooden grill, observing things, her nascent mind trying to make sense of the fridge placed at an odd angle in the living room. There was no place for it in the kitchen, and the reason for its odd angle was that the latticework that carried the freon heated up if placed right next to the wall. It had to be at an angle for the fridge to keep things cool, to keep the meat cuts preserved. There was a Puerto Rican flag hanging from one side of the fridge, a banner for all to see the minute they walked in through the door. On the other side were clippers from which hung herbs, drying in the heat, their aroma perfused through the air.

The child looked at the TV and then, becoming bored with Tonto, watched the bedroom door with much interest. There was a bed inside, paired with two bedside tables, a dressing table, and that was it. There was no more room in that little cube for anything else. But Lucia's eyes were not interested in discerning the Hispanic-themed bedsheets or the artwork hanging from the wall. Self-made artwork by her mother when she was a young woman and dreamed of being a big-time artist in the Big Apple. Depictions of spirits and trees, nature and night.

What Lucia was interested in was the closet door adjacent to the bed. A walk-in closet, it had given quite a scare to her parents when she'd once crawled into it when neither of them was looking. And then she'd somehow locked herself in there and started to wail at the top of her lungs when the dark surrounded her. Her parents, aware that this was a rental property, tried to be as careful as they could with the door, but in the end, her father had to yank it and damage its bolt in order to rescue his daughter from within. A new closet door was installed, and even this one, at this time of the afternoon, was up to no good, creaking insidiously, begging to be opened.

The pressure cooker that Maria was using to tenderize lamb gave a huge hiss, drawing Lucia's attention away from the bedroom and toward the kitchen. While her attention was traveling, it caught onto the window and stayed there. Where there should've been a window air-conditioner installed (as per the notches left by the previous tenants), there was a barebones exhaust fan that served only to make the humidity and heat a little bearable. Any more, and it'd stop being an exhaust fan and be some sort of miracle device with four blades blowing heaven's cool wind.

Some evenings, when Maria was far too exhausted to take a bath, her back aching and her body drenched in sweat, she'd look at the exhaust fan and say a prayer, sometimes to Saint Michael, sometimes to something more ancient, and she'd feel the difference in the air. It would become cool, and that was indication enough to her that the forces she believed in were real and heard her loud and well.

And it was good that there was evidence, because

Espiritismo and Santeria were both belief systems that punished the doubtful. Being a practitioner of both, and her husband a quiet accomplice if not an outright believer, there was a small altar in the living room with candles, cigars, rum, dried flowers, and little jars containing herbal essences and oils. Last night's sourdough bread was also placed on that altar as a food offering to the orishas. A pack of reading cards, her old rosaries, and a bottle of small bones also adorned that altar, along with no less than six candles of different colors. The book, a lengthy tome bound in ancient leather, was placed below the altar, on the bottom shelf, making it the centerpiece.

Hanging up on top of the altar, a good distance away to make both things distinct, was her mother's picture. God rest her soul, and may the saints cling her to their bosoms in heaven. It was her mother who had raised Maria after her creed, a faith so specific and secret that only those initiated to it were allowed to use it as intended. Maria was one of the initiated, naturally, and had learned early on that you did not whisper incantations into mirrors after midnight nor sweep your house after dark, for doing so would sweep away any and all blessings. Dreams were never meaningless; more often than not, it was your ancestors trying to tell you something important, and you'd best heed them or they'll make themselves heard by other means. The previous week, Maria had dreamt that her youngest uncle's teeth had fallen out. Three days ago, she'd gotten the news— no surprise there—that he had passed in his sleep from emphysema. And yet, as tragic as that was, it could not keep her away from her Marlboros. There was an act of worship to smoking in and of itself.

You breathed in what killed you, and instead of killing you, it comforted you. Like Eleguá, who promised mischief but also granted new openings. Like Chango, who was thunder as much as he was justice. Like the *espíritus guías* who walked with you wherever you were, and sometimes scorched you a little so you could save yourself from a lot of fire. A sweetness to bitterness, a tenderness to the harsh smoke annihilating your throat one drag at a time.

There was another dream, this one last night, and it had prompted Maria to cook lamb, partly as an offering, partly as tonight's dinner. In the dream, Uncle Roberto stood in the dark of their bedroom cabinet, eyes gouged out, grave dirt spilling out of those holes. He stood in his funeral suit, a single rose in his coat pocket, a locket in his stretched-out hand, the locket swinging like a pendulum. Gray, this man, yet bearing complete resemblance to Uncle Roberto, he groaned without forming a word, for instead of a tongue in his mouth, red hornets were buzzing, stinging, sitting angrily.

Maria had woken up covered in not just sweat. The next morning, she told her husband that it was Lucia who'd peed in the bed to save herself from embarrassment. Walter merely nodded in understanding and went to attend his business wearing his plaid shirt, his corduroy pants, and his felt hat, looking more Cuban than Puerto Rican, but Maria knew that in his mind, he was dressing himself as an American. A cultural hodge-podge, but underneath, his own man.

With the lamb done, seasoned, still hot and simmering in the pressure cooker, Maria came out of the kitchen, her chest drenched, her sleeves pulled back, and sat there under the fan, lips pressed together at the little tug of guilt every parent feels when they see that their child has fallen asleep in their absence.

A moment of relief from being a stay-at-home mother, wife, and her other business. She was eager to take any relief that came her way, even if it came with its share of July hum and heat and the sound of protestors on the street below carrying peace sign placards and wielding loudspeakers.

But the moment of relief was cut short with a fast knock at the door.

"*¿Quién es?*" Maria called out, too tired to go to the door herself.

"*Soy yo, Pilar,*" the woman from two stories down spoke from the other side of the door.

Maria rolled her eyes while she still had a chance to do so. Maria and Walter's family was from San Juan. It just so happened that so was Pilar's, and that was enough for the woman to impose herself upon them, especially after learning of Maria's reputation as a Santera.

"Tia Maria?" she called out in her singsong voice. "I brought mofongos!"

"Ay, I'm coming," Maria said, getting up with a grunt and making sure that the black azabache stone locket was still there on Lucia's neck to protect her from the evil eye. The apartment was a little bit all over the place, but what did that matter to Pilar, who was herself a woman in constant shambles who relied upon Maria's prophecy and divination to make sense of her life? How she'd survived before her was something that Maria often thought about at the expense of her sanity.

Pilar was a walking, talking disaster machine, both causing it and attracting it, from her husband's third cardiac episode to the time when her son had nearly choked to death on an apricot seed of all things. But she was good business, because with every reading and portent, Pilar gave Maria a dollar, and between Pilar and the other women who came to her from all over the block for readings, each of them giving as much as they could afford, Maria made around ten or so dollars every week, which wasn't bad at all.

She saw people on Friday afternoons, charging twenty cents for twenty minutes, and for twenty cents she helped them divine their dreams, talk to their dead loved ones, or have protection spells put upon them from what they deemed wicked.

Pilar had a face that was better suited to a hyena. The moment that Maria opened the door, Pilar shot a look at Lucia, a darkness shifting in her irises. Maria reminded herself to say a prayer of protection for Lucia when Pilar was gone, and then allowed Pilar in.

"What are we doing this time then?" Maria asked as she took the tray from Pilar.

Pilar's husband was a construction worker, whom she was certain was having an affair with some Mexican broad in Brooklyn. "Why else would he give me so much spending money?" she had said repeatedly.

"Maybe because he loves you?" Maria had commented once or twice.

"No, that can't be it." Pilar would dismiss the obvious and choose to run after doubts and rumors.

"I had a dream, Marisol," Pilar said, seating herself rather comfortably on the sofa. She took out a dollar bill before Maria could say a word and placed it on the coffee table.

"Do tell," Maria said, facing her altar, readying herself to listen to Pilar's existential rant wearing the guise of a dream. As Pilar began, Maria said a prayer to Santa Maria, the woman she was named after. It did enough to still her racing mind and put her in her "espiritista mode," as her husband liked to call it.

He was really happy with what she brought in from her readings. With what he earned from his daily toil as a construction worker by day and a bartender by night, and with what she earned from her divination, it had made the Morenos' life very comfortable.

1952

Walter Moreno did not look like it, but he was a thinking man's thinking man. Where others saw culture and music and protest and literature and commerce and communism clashing with capitalism, Walter saw opportunity in a way that shrewd men do, at first glance, and with great certainty.

First, he worked among the working class, relying upon his experiences from back home, working on construction sites, tending a bar in Harlem, and within a year, thanks to Maria and her under the table income from her psychic readings, he had enough saved to set up his own establishment. An establishment in Manhattan instead of the Bronx or Brooklyn, because, as per his experience, the working-class stiffs liked to get loose around their place of work. So, construction workers by the hundreds who toiled in the sun all day in Manhattan didn't have the stamina to go to another borough for a cool drink and some good music; they needed an affordable, unpretentious joint right there in Manhattan. Similarly, people who worked in the docks and the warehouses needed somewhere close by for some rest and recreation.

And that is what Walter Moreno offered them. On the corner of Hudson and Jay Street, amidst the cobbled sidewalks of Tribeca and looming old architectural landmarks, there was a dark establishment with an exterior marked by glossy black paint, smeared on thick as if additional coats had been added periodically.

The windows were dark too, boarded up by something inside that wanted to protect its patrons. It had no name; it simply was. On the corner of the exterior stood a large plinth that seemingly held the side of the building upright, and in a little alcove behind it was the entrance door to the establishment. The tiles outside the door were a worn checkerboard of black and white, with a single letter (an S) etched in the center. No one remembered what it once stood for.

The building had about a hundred code violations and was a liability for the landlord, but a profitable liability. He rented it to Walter for quite the bargain, the unsaid part of the bargain being that if the city authorities came snooping by, they'd find a colored man inside, and any consequence would be upon the shoulders of the man whose name was on the lease, not the landlord himself. But Walter, being a thinking man's thinking man, had spent a month and a half after renting the place to bring it up to code. After all, he had jumped on the hustle of the American Dream with an eager spirit and strong forearms.

To those not in the know, it was just another watering hole. Quiet, narrow and dusty. Eight stools lined along the bar. A dusty jukebox that worked when it felt like it. A bell over the door that jangled with every soul brave enough to walk in.

But Walter kept the place clean. His wife came by every now and then (when a sympathetic woman who lived next door was willing to watch over Lucia for two hours or so; a trustworthy woman with a kind heart and a caring touch, older than both Walter and Maria) to help him stack the bottles and stock the shelves. What Walter did not see, or, if he saw, he *pretended* not to see, was Maria sneaking in her amulets and protective charms and hanging them in discreet corners of the bar to bless and protect the place.

But for the most part, Walter tended the bar on his own, pouring drinks to the people he'd once worked alongside, listening to their woes, offering his solace via consolation and affirmation. A thinking man's thinking man, when not presented with the opportunity to help in an official capacity, such as a therapist or a professor, becomes a bartender, for that is a help in its own. You don't just serve drinks. You serve advice, and everyone, even the freeloaders, is free to take it. The man might not have been a bona fide practitioner like his wife, but there was a strange kind of comforting magic in him, in the way he greeted those who frequented his bar, in the way he poured drinks, in the way he whispered to the jukebox to work, for the love of God, in the way he listened, and truly listened with an intent to understand instead of to escalate.

And now that he had his place of power, a place with small baccarat-style red sconces, a small strip of light behind the bar illuminating cheap liquor in cheaper bottles, and stools that were compressed from overuse, Walter Moreno was not just a thinking man. He was an acting man.

And he acted to preserve his family. Preserve it from poverty, from a lack of a roof over their head, from starvation, from purposelessness, and most importantly, from the darkness he had seen lurking in the closet's self-contained abyss.

After last call, a tired Walter would drive his beat-up Ford (he joked that it was the only thing he could a'ford) to the Bronx, park it across the street, and then climb the stairs to the top floor. He'd unlock the door, let the waft of whatever Maria had cooked envelop his being, maybe take a bite or two before heading into the lounge.

As a bartender, the biggest irony of his life was that he could not drink on the job. Not while he was the property's sole server, bouncer, and cleaner. And it was no easy feat, not to mention illegal, to drive drunk. He had something to look forward to every night: Lucia, Maria, their little life in that little apartment. And that kept him sober while he served gin and bourbon and vodka and good old whiskey.

He drank his first drink of the day on the sofa in his living room. One bottle of beer, enough to drown his heat and any sorrows that he'd accumulated during the day.

Around this time, Maria would wake up, walk to the kitchen while rubbing her eyes, and warm his food for him. He'd go into his room, peer into the crib, and find his daughter sleeping. He'd kiss her forehead, then prepare himself for what was next.

While no longer empty (in fact, with Maria and Walter's clothes, it was as packed as possible, nearing spillage), the closet still contained the darkness he had locked gaze with on their first day here. And while he'd stand there, rifling through clothes on hangers, he'd peek behind, and find the darkness waiting.

1960

Ten years later, in that already ancient room that was now weathered further by being lived in for a decade, Lucia stood there staring at the same open closet, almost as if she was in a trance. Everything around her was silent. No voice came intruding in the bedroom.

With a bob-cut that moved as if it had a life of its own, keen eyes prodding into the dark without fear, and her hand on her waist in perfect imitation of her mother, Lucia stood in front of the closet in the middle of Saturday, wondering where her mother's special book was.

While she searched for it, she took a maroon scarf from one of the hangers and wound it around her neck.

There, now she looked older and more distinguished, the perfect guise for her plan.

After all, no one really paid attention to a ten-year-old in matters of fortune-telling, did they?

"There you are," Lucia said, grinning as she spotted the book's deep tanned leather jutting out from under the top shelf, tucked away underneath folded laundry. The book was leather-bound, a pale shade like pigskin, and thick with weight. Its cover gave off the faint scent of dust and something older—like library stacks no one visited anymore. But the pages inside looked untouched, pristine, almost damp with ink. A single thread stitched into the spine served as its bookmark, and it was always in a different place whenever Lucia stole it from her mother's domain.

She had seen her mother use it all her life, on Fridays when women swarmed the stairway waiting for their turn with the Oracle of Brook Avenue. Her mother would close her eyes and let the spirits guide her as to which page to open, and then she'd share the details to her clientele.

For Lucia, it was certainly a lot more interesting than her fifth-grade schoolbooks. Those books told her about how gases were basically just boiled liquids, but this one, this big, heavy tome that was now in her hands, told her what the boil meant.

And no way she was touching her schoolbooks. It was July. School was out, thank you very much, and it was plenty hot enough inside the apartment to put her mind off reading any school-related stuff. She needed to be out, and she needed to be out with the book.

Lucia took the heavy book with its engraved leather and hid it under the shawl. She casually shut the closet door, not even bothered in the slightest about the darkness behind the clothes or the fact that she had undone the folding of a lot of laundry in her attempts at getting the book out.

Her mother was asleep in the air-conditioned room, *her* room, and her father was tending to the bar. These grown-up matters were not Lucia's concern, and even though she really wanted them to be, to jump happily up and down when her father came home one day and told her mom that he now owned the bar and the apartment above it, thanks to ten years of saving every penny, the fact remained that she was just a kid. And kids needed money to buy ice-pops. Kids needed their friends to read comic books and talk about what was on TV yesterday.

Not having either as of this moment, Lucia walked out of the apartment cat-footed so as not to wake her overprotective mother, and descended the flight of stairs. There might not be friends waiting outside that apartment, or fat stacks of cash, but there was a haven, and sometimes, a haven was good enough.

The haven in question was a series of tin sheds that the residents of the apartment building had built for themselves in the empty lot behind the building. The reason for the transient nature of the construction was that this was New York. You never knew when one empty plot of land was cordoned off and filled with construction material for yet another building project. Another reason was, tin sheds were almost all that most could afford to build, what with most of the people living here living hand to mouth, even the ones who didn't really have any reason to do so. This was New York, and if you didn't live below your means, then the city would have all the more reason to swallow you whole.

Lucia could not give less of a damn about the city's transient nature or why her father and mother chose to live a whole class below their means when he was earning enough money for them to shift to a better neighborhood. There were some things that did not enter a child's mind, such as that this place, as wondrous as it was, was not a welcoming place. Here, people took one look at the shade of your skin and decided your fate within that instant.

But these were all bridges that she would cross when she got to them. For now, she was all too happy to walk out of the back door of the apartment building into the empty lot.

A chain link fence bordered the lot on three sides, the fourth side naturally closed off by the back of the building. Beyond the fence, there were other lots of other buildings, and the children had done as they do, made holes in the bottoms of fences so that they could cross over into the territory of other lots where their friends were.

Because of the foot traffic, the grass was all but gone in the middle of the lot, leaving a bald, dry patch of dirt that had sunken a few feet into the ground. Lucia walked around it, unperturbed by the heat or the buzzing of insects in the air. The cigar smoke coming from the tin sheds and the sound of conversations in six different languages were none of her concern. Her father smoked in the apartment, so cigar smoke was more of an aroma than a nuisance. And all these people talking in their different accents were people she knew on a first-name basis on account of sharing an apartment building with them.

They gave her a nod, peeking from within their sheds, and no more. Then they went back to their business as Lucia walked over to the little rusty shanty her father had set up in the corner of the lot. Here, he had placed his tools on a half-bench and bolted it out from outside so that no one would steal anything from within. Lucia knew where he hid the key in the apartment, and as such, had it with her.

She opened the tin door and went inside, finding her trusty pillow on which to perch, and then sat there with the book laid out on the sawdust-covered floor. She always made sure to clean it up afterward so that her mother wouldn't know she'd taken it.

The book was a boon for her budding career as an oracle in the making. Lucia would stand in the sweltering heat of the hallway or on the stairs, arms outstretched and hope to divert some traffic toward her business, saying advertising lines such as, "It is I, Lucia, Daughter of the Oracle, Maria Moreno, the All Knowing. Let me read your palm and tell you what waits tomorrow."

Those who were far too desperate and exhausted enough to wait a moment longer sometimes took her at her word and followed her down into the shanties. There, she'd have them sit on her father's stool and she'd attempt to read their fate while sat next to the burning candle.

Lighting candles and whispering to them was something that she had been practicing for as long as she had gained cognizance. She had seen her mother do it, and sometimes her father, and it was second nature to her to treat the fire atop the candle as a living thing instead of just as a source of light and heat.

But the flame did not talk back, and after the first few rounds of nothing, some folk thanked the girl for her time, chuckled at her efforts, and then lambasted themselves for losing their place in line.

This did not deter Lucia. She continued to poach people on the stairs and offer them a faster service to talk to passed loved ones or answer their questions about missing relatives. She knew better than to lead people on. To lie. Her mother had told her that a lie told as a fortune would come back to haunt you for the rest of your life.

Lucia knew that she needed to up her skills as a fortune teller the same way as how she'd gotten an A in math. By studying. And with the source material sitting right there on the floor, what better time than now? In another hour or two, people would gather on the stairs, and if she'd learned enough by then, maybe this time she wouldn't tell dud fortunes.

The bookmark in the book was in an unusual place today. All the way toward the back, in a section that Lucia had never explored before. The book was big, thick with weight, and from what she had gathered, the instructions on candle-reading were at the beginning of the book.

But the leather bookmark tucked all the way in the back was far too inviting for her to ignore. With considerable effort, she pulled the book open to where the bookmark was.

The book slipped from her hand and turned to the first page as it thudded on the floor, raising sawdust in the air. Coughing, Lucia read the page that she'd read countless times before.

This book has no name and should never have one. It was not written, after all. It was passed down, page after page. These are lived experiences, and books with lived experiences, magic, mystery, the Madam, whatever you want to call it, are not mass published or meant for the eyes of the public.

Understand this, practitioner, my descendant, that conductive research can lead to harm. So practice with caution. And when you are done, at the end of your long road, add a page, add a chapter, write your findings, and pass it on to the next of your kin.

Nodding as if she understood everything, Lucia made another attempt at opening the book where the bookmark was and succeeded. The chatter from the other tin sheds quietened as her focus intensified. Although that was not all it was, Lucia did not notice. She did not see the way the sun was blotted out by clouds that had rolled out of nowhere, and yet, they weren't all that unexpected given the hurricane warning. The tin sheds in an uneven row began to creak. One by one, the people who were occupying them went back into the apartment. The singular bulb hanging in Lucia's tin shed swayed and clanged with the walls, but Lucia was already pulled in by the book.

The page that the bookmark was sticking to had a title.

The Witch

She had never once referred to, or heard anyone call, her mother a witch. A *bruja*, maybe, and that too in whispers as they waited for her outside the apartment. But never to her face. Her mother never claimed that title. And yet, here it was.

She read on.

She came with the storm breeze, in a black dress the rain couldn't wet.

Her eyes were ancient, and her voice was older than the language we spoke.

She called me by name. Not the one men used,

but the name my mother spoke when healing me with smoke and prayer.

She said she came from the West, a bridge over water, but had no home.

That she had loved once, but what she loved was dying... in a city made of steel.

"The Devil walks there," she told me.

"But not with horns. With hunger. And a man's name."

I asked her if I should be afraid.

"No," she said. "Not you. But your daughter must."

Upon reading the end of the page and finding that there was nothing written on the next one, Lucia pulled her neck back and noticed just how quickly and unnaturally the weather had shifted outside. She could see it from the makeshift window, and made nothing of it, thinking it was yet another summer storm. In her mind, it was a good thing. A summer storm meant that the air would be cool, and her parents would not occupy her room as much and instead sleep in their own with the windows open and no air conditioner. It still boggled her as to why they didn't get an air conditioner for their room. Something about the electricity units unfairly multiplying.

"Lucia," a hoarse voice called from outside.

A customer? Lucia wondered and tried to pry the door open to see. The door didn't budge. Instead, the wind blew and wedged it even harder in the wooden frame.

"Hey, can you help me open the door?" Lucia asked.

There was no response other than the shriek of the wind, and after another few seconds passed, the shriek died down, leaving only silence. In that silence, that voice called out again, "Lucia!"

Her heart started to beat arrhythmically at first, and then, when the door didn't give, it started to beat like a jackhammer in her chest, shaking her entire torso with its frantic beat.

"Help!"

"Lucia!"

Lucia stood up on shaking legs and did the only thing that made sense to her mind. She threw her body against the tin door and fell on the other side on long, wet grass face-first. The door angrily shut behind her as if it were sentient, claiming the book for itself, along with the candle that Lucia had brought but hadn't had a chance to light yet.

But Lucia was not concerned with the tin shed's erratic behavior.

It was unnaturally dark for mid-noon. The multi-gray-layered cloud curtain in the sky groaned, as if it carried all the dread of the universe within it. A lightning bolt crackled on the horizon, and as its flash died down, the shadow of the trees all around her seemed all the darker. Shadows upon shadows gathering and intruding from every direction in the abandoned backlot, all the windows of the building in front of her closed down in anticipation of the storm.

"Lucia."

This time the voice was softer, nearer.

Lucia's head snapped right as she pushed herself up, brushing dirt from her pants. That's when she saw it. A dark figure stood at the edge of the clearing, watching her. Its arm stretched out, one finger aimed straight at her. The hand looked wrong, long and jointed, ending in clawlike tips that caught what little light there was.

She froze. The air thickened in her lungs. Every instinct said *run*, but her body wouldn't move. It felt like a dream that wouldn't break.

The figure took a step, then another, unsteady, as though learning how to walk, or remembering. Each movement carried the weight of something that had only just found its footing.

"Lucia," it spoke again, the word rattling in its throat like crunching bone. The shadow had more shape now, and more width, the spectacle of which injected raw terror in the ten-year-old as she squealed and made a break for the apartment building.

"Mama!" she called out, not knowing just how close the horror was behind her. She had seen enough to fuel her nightmares for a lifetime.

The stairs shook violently, not under her weight but under the weight of her pursuer, the lights in the stairwell flickering and going out, leaving her scampering in the dark.

A guttural voice pulled harsh breath as it closed the distance behind her, its black-soaked hand pinching at her sneaker and missing at the last instant. Light or not, Lucia knew this place like the back of her hand. She climbed for her life, her lungs burning, sweat pouring out of every pore, and her heart shrieking with pain as it beat. She reached the top floor somehow, and still the darkness and the haunter draped within it did not relent.

"Mama!" Lucia whimpered, throwing the apartment door open and then clanging it shut, bolting it. Strange, she thought, that she could not feel any sanctuary here, even though she was in the place every child thought of as the safest place to exist.

Behind her, the door started to shake in its hinges, a loud force pushing it and pulling it in hopes of yanking it off.

"LUCIA!" the voice roared in anger from the other side as liquid darkness began to seep from under the doorway and toward Lucia's feet.

"MAMA!" Lucia yelled and felt a hand fall upon her shoulder. She screamed, but another hand wrapped around her mouth.

It was her mother, bleary-eyed from sleep, weary-faced from a day's worth of toil. Her mother released her face and then brought a finger to her own lips, signaling quiet.

"*El...el diablo*, Ma." Lucia pointed to the door that shook with all the violence in the world.

Maria moved Lucia behind her, protecting her from the darkness that flowed underneath like spilling gutter water.

"I took your book to read," Lucia cried, hot tears scaling her cheeks as she grabbed onto her mother's shirt and watched from behind.

"Tell me what you saw, *nina*. Tell it to me now," Maria said, not backing away from the door.

The haunter intruding upon the door ceased its relentless barrage for just a moment.

Lucia hiccupped and sputtered, "It was black...like coal... Its eyes were red. And, Mama, it was calling me, watching me."

"Did you see anything upon its forehead?" Maria asked, still standing sentinel in front of the door.

"A star, glowing orange like fire," Lucia sobbed.

"Him," Maria whispered, before reaching into her pocket and retrieving a jade amulet.

Then, standing tall, she took a step toward the door, driving the darkness out, speaking firmly, "Now you listen to me. You are not welcome here."

A low roar carried through the air as whatever it was that stood on the other side of the door listened.

"You are not welcome here. You are not to haunt my daughter. Her bloodline, my blood, is sanctified.

Protected. Leave now, and I may let you be. Stay, and I will tear your name from every shadow that you ever touched."

There was a loud, high-pitched yet deep scream from the other side of the door as Maria pressed the talisman deeper in her fist. Then the door shook one last time as if angrily kicked, and the noise ended.

Outside, the dark of the clouds began to give way to the beams of the noon sun. The air became lighter, and in the absence of dread, Lucia burst into tears and clung to her mother, not seeing just how much of a toll this confrontation had taken on Maria.

Maria put her hand on Lucia's hair and caressed her, saying nothing. She walked over to her daughter's still cool room and put her to bed wordlessly. She sat there for as long as she needed to, until Lucia fell asleep, and then covered her daughter with a handwoven patchwork quilt.

Once enough time had passed between the incident and she was certain that Lucia was deep asleep, Maria went down to the tin shed, retrieved the book, brought it back into her apartment, and put it back into the dark closet.

"Not again, you hear me?" she spoke into the darkness of the closet. "Never again." The impenetrable blackness in the closet sat still, releasing no sigh nor any cold draft of acknowledgment, and that was good enough for Maria.

She pushed the closet door shut after making sure that the book was tucked deeper than Lucia could reach.

When Lucia woke up, it was as if she'd woken from a fugue state.

Neither mother nor daughter talked about what happened.

Sanctuario

Of all the transient things that Lucia experienced in her life, perhaps her childhood was the most fleeting of all. There she was, a ten-year-old, sleeping a dreamless sleep while her mother sat beside her, and a mere nine years later, time that flew by with a sparrow's urgency, she stood by the fresh dirt that was the mound underneath which her mother was buried. It rained on that day too, but her father's umbrella helped keep her dry.

There was a large crowd attending the burial, most of them people from the block, and some of them people whose lives had been changed for the better thanks to Maria's prophecies and guidance. A few relatives from Puerto Rico even came. The pastor spoke kind words, quoted the Bible half in Spanish and the other half in a thick American accent, his voice muffled by the roaring of the wind, the grumble of the clouds, and the sobs of those who stood around her.

Lucia herself did not cry.

It made no sense to her as to how anyone could just... cease to exist so nonchalantly. Yesterday her mother had made tacos for Taco Tuesday, and she had invited her high school boyfriend over. They were still going on, but that relationship was headed for the rocks. Juan had no interest in pursuing college, and Lucia had taken a gap year to figure out what she needed to do. But they still saw each other. In fact, Juan was standing on the other side with his mother, who was her mother's oldest friend in New York, Pilar.

Last night, she had kissed her mother, something that she did less and less of, and now there was not enough sorrow in the word to punctuate the remorse she felt as to why she'd drawn away from the woman who had loved her most, loved her truly, and her mother had told her, "There's always something light lurking behind an endless dark, girlie. You'd best remind yourself of that once in a while."

Not understanding this was a mother's parting message to her daughter, Lucia had only kissed her mom on the forehead and had gone out of the room to fix up a late-night snack for herself.

In the morning, her mother hadn't woken up at her usual time, but it wasn't *that* which alerted them to her passing. It was her father's loud scream as he woke up in bed next to a dead woman that told the whole apartment building that the Oracle of Brook Avenue was no more.

Standing there in the rain, Lucia's mind traveled in every direction where her mother was. The past, the distant past, and the past beyond the distant one. Back to when she was sixteen and told her mother that she could sense illness before it struck, smell death on a stranger's coat, and speak to things that had never been born. That was just three years ago, and her mother had smiled at her while she stirred her soup. What did she say?

"Let this power sit with you, *nina*, like a quiet guest. Ever present. Never demanding."

The cautious nature of her mother's advice had made

Lucia grow distant in terms of sharing her curiosities and discoveries with her. Sometimes, her grandfather spoke to her in her dreams. She didn't tell her mother that. Sometimes, she'd see bones on the floor of a slaughterhouse and know without any effort that someone was going to die. The bones told her so. She did not tell that to her mother. She never called herself an oracle. In fact, that whole stint of her trying to read people's palms ended after that noon when reading the book had summoned something dark.

Her father's hand pressed harder on her shoulder. There was not a drop of rain on his umbrella-covered face, and yet, enough tears had made his just as wet as the rest of the people's. He sobbed without holding back, his eyes closed, his chest heaving.

He's going to live another five years, growing weaker with each passing day, until he dies and is buried next to Mom. Lucia didn't even have to try; this thought came on its own, and given that it had come at such a calamitous time, it didn't shake her as much as it should have. Instead, it prepared her.

It struck her just how powerful a practitioner of the old ways her mother was that she did not let her own daughter divine her time of death. And now all that magic was gone, buried six feet under with her book of song rested atop her chest.

All's not gone that might seem dead, nina, a voice called out to her, almost as if from the grave. *Remember what I told you? The dead are with us, whether we want them to be or not. You are still not getting rid of me that easily.*

Whether it was imagined or entirely real, it did not

matter. Lucia, who had been holding herself strong up until now, burst into tears, every pain she had ever felt kindled fresh for her to feel in that very moment as she stood by the grave.

AND THEN, even that time passed, and she was in her early twenties, knowing but choosing not to obsess over the fact that in another year or two, her father's time would come. To brace herself for it, she had left Walter in his own apartment, where, when he was not reading the news or watching TV, he was smoking his cigars and helping himself to canned meals, gaining weight, enjoying his retirement money, tending to the bar every now and then.

Lucia, on the other hand, had moved into an apartment with a man whom she figured she could change if she spent enough time with him. A younger man with a temper and a tongue to match. She could not change him, nor his short fuse or wandering hands. He spent more time in bars than he did at home, and then, on one occasion, when she did find him at home, it was with another woman in their bed.

She let him have her Moreno wrath for the first and last time, and sent him packing.

And then she sent herself packing, because this shoddy studio apartment in Harlem wasn't doing it for her. She knew that her father owned the apartment over the bar, an apartment that had been used up till now for storage purposes. Six months before her father died,

Lucia moved into that apartment, clearing all clutter and selling all old and no-longer-useable equipment.

It was good that she was away from Brook Avenue, away from the darkness, from the voices that imposed their will upon her if she didn't listen. Here, all was quiet, all was calm, and she was free to be the person she wished to be. To be able to break tradition in public, cutting her hair short, wearing American dresses, singing in Harlem supper clubs. She enjoyed this new part of her. And yet, she stuck with the old ways in the quiet of her apartment, still lighting her candles.

In time, she learned how to create a door that would keep the dead on the other side so that they wouldn't intrude upon her as much. But they came to her anyway, sometimes sharing their plight of loneliness, sometimes asking for her help, and sometimes not knowing that they had died.

Although she did not have any explicit memory of the tin shed and the demon she'd come across (for some terrors are so scarring that the brain pretends to have forgotten them, while forgetting none of the lessons that came with the terror), she was never off guard when practicing the old ways.

When her father died, and when she was done burying him next to her mother, there was no formal handoff. Just the estate lawyer giving her an envelope and keys. She'd inherited the bar and the apartment above it, following Walter's purchase of it many years before.

The first order of business was to rename it to reclaim it. No longer would the singular S be the name and marker of this place, even though it was built solely for those who knew how to find it.

It would be called Sanctuario, and once she was done finishing its remodeling, she'd open its doors to the world once more.

For something was already on its way.

CHAPTER 2
AMSTERDAM

1977

At first glance, the city did not feel like it belonged on earth.

With its tilting canal houses, cobbled lanes, and the clatter of bike bells cutting through the soft lapping of water against stone, Amsterdam played a symphony where both the old and new harmonized with each other.

A symphony of gabled rooftops and spires like the Westertoren rising above them, watching over bridges arched like eyebrows above the Prinsengracht, Keizersgracht, and Herengracht.

Glass-roofed tour boats glided past houseboats that were festooned with flowerpots. The scent of weed smoke and stroopwafels wafted from the Nine Streets, where the bakeries, eateries, and cafes of this city were found right next to quaint antique stores and bookshops.

Trams hummed along the Damrak toward the Dam

Square's royal palace and the Nieuwe Kerk, while a little farther down, the Rijksmuseum's archway framed cyclists and pedestrians alike as they moved past Rembrandt's painted ancestors, and the Van Gogh Museum spoke in colors of beautiful psychosis.

Pigeons pecked about the bronze of Spinoza near the old Jewish Quarter, and somewhere near Vondelpark, jazz poured out of an open window above a bar where the barkeep poured Heineken as if it were balm for all the many ails of the soul.

It was a city that did not tolerate inhibitions. And you could tell by the way people breathed freely as they drank, as they smoked marijuana on street corners, eyeing the dancing women in red windows.

While there were no laws explicitly passed to allow such lasciviousness, the lawmakers and the upholders of law did nothing to stop it. When the police were not busy turning a blind eye, they were participating in the debauchery themselves.

Jerry loved the city for what it was: a welcome respite from the cultureless wasteland that was America, a different flavor of European life, one that was not found in the streets of London or Munich.

A well-travelled man with quite the diverse cultural palette, he appreciated Amsterdam for what it was and hung over it like a cloud of smoke, casting his presence over the tall and narrow canal houses of the old city center, watching the tourists floating down the canal, making note of the city's bustle, his sharp senses registering everything.

Amsterdam was not yet aware of his malevolent

presence. When something out of the ordinary transpired, such as the sudden disappearance of a prostitute from a window in the back alley, the town assumed that yet another lady of the night had moved on.

But in the winter of '69, the town started to talk about the Shadow on the Herengracht. No sooner did night fall than men and women started to vanish with increased frequency, and what the detectives and the fearful public did not know was that one human body could feed a vampire for up to three days, but the taste of cold blood was not necessarily appealing.

The city folk, wanting to ascribe it to some ordinary phenomenon, blamed drugs, the Polish immigrants, or, if not either, mental illness claiming the lives of the morbidly depressed.

Professor Haden Moore, an expert on the subject of theology, religious iconology, and symbology, a man who had lived long and traveled wide, recognized the pattern of disappearances, having read about it in Vatican archives and Sumerian texts, having witnessed this controlled chaos before, where creatures killed methodically and then cleaned up after themselves.

He had not dyed his hair gray sitting in the sun, after all. Before he wore these tweed jackets with elbow patches, before he delivered lectures on kabbalah, the ten sephirot, and helped differentiate between the Catholic and Orthodox icon traditions to indifferent students, Haden was a man the Vatican called whenever it had questions that had no answers written in any of the books they possessed.

As a hyper-gifted man with a photographic memory

and deep understanding, he had already consumed most of the books that he could get his hands on in the Secret Archives when he had interned there in his youth. And that was just his internship. What followed was an illustrious career in understanding the darker realities that thrived on this planet and hunting them.

Haden Moore, despite his seemingly close ties with the Vatican, was no priest. His name was never mentioned on official rosters, and yet, when a convent in Lyon went silent for forty days, it was Haden that the Vatican sent to investigate.

When an ossuary in southern Italy began growing new bones, it was Haden who put an end to that necromancy. He was the non-exorcist that the church never wanted to admit they employed, but had no choice but to do so when push came to shove.

He did what he did best. And his job was to make problems disappear without fuss. With a knack for persuasion and enough charm to boot, he could convince men to join his group of vigilantes to hunt and take down the things that went bump in the night.

Hunter Haden was the nickname they had for him, but he referred to himself as a professor. He believed in observation, in the repetition of patterns as they repeated across centuries and continents.

Monsters, for instance, did not just operate on instinct. They followed, even in their chaos, rules and rhythms. Their feeding habits held signatures that never changed. And Haden had made it his life's work to trace them.

And unlike the actual hunters, who charged in with

silver and fire, Haden waited, sitting in dark pews and counting the wolves that howled during certain hours.

He'd catalogue weather anomalies and connect them to disappearances. He collected newspaper clippings from the remote towns in Tinjan, Peru, Madagascar, and pinned them on a corkboard. He knew the names of men who had no birth certificates, whose lives predated official record-keeping, but who were still out there, somehow still breathing.

A modest man in his craft, Haden charged a handsome fee, not for his own luxuries but for the recruiting of people, for the purchase of weaponry, and for renting abodes as he rid the earth of the ghouls that haunted it.

He worked simply and primitively, finding modernity to be nothing more than a complexity. And so, he relied upon maps, newspaper clippings, and the grimoires he had retrieved from monsters gone by to give him clues. Master charts of patterns that, once realized, could predict the next outbreak before it started.

Haden had gotten close to the truth so often that the Vatican had pulled him back time and again, lest his findings suggest that some monsters were not in hiding. That, instead, they were evolving and learning to adapt, avoiding detection in a rapidly modernizing world.

BY THE LATE 1960s, the Vatican's interest in Haden had fizzled out. They kept tabs on him, certainly, but there were fewer and fewer calls from Rome. Haden's role as a professor at the University of Amsterdam was a soft retirement of sorts, one in which he could live a quiet life surrounded by books and solitude.

The city's calmness, its orderliness, were something that spoke greatly to Haden after spending a life that had little of either. Here in this city, people did not hold to superstitions. They believed in infrastructure and treated religion as folklore and nothing more. Or so Haden had observed.

The classes he taught each week were on ritual symbology, medieval apocrypha, and cult doctrines of old. His students were a mixed bunch, most of them indifferent to the subject matter and only choosing to attend his classes because he passed them easily, which bumped their GPAs a few points up.

However, some students clung to his every word as if it were gospel, and he was kind of irritated with them by now. They did not respect the electric bell as it rang in the halls. Instead, when the lecture finished, they flocked around him, asking him questions that belonged in tomorrow's lecture. He had considered buying a broom to beat them with.

Lisa Vicenza, twenty-one, a blonde-haired girl from Italy, was one of those pestering students who always looked like they were on the verge of a religious epiphany. He admired her spirit, but did not have the heart to tell her that there was nothing but disappointment at the end of this road. The answers that she sought in religion were not altogether that neatly packaged for someone like her.

What did it matter anyway? She was going to graduate in the fall. And then he'd have the next batch of students. This Lisa would be replaced by some Julia or some Matilda, and...

Oh, who am I kidding? I have a good life here, thought Haden as he sipped his morning cup of bitter coffee and looked outside the window of his canal house. He could technically own the canal house if it came to it, but it had five stories, and he didn't really need the other four. So he rented it, likening himself to Sherlock Holmes, given how nosy his landlady was as well. She was always climbing the flight of stairs with a tray of baked goods.

Ms. Grisham, a woman who spoke fluent German and French, never really explained why. When she was not busy pestering the good professor, she was behind the counter at the bookstore below, selling secondhand paperbacks to tourists and broke academics alike.

It was barely five in the morning, and Professor Haden Moore, resting both elbows on the window sill, his torso out, could see that Ms. Grisham, sixty-five years young, was busy and about, throwing bread into the Prinsengracht for the flock of ducks that were swimming idyllically while they still could, while the water was not disturbed by the constant boats.

It did his health well to take in the morning air, really feel all the breeze freshened by the leaves of the lindens and elms, and drink his coffee with, ironically, a cigarette. But men of Haden's ilk were cut from a different cloth. The cigarettes had not done his health any harm up until now, and he was certain that they were only going to invigorate him, not debilitate him in his twilight years.

Today was a Sunday morning, and in another hour,

Professor Haden would get ready, don his trench coat, fill his pocket with breadcrumbs of his own for the geese and pigeons that flocked around him by the canal, and pick a Vonnegut novel to read in the early hours of the morning.

Next, he'd take a walk through Jordaan with a leather notebook tucked under his arm, a notebook that he'd stop and scribble in every now and then. If the butcher near Dam Square was sitting in the park with his chessboard, Haden would play a match with him. If not, then he'd go to the mailbox and deposit letters to a handful of his old colleagues in different parts of the world. And then he'd come home and rest before his evening tea.

But none of that happened today, and Professor Moore had only taken the first sip from his coffee and the second drag from his cigarette when he witnessed his Sunday (and the rest of his days to come) being mercilessly robbed from him.

It started with a scream from Ms. Grisham, the old landlady who had never married yet knew more about men than a whole block of housewives put together. She screamed so loud that the flock of ducks that were circling the breadcrumbs she had thrown in the water immediately started to quack in alarm and flew off.

There were only five or six people in the street below, all of whom shared in her alarm as she screamed again and pointed a finger at the water, yelling, "*Oh mein Gott!* There is a corpse in the water!"

The cup nearly fell from Haden's hand as his eyes followed Ms. Grisham's finger. There it was, unmistakably, indeed, a body floating upside down in the water, carried down the canal. In the meager light of the rising sun, he spotted the woman's ripped garment and her ashen hair.

By the time he had reached downstairs, the corpse had floated under an arching bridge. But there were two policemen on the other side, reaching by way of hooks attached to the end of wooden sticks, normally meant for dragging something out of the water.

Haden quickened his pace just in time as the police officers pulled the body of the girl out of the water and placed her upon the sidewalk.

It was Lisa Vicenza, her entire body three shades paler than when he'd last seen her on Friday, eyes closed, lips blue, and two distinct puncture marks on her carotid.

"Back off, sir!" the police officer snapped at Haden, not knowing who he was or under what authority he was standing here. Haden did not argue. Instead, he backed away, his mind beginning to spin gears that had been gathering dust for far too long.

As a small crowd of eye-rubbing citizens and early morning joggers began to gather around the police, Haden heard something.

"Twelfth one this month," a woman whispered as she clung to her boyfriend's arm. He patted her head and turned her face away from the dead body.

Haden took hold of Ms. Grisham's arm and said, "Come along, Ms. Grisham. This is a matter for the police."

"Oh, how…utterly…horrible," she whimpered, standing there resolutely.

Above them, above the canal houses and the towers and old building fronts, a pink-hued sun rose, its many shades reflecting in the canal water, shedding soft light on the over-eager theology student.

As Haden escorted his landlady back into her bookshop, he made a mental note of what he was going to do next.

Twelve deaths in a month were no coincidence. How had he missed this? He was a meticulous man. Was it a symptom of age-brought senility that the first eleven murders had flown under his radar? Or was it a different sort of predator, which made it harder to detect the pattern?

Something was here. And if he didn't confront it, it was only a matter of time before it would confront him.

IT WAS around the evening of the same day that Professor Haden made his move. Between the morning and the evening, he kept himself busy. First, he made a trip to the press office, where an old journalist friend of his by the name of Horcoff sat in the senior editor's office.

A balding man with beady eyes and glasses altogether too big for his face, Horcoff Sigmund was *De Telegraaf*'s oldest employee, and had seen to his meteoric rise from one office to the other the hard and long way, starting as a photographer, then a copywriter for those fluff pieces in the back of the newspaper, and then toiling around the Netherlands reporting on this, that, and the other, before settling down in Amsterdam and taking the helm of the editorial office.

"It's not a good day today." Horcoff shook his head before Haden had fully entered his office. "Not today, Moore."

"So soon you forget the trenches." Haden clicked his tongue and shook his head, taking his felt hat off and placing it upon Horcoff's scattered desk.

"I never," Horcoff said, raising a finger of self-preservation, then nodding at the picture on the wall, one with a framed picture of Allied soldiers standing victorious in Stalingrad. In the corner of the picture, two men stood with grins on their faces and fire in their eyes. Only now, twenty-six years later, were both those men in this office, their faces bearing grimness instead of grins. And the light that was in their eyes was dimmed by age, yet still burned somewhere in there.

"Then help me out, and tell me why you've been holding out on me," Haden said, his voice slow. "You know I am in town. Have been for some time now. When was I supposed to know that there had been eleven disappearances in the city?"

"Deaths, not disappearances," Horcoff corrected him. "And like everyone else, you'd have read about it in the news."

"Except, I've been reading the paper every morning, and only three were mentioned. What about the others? What about the fact that you promised me that if something of this sort happened, you'd reach out to me?" Haden knew where to apply the pressure when needed, but this wasn't pressure application. This was remorse. His friend had grown lax.

"I..." Horcoff sighed. "I have had my arm wrung by, let's not say who. I can't quite publish the news, and I was explicitly told not to involve you."

"Who?"

"The mayor. The alderman. Police chief. They pretend not to know you, but your reputation precedes you, Professor. They'd rather you not get involved prematurely."

"Prematurely? Horcoff, twelve is not a number that should be considered premature. Did all the bodies have..."

"I'm going to stop you right there so that I am not implicit. There's politics involved, Haden. The offices would rather this 'problem' did not exist. And the concerned parties know that you do tend to charge quite the fees. If it's just another killer, they have the police on it. And if it's not, then God help us all. Because the election is due in another month, Mayor Shiloh is going to be re-elected. He cannot have a crisis on his hands before the elections," Horcoff said. His eyes said something else. He was pointing at a file that was set apart from the rest of the unarranged stuff. He nodded at it again.

Haden nodded in understanding and took the file containing the pictures of the victims.

"We should have coffee sometime, eh, Haden? I like how you make it. Reminds me of MREs."

"Be seeing you then, Horcoff."

With the file tucked away in his coat and with more questions than answers, Haden walked out of the office, aware that there were eyes on him. The people standing around the press office were not just bystanders.

He took the longer way home and waited with bated breath till the foot traffic had thinned out below. After the most recent body was discovered, a curfew was imposed. In the meantime, Haden looked at the pictures of the bodies, finding the same puncture marks on the necks of all the victims. There was journalist shorthand written behind every picture, detailing what Horcoff had learned from the autopsy reports.

That each body was completely bloodless when it was discovered.

HADEN WAS TALLER, even by Amsterdam standards, and despite the fact that he was middle-aged, he was well-built. That, combined with his felt hat and his trench coat, gave him an air of authority in every room he walked. His deep voice did the rest.

Aware that he was breaking about a dozen city laws as he walked into the police station after curfew hours, Haden barged through the door, noticing the haphazard state of the bullpen where young cops were scampering from desk to desk with files in their hands and panic on their faces.

Haden blinked and acknowledged the armory, where firearms were displayed in a blue cage. It was too easy to just jump over the counter and enter the armory, but that was neither here nor there. He ignored the police officer at the reception calling out to him, pushed past the two younger cops barging his way, and headed straight into the police chief's office.

The police chief, Coenraad van Vliet, a white-browed man with a smooth face that made him look like a cognitively dissonant painter, had created a portrait of an overlarge baby. A baby with a bulging pot belly and pink skin.

He glared at Haden, who glared back as he strode into the office and slammed the door shut behind him.

"You got ten minutes," Coenraad said in resentful acknowledgement of authority that surpassed borders and governments.

Haden took the file and slammed it on Coenraad's desk.

"Do you mind telling me why I haven't been made aware of this?" Haden snapped as Coenraad took the pictures out of the files.

"Horcoff gave you these? Son of a bitch will have what's coming to him."

"You will not touch a hair on his head," Haden growled, putting his fist on the table and leaning closer to the police chief. "You should have been the one alerting me, not him."

"The fact that you need alerting means one of two things, *hunter*. Either there's nothing wrong or you're growing old, slow." Coenraad smirked, taking a pack of cigarettes out of his desk cabinet and lighting one up without offering it to Haden.

"This woman was found dead earlier today," Haden said, pointing at the picture of Lisa Vicenza. "Today."

"And my men are on it, as I am sure you saw."

"What's that supposed to mean?" Haden growled, scowling at Coenraad. Coenraad coughed, the smoke catching in his throat.

"I mean," Coenraad said, his eyes watering. "These are whores, druggies, runaways, alcoholics. People die every day, Moore. And sure, maybe someone's dumping their bodies in the canal, but it doesn't necessarily mean it's connected. Not everything is a conspiracy."

"Only this wasn't a whore or a junkie. She's Lisa, a student of mine. She was a phenomenal student, not some druggie," Haden said.

"Ah. So it's personal?"

"No. It's a warning. She's not the first. And she's not going to be the last, Coenraad. She was drained of blood. And the reports say that so, too, were the other bodies."

Coenraad shrugged. "You're far behind the times. I mean...wait until the autopsy report arrives tonight. It'll just reveal that she was a drunkard, high on a cocktail of pills when she died."

Haden gritted his teeth. Lisa was a good kid, someone who had grown up in a conservative household and had not turned away from that religiosity; instead, she'd chosen to pursue it at an academic level. Hardly her MO to be doing drugs or drinking away in Oudezijd.

"What about the puncture marks? Neat, precise, no tearing, no bruising? There was no struggle, from the signs of it. It seemed more like a ritual," Haden said, looking at the picture again.

"Needle marks," Coenraad said flatly. "A big enough needle hole will drain away quite a lot of blood, but then again, I'm not a doctor, just as you're no police officer. Go talk to your colleagues, or write a letter to the Vatican. I hear they like stories, the kind you're peddling."

Haden picked his file up from the desk and pointed a warning finger at Coenraad, saying, "You're going to believe me when the next one shows up. And the next one after that."

"How can you be so sure? Are you, by any chance, committing these acts? Has the hunter become the very thing he once hunted?"

"Fuck you, Coenraad," Haden said, turning heel to walk out of the office. "And don't get in my way."

He only heard Coenraad's resigned sigh behind him.

JOURNALIST SHORTHAND WAS fine enough for perusal, but if Haden wanted to confirm his suspicions, he needed to get in touch with the coroner.

Haden walked out from the station in the empty streets just as the rain started to beat down, wiping away evidence, wiping away the city's dust and its sorrow. He tucked the file deeper in his trench coat so it wouldn't get wet. His felt hat got soaked, but for the most part kept his face dry. Haden was not a man who was afraid to get wet. He enjoyed the added weight of the rainwater on his clothes.

In the abandoned yet still-lit streets, he walked along the curving Warmoesstraat, appreciating the shimmery sheen of rainwater on the cobbled stone as it glowed golden in the lamplight. He ducked under the striped awning of Café de Toog, a corner place he'd favored since his move.

The owner knew him from years of serving, years of coffee and water, accompanied by scores of cigarettes. As Haden knocked at the window, the man nodded from behind the bar. Curfews did not matter to old men such as him or Haden, and if his old patron wanted a coffee, a coffee he would get.

Outside, Haden took one of the round iron tables, wiped it down with the back of his glove, and sat with his collar up against the chill. He lit a cigarette, the paper hissing briefly in the wet air, and when the waiter came, he didn't need to ask for anything; the waiter already knew his order.

Inside his coat pocket, folded once and sealed in a plastic sleeve, was the name and number of the coroner who'd done the autopsy on Lisa.

He finished his cigarette in silence, his eyes tracing the street. He had pondered the times at the Vatican, Romania, and his traversing of Europe to track down the creatures that were sworn to the night. He had stared death in the face, but still had trouble believing himself that evil existed, for he wanted it not to.

He wanted to believe that the work of these creatures was simply madmen who would do anything to satisfy their sick minds.

He was deep in thought when the honk of a truck driving by broke his gaze. He realized that he'd finished his coffee and his cigarette had all but gone unsmoked, the ash holding onto the butt for dear life, like a building that was about to crumble.

He stood and walked into the cafe, where the scent of yeast and damp coats reminded him of home, and walked casually to the owner.

"May I use the phone?" he asked.

"Of course, Professor. Office in the back. You know the way."

Inside, with the door closed and the rotary dial humming beneath his fingertips, he removed his jacket. It was still wet from his walk, and he did not want to drench the cafe owner's desk with water. He waited for the coroner to answer, and when the voice came through, gravelly and tired, Haden spoke simply:

"This is Professor Haden Moore. I need to meet you tonight," he spoke into the phone. "I will need you to bring a certain file. And I shall need you to be at the cemetery gate tonight at eight sharp."

The coroner responded with an affirmative after a minute of silence.

IT WAS JUST past eight when Haden reached the edge of De Nieuwe Ooster. The cemetery gates were wrought iron and flanked by stone pillars gone soft at the corners with lichen. The rain had stopped, but it left a lingering smell in the air, iron mixed with mud. A cold and unappealing smell. Haden stood just outside the threshold, gloved hands in his pockets, the collar of his trench still turned up.

The coroner arrived a few minutes later, slower than

Haden remembered, with a folder tucked under his coat and a plastic bag hanging from one wrist.

He didn't speak immediately, for he was too concerned with scanning the horizon and looking behind him as if somebody had been following him the entire way.

He was a tall, slender man with jet black hair slicked to one side. He had an Aryan mercilessness etched into his face. The last thing a dead body would want to look up at.

"You said bring the file," he muttered and handed over the file. "Why are we at a cemetery? Please tell me it's not what I think it is."

Haden took it with a nod, flipping through the autopsy photos quickly, not to study them, just to show that he already knew what he was looking for. He had already seen the puncture marks in the photograph that he showed the police, but he wanted to ensure there were no other marks on the body.

The hallowed ground confirmation provided a moment of relief for the coroner, but it would be short-lived, as the confirmation of needing hallowed ground only meant one thing: monsters had made their way to Amsterdam.

"She had no blood," the coroner said; he looked scared and desperate, and said it as if it needed repeating. "Not just exsanguination. The veins were dry. Entirely collapsed. Like her body had been drained through pressure rather than injury."

"No defense wounds?"

"None. Nails clean. No bruising on the wrists or face.

No semen. No struggle. There is an indication that she had sex, but that could be anyone's guess."

"And the bite?"

"It was too clean, Professor. Two unbelievably precise punctures, you see?" he said, pointing at the photograph. "No tearing or anything around it, and look at this..." He pulled something from the plastic bag and handed it over. It was the woman's blouse.

"It's ripped," he added, showing Haden the claw marks in the blouse. "She was wearing it. Whatever this was wasn't...human."

Haden studied the small blouse, bunched it up, and then tucked it into his coat.

"The police got in touch with me, telling me they're going to close this case hush-hush, a suicide, if you can believe it," the coroner said, clicking his tongue.

"But the bite marks and the shirt," Haden insisted.

"I didn't say it made sense," the coroner said, his voice lowering as he looked around. "But there's already pressure. City council, tourism board. It's not good optics, having corpses bobbing up near the Jordaan. With the blasted election a month away, the police won't do a thing about it."

They stood in silence, and somewhere beyond the gate, a crow gave a single, drawn-out caw. Crows cawing in the night were never a good omen, especially not when the linger of murder was still heavy in the air.

"Five more cases came across my table this week," the coroner added. "All with similar signs. You think I'm crazy for meeting you out here?"

"I think you're smart," Haden said. "And I think we're

running out of time. I am meeting with some other professors and a Vatican archivist who has joined me on other expeditions before. Come, let us talk in the church."

The two men walked slowly toward the church doors, which were open, as they always were. Ready to accept anyone who wanted to bring God into their life. The crows were dancing and singing in the background. They paused outside the doorway, under the archway where the stone saints looked down on them.

"I often wondered who crafts these statues; they always look more evil than good." Haden chuckled as the two looked up at the cherubs staring at them. He turned to the coroner, his voice lower now.

"I've seen a village in northern Italy where an entire generation vanished. Twenty-seven people, gone. Only a priest was left behind, mumbling numbers that didn't make sense until we realized they were dates. Feast days and breeding cycles."

The air between them became more palpable with tension. Haden wanted to trust this man, and in coming here with the file, the coroner had proven that he could be trusted. But there were secrets that Haden knew that would put the fear of God in the man who dealt with dead bodies for a living. A man who, in his own mind, had seen it all. And yet, Haden had enough to tell him that would make him reconsider that stance.

"In Medjugorje," Haden continued, deciding that trust was a two-way street and that he should at least attempt to build it before assuming otherwise. "I saw a child aged overnight. Skin like parchment, eyes black from the inside. She spoke five languages, none of them spoken on Earth. Her mother tried to drown her twice. They said the Devil had come to claim her soul because the Virgin Mary was planning a visit."

"You're not talking about who I think you're talking about," the coroner spoke, his face perplexed.

"I'm talking about things that existed long before anyone called them vampires." Haden's eyes held the coroner in grave regard. "And this, whatever is happening here, feels worse. Vampires leave bodies around. These ones are cleaning up. That takes organization. I'm sensing that a family has moved to town, but that means a leader is with them, someone older than water."

The church bell above them rang once, low and off-tempo.

"We should go inside," Haden said, looking over his shoulder. "They might not be gods, but they have spent enough time among us humans to imitate us."

The coroner blinked at him, unsure if he should respond as they both walked inside. Inside, the church was quiet but not empty. A nun passed them without a glance, her rosary beads clinking softly at her side. Toward the back, they settled into one of the pews beneath a fading fresco of Saint Michael casting out the devil.

"They don't just kill to feed," Haden said. "They kill to erase and to stay hidden. Everybody you've seen is one step away from no longer existing. And I'm afraid, Jonatan, that includes you too."

The coroner sat rigid, his coat damp at the shoulders. "You think they'll come for me?"

"I do. I've seen this too many times before. You are a link between them and their secrecy. And that makes you a liability," Haden replied. "This all has happened so quickly, but I am also quick. I'm going to call in reinforcements, men who reside in Amsterdam. Speed is of the essence here, and these are men who hunt for pleasure, who are methodical, and won't let their town be overrun by vampires and monsters. And you, Jonatan, you notice things, you don't accept the status quo, that makes you useful. I'm hazarding a guess that one of them has either threatened the police sergeant or paid him off."

"And if I say no?" the coroner asked with a frail voice, a voice completely unbecoming of his person.

"Then you'll leave this church, go back to your life, and in a week or a month, someone will find you in your own autopsy room. And your report will vanish before it's filed."

The coroner didn't answer immediately. He stared up at the fresco, eyes lingering on the flaming sword in Michael's hand, as he took a deep breath.

"I'll come," he said quietly. "But I don't know the first thing about killing."

"Neither did I, once," Haden replied, standing. "Not until my hand was forced."

He placed a hand briefly on the man's shoulder, saying, "We meet tomorrow. At ten p.m. The old catacombs beneath the university archives. You are to tell no one, not even your wife, understood?"

The coroner looked up at Haden, the mercilessness

gone from his face, leaving behind worry and age. He nodded briefly, and Haden nodded back.

And once that business was concluded, Haden walked out into the rain, disappearing between the downpour as yet another shadow in the cemetery.

THE CATACOMBS beneath the university were not meant for meetings. They were places where forgetfulness dwelled. Bricked-in hallways from the seventeenth century, stone sweating under the pressure of the city above.

A trickle of water echoed every few seconds as it dripped from the ceiling into a rusted drain, the sound carrying farther than it had any right to in the stillness. The air was cold enough to remind a man of what lay beneath the ground, but not cold enough to preserve a body. A place of in-betweens. Between history and oblivion, between faith and what it had buried.

Candles had been set along the alcoves in iron sconces, their flames wavering, throwing shadows across statues whose faces had already been half-consumed by mold. The scent of wax and old limestone hung thick. At the center of the main chamber, a round oak table had been dragged from somewhere else, its legs scarring the stone floor on the way down.

It was too big for the room, too heavy, and yet it belonged here, the way an altar belongs in a church. Maps and papers were already scattered across its surface, pinned down by coins, a compass, and a single rusted dagger.

Haden Moore was already there, waiting, trench coat draped over the back of his chair like the discarded skin of some animal. His broad hands rested on the table's edge, fingertips smudged with ink and candle soot. He didn't look up when the first footsteps arrived. He'd expected them.

Jonatan came first. The coroner walked as if afraid the ground might give way, each stride hesitant, hands clenching and unclenching at his sides. His clothes still carried the faint antiseptic smell of embalming fluid, though beneath it was the sour tang of fear.

Then Paulo. Professor of medieval languages, shoulders hunched against the damp, leather satchel banging against his side. His hair, once black, had gone streaked with gray, but his ink-stained fingers still twitched with the nervous energy of a man who lived among books instead of people.

Tomas followed. The archivist. His steps were steady, though he moved like a man accustomed to dim cloisters and library aisles rather than wet stone chambers.

And then the last one came. Lars the brute. His body was blocky, shoulders filling the narrow passageway, tattoos twisting like sailors' ropes up his forearms.

The five of them were assembled.

Haden raised his head slowly, letting his eyes settle on each of them in turn, the way a priest looks at a congregation before the sermon. He didn't speak immediately. He let the silence fill the chamber, let the candle flames flicker against stone, let the sound of dripping water remind them all of where they were: beneath the city, beneath the living, at the threshold of something older and hungrier than all of them.

When he did speak, his voice was low, but it carried through.

"Victims converge here," he said, tapping the map. "This brownstone, number ninety-two. The baker across the way swears he only ever sees them at night, curtains closed by day, figures at the door after sundown," Haden now rested his hand on the map. "I've done more digging. They'll leave by water, they always do. Every city I've chased them through, they vanish through the docks once they've been found out. A moving truck's been running between the brownstone and slip twenty-two for a week now, hauling crates at dusk and returning empty before dawn. That's their exit. When they move tonight, it'll be from there."

Jonatan let out a small murmur.

"Let it be known, gents," Haden continued, "that this isn't a demure council where tongues will wag idly and parliamentary ideas will be argued. Our survival hinges upon this meeting, and unfortunately, we don't have the luxury of time. We have this one night to plan our hunt. Understand?"

The men first looked at one another, then all eyes converged on Haden Moore. They nodded with deliberation, each understanding the gravity of the situation.

The hunt had begun, and Amsterdam did not know it was already burning.

CHAPTER 3

HOUSE OF HORRORS

Jonatan leaned on the iron railing beside his bicycle. His flat cap was pulled over his brow, and his long jet-black hair struggled to hide underneath it.

Christ, I might die tonight, he thought, standing there across from the brownstone. The morning had come and whispers of sunshine shone through the looming clouds above. It interrupted the occasional drizzle that overshadowed the city, giving a stark warning not to get too comfortable, and Jonatan felt the same way.

But what choice did he have? He could certainly go back to his day-to-day life in the morgue, slicing and dicing bodies and taking his valium at night so that he could sleep. Or was Professor Haden correct? If he said no, he could very well be the next victim laid across his own table.

He'd never faced his demons head on, but right now as he stood watching the brownstone, knowing that vampires were dwelling inside, he'd never felt more cornered. It was an odd juxtaposition for him.

All around him, life was thriving. Geese flocked in the canal, tourists and residents alike rode their bikes along the riverbank gleefully, commuters struggled running to the bus stop in the hope not to miss the seven a.m. arrival, because the bus driver wouldn't wait longer than he had to. Yet, right in the center of it all stood this decrepit mausoleum, a testament to all things sullen and fitful, and Amsterdam had no clue.

He trailed off, thinking about his work, where he would regularly confess his sins to the dead and find them more empathetic listeners than most living people he'd come across. They didn't talk back, although some nights (because his work often revolved around the midnight hour when a body would be delivered to him from the hospital) he wished they would. He remembered right now about the last girl.

Her skin was the kind of blue that only came from embalming, or blood being drained entirely from one's body. Her eyes were a milky white, nothing out of the ordinary, but it was the puncture marks on her neck. These were different than the others. They looked bigger, with additional marks around the prominent two, as if other teeth were fighting for space on the girl's skin.

"Oh, you silly, silly girl, why did you have to go and get caught up in this mess? You were so damn young," he asked her, hoping for some kind of response. Some kind of nod to what was happening in the city that brought eleven other humans to his metal table. But she didn't respond. A simple twitch in her left index finger, a mix of chemical and muscle reactions in the brain, always told Jonatan the same thing. That while the dead couldn't talk back, they could certainly hear him.

Haden stalked the street with a cigarette gritted between his teeth. His effortful casual gait was betrayed only by the sharpness of his eyes, the way they cut through the noise, analyzing everything. And while most dreadful things hunted in the dark, the daylight did nothing to quell Haden's alertness. After all, most vampires, werewolves, and other demons usually employed a handler. A familiar. Someone who would watch over them when the sun was up, and if these godless horrors moved in herds, then it was likely that a group of familiars or family members watched over them.

It wasn't uncommon in the underworld for hunters like Haden to go missing during the daytime either, and this always kept Haden on his toes. Random kidnappings on the street, a bomb hidden under a car, or simply a murder in a cafe restroom. Familiars would stop at nothing to put a problem to bed, and in the spring of 1962, Haden nearly fell to a similar fate.

When Haden was talking to the Vatican about the Medjugorje case, he almost fell foul to a group of familiars who had seemingly been employed by some ungodly forces. He had decided to take a stroll in Vatican City after meeting with officials who wanted him to solve a case in an apparent return of the Devil. It was said that six visionaries had been visited by Satan—he told them that in twenty years to the day, on March 18th, a false prophet in the form of the Virgin Mary would appear and try to poison them.

And that the only way out of this calamity was to birth the son of the Devil, who would help them fight back and destroy the apparition. One of the women to whom Satan had appeared was a nineteen-year-old virgin called Armina, who the Vatican said had gotten pregnant by way of undivine intervention.

It would be Haden's job to investigate, to see if there were any truth to the rumors, and by way of his own discretion, Armina and the unholy child were to disappear. For the alternative could spell a far worse fate, not just for the visionaries, but for humanity itself.

Haden had agreed to take on the case, but shortly before he was due to board a flight, as he was exiting his hotel, a camper van screeched up alongside him. Three men in black balaclavas jumped out of the van and tried dragging Haden into it. If it wasn't for the hotel door staff and a passerby, they could very well have been successful and Haden wouldn't have lived to see another day.

It was this event that always kept him on his feet. A small army knife, a bottle of pepper spray, and his cigarettes became his *trois de resistance*.

It was around late afternoon, the lazy sheen of golden light on every building, sunlight reflecting off of every window, as if sanctifying the city while it still could. Lars squinted in that sunlight, his voice hoarse but steady.

"They've got a private boat prepping at slip twenty-two. I was talking to the crew. They said it's pulling out just after midnight."

Static hissed, then Haden's voice cut back. "This boat has a manifest, yes?"

"None that's listed officially." A pause, which was then followed by the faint grind of ice crates in the background. "But I've seen two unmarked loads. And if I didn't see it I wouldn't believe it, but these crates are tall and broad enough to fit a body."

Silence hung over the line, the kind of silence that meant everyone had reached the same conclusion. Then Haden again: "Okay, keep your eyes on it. I doubt anyone will be leaving during the daylight."

"Roger that," the brute grunted, and the channel went dead.

Had the gang of hunters been ordinary folk, bar Jonatan, then the plan wouldn't have come together so quickly. Haden was good at that. He had spent enough time over his years making good connections, learning who he could trust and who he could bribe. These men had been embroiled in battles with the undead in many a situation, and while their brain cells didn't always fire on all cylinders, it somewhat added to the bravery and camaraderie that helped them defeat creatures of the night with gusto. It was Jonatan and Haden who were responsible for most of the intelligence, and it was evident in the execution.

It was also a shared commonality between the group that Amsterdam had been their choice to take a back seat from the underworld. Each one of them had their own reasons for retreating here and making life a little easier. It was one of the only places on the planet that afforded acceptance, cultural differences, and hedonism.

Lars preferred the company of ladies of the night. It was a sweet uncomplicated distraction, and when he wasn't parting their legs wide and gorging upon their tender wetness, he was munching on medium-rare meat at cheap steakhouses across town.

Tomas preferred the company of the same sex. He was on a similar train as Lars in that he wanted zero distractions. He enjoyed the random sailor or tourist so that he wouldn't get lost in a love affair that could raise eyebrows in his somewhat religious family household. He was old for his twenty-seven years, and in that short time had accompanied Haden on three expeditions involving things that were better off not being mentioned.

"They're going tonight, aren't they?" Tomas's voice was a bare murmur into the mic, almost drowned by the hiss of rain.

Across the city, Haden didn't hesitate and quickly chimed in, saying, "Yes." He dropped the cigarette into a puddle, the ember hissing out. His eyes never blinked as he scanned the brownstone's upper windows.

While the hunt wouldn't begin before midnight, the hunters were already laying the trap and closing in around their prey.

By ten thirty, the streets had gone quiet, a little unnatural for a city as lively as Amsterdam, but given these uncertain days and the curfew, people opted for their safety over any touristy matters such as enjoying the nightlife or spending their money on bodily pleasures.

Amsterdam was heavy that night with thick fog (another reason why the streets felt subdued and silent); it had rolled in low along the canal, turning streetlamps into dull orbs. The rain had stopped, but the cobblestones were still slick, reflecting the amber glow of shop windows now closed for the day's business, but still keeping a flicker of lights on. The brownstone stood dark, looming and threatening, save for the moonlight that stood behind it. *An omen if ever there was one,* thought Haden.

Across the canal, Haden and Jonatan sat on a bench facing the house with their coats turned up against the mist. They weren't the only people out and about at this time of night, but they were one of the only few.

It was a weeknight. Pubs and nightclubs in the center vicinity wouldn't be open late, closing around eleven p.m. for the night. The bench was hidden behind a large oak tree that shielded the two from any view of the house, even if it was across from the water. The pair sat almost a foot apart, like two lovers shrouded in secrecy, and both of their radios were turned down to the minimal volume allowed so as not to alert anyone.

∾

At 10:58 P.M., Haden's voice crackled over the comms as he sat like a statue, unclenched and unnerved. "There's movement at the front door."

The others replied with acknowledgement, yet Haden's nonchalant attitude caught Jonatan off guard. He was, after all, new to the game of the hunt, and he was almost certain that this would be his last night on earth.

Jonatan hissed, "Now what?" but Haden gave no reply, his eyes fixed on the brownstone's front door as it eased open, then creaked to a stop.

For a moment, Jonatan thought the dwellers were about to emerge, but the pause lingered, too long for chance. It felt like someone inside had misjudged the timing, or worse, had cracked the door to search for them. Haden didn't move or breathe, his stillness so absolute it looked less like patience than possession.

The vampires emerged wordlessly, their quiet and swift movements carrying the mechanical grace of something rehearsed, as if this departure had been performed a hundred times before. A tall man stepped out first.

It was Jerry.

Haden let out a small breath of air, enough to make a noise somewhere between a whimper and a whisper.

Jerry's features were too precise to be natural, a face that seemed carved rather than born, the effect made stranger by the long gloves and an antiquated coat that hung from his frame. Three others followed, each burdened with a case or trunk, their pale skin glowing faintly in the moonlight, an unnatural sheen even for Amsterdam. Last came Billy Cole, who eased the door shut as if not to wake up his neighbors before turning to sweep the rooftops and street below.

From his post two blocks up, Tomas tensed as he raised the walkie, his voice hushed but urgent. "It doesn't feel right. He looks like he knows something."

"Let him know we know," Haden said quietly into the comms. "They might be soulless, but they're not mind-less. At least not all of them anyway."

Meanwhile, at slip twenty-two, Lars leaned against a post near the rippling water, his coat wrapped tight and hat pulled low. He'd been there an hour. The boatman had arrived just after sundown, a middle-aged man with a limp and a quiet suspicion in his eyes.

"You the chump who got dealt the graveyard shift?" the man had asked, nodding toward the sleek black boat moored at the end of the slip.

"I was ordered to," the brute replied in Dutch, flashing the forged pass. "Said I'd cover for a friend. Something about a last-minute runner."

The boatman gave him a once over. "Know how to keep logs?"

"I know how to stay warm and quiet, and not ask questions. That good enough?"

The man gave a grunt and a shrug. "You'll be waiting a while. They said midnight, but that crew looked like the kind to show up late."

"That's not a problem for me. I'm used to shifts late in the night, but you don't look like you are. My bet's you've got a wife and she's waiting for you at home. My experience has told me that around this hour, wives want their husbands in bed with them, not out in the city, especially one such as this," Lars said as he threw a stick of gum into his mouth.

That got a laugh from the boatman. "Someone paid me a small fortune to stay here until that boat left the dock."

"Funny you say that, because I got paid an arm and a leg too by that same someone. Trust me, I've dealt with these guys before when they moved here. Head on out and I'll take care of them. They won't ask questions. They never do," the brute responded.

The man had agreed in that he was old, tired, and wanted to be warm. And who would care if this big muscular brute was taking over for him anyway? He gave it a brief thought, weighing both options, then, looking at the brute and his tall stature, his wide brawn, he nodded, thinking to himself that the same party who had paid him must most definitely have paid him. *This guy was born to be a henchman*, thought the boatman with a dry chuckle, and waved at the brute before departing toward his home.

By the time the man had limped off into the mist, the brute was alone on the dock, tendrils of fog and smoke sweeping at his feet, lingering low over the water. He waited another half-hour, walking the perimeter twice, then returned to the boat. A small container of gasoline sat in a canvas bag behind the wheelhouse; he'd planted it earlier that afternoon.

At 11:03, he slipped the rag into the neck of the bottle

and made it snug, admiring his handiwork even though there wasn't much to it. As a Russian soldier had once told him with a vodka-drunk smile, "A Molotov works fine in a pinch, da. It isn't grenade. It isn't spring mine. But in the moment it explodes, it reminds the victim that if flames are real, then so must be Hell. And then he burns, comrade."

"Ready here," he whispered into the walkie. "Boat's all rigged."

"Hold," came Haden's voice. "Is all of the stuff on the boat?"

"Yeah, they must have loaded it earlier. This vessel is all set to sail."

"Then make sure it doesn't. Set it the fuck alight and get the hell out of there," Haden commanded.

Paulo had walked over to Lars once he saw the old man leave the docking station. They watched the boatman climb into his rusted little car, the kind of manual transmission relic that jerked forward with every shift, coughing smoke as it limped away from the docking station. A small yellow tin thing that reassured Lars the man really did want to be home, he didn't want to be sat here in the cold any longer.

They lingered, saying nothing, their eyes on the barge as it rocked gently against the pilings. In the shifting beams of the night's fog-refracted light, the contents of the barge came briefly into view. Crates stacked two deep, tarpaulin half-drawn across them, the outlines too obvious, too heavy, the unmistakable shape of coffins disguised as freight.

To the untrained eye, this was simply another freight

headed for some offshore vessel, but to the hunters, the sight held them both still. Paulo stood mesmerized by the boat in front of him, the swaying of the boat sending him into a momentary lull as he meditated on what was to come, for this was only the beginning. Lars drew deep on his cigarette, toying with the smoke leaving his mouth in a sort of ceremonial dance, the smoke acting like a thin ribbon that danced above him, reaching for nothing before evaporating.

For a long moment they simply looked at each other, the silence thick with everything unspoken: fear, certainty, the knowledge that this was the right place and the right time. Then Lars drew once more on the cigarette, held his breath, and looked at the glowing ember of the stick.

He flashed a look to Paulo, who looked back and gave a simple nod, then, with his dirt-stained fingers, he pressed it to the rag-stuffed mouth of the waiting bottle. The flame caught fast, and Lars turned the bottle in his hands as if to study it, and with a flick of his wrist he sent the Molotov arcing out to the middle of the boat.

It broke against the hull and the fire immediately spread across the tarpaulin, racing up the stacked boxes. It started low at first, until it reached the coffins, then it erupted into a pyre that lit the dockside in a flickering orange haze.

"Let's get to it," Lars said, as the fire drifted up into the mist like a signal to anyone watching that the way forward had been cut off.

～

THE SUV HAD ROLLED off from the brownstone and started its slow drive to the dock. Haden and Jonatan ensured it was out of view before standing up and walking across the bridge to the house. Tomas had skipped over to them fast, looking around as he was running across the street. His stomach grumbled uneasily, and his wasn't the only one doing so. Nervousness met them each in its different forms, manifesting in odd quirks—twitching eyelids, trembling lower lips, tapping feet, shaking hands, and a terrible case of heartburn that had nothing to do with indigestion.

They met at the door to the home, and Haden pushed down on the brass door handle. The door popped open with ease.

"Kind of runs antithetical to the whole 'meticulous' myth if he's not locking doors behind him," Tomas whispered.

"Kind of doesn't. It's basic bait and switch, perfectly in line with his character. He'd rather we waste our time here, comb through the place. As for them, they don't intend on coming back," Haden replied with impatience.

"Might be a trap then," Jonatan chimed in, worried that once inside they would meet their peril, causing Haden to pause.

"Highly likely," Haden said, voice coarse with grim realization. "Jonatan, head back across the street and take watch. If you see anyone coming back, you radio us immediately. Here. Take this cross."

Jonatan shot Haden a look as if to ask if he was serious. Decades as a coroner did little for religious beliefs, and regardless of their fight against the undead, Jonatan was still unconvinced these people were anything but aberrations, mutations—scientifically explainable.

"Christ might have fuck all to do with this, but the cross works. Wear it!" Haden continued, as Jonatan skipped off to the railing against the canal.

The door groaned as it swung open, and the hallway stretched ahead, narrow and dark. The walls inside were painted black, the only lighted fixture being the blonde floorboards beneath them, which creaked with each step. The tiles in the entrance hallway were black and white, checkered like a chess board, giving rise to the grandness of the abode, their surface worn but still gleaming faintly in the light of Haden's flashlight.

To the left, a staircase climbed straight up, wide at its base before winding into the shadows above, each turn visible until it disappeared at the top of the third story. The banister was heavy, polished black, its surface chipped where countless hands or something more sinister had once gripped. And the air? The air smelled of damp brick and dust, stale in a way that suggested the windows hadn't been opened in decades.

"Screw the flashlights. Just turn the lights on," Tomas insisted. "Lightbulbs won't alert the police, but flashlight beams will if they catch sight of it from outside."

Haden agreed. This was why he brought these people with him. They complemented each other rather than complicating each other. Haden switched the lights on, and it came as no surprise to him that they still worked.

They had imagined that the vampires had simply abandoned the house rather than going through the mundane nuance of calling the energy company to turn off the connection.

Or, their shell company would deal with that later.

If there was one thing vampires were, it was calculating.

The lights buzzed and flickered for a moment, as if they weren't sure of their new guests. For a mere moment, Haden and Tomas stopped to catch their breath.

The air proclaimed what the ungodly stench was already exclaiming. This was it. They were in the nest.

Haden took the reins and stepped forward. The first doorway on the right led to a large room. It had large ceilings and was also painted black; for all intents and purposes, it looked like a living room.

Crown molding covered the angles, and a large chandelier adorned the middle of it. A sumptuous sofa sat immediately to the right with two armchairs on the opposite side of the room. A television stood in the corner near the large window. The large windowpanes felt like a dichotomy of sorts, but a set of large purple velvet curtains would ensure that during the day, no light would be flooding into this room.

There came a belabored creak from the floorboards above them.

Tomas nudged Haden, asking, "Reckon someone's here?"

"No, it can't be. They'd all have left. It's just an old house settling down in the night wind," he whispered back.

Haden crossed to the fireplace, its hearth still dark

with the trace of a fire that had only recently gone out. He set down his tote bag and knelt, opening it wide as his hands worked inside, fingers brushing against the coarse fibers of the burlap sack that held the charges.

Tomas watched him pull one free, the expression on his face tightening when he realized what it was.

"You had the bombs in a fucking tote bag?" he hissed, agitated. It looked careless, almost reckless, the kind of choice that could have ended the job before it began.

Haden glanced up at him, unimpressed, then shifted his focus to the living room doorway. Still clear. He paused just long enough to throw Tomas a quick wink before peeling away one of the adhesive panels on the detonator casing. Rolling up his sleeve, he reached into the chimney's narrow chute and pressed the device into place, securing it where no one would think to look.

Another creak came from above, and this time both men froze, their eyes lifting toward the ceiling. Before either could speak, Tomas's radio burst to life with Jonatan's voice, the volume turned too high. The sound cracked through the silence, echoing in the living room and making them both flinch.

Tomas hurried to the window with Haden close behind, and there, across the street, Jonatan sat half-hidden on a bench beneath an oak, the radio still in his hand.

"You don't need to respond. Quiet as it is here, you might as well scream," Tomas whispered, nudging Haden. Haden gave a quick nod and raised his flashlight, sending a sharp flicker of light through the glass.

But Jonatan misread the signal—saw panic where

there was none—and in an instant he broke cover, leaving the bench behind as he sprinted across the street toward the house.

"What is he doing?!" Tomas hissed.

"He's either seen something out there or he thinks we're in danger. Quick, back to the front door... Let him in quickly."

By the time Jonatan reached the front of the brownstone, he was already out of breath from the sprint. Haden and Tomas opened the front door to a heaving Jonatan and ushered him in fast.

"Jesus, man, how out of shape are you?" Tomas asked.

"Quiet, the both of you!" Haden snapped.

Another creak, and the three of them whipped around before standing still, their eyes fixated on the top of the staircase. The house imposed upon them with formidableness, alive in a way all old houses are with haunting, violent memory. Even in the short time there, Haden and Tomas felt like shadows were moving all around them.

Haden held his palm out against Tomas's chest, forbidding him to follow as he stepped forward. His gaze followed the creaks above as he moved toward the foot of the staircase, trying to make out what was lurking in the dark.

He saw nothing.

The three breathed a sigh of relief and walked slowly back into the living room, where Haden picked up his bag of bombs.

"Upstairs, now!" Tomas whispered, signaling to Haden.

"Nope. We need to get the fuck out of here," Jonatan snipped back.

"Jonatan, go wait outside and keep watch. You're no good to us in here," Haden instructed dismissively.

"I am not going back outside alone. It is pitch black, and on top of that, it's wet, and if that's not enough, then let me tell you, I can feel them watching me from afar," he said, shaking visibly.

Haden accepted defeat; the coroner had done him enough favors these past few weeks and it was unfair to put his life at risk for the case of being the lookout guy. With the first bomb planted and the bag of bombs back in Haden's hands, the three of them walked briskly back to the hallway.

The Edison bulbs in their sconces gave off a weak, amber light, enough to mark the kitchen at the back of the house and the dining room that opened off the living room. Haden let the beam of his flashlight sweep briefly, but stopped when it fell across something he hadn't noticed before. Beneath the staircase was a door, full-sized and fitted with the same dark wood as the others.

At first glance, it could have been overlooked, but the proportions told a different story. A closet door would have been narrow, an afterthought in the design. This one was tall, broad, and built with purpose. It led somewhere. The air around it seemed heavier, as if the house itself recognized what lay behind it and had drawn the lines sharper, made the space impossible to ignore.

Haden lingered on it, silent, already certain of where it went.

He glanced at the others. Tomas gave a short nod; Jonatan shook his head. Haden shut his eyes tight, gripped the knob, and turned. The door gave way easily, releasing a gush of cold air that howled through the narrow gap before spilling into the hall.

As he pulled it wider, a single cord hung down, a bulb swinging faintly in the draft. Haden tugged it, and the light snapped on, dim and yellow, spilling across the stone staircase that dropped into the dark below.

"What's down there?" Tomas grunted.

"Their resting place. Dark, cold, desolate, stowed away under earth," Haden said. "They dig fast, and they dig deep. If we want to make sure they don't escape, we seal the holes. A charge in front of every tunnel."

"That would decimate the house," Tomas said.

Haden gave him a look. "So? What other course of action do we have?"

From the back of the hall Jonatan's voice broke in, sharp and unsteady. "Gentlemen, we're running out of time here." Sweat streaked his face as he wiped at his brow.

Haden and Tomas exchanged a long glance, then both nodded.

"Give me one," Tomas said, reaching for a charge. "I'll take upstairs."

"Very good then. I'll take below."

Haden motioned for Jonatan to follow him as he stepped to the basement door. Tomas turned away, already climbing the staircase. Jonatan rolled his eyes, muttered a curse, and crossed himself for the first time in years before stepping after Haden into the dark.

TOMAS WAS FEARLESS, maybe too much for his own good. He hadn't always been a field man. In Rome, he lived beneath the archives, literally. His quarters were tucked beneath the Bibliotheca Secreta in the Apostolic Palace, a stone room with no windows and shelves packed with vellum-bound codices.

For years, he was the Church's ordained reader of forbidden texts. If it was written in dead languages, sealed with wax, or stitched with human hair, Tomas had read it. He knew every heresy by name, and every name by bloodline.

But it wasn't knowledge that made him fearless. It was what he'd seen on the Vatican's blacklist of unsolved cases.

He'd accompanied Inquisitors to remote villages in Romania and southern Italy, places that still buried their dead with stones in their mouths and crosses made from wolf bones.

He'd seen the remains of entire parishes drained overnight.

He'd watched a priest burst into flames after performing a mass in a desecrated chapel. And all of this was just during his teenage years.

Haden had accompanied him on the trip to Romania, and the two witnessed unexplainable horrors that they pledged never to repeat. So, when the call came from

Haden, he didn't hesitate. He packed a bag and boarded a train headed north.

Now, as Tomas stood at the stairwell, one detonator in his hand, his posture was relaxed, serene, but alert.

Not because he feared death.

But because he had already faced it and lived.

HADEN DESCENDED FIRST, his boots slow but firm, the concrete beneath them making a sharp smacking sound with each footstep. Jonatan followed, his breath catching in his throat as the door at the top closed behind them. The air changed immediately; it was thicker and colder, but surprisingly to them, not damp.

It wasn't what they expected. No mold or mildew crawling up the walls. Instead, it felt preserved. Like it had been kept dry and ready for use. The walls were thick concrete, smooth but aged, with faint hairline fractures running like veins through the grey.

"There's no coffins here," Jonatan said. That was the first thing he noticed. But across the cracked floor were loose scatterings of dirt, fine and dark, arranged in deliberate lines and shallow humps. It wasn't natural. These weren't piles from shoveling or dragging, this was placed or left accidentally in a hurry. As if something had been buried, then lifted and carried away.

Haden crouched beside one of the dirt rings, brushing his fingers gently through it. "This soil's not native," he murmured. "It's the same soil they slept in."

Jonatan stepped farther in and pulled on the light

switch in the middle of the room. It lit up the basement enough that Haden could switch off his flashlight. The two looked around. Furniture lined the perimeter, old, heavy things were draped in thick cloth.

A mirror was turned to face the wall. And on the far wall, near what should have been a utility box, was a poster. At first glance, it was nothing, a faded travel advertisement for the Trans-Siberian Railway. But the edges curled in a way that suggested they hadn't been glued down properly. Jonatan stepped closer.

"There is no tunnel here!" he called out over his shoulder.

Haden didn't respond. He was already walking toward the poster.

"Jonatan," Haden said quietly. "Bring the light."

Jonatan unclipped the flashlight from his belt and leveled the beam. The poster brightened under its glare, colors washed out and its edges curling inward. For a moment it looked like nothing more than an old advertisement, but then the light caught a faint shift behind it.

Haden stepped closer and pressed his fingers against the paper. It flexed, then tore under his touch. What lay behind was not concrete. It was a door.

The wood was crude, fitted low into the concrete, its hinges orange with rust and a latch bolted into the frame. It looked hand-built, the kind of work done slowly, someone shaping hours of hiding into the shape of an exit. The fit was tight, but above it the wall bore faint marks and lines carved shallow into the concrete.

Etchings. Baltic or Uralic in form.

"They must've used this before," Haden commented.

He turned to Jonatan, who stood rigid with the detonator bag heavy in his hands.

"That's why we plant the charges here. If they fall back inside, this is where they'll run off to. And we finish it before they vanish underground."

Jonatan stared at the low door. "Where do you think it leads?"

Haden's mouth didn't buckle. "I don't think we want to know."

He grabbed the bag from Jonatan and set it on the floor, his hand lingering on it for a moment. "Let's make sure they don't escape."

At the top of the staircase, Tomas found a hallway that mirrored the one below, narrow and dim, with three closed doors set along its length. Another stairwell climbed from the far end toward the third floor, vanishing into shadow. He started toward the first door, but stopped short. The earlier creaks had been too deliberate, too heavy to dismiss as settling wood.

Someone else was here.

He pressed his ear against the door. The wood was cool under his cheek. Nothing. No breath, no shuffle, no whisper of movement.

His eyes strayed to the switch on the wall. He flicked it, and the hallway stayed black. The wires were dead, or cut.

The silence closed in around him, deeper now. Then

came the sound. A long, heavy creak from above, followed by something softer, dragged out of the dark.

A moan stretched into the silence.

Tomas froze at the sound, his breath tight in his chest, every muscle locked toward the stairwell above. It wasn't loud, but in the stillness of the house it carried farther than it should have. His hand closed on the railing as he turned toward the second-floor hallway. It ran parallel to the one below, narrow and dim, the sconces fixed along the walls dead and cold.

He stood facing the three doors. They were evenly spaced, all of them shut. He'd faced monsters head on in his past, but never had the misfortune to be willingly trapped in one of their nests. And he knew better than to explore each room, because behind each door, evil most definitely lurked.

He continued his trepid walk down the hallway, the only light coming from the skylight at the very top of the house, above the third-floor landing. *Odd*, he thought. *Why would vampires keep a source of light that poured through the entire interior?*

He moved forward carefully, the weight of his boots pressing a groan from the boards with each step. He passed the first door without stopping, but his eyes lingered on the doorknob, waiting for the moment when a monster may surprise him.

The second he studied longer, his pace slowing, his ear turned to catch even the faintest sound. But it was nothing other than the sound of his own pulse, vibrating through his head as he continued on his journey.

He stopped at the last door. The coldness of the wood

felt like ice as he pressed his ear slowly against the door, waiting to hear if something was inside. Still nothing. He reached for the knob and turned it slowly, the hinges answering with a drawn-out squeal. He leaned in, his body half in the hall, half in the room, one hand gripping the frame.

His other hand found the switch. The bulb above flicked on, casting a dim wash of yellow across the interior. The room was bare. A small fireplace stood where the one in the living room sat below, its bricks stained dark with soot. Dust filmed the floor, but the corners showed signs of use. The air was cooler here, not the untouched stillness of a space left empty, but the feeling of something that had passed through only recently.

He decided that this would be a good place to set a charge.

As he continued to scan the room, another shadow formed back in the hallway. The first door that he'd passed was slowly opening.

The nightmare emerged like a liquid, peeling itself from the doorway. One clawed hand gripped the wall, another curled talon anchoring to the ceiling, each movement defying physics and grace alike, but it made no sound. It was almost invisible. A leg followed, the foot pressing flat against the vertical surface as it made its way to the ceiling and down the hallway toward Tomas.

He hurried into the room and quickly set down the detonator, kneeling in front of the fireplace. He ripped off the sticky covering so he could place it inside the chute, attempting to arm the detonator so that Haden could fire it off later.

As he fumbled with the bomb, the horrendous creature bathed in silhouettes reached the threshold between the hallway and the room. It moved slowly and gracefully, swinging slow and confident like a sloth in the jungle, its yellow eyes glowing in the dark.

It paused for a moment as Tomas was reaching inside the chimney. Then it glided inside slowly like gravity continued to mean nothing. Jet-black skin and elongated limbs. It crawled across the ceiling, its clawed fingers splayed wide as it repositioned itself directly over Tomas, silent and weightless.

It watched as the chimney swallowed most of Tomas's attention as he positioned the device. But something pulled at Tomas, an instinct, a change in pressure, the drop in air temperature.

A soft plink rang through the air.

A drop of saliva hit the floor inches from his hand. Tomas knew exactly what was happening. He'd prepped for this moment already. He knew the kind of fiends that waited for their moment. Wolves in the shape of men with their conniving grins, aberrations that showed their teeth before they attacked.

As it happened, this aberration was beginning to show its teeth now.

THE BARGE BURNED BEHIND THEM, crackling flames roaring high into the night sky, mixing thick smoke with the fog. The smoke would also serve as a signal, and it would only be a matter of time before authorities caught on to the blaze.

Being that the port wasn't used at this time of night, and that it was far enough from the town center, it would take a fire engine at least twenty minutes to get to the dock, and it would be unlikely that anything would be salvageable. If anything, the boat had started to slip lower into the water, something Paulo could faintly make out as they drove off.

Lars kept his hands steady on the wheel, chewing his gum and rolling it slow between his teeth as a form of meditation. The simple rhythmic chewing was akin to box breathing, something he'd learned a long time ago to keep sane under pressure. The truck rattled down the black road with nothing but the rain and occasional thunder in the distance to light the way, save for the random streetlamp.

The noise of the engine groaned with every gear shift, threatening to give out and push the men into the meadows that flanked the small road to the dock. Paulo sat tense beside him with his shoulders drawn in and his walkie clutched to his chest. He kept sneaking glances at the brute, unsettled by the calm on his face. But Lars wasn't pretending.

Fear had been burned out of him long before Amsterdam, in a jungle half a world away.

He had been part of a convoy running supplies north of Pleiku, a thin line of trucks dragging themselves down a narrow trail with green pressing in from both sides. It was hot enough to melt the air. Sweat glued the shirt to his back, and when it wasn't glueing things, it ran the dirt from his forehead down into his eyes, blinding and stinging them.

The convoy rode quiet, the only noise coming from the cicadas screaming louder than their thoughts. If anything, it blurred out the noise of the military trucks that were barraging through the jungle. Or so they thought.

Lars had three of his squad with him in the back, their rifles across their knees. Boys, mostly. Nineteen, twenty. Still joking about girls back home, still believing the war was something they could walk out of when their time was up.

The cacophony of gunfire cut through it all. First from the left, then the right. Muzzle flashes stitched through the green, jolting the convoy and causing the tires to spin mud when they tried to bolt out of there faster. Lars swung his rifle up, but the sound was everywhere, the jungle alive with noise. Then the truck lurched to a stop, and hands came out of the bushes.

A rifle butt cracked his skull, and here, his senses betrayed him.

When he came to, he was tied to bamboo in a clearing with his wrists lashed behind his back, the cord cutting through his skin. But that wasn't what bothered him. Neither did the smell—kerosene, dirt, and sweat. But not his sweat, nor his comrades'.

War or not, they ensured that sweat sticks were ground under their armpits before they even left their tents. This sweat belonged to someone else. As he glanced over, three of his men were with him, bound the same way, their eyes wide and wet in the dim light. They were kids again, stripped of all the bravado.

The captors wanted information from Lars. They had sensed he was the leader of the convoy and knew that torturing some of the younger crew members would deliver results. The nineteen-year-old was the first to go. They dragged him away from the pole he was attached to and placed him in front of Lars.

An enemy soldier knelt behind him and using his thumbs and index fingers prized his eyes open, but Lars offered no resistance. He watched as the enemy started slow, ripping off the fingernails of the young soldier.

His face didn't move, nor did he try and blink. It did nothing to ail the frustration of the enemy, who only sought to tougher tactics. The fingers were removed next. But Lars just watched and listened to the screams of the young soldier, pleading and screaming for his mother.

One by one they gutted the rest, leaving him to feel every sound grind deeper into his bones. He didn't flinch. Not when blood sprayed, not when the dirt drank it up, not when his friends' eyes went glassy under the stars. That was the moment the last of his soul died, when he realized there was nothing in him left to break.

When they came back for him later, he was ready. They untied him to drag him outside the hut, but he moved before they could blink. His hands found a chin and a crown, and he turned hard, the man's neck snapping like kindling.

The second tried to lift his rifle, but Lars drove his elbow into the throat, jammed him back against the wall, and twisted until another wet crack silenced him. He took their knife, cut the ropes from his ankles, and stepped into the night.

Lars walked through the camp barefoot, the blood not yet dry on his chest as his rifle was clutched in one hand. By dawn he had found the river. By dusk he was back with his unit, though something in him had stayed behind in that clearing, tied to bamboo beside three boys who never made it out.

Now, as the truck carried him through the city's mist, Lars's twitching nerves and the thought of vampires didn't stir him. He had already seen the worst a man could see, already lost the last piece of himself that could feel horror.

The only thing that mattered was the truck beneath him, the way it groaned when he pressed the pedal. If it failed, if it cost him his place in the fight, that would be the ultimate failure. Missing the action was the one thing left in the world that got him out of bed in the morning.

"Radio the guys and let 'em know we've set it alight," he said to Paulo, who sat beside him in the passenger seat, stiff as a board. His hand wrapped tightly around his walkie talkie as his elbow rested on the window. He agreed and went to switch the circular button to turn up his volume.

Yet his moment of staring down at his transceiver was interrupted when strong headlights appeared ahead, strong enough to pierce the thick dense fog. A black SUV was approaching in the opposite lane, as if it had been waiting for them on this lonely road. The light from both vehicles flared at each other in the fog, bleaching the night into a hard white glare that left little room for shadows.

For several long seconds the street narrowed to nothing but glass and light, until at last the SUV drew level and passed close along their flank. Through the windshield Lars saw the driver. Billy Cole. His face was calm, his posture loose, as though he were out for a casual drive. Yet he turned his head enough for the light to catch his features, and his expression bent into a slow smile.

Not a grin of surprise or pleasure, but something calculated. A smirk that carried intent. It was aimed directly at the brute.

Lars tightened his grip on the wheel until the plastic groaned beneath his hands. Paulo shifted uncomfortably in his seat, his chest tightening as the SUV slipped back into the fog behind them.

"They're onto us!" Paulo grumbled, his voice dry in his throat as he stared forward.

Lars didn't respond straight away, he just looked at the glow of the fire still lighting the mist in the rearview mirror. A column of smoke climbed into the distance, but the road ahead remained dark. He knew as soon as the SUV was out of sight, he would slam his foot down on the accelerator and race toward the brownstone. Paulo shook his head once, as Lars finally responded, "No. He knows."

"Come in, come in," Paulo said. "Haden, we just passed them. The main guy was driving."

Static hissed back from Paulo's speaker, and Lars checked the mirror again: the lights were gone. He pushed down on the clutch, pulled the gear stick into fourth, and pushed hard on the accelerator. The truck felt like it was on fire, a blast of engine oil and gasoline fumes blasted through as Paulo's head was glued to the back of his headrest.

Then something flared in the distant background. Two headlights pierced through the dense fog. The SUV had realized the fire was for them, it swung around and began its chase of the truck.

"They're coming," Lars said, his voice confident and low; his eyes looked in the rearview mirror but his head never moved. He pushed the pedal harder, though he had already been flooring it. The truck jolted forward and Paulo flew back into his seat once more, nearly dropping the handheld radio.

"They picked us up," Paulo whimpered. His grip tightened on the radio. "They know."

"Aye," Lars said, his jaw still tight. He checked the mirror again, watching the lights behind them carve through the mist, disappear, then reappear as the SUV hugged each turn. It wasn't close, not yet, but it was tracking them, every move matched, every street chosen with intent. It was catching up.

Lars snapped, "Tell them to get the hell out of there now."

Paulo raised the radio, voice sharp into the static. "Haden, come in. They're behind us. Billy's SUV is heading your way. Do you copy?"

The response dissolved into static. Lars pressed harder on the accelerator, guiding the truck through the tight lanes, every corner now a test of traction. The mist thickened ahead, camouflaging the road, but he could still see the headlights behind them, small in the distance. The SUV was pacing them, gaining ground one block at a time.

TOMAS SCREAMED and retracted away from the fireplace as quick as he could when he saw the demon dropping from the ceiling and crawling on the ground in front of him. He'd seen Hell before, but this was something new. Now he was alone, trapped in a room with a demon that he didn't recognize.

At first it was studying him, as if it wasn't sure who or what he was. Was it a meal? Was it a vampire? The beast stood small, around four feet in height, and Tomas still couldn't make out any of its features apart from its jet-black skin and its yellow eyes.

It crouched down to the floor, as if adopting a wolf-like stance, and slowly reached its left claw out to try and grab Tomas's foot—testing him—like a shark taking a test bite. Tomas kicked at it, and it jolted back.

Now it understood that this was prey, for it flared the most grimacing smile.

He reached for his handheld radio that was attached

to his belt and fumbled with it, but the sweat running on his fingers only made the device ever more slippery. The ghoul tested the water once more, clawing at Tomas's foot menacingly and playfully before stepping forward.

"Haden! Haden! I need your help now!" he shouted into the device.

Haden and Jonatan had already raced out of the basement as the call came in from Paulo. They were exiting the steps when Tomas's call came through, albeit they could already hear his screams.

The thing clamped onto Tomas's ankle and yanked with a force that sent him sprawling across the floorboards. His boots scraped for a grip as it dragged him out of the room, its small, wiry frame no taller than four feet but pulling with the strength of two men.

Tomas kicked and twisted, every muscle straining, but the creature hauled him with steady, jerking tugs toward the threshold of the bedroom it had crawled out of.

His hands clawed at the railing along the landing until his fingers found hold. Wood groaned under his grip as he locked on, his hands dripped with sweat as he barely hung onto the wooden railing.

The horror hissed, jerking harder, its jaw unhinging wider as a row of teeth that extended to the holes in the side of its head were exposed. The thing wasn't curious anymore, it was hateful.

Haden and Jonatan charged up the stairs at the sound, their weapons raised in front of them, just as the creature dragged Tomas another foot closer to the open door from which it emerged. Its face turned toward them, its mouth still stretched impossibly wide, a sound spilling from its throat that was less a hiss and more the raw scrape of metal. The fury in it was clear, every tug on Tomas's leg a violent declaration that this was its victim, and no one was going to take him from it.

Haden pulled out a pistol and aimed it at the demon. The dark abomination didn't flinch, for it hadn't ever seen a pistol before, let alone understand what one was. He pulled the trigger and let four rounds of fire into the phantasm's head and chest, killing it. The gunshots' explosive force threw it back against the other side of the hallway and made its limp corpse slam against the wall.

"Tomas! Jesus Christ, let me see!" Jonatan said, racing up past Haden and crouching down to Tomas.

"I'm fine, brother. That cunt just had a good grip on it, whatever the fuck it was," he said, panting, out of breath, looking at the demon laid cold against the wall.

The three of them stood over the dead demon; its body had almost deflated and it looked even smaller than it did before. Its tongue was hanging from its mouth.

"What is it?" Jonatan asked Haden.

"No time to explain!" he replied. "Quick, downstairs. They're wise to our act and they're on their way back. Tomas, where did you place the other explosive?"

"In the fireplace, same spot as downstairs," he responded in agony from the tugging on his ankle.

"Then we're fine! We already have three bombs in place. We need to leave now!"

The three of them made their way down the hallway, Tomas limping a little, and then they heard the moan again. It was the moan that Tomas had mistaken earlier for the demon.

"There it is again!" he whispered, as the three of them looked up to the third floor.

"What?" Haden barked.

Tomas turned to look at Haden, and got close to whisper even further.

"When I was walking up the stairs, I heard moaning, whimpering. Then that thing came through into the room I was just in. I thought it was that thing trying to trick me. But there's something else up there."

"We have zero time; we must get out of here now," Jonatan said.

"No, we must see what...or who...is up there. I imagine they must have prisoners," Haden stated. "Quickly, you two get out now. I'll stay behind and go up there."

"Just blow up the house now! It's not even one a.m. They have all night to hunt us down once they return," Jonatan said.

He raised a valid point; for a professor that spent most of his life hunting the unknown, he hadn't planned for a hell-fiend to be hiding in the house to stall them. He hadn't planned for a hideaway once they had removed themselves from the house. He had planned on them not knowing they had even broken into it and set the detonators.

"You guys have about five minutes before they get here," Paulo snapped into the transceiver, as the truck came to as slow of a halt as it could outside.

"Haden, we can't save whatever is up there," Jonatan pleaded.

"That doesn't mean that we shouldn't try. You two, go with Paulo and Lars and drive as quick as you can to the church on the other side of the canal. They're not going to follow you; they'll be too busy trying to get back here."

Jonatan ducked under Tomas's arm and took most of his weight, guiding him step by step across the landing and down the staircase.

His injured ankle barely touched the floor, each brush of it sending a hiss of pain through his teeth. His hand clutched the rail as if it were the only thing keeping him upright. But Jonatan kept him moving. His eyes fixed on the door ahead where the cold night waited like a promise of escape.

"Haden?" Lars asked as they piled into the truck.

"He's not going to come. There's something inside up the stairs that he wants to investigate. He told us to go to the church."

Lars unbuckled his seatbelt and opened the door, getting out hurriedly.

"Where the fuck do you think you're going?" Paulo asked.

"I'm not leaving him alone in there. If he stays back, he's going to die."

"Hey, we have to get out of here right now. You said these guys are on their way," Tomas interjected.

"No comrade left behind. Haden's my brother. I'll be back."

"He's on the third floor," Jonatan shouted after him.

"You've got to be fucking kidding me!" said Tomas, as he watched Lars jump out of the truck and hurtle toward the front door of the brownstone.

Lars had the ability to bulldoze through most things, both mentally and physically. He didn't listen to the others.

He didn't even bother slamming the door behind him. Once inside, he knew where to run, and given time constraints, he didn't stop to even notice the shadow-swept, looming, glowering-eyed, demonic presence on the second floor either. He reached the loft and immediately pushed the heavy wooden door open.

But no amount of witnessing a wide array of terrors, from the horrors of war to the malevolence men in power bore upon the helpless, could have prepared him for this.

A jolt slammed his stomach like someone had taken a sledgehammer to it, a wave of nausea traveling up his esophagus as he stared bewilderedly into the room. His cheeks dampened by the slow roll of tears that couldn't be contained any longer.

Five frail, withered bodies were tied to makeshift crosses on the floor, their hands and feet bound. Three men and two women.

They looked younger than they should, early twenties at least, their hair matted as if it hadn't been washed in weeks, their bodies completely naked.

Used syringes lay scattered around the floor, and some of them were connected to IV bags, further evidence that the vampires were using the humans as a constant food source, feeding them via liquid nutrients so that their blood would regenerate.

Lars's eyes scanned the bodies as he slowly closed the door behind him, wiping tears with his other hand. Their skin looked pale and malnourished, almost translucent, save for the bloodied and bruised sections on their wrists and necks.

Then, one of them moved, stirring the room from its menacing quietness into panicked realization. These tortured men and women were still cognizant.

"Kill. Me." The younger man was crying, his drained hand faltering and shaking as it tried to reach forward. "Please. Kill. Me."

"It's not too late, Haden. We can save them," Lars groaned, unwilling to give up just yet.

"No, we cannot. They are dead already," Haden responded, the grim pessimism, the admission of defeat, his uncontainable terror, all of it apparent in the way he uttered each syllable as he beheld this ghastly sight.

CHAPTER 4
THE GETAWAY

The A-frame loft pressed down on Haden and Lars, the ceiling low and the air stale. Rafters showed their age in splinters and sagging wood, the gaps between them filmed with webs that caught faint flashes from the floor below.

The space felt both abandoned and lived in at the same time; a nest held together by neglect. Lars scowled at the filth, unsettled that vampires would choose to hole up in a place like this. Haden knew better. Every ruin had its twin, a palace somewhere else in the world.

Haden thought about putting a bullet through each skull. A quick mercy, the kind of soldier's end he'd granted too many times before. But he'd already laid four bullets into the demon downstairs. He was lucky that no neighbor was knocking on the door yet. He holstered the thought and his weapon and turned back to Lars.

"We need to leave," Haden grunted. Lars heaved a breath in response.

They turned toward the door. Then it came, the

sound of glass breaking somewhere deeper in the house. The crash rang up through the beams, bouncing off every floor until it felt like the walls themselves had flinched.

Haden's hand stayed on the doorknob, his grip turning his knuckles white as he listened. A scrape followed that felt purposeful, not the stumble of an accident but the tread of someone who already knew the house. The silence that followed imposed menacingly, broken only by the sound of steps climbing from below.

"What's that?" Lars called out, his eyes flicking back to the young man on the floor, still whimpering and begging for an end. Haden gave no reply. He only raised a finger to his lips, a sharp gesture for silence.

OUTSIDE, the fog smothered the street, turning lamps and houses into vague shapes behind the glass. Given its peculiar arrival and its persistent prevalence, the fog felt as if summoned by the vampires themselves. Paulo sat behind the wheel, the key cold between his fingers, waiting to twist. His grip ached from holding still, but his eyes never left the brownstone door.

Beside him, Tomas held a hand to his leg, each press sending jolts of pain up through his body, leaving sweat to bead on his temple. In the back, Jonatan coiled strands of hair around his finger, then set them free, over and over. The cab smelled of damp clothes and oil, as their weapons lay within reach.

Paulo's thumb pressed the radio. "You guys need to get out of there now. They were chasing us and now I can't see where the fuck they are. I can't see them behind us anymore. Haden? Do you copy?"

"Fuck!" Tomas growled. The others looked at Tomas, his face paler than it was mere moments ago. His lips trembled as his eyes continued to fixate on what was in front of him.

Jerry the vampire stood before the truck, coat collar high, hands sunk in his pockets, as if he'd wandered there on an evening stroll. His gaze never shifted, calm but hungry, fixed on the three men inside. Tomas's breath hitched when he saw Billy Cole slip from the fog at the truck's side.

The glass went first, Billy's fist blasting through the window in a spray of shards.

The hand followed, fast, clamping around Tomas's throat. Before Paulo or Jonatan could react, Tomas was wrenched upward as his body was dragged halfway through the window. His legs kicked against the metal, heels drumming the door, arms thrashing in frantic arcs like a bird broken in flight.

Billy dragged him across the hood, holding him down as he presented his prize to Jerry.

"You've cost me dearly tonight, gentlemen," Jerry said, taking a step forward. His tone was almost conversational, like a man scolding a group of boys for playing ding-dong ditch. "Those coffins that you so recklessly destroyed were centuries old. Not to mention you've ruined this city for me. But one mustn't get attached. As a family member reminds me often, there are many places in this world to lay one's hat."

Beneath the dashboard, Paulo kept his finger firmly

on the transmitter, allowing Haden and Lars inside to hear some of what was being said, although the sound was quite faint.

"I think it's about time we take this inside, don't you?" Jerry stated, it wasn't a question. The men had nowhere else to go but inside.

Haden and Lars slipped from the room and eased toward the second staircase, careful not to let the old boards groan under their boots. The ghoulish creature was still slumped in the hallway below, its body twisted and unmoving. They traded a glance, then looked back just in time to see something stir.

From between the railing spindles, a hand pushed up from the stairwell below. The fingers were too long, the nails longer still, clicking against the wood. It reached higher, stretching past what any human limb should manage, and clamped onto the demon's leg. With a violent yank, the corpse was dragged through the railing.

Wood splintered violently, its cracking sound echoing through the house.

The demon's body crashed down the steps, bones thudding against every riser until both vanished into the darkness of the first floor.

They locked eyes and, without saying a word, rushed back up the stairs to the loft. Lars, with his large meaty hands, grabbed the rickety brass doorknob and twisted it softly, wincing as he did so, hoping it wouldn't make a sound.

Haden searched for a window. He remembered seeing it earlier in the day when he was monitoring the home. It was a large enough square window that the two of them could easily fit through, even if it meant a potential drop to their untimely deaths.

Behind the large heavy curtain that draped wall to wall could be the only place for the window, although, in the dusty loft, it was hard to tell which way pointed to the front or the rear. Haden didn't waste a second in trudging toward it and pulling it down, revealing a single sash window, its glass darkened almost to black.

You couldn't see out of it that well, and the frame was nailed shut.

"Psst! Lars! The window; I need you to open it." He beckoned in the window's direction.

Lars, still pre-occupied with the dying victims, walked over to the window and saw the nails. He pulled out a small Swiss army knife, the type that had more bells and whistles than the standard hardware store; he used one of the attachments to jimmy open the nails that were roughly hammered into the wood, before flinging the window open.

Down below, Jerry and Billy were escorting the men into the brownstone.

"Fuck," Haden said, frustrated, afraid for his fellows.

"What now?" Lars grunted.

"Let me think..." Haden replied, but was interrupted by a knock at the door to the loft room. The knock had come almost as fast as the men had walked into the house.

"Professor, I suggest you, err, come out and say hello. Otherwise we might have to break down this door and... wring your neck."

It was the voice of Jerry. Haden knew he had no other option but to face the vampires head on. He looked at Lars and handed him the detonator to the bombs that had been placed throughout the house.

"Follow my lead," Haden mouthed to Lars.

"Very well then. We surrender," he announced to Jerry.

He crossed the loft, turned the lock, and stepped back beside Lars at the window. The door opened, and Jerry entered first, Billy Cole at his shoulder, another vampire behind them.

"Haden, old chap," Jerry said, smile broad and wicked, the dim lights casting a shadow on his face, making it pull up and appear even more sinister, if such a thing was possible. "How have you been?"

"Gellert," Haden replied, his tone lacking emotion, "I've seen better days. I could say the same about you."

"You know, I thought you'd have the sense to keep your distance," Jerry said, voice light, deriding. "You live your life, I live mine, and never the twain shall meet. A mutual understanding."

"I was prepared for that," Haden answered, nodding gravely. "In fact, I came here seeking retirement. You knew that. But I was here first, Gellert. And when bodies started turning up, I could only assume you'd come for me. That I'd be next." He pulled out his lighter, lit a cigarette, and let the smoke curl out before he spoke again. "If you were me, wouldn't you have done the same? We are, after all, creatures of survival, you and I."

Jerry's smile faltered into silence. Billy Cole hovered at his side, the usual grin fixed on his mouth. The woman behind them leaned against the doorframe, half-lidded eyes watching, her pose more languid than wary. Haden drew again on the cigarette, the ember flaring between them, refusing to look away.

"Lars," Haden said, "Allow me to introduce Gellert. And William, is it?" He slipped the lighter back into his pocket and drew slow on the cigarette.

Billy's smirk broke into a hard grin. "Billy."

Jerry spread his hands as if in mock courtesy. "So what now, gentlemen? I can't let you run off into the night. You destroyed my belongings. You burned a coffin my sister entrusted to me. You burned another Billy built with his own hands for one of the younger ones below."

"Well," Haden said, letting the smoke curl from his lips, "I'd like myself and my men to walk out of here alive. We could call a truce, but that's not really your style, is it, Gellert?"

Jerry's grin widened as he shook his head. "You've wrecked what I built here, burned coffins, tore my home apart. You're right, Haden. A truce wouldn't really be my style. Your actions can't go unanswered." He tapped the door with a fingertip, then slammed his palm flat against it, the crack echoing through the loft. "Since you took something of mine, I suggest I do the same. I keep the boy you call Tomas. The rest of you can leave, and that's all the truce you'll ever get from me. If I see you again, I reserve the right to end your puny existence. I'm a fair man, Haden. You know this. But you've caused me… So. Much. Trouble."

"Well," Haden said evenly, "in that case, it looks like

we're at an impasse, Gellert. Where are my men by the way?"

Blue and red lights bled through the curtains, filling the loft in shifting color. Outside, three police cars idled at the curb. Six officers stepped out, two from each vehicle. They moved slowly, jackets pulled tight against the cold, their faces drawn with the look of men dragged from sleep. None of them reached for their guns.

Haden and Lars leaned to the window. Jerry joined them, stepping into the gap between. For a moment, the three stood together, watching in silence as the scene below unfolded.

Without breaking his gaze, Jerry repeated himself, voice almost a whisper. "You continue to cause me... So. Much. Trouble."

Down on the street, the officers finally looked up. Six sets of eyes found the three figures at the window. For Haden and Lars, it felt like a chance; razor-thin, but real nonetheless.

Officer Renfold shouted up. "We had reports of gunfire. There's broken glass outside. Everything all right in there?"

The vampires escorted Lars and Haden down to the entrance of the house. Jerry moved first, strolling toward the front door, as he passed Jonatan and Paulo in the hallway. He pulled it open, calm as ever, and smiled at the uniforms waiting in the hall. "Yes, Officers. There was a disturbance. My family and I had planned to leave town this evening, but we heard the same reports you did. A robbery, perhaps, or some nuisance. We've abandoned our plans until the matter is resolved." His tone was smooth, almost apologetic, the picture of a man inconvenienced at the wrong hour.

"Is that so?" the officer shot back. His eyes shifted past Jerry. "And you, Haden, what are you doing here?"

Haden forced a smile. "Officer Renfold. A sight for sore eyes, if there was one." He tapped ash from his cigarette and gestured toward the stairs. "The five of us were just leaving. Mr. Gellert asked us to keep an eye on the place while he was gone. Me and the others were on our way out."

"Who's the fifth?" Renfold asked, eyes narrowing. "Mind if we come in, Mr. Gellert?"

Jerry's smile didn't waver. "Please, it's Jerry. And of course, come on in." He stepped back from the door, gesturing them inside as if they were honored guests.

Renfold crossed the threshold, gaze sweeping the hall once more. "I'll ask again, who's the fifth, and where is he?" he insisted, his voice harder this time.

Haden felt the knot in his stomach come undone. If ever there was a time to save Tomas, it was now.

"I believe he'd gone to inspect the basement, to check and see if all was in order," Haden said, voice steady. He glanced at the officer, then back at Jerry. "That's where you took him, right, Jerry?"

Jerry's smile held, and yet, the masked rage in his eyes glinted red hot. "Indeed. I do believe he was checking on our...basement. Billy, would you be so kind as to fetch Tomas, please?" His eyes never left Renfold, his tone all civility.

"Aye," Billy said, already headed for the stairs.

"Mind explaining the gunshots and the broken

glass?" Renfold inquired. "We had reports. Would any of you fine gentlemen know what that's about?"

"A fire broke down in the docks tonight," Lars chimed in. "It could've been that."

The officer's brow twitched. He glanced at the group, then let his shoulders sag with fatigue. It was one in the morning, and his weariness was apparent.

The basement door opened. Billy stepped out first, then shoved Tomas into the light. His hair was mussed, shirt half-unbuttoned, breath ragged. Paulo, Jonatan, Haden, and the vampires crowded the hall, their bodies closing ranks in front of the basement door, forming a wall Renfold couldn't see past.

"Is everything okay back there?" an officer asked, peering around Jerry.

"Oh, everything's just fine, wouldn't you say so, Tomas?" Billy smiled, his arm around Tomas's shoulder as he looked at Haden. He was confused and wondering what was going on, although he'd been around Haden on enough expeditions to know when to play the game and read between the lines.

"Fine indeed, Officer," Haden said smoothly. "It's been quite a night. Now that the family is back, there's no need for us to linger. I suggest we can all call it a night."

Renfold gave him a flat look. "Sure. Listen, whatever this is, some kind of late-night swingers party, keep it down next time."

The officers turned for the door. Haden and the others moved with them, careful to stay close. Tomas limped in the rear, his face drawn tight with pain. As he reached the threshold, Billy slid into his path, leaning down so close Tomas could feel the heat of his breath. Billy's grin widened, teeth bared, a silent promise of what would come if they crossed paths again.

"Haden!" Tomas called out, his voice carrying shrill notes brought forth by pain, forcing them all to turn. "I... might need a hand getting to the car. My foot's shot to hell."

Renfold glanced back, eyebrow raised. "And how'd you manage that, son?"

"It was the damn basement," Tomas said quickly. "Slipped on a rock down there. You should get those cleared out. Felt like someone was digging a tunnel." He gave a strained laugh. Billy only leered at him, the kind of smile that promised he'd heard every word.

The group moved for their vehicles. Engines coughed, headlights carved through the mist, and the convoy eased away. From the doorway, Jerry watched with Billy at his side, the others fanned out behind him. He bit into an apple, the crunch carrying in the quiet street, and raised a hand in a casual wave as the taillights sank into the fog.

"Holy fucking Christ," Paulo exhaled a sigh of relief.

"I wouldn't want to go through that again," Tomas grunted.

"What's the range on the trigger?" Lars asked.

"Not far enough! Around five hundred feet if we're in plain sight and we're lucky. Right now, let's thank our lucky stars that the police showed up. If I hadn't fired a bullet into that blithering creature, they wouldn't have," Haden said, the strain lifting from his voice a little. Now that they were out in the open, away from the vampires, he was regaining his self-assurance one step at a time.

"So what now?" Jonatan asked.

"We lay low. The plan to blow the house up in the morning has now been somewhat fucked thanks to the cops. A dichotomy if ever there was one."

"We can't let them live, Haden. What if we set off the bombs in another hour or two?"

"They won't be home. I don't doubt that they'll head out and start feeding for the night, and given how we've rubbed them the wrong way, I can hazard that we'll be on their fucking menu. I'd suggest that we sleep in the church tonight and continue our plan in the morning. For if we don't, then we all have to find a new place to live by sundown, and like I said, vampires are vengeful bastards. They'll come looking for us wherever we are."

"THINK there's anything to worry about?" Billy asked.

Jerry leaned against the frame, thoughtful. "Hard to say. They came here with a purpose, but I don't know what. They can thank whatever God they pray to that they didn't go into the tunnel."

"What about the grimoire?"

He shook his head. "No. Haden knows I'd never leave that behind."

"Then maybe let's pay them a visit. Take flight."

Jerry smiled faintly. "No. They've had their warning."

Billy snorted. "Told you Jimmy wouldn't do much good."

"Jimmy was supposed to devour them and enter that tunnel once he was finished."

"You give that thing too much credit. It's always been a liability."

Jerry let the smile fade. "Perhaps. But it's devoured plenty in its time. I'll check the loft again myself. And Billy, plan B was the right call."

HADEN and the crew pulled over beside the church on the road toward the station. The cop cars were silent, there not being the need for the blaring blue and red signals above any longer. Two of the cars continued on as Officer Renfold pulled up behind the truck. His tires released a small screech as the white sedan came to a pause.

"Thank you for accompanying us here," Haden said to Renfold, leaning on his car mirror as if he had the authority to do so.

"Don't sweat it. I owed you one, after all," Renfold replied as Haden tapped the roof of the car and began to walk away. "But hey, Haden... Why the church?"

"I need to pay an old ghost a visit."

The cruiser idled a moment, then pulled away, its lights dwindling down the road.

The hunters stood quiet as the medieval church hung over them. The building felt protective yet daunting at the same time, as if once inside, they could never leave for fear of being devoured. In front of them, a dozen or so stone steps that looked like they'd carried the confessions of half the town for centuries beckoned them in.

Large red doors set in an arched frame were the only solace between the hunters and the vampires, and the men didn't stall in crossing the threshold to safety.

"Come on, come on, come in!" Haden signaled with urgency as the group looked back to ensure no vampires were following them.

Inside, the church was lit by candlelight. It was large, immaculate, and ornate. Every window glass stained, every detail thought out. The wooden pews flanked the aisle; at the end, a marble altar commanded the room, and above it, a gold cross with Jesus crucified on it. The group was tired. Jonatan walked around the church trying to find a back area with a kitchen, somewhere he could grab some water for everyone. Tomas had his ankle dipped in the holy water basin, and Lars, Paulo, and Haden sat around each other in one of the pews closer to the altar. They whispered as they talked about their next move.

"Where do these things come from?" Paulo asked.

"Paulo, we've seen these things before, and does the answer ever change? They are born straight from Hell, from the Devil himself."

"So all of this is real, huh? As above, so below? God on high, the Devil down nigh?" Jonatan chimed in.

"There are things in our world that we cannot comprehend. Different dimensions, different Devils, different universes. By God, there's things that the Vatican has brushed under its many velvet carpets that if you found out, you wouldn't sleep a wink again in your life," Haden said grimly, staring at the statue of Jesus on a stone cross, Christ's mournful eyes looking down at him, the marble sculpted into beads to indicate blood dripping down the crown of thorns.

"Where did he come from? Jerry?" Tomas asked, still soaking his foot. "He doesn't feel like the others."

Haden leaned back in the pew, his eyes still fixed on the crucifix above the altar. He didn't answer right away. A cold wind scraped against the stained glass, howling as if the vampires were hovering outside. A chorus of heads turned to look at the window before diverting their attention back to Haden.

"He's not," he said. "He was once human. But centuries ago, during the time of Vlad the Impaler, he immersed himself in occult and esotericism, which culminated in him summoning something that should've been left well enough alone. A fallen Watcher by the name of Samyara. It gave Jerry what he craved most—power, eternal life, and knowledge forbidden even to the angels."

"Why?" Paulo asked. "Why would anyone want that?"

"Before he was a vampire," Haden said, "he was a nobleman by the name of Gellert cel Catura. I believe they fought together, but they had disagreements on how to fight. Gellert... Sorry, *Jerry*, was actually the nicer of the two. Vlad was the reckless one. Jerry was calculating. Vlad enjoyed carnage and menace. Jerry preferred meticulousness. Guess which one all the history books make mention of? Jerry learned early on that the best camouflage is discretion, and it has allowed him to live as secretly as he's done all these centuries."

Jonatan looked down and Paulo said nothing.

"Christ," Lars mumbled, as if expecting the figure on the cross would respond.

Haden continued, "Gellert was a rich man even back then, before he became a vampire. And one can even imagine him living a normal life, one with a loving wife and a sprawling palatial estate. Back then, Vlad wanted it all, money, power and fame. His soldiers tore through anything that was in their way, and unfortunately that meant Gellert too, while he was away in Buda. They took his castle, raped the servants, burned the chapel, and—" He stopped himself, jaw flexing. "They found his wife. She slit her wrists before they could have their way with her. When Gellert returned, all that was left was ash and the bloodstained silk of her nightdress."

Tomas slowly looked up.

"From what I know, Gellert did not cry," Haden continued. "And he most certainly didn't bury her. He burned everything. Every relic. Every symbol of God. And then he locked himself in the ruined crypt beneath the chapel. He opened every book he'd ever collected—pagan, Sumerian, Babylonian—and he began the rites."

"What rites?" Jonatan asked.

"Dark rites written by those taken by despair, rites of blood magic, witchcraft, black rituals, whatever you want to call it," Haden whispered, each word shaky, his fingers trembling against the pew's back. "Summoning spirits, raising the dead, selling your soul in return for favors from the hellbound. It is when a man feels like he's got nothing left to lose, and all redemption is beyond him, that he turns to this."

Tomas leaned forward. "So he summoned Samyara?"

"He did," Haden said. "A shadow in the dark appeared to him with a voice that would make your knees go soft. It offered him power, immortality, vengeance. But with one price."

He looked at each of them.

"He would never know love again. The love he found in his wife, the demon used against him. Jerry was so devastated, he never wanted to love another human. He only wanted his wife, and he wanted revenge. Alas, the memory of his true love would stay. The heartache too. But the ability to feel it, to feel anything but hunger and rage, would be gone. Jerry would be damned to a life of finding his true love over and over, only for her to die."

"Jesus Christ," Paulo whispered.

"He agreed," Haden said. "Without hesitation. The next morning, Gellert no longer existed, and Jerry was born from dirt, forced to feed on the blood of the living to survive. Never again would his skin touch the sun either."

An air of silence washed over the men. Except Jonatan, these men had been in supernatural battles before, but never received the answers to their deepest questions. The how's and why's of the underworld.

After a moment, Tomas asked, "Did you hear about the grimoire?"

Haden shifted his head slightly. "What do you know about that?"

"I've heard the name," Tomas said. "Roman archives mention books tied to the beings they choose. A book that isn't read as much as it reads you."

"This one is worse," Haden said. "It's sentient, bound

in human skin. It speaks to you, through visions, voices, compulsions. It shows you the outcome before you even act. And if it likes you…it changes its ink."

"What does that mean?" Jonatan asked.

"It rewrites itself," Haden said. "It adapts to the wielder, blood spilled becomes ink. And it's old. Older than the Bible. Older than language. We think these books came from the East, before Babylon, maybe even Sumer."

"And Jerry has a grimoire?" Tomas asked, his voice barely above a whisper.

Haden nodded.

"He keeps it close. You'll never find it lying out in the open. If I had to guess, it's not even on this plane half the time. He pulls it through when he needs it. Like a tether between this world and something far worse."

"Can we destroy it?" Tomas asked.

Haden shrugged. "Everything can. Untransmutable laws of physics are on our side. But I dread to think what would happen if this book got into the hands of the wrong person. You know, all that Newtonian jazz— energy not being able to be created or destroyed, but being capable of transferring from one form to another."

"And Jerry?" Paulo asked. "Can he be destroyed? Laws of physics still on our side with that one?"

Haden turned his eyes to the crucifix.

"Of course, though not laws of physics as much as laws of death and undeath. Tonight, as I was in that basement, I looked hard for his grimoire. I wouldn't want to yield the power myself, but I know of a witch that I'd trust with it."

The church creaked around them. Somewhere in the rafters, a pigeon fluttered, causing the men to look above and the waft of incense to dance around the church hall.

"That's why you must not think of it as a mere hunt," Haden said. "It's containment. If Jerry is killed and the grimoire finds someone new..." He didn't finish the sentence.

"What does the book want?" Paulo asked, as the conversation transitioned from catching a vampire to the grimoire.

"Chaos," Haden said defeatedly. "Desire. Evolution through suffering. It doesn't want a quiet world. It wants one that burns, because fire clears the land for something new."

"And if we kill Jerry?" Jonatan shifted uncomfortably.

"We pray the book doesn't choose one of us. Now, everyone try and get some sleep. Tomorrow we go to war."

THE FIVE A.M. morning rays of light bled through the stained-glass windows, slicing the gloom of the church into fractured rainbows that dripped across the pews like blood through a prism. The five men stirred slowly from sleep, sore and crumpled in their jackets. The pews creaked beneath them as dust danced in the golden shafts of dawn. But one figure was already awake.

She sat silently next to Haden, robed in black, her white veil bright against the light. In her hands she cradled a vial, a fat, bulbous object with metal banding around the neck and a wax seal pressed into its lid. Her eyes weren't on them, but on the far right of the altar. It was Paulo who noticed her first, his breath hitching as he elbowed Lars awake.

Haden opened his eyes slowly, a twitch behind his forehead, his neck crooked and aching. He sat up, blinking the sleep from his eyes. The nun smiled at him.

"*Le génie du mal,*" she said, her voice a hallowed whisper.

Haden followed her gaze to the marble statue in the corner—the horned Lucifer, cast down and chained, half-buried in flowing robes, his body muscular, his wings furled around him.

"The genius of evil," he said, watching her carefully.

"Indeed," she whispered, then turned to him and pressed the vial into his palm. Her grip was firmer than he'd anticipated.

"You'll need this," she said. "But not for when you think you will."

He looked down at the vial. The liquid inside shimmered unnaturally, refracting light in a way holy water never did.

"What is it?" he asked, some part of him already knowing the nun wouldn't answer.

The nun didn't respond. Her gaze returned to the statue.

"Beautiful, wouldn't you agree?" Haden said, trying to gauge her.

"A heavy distraction." Her voice echoed slightly. "Just what Lucifer would want. Look too long, and you forget the true danger is always behind you."

"Who is she?" Paulo whispered to Lars from the pew behind them.

"No one important," the nun responded without turning around to face them.

The church suddenly got darker, the vault around them blackening as the sun dipped behind clouds outside. The group looked around as if a force had entered the church with them.

"He'll flee to another land if you don't stop him. Find the book and you'll know what to do. But be warned, it knows what scares you, it can reach into the very depth of your soul, read your secrets, your innermost desires. A book such as this, it will lie to you, trick you to get what it wants," she said, her voice firmer now, stronger.

From the shadows at the edge of the nave came soft, broken cries. The sobs were muffled but carried through the cavernous hall, bouncing from stone to stone until it felt like the walls themselves were grieving. The men turned toward the entrance. Five nuns drifted into view, their habits brushing the ground though their feet never touched it. Their faces were hidden, lost in folds of cloth, and still the sound poured from them—a chorus of quiet weeping. Their hands were locked in prayer, fingers rigid, and the farther they floated down the aisle, the clearer it became that nothing cast a shadow.

"I must go now," the nun stated as she rose to join in the floating procession, effortlessly entwining herself in the movement of the ethereal nuns.

The men watched as they floated toward the altar, their eyes locked on the women. Until a large horn outside rattled all of them, prompting them to look back toward the entrance.

"The truck!" Lars shouted.

And as they looked back to the altar, the nuns weren't there anymore.

OUTSIDE, Lars was bartering with the tow truck company that was attempting to remove the vehicle from the front of the church steps.

"How did you stop him from towing the car?" Paulo asked.

"I knew him, old buddy of mine." Lars laughed back.

"Of course you did." Paulo chuckled.

"Okay, so what now?" Tomas asked Haden.

Morning light did little to clear the fog in their heads. The pews were cold, their backs sore. After everything that had happened, the adrenaline had worn off, and all that was left was doubt. The plan had been bold. And now, after the fire at the docks and the surprise arrival of the police, they were on the radar. If they went ahead with destroying the brownstone, they wouldn't just be vampire hunters, they'd be arsonists. Murder suspects. Fugitives in a city where they had built roots.

They could all feel it coming, the comedown.

"We continue with the plan. If we stop now, we'll not only be dead, the vampires will continue their reign of terror in the city," Haden stated, each word seeped in grave understanding of the severity of the mission that lay ahead.

"Professor, I've got one thing I want to say. Let's blow these fucks up!" Lars said.

THE TRUCK STARTED WITH EASE. Its window shattered from Billy's blow. All five men climbed inside and Lars started the ignition, putting the gear shift into first. He pressed the clutch with his left foot, slowly lifting in unison with the accelerator pedal. The truck rolled off quietly from the front of the church as they made their way to breakfast.

Fred's Café sat on the corner of Brouwersgracht and Prinsengracht, with a deep red awning stretched above the windows, its fabric still wet with dew. The glass beneath glowed with an amber light that spilled out, warm against the grey of the street.

Inside, the lamps burned low and steady, their glow carrying farther than the half-risen sun outside. It was the kind of light that pulled you in, promising warmth, food, and quiet.

Lars killed the engine and the men climbed out, shoulders hunched, collars turned up. They looked worn down from the night, but the café drew them across the sidewalk like moths. A small bell jingled above the door when they stepped inside.

The air was thick with the smell of coffee and frying eggs, and a row of polished tables stretched across a narrow floor. Only a handful of locals lingered over their cups, jackets draped over chairs, the low murmur of their talk a welcome cover for the hunters' silence.

They chose a table at the back, large enough to seat them all. Worn-down laminated menus lay stacked, corners curling from years of use, but the words inside might as well have been scripture. Omelets, rye bread, cheeses, steaming eggs.

They ordered fast. When the waiter returned with a heavy pot of coffee, its handle wrapped in cloth, all five pairs of eyes locked on it. The cups clinked as they were filled, steam rising in thin spirals. For the first time in a few hours, they let themselves breathe.

Haden ordered orange juice and a plate of Edam cheese with rye bread. Lars ordered two omelets. Paulo, Jonatan, and Tomas ordered more of the continental variety, ham slices with gouda. There continued to be silence around the table as everyone replenished their minds and bodies.

"You know," Lars stated as he waved his fork to the group, "it wasn't our skills as much as it was luck that we made it out alive last night. Especially you." He pointed toward Tomas before shoveling the egg omelet into his mouth.

"Precisely why we need to nail these fuckers today," Jonatan growled, prompting the group to stop eating and stare at him in surprise, before all of them burst into laughter, trying to keep their food in their mouths.

Lars slapped him on the back. "Welcome to the dark side, buddy."

"I see the dead every day, I've seen the dark side plenty," he responded.

They finished their breakfast in silence, left a scatter of bills on the table, and stepped back into the fog. The café's grease clung to their clothes, a sour film that filled the cab as they climbed in. No one spoke.

Each man sank into his own thoughts as the truck rolled forward. Some thought of home—sisters, brothers, lovers, children—and pressed the memory close. Hands moved in silence, crossing their chests. Lars made his quick, half-hidden, ashamed to let the others see. In the back, Jonatan's lips worked without pause, whispering prayers so low only he and God could hear.

The fog grew thicker as they rolled into the street. The brownstone loomed through the haze, silent, its windows dark. They parked at the far end, close enough for the signal to carry, far enough that Billy Cole's eyes couldn't catch them from the glass. The truck idled, the sound of its engine muffled by the weather.

The men in the back leaned forward, elbows on their knees, watching Haden. He sat stiff in the passenger seat, his eyes on the satchel at his feet. He had fought worse than this, faced worse things, but never like this. Not on a quiet street, not at six in the morning when the rest of the city was waking to coffee and work. He reached into the bag and brought out the detonator.

It was small. Too small to hold so much weight. Plastic casing, one red switch. It looked ordinary in his hand, but the cab grew still when he set it on his lap. The others leaned closer, not to see the device, but to steady Haden as his thumb hovered.

A deep breath emerged from his lungs as he looked up to the window and out into the street. Looking down again, he flicked open the plastic shield that prevented any mishaps or accidental activation of the detonator. The small red LED lit up—it was ready to go.

"Push it," Jonatan said from the back, prompting everyone to look around at him again. They were loving his newfound confidence.

The moment had come. Haden would push the button, the explosions would go off, and that would be the end of Jerry the vampire and his family.

Easy.

The street was quiet, save for a lone woman walking past the brownstone with a satchel bag across her shoulder. She was younger, twenties, and likely walking to her day job. Haden waited for her to pass. The explosion would no doubt knock her on her ass if she was caught in the crosshairs. And civilian casualties were never on his playing cards. He was to hurt the monsters that hurt civilians, and nothing more.

The woman had moved on, turning the corner onto the adjacent street at the other end of the block, and now the street was empty. Haden looked to his left once more, noticing a few tourists on the bank side of the canal.

He stared at them as they admired the canal, the ducks, and the fancy houses that lined the water. They were far enough to not be hurt by any exploding glass, yet for a moment Haden hesitated once more, his finger over the trigger, and he lowered his head as his eyes continued up the street.

"Push it," Lars stated.

And with that, Haden pushed the trigger on the detonator.

Nothing.

"Fuck," Haden snapped.

"What's wrong with it?" Lars asked.

"I don't know!" he said, agitated. "Maybe they found the charges!"

Jonatan reached forward and snatched the device from Haden. It was lighter than he expected. It looked like something he would pick up at the local toy store for his son.

He smacked the side of it with his hand twice, as if banging it would make it work, then, slamming his finger down on the trigger, the little red LED lit up. Everyone in the car looked in surprise at the light, before looking up in anticipation at the house.

For a moment, nothing happened. Then a brilliant burst of light lit from the basement, followed by the deep roars of the explosion.

The street shook under their tires as a blast of orange light punched through the stonework, spitting brick and fire into the air. The windows above shattered in sequence, glass raining down like shrapnel. Smoke poured out thick and fast, grey, dirty, laced with something darker, curling up and out of the house as if someone had been holding their breath for too long.

Three bodies were thrown through the fog, hitting the asphalt with wet, bone-heavy thuds. One skidded halfway across the sidewalk as its limbs twisted. Another rolled into the gutter. The third didn't move.

Haden and the other men rapidly opened the car doors, jumping out as if the horror had exploded inside the car instead.

They hurried over to the rubble, the fog blocking

their view as it extended into the sky, dust and shrapnel continuing to fall down on them. Glass from neighboring homes crunched under their feet as they crept heel to toe toward the wreck.

"Wait," Haden's voice cut through the panic as he stepped in front of them, arm outstretched. His eyes locked on the smoke. "Just wait."

Three vampires stood up slowly as if gathering their bearings, one of them the woman that greeted Haden and Lars in the loft.

They were naked, yet baked in the dirt that had afforded them a good sleep. Their bodies curling up as if they had been laying in a tunnel, as if wings were about to unfurl from their backs. The first vampire stood tall, his neck arching back, stretching himself out of the madness as he started to understand what had happened. The other two joined him.

And then it began, the horrible dissolution, the consecration of unsacred skin by the light of the sun itself.

The fog started to lift, its shroud of protection wearing off as the sun's rays pierced the smoky veil, illuminating itself on the three undead. The female looked at her hands as they started to singe, still unsure but coming to her senses on what happened.

The smoke emanating from her skin couldn't be distinguished from the smoke rising from the ashes, yet it caused an immense pain. She screeched as the rest of her body set alight. Her fellow compadre, the other vampire, howled as he slowly turned to ash. Jonatan and Lars covered their ears as the high-pitched horror threatened to break their eardrums, for it certainly ricocheted off the walls of the neighboring homes.

The taller vampire turned, his black eyes locked on Haden. He knew he was done. The right side of his face melted under the power of the sun as he moved toward them in an attempt to right a wrong, but it was too late, his legs gave out and he fell to the ground.

It was his knees that hit the ground first, cracking like smoked ribs as the men watched on. All five of them took subtle steps back as if to signal, *I'm afraid, but not too afraid.*

But this vampire was not giving up that easily. He crawled on burning limbs, leaving skin and flesh in his wake, like a butterfly escaping its exoskeleton. The men knew he could do no harm; they stood still like statues as they witnessed his body slowly turn to ash and dust.

"Haaaaidennn!" a voice screamed from the hole in the basement wall. It was Jerry, standing there, his eyes a piercing red that could be seen from at least thirty feet away. The teeth in his mouth looked aggressive, jagged at all angles, the fangs searching for anything that could graze them. Haden and the men looked at Jerry, knowing he could not step outside of the basement, lest he fell to the same fate as the three undead in front of him.

And in the blink of an eye, he was gone.

"What about the other bombs?" Tomas asked.

"I don't know, goddammit. Either they found the charges or the charges failed," Haden replied, still in shock from the scene before him.

In the distance, sirens began to wail, and closer by, people had come out of their buildings to look on at the horror. The ground was disheveled, it looked like a gas explosion or a terrorist attack; whichever would have done just fine with Haden.

As the men started to notice more people walking over to the wreckage, a noise behind them murmured. The garage door was opening slowly, the engine of the vampires' SUV inside growling, as if ready to mow down anyone and everything that stood in its way. The headlights were on, flaring through the mist of the fog and ready to go.

Lars locked eyes with Billy Cole once more. The smirk was still there, but it had curdled. Rage bloomed beneath it. His pupils were red and glassy, his jaw locked, his hands twisting tight around the wheel like he wanted to break it in half.

The men edged back, careful not to trip over the rubble scattered like bones across the sidewalk. The blast had cleared a perfect path, almost as if Jerry had planned for it, and the men knew that Billy was about to launch out of the driveway like a bat out of hell.

The garage door hit its apex with a final shudder, and from down the street, the first ambulance screeched around the corner. And that was Billy's cue. He slammed his foot on the pedal and the SUV lunged forward like an animal loosed from a cage. The men dove aside, barely clearing its path.

They lay face down for a moment, covering their eyes should any loose debris be thrown at them as the speeding black SUV swooshed past them. Haden jumped up first, his trench coat dusty from the scattered concrete. The others quickly followed suit as they all stood and looked toward their truck. Billy's SUV had stopped alongside it.

Jonatan was the first to sweat, beads running down his forehead as they looked on in horror, wondering what was about to happen. They saw Billy winding down the window. Would the SUV reverse into them? Would Jerry emerge from the back, defying the sun, and sink his fangs into their necks one by one?

As soon as the window was fully down, Billy's arm slowly exited the SUV. He was holding a Smith and Wesson Model 10 pistol. His thumb cocked the hammer slowly, like he had all the time in the world.

He wanted to make sure that the five men knew what was going to happen next.

"Get down!" Haden screamed.

But the gun wasn't for them; at least, not their souls.

Billy fired two rounds into each of the tires on the left side of the truck, rendering the car disabled, then his arm slowly retreated back into the SUV.

As the men looked on from the ground, Cole poked his head out of the window. There was no humor this time, no smiling. He stared with dread and daggers at them as his SUV drove away.

And then he was gone. The SUV tore down the street and the tires shrieked, just as the first sirens screeched to a stop beside them.

CHAPTER 5
WELCOME TO NEW YORK

If ever there was a place that could be called the Devil's playground, it was Manhattan. This great concrete city with its tall towers competing with each other for height, leaving the grandest structures of older civilizations in the dust, this jungle of skyscrapers a testament to the resilience of the human spirit and the sin that rotted it.

During the day, the thousands of people who walked its streets, worked tirelessly behind the glass windows of its buildings, and ran their businesses created a symphony, one that sang of the ambition that flowed through the veins of these New Yorkers.

The air came alive with this symphony, the music a form of electricity, its many notes comprised of people talking loudly over one another, the stomps of boots on the sidewalk, the horns of taxis and cars, and construction workers cursing at each other while also indulging in their fair share of tomfoolery.

Outside of bodegas, inside the crammed Macy's, on

5th Avenue, on the Upper East Side, in the Financial District, underneath the many canopies of Central Park, the desire to fulfill the American Dream had never been more charged.

But at night, the shroud of darkness fell upon this great city, and while it tried hard to subdue it in shadows, New York fought back with its hundreds of thousands of lights, whether they were lit behind the windows of all these blackened buildings or in the streets, as if proclaiming, *Day, you had your fair share of say in illuminating matters. Now watch this.*

Times Square would come alive with a cacophony of sharp colors; Columbus Circle would glimmer with the headlights of all the cars circling the statue of the Italian explorer who had set out to find India and had found America instead.

Amongst this battalion of stone sentinels stood the Empire State Building, guarding the island from the night and its many terrors. Its spire a banner, a symbol of hope for what the city and its people stood for. Even the newly arrived citizen of New York would look up and ask, *Will I make it here?* And somehow, they'd find comfort in the oxidized green of the spire, as if it was saying, *You shall, but it won't be easy.*

But unbeknownst to the city and those who dwelled in it, New York was on borrowed time.

September brought rain that hammered the rooftops and scaffolds, rattling against the tin tops of cabs that were lined up in rows. They hadn't moved for hours. Neon lights burned in fragments—BAR became B R, HOTEL sputtered to HOT L—letters failing one by one was nothing short of poetic, a symbol if ever there was one of how the city was operating, half in the dark.

No city exists on earth that does not have its pestilence. And New York, jewel of America though it was, was plagued with robberies, muggings, and in the darker hours, even murder. Take the Torso Killer, for instance. A headline in the newspapers for well over a week.

Brutal murders of younger girls that only added more terror to those that had shift work. Cafe workers, barbacks, and waitresses who, because of their jobs, had to head home in the dark. Those that had no choice but to ride a volatile subway because the rain above drove everyone underground.

Jennifer stepped out of the diner just after midnight, the door clattering shut behind her, the smell of coffee and grease clinging to her skin. Her feet were swollen from the shift, and her hair still carried the faint odor of fry oil that no shampoo could completely wash out.

The rain had been steady all evening, but now it had worsened into a downpour that blurred the avenue into streaks of white light and shadows. She pulled her heavy woolen coat tighter. As much as it had its own share of not so optimal things, Jennifer missed the Windy City.

It had rain, of course, but not like this. Chicago's storms blew in quick and wild, then vanished as fast as they came, leaving the air sharp and clean. New York rain pressed down, heavy and relentless, fermenting exhaust fumes and rotting garbage, until the city felt more like a punishment.

While Chicago was called the Windy City because its people were so wound up and full of hot air, at least they stopped on the walkway to give you an earful about how you were being a jackass with buttons for eyes. In New York, if you shoved into someone, it was a quick, "Fuck you, I'm walking here!" and they'd be on their business.

Her apartment was in Harlem, and the subway was only a block away. But she couldn't face it tonight. Not the underground at this hour, not the echo of footsteps in tiled tunnels, not with the papers full of torso killings and missing girls. She had taken the A train once past midnight, months earlier, and had realized that day that silence was a sound unto itself, more terrible than all other sounds.

She'd heard herself walking, the staccato of her heels, and it had carried like gunfire chasing shadows behind her.

Columbus Circle was a few blocks west, its lamps bleeding through the curtain of rain in soft, muted orange.

For a moment, the scene resembled a postcard—umbrellas bent against the wind, puddles shining under the lamps, a horse-drawn carriage dragging itself through the storm with a driver hunched deep in his coat.

Jennifer smiled wearily at the thought. She could almost pretend she was looking at one of those old-fashioned Christmas cards, the kind her mother used to pin to the wall.

But this wasn't Christmas. This was New York. And she was eighteen, standing alone on the street in a yellow dress that was already too thin for the weather.

The heavy coat dragged on her shoulders, and by the time she ducked beneath a stretch of scaffolding, it felt like she was carrying an extra body across her back. Jennifer hated the scaffolding that boxed in the sidewalk, always looking like something wasn't finished, making you feel like you were walking under a cage.

Once, in Chicago, she'd read about a woman killed when the whole thing crashed upon her. She thought about that every time she stepped under one, and every time she promised herself she wouldn't.

But tonight, it wasn't like she had another choice.

The rain hammered the tin above her, and she took the moment to slip the coat from her shoulders to wring it out, sleeves first, then collar, squeezing water onto the sidewalk. The wool clung to her wrists, heavy and limp, as her arms trembled with the effort.

She held it up by the scaffolding, twisting it hard until streams poured down in thin rivers. It gave her a moment's relief, but only a moment. The thing was soaked through, and the rain was waiting the second she stepped back out.

That's when she heard the car coming down the street.

The hum of tires through water, the splash of puddles parting, then headlights rolling up behind her in a slow crawl. She turned. A red sedan edged to the curb, its paint chipped in uneven patches, as though someone had started to strip it years ago and never finished the job. The window rolled down with a groan, and a man looked out the window, his voice raised through the storm.

"Hey there, darlin'. Need a ride?"

Jennifer froze, her heart thudding against her ribs. She knew that voice. He had been at the diner tonight. A big man, broad in the shoulders, who had kept her table for hours. He'd insisted the coffee pot stay with him, had her pour cup after cup, and he'd tipped far more than he should have. She had smiled, said thank you, and thought no more of it. Now, standing in the rain, she wished she'd used the money for a cab.

"Oh, hi," she called back, forcing her voice to sound friendly, even though that was the last thing she felt right now. Alarmed, sure, but not friendly. "It's all right. Thank you for offering though. I'm just on my way to meet a friend."

The man frowned, as though not buying it. Or maybe it was that he'd perceived her rejection as rude. "Are you sure, sweetheart? I'm headed down Harlem myself. You said that's where you live, right? I can just drop you off. Honestly, it's no trouble."

Rain streaked down her face, plastering her disheveled hair to her cheeks. The coat dragged at her arm like a dead weight as lightning cracked overhead.

The man looked harmless enough. Big, yes, easily two-fifty, with curling hair and a face that could have belonged to a friendly uncle, but not threatening. She felt a strange warmth in his expression, something that reminded her of sneaking cookies as a child, of someone pretending not to notice.

She hesitated another moment, trying to reason with the part of her mind that was blaring a red alarm. Then, finally, when she'd manually overrode the alarm, she said, "Well, all right then. It's just, my coat's all soaked and I don't want to ruin your seats."

"Throw it in the trunk! It's what they're for anyway," the man said, a grin on his face, cheer in his voice.

Jennifer grimaced as she struggled with the dripping wool, sliding it in the trunk and slamming it shut with a hollow thud. For a moment she thought about turning away, about braving the subway after all, but the sky opened up again, lightning flashing as the storm poured down harder, causing her to surrender.

Inside the car, the heater breathed a low hum, stale air tinged with the smell of old upholstery and cigarettes. Jennifer ran a hand across her forehead, sweeping damp hair from her eyes. She tried to relax, imagining herself already home in Harlem, boots off, dress drying on the back of a chair, and sliding into her single bed with a comfort that smelled of lavender laundry detergent and that warm cottony scent that invites a deep, safe sleep.

The driver gave her a quick glance, his hands loose on the wheel, a smug smile on his face, as if he was doing her a favor. "Harlem, right?"

"Yes," she answered, though her voice sounded small to her own ears. So she raised her voice and said, "That's right, Adams Avenue."

The city slid past on either side, the tall buildings giving way to shorter ones, neon signs thinning until the windows were dark more often than lit.

Jennifer leaned against the door and pressed her palms together in her lap, the yellow fabric of her dress already clinging to her knees. Something about the long and undisturbed unnatural silence in the car began perturbing her, forcing her to make conversation.

She tried to fill it. "I really appreciate this, you know," she said. "The rain came out of nowhere, and now my coat's all ruined, and so is my day."

He chuckled softly, almost kindly. "Hey, coats dry. And let's not fret about days. There's always the next one to look forward to."

She nodded, though her eyes stayed on the glass. She couldn't tell if they were heading north anymore. The streets all looked alike in the blackout, a blur of wet asphalt and traffic lights that changed for no one. She thought about asking again, about checking a sign, but kept quiet.

When he spoke next, the cadence of his voice had altogether shifted.

"So," he said, almost conversational, "tell me about the guy who stood you up. Big guy, I'm sure? Strong?"

The question caught her off guard. Jennifer's head turned slowly, her hands tightening in her lap. "I beg your pardon?"

He smiled again, but this time it felt different. "Begging doesn't befit you. Besides, I said what I said. A pretty girl like you doesn't stay out this late without waiting for a date to show up. Am I hot or am I cold?"

Jennifer pressed her knees together, tugging at the hem of her skirt to cover them. Her throat felt dry. "I believe that that's none of your business."

The man's eyes lingered on her longer now, his hands still loose on the wheel but his mouth pulling into something between a grin and a sneer. "My mistake. Line drawn in the sand. I apologize. If it's anything, I was just trying to make some light conversation."

The hairs on her arms lifted. She turned back to the window, watching the rain streak across the glass, and realized she no longer had any sense of where they were. The buildings were too low now, too spaced apart. This wasn't Harlem.

"He's big enough," she replied, thinking that this might disarm him.

"Well, good for him. Pretty little thing like you, I bet you have a real tight little nice shaven cunt."

Jennifer's head snapped toward him, her voice breaking sharp in the damp air. "Stop the car right now and let me out!"

He smirked, his lip curling as he kept his eyes on the road. "Not until I've had my way with you. I bet you taste sweet as cobbler pie down there."

Her body went rigid. Death didn't cross her mind, but rape did. She forced herself not to move, only let her eyes flick down toward the door handle.

"Don't bother, honey. They're locked," he said quietly, the words so casual they might have been an afterthought.

A wave of cold rushed through her body, the kind that seemed to come from inside rather than out, freezing her in place. She thought of the girls she'd read about in the papers, the ones found in dumpsters or not found at all. She thought of her parents warning her when she left Chicago: don't move to New York, it isn't safe, girls disappear there.

She tore the seatbelt loose and reached for the window crank, her wet hands slipping on the metal as her knuckles trembled with the effort.

The blow landed before she saw it coming. His fist caught her cheek and slammed her head into the glass. A dull thud rang in her skull and her vision burst into white sparks, and her fingers fell away from the crank as her eyes rolled back in her head.

Half-conscious, she felt the car slow down and turn, the tires rolling onto gravel. The headlights caught a line of garages, their corrugated doors gleaming with rain. The man's profile loomed beside her—massive shoulders, thick forearms, hands that looked like they could shovel earth. He swung the car into a dirt drive and yanked the gear into park.

Jennifer came to with a cry, hands clutching her face, realizing the window, the door, everything around her was useless. Panic swarmed her chest, hot and suffocating. The driver's door opened, the weight of it shifting the whole car, and then he was outside, his bulk passing across the beam of the headlights.

She noticed just in time and snapped her lock down, catching him off guard. His size worked against him; he didn't sprint so much as attempt to lumber back to the other side of the vehicle, a thick shadow circling the hood. Jennifer scrambled across the seat and grabbed the armrest to his door. She slammed it shut with all her strength and locked it.

The headlights painted him in yellow. His hair hung

ragged, plastered to his head in ways that looked like horns. His white shirt clung like second skin to his chest, torn open, his fists clenched so hard the knuckles gleamed. His eyes burned with rage, fixed on her, and she thought in that instant he looked less like a man than something that had stepped out of Hell.

Jennifer crouched on her knees on the seat, heart thrumming in her throat, the adrenaline turning her whole body to tremors. Inches separated her from him, only a pane of glass, and she knew it would not hold.

They stared at one another. His face pressed close to the glass, rain streaking down it like tears. His eyes were pale and glacial, cutting into her.

She realized something and turned her head slowly, knowing that his eyes were following her gaze. The keys still dangled in the ignition. He couldn't believe he left the keys in there. His grin widened, savage now as he leaned back, cocking his arm, and he drew his fist wide in preparation to smash the glass.

Jennifer's scream never got a chance to escape her throat. Instead, her palm slammed down on the horn. The blare filled the void, shocking him and breaking his rhythm for just a second. A second was all she needed.

Her shaking fingers caught the keys. Her hands were still wet and she slipped grabbing them, before latching on, turning them hard, and starting the car.

The engine coughed, then caught with a roar that made her laugh through her tears, half-disbelieving. She wrenched at the shifter, thumbed the button, dragged it down two notches, and the car lurched into reverse. The killer hurled himself onto the hood.

The tires spun on wet mud, gravel spraying against the garages as she craned her neck over the seat, steering blind through water and tears. The sedan shot backward until it smashed into the chain-link fence, the metal shrieking as it bent. The impact hurled the man off the hood, his body slamming into the fence with a rattle that echoed through the night.

Jennifer's hands slipped on the wheel, slick with sweat, her arms aching with effort. She jammed the shifter into drive, but before she could floor the gas, glass exploded beside her. His hand punched through the driver's window and clamped into her hair.

Fingers tangled deep, yanking with brutal strength, he dragged her upward until her shoulder scraped against the jagged edge. Pain seared her skin and she screamed, raw, piercing, as she stomped her foot on the accelerator.

The car lurched forward, bounding out of the driveway and back onto the street. The horn blared under her palm, one long cry that merged with her own, echoing through the empty blocks.

And then, when she looked back, there was no sign of him.

In Midtown, an arsonist indulged in deep arousal, setting fire to a building and gazing upon the flames with reverence.

The glow was faint through the fog, but the stink of wood and plastic carried far, acrid on the wet air. People on the stoops smelled it, turned their heads, and said nothing. Fires were just part of the new routine, like muggings, union strikes, and rats spilling out of garbage that hadn't been collected in weeks.

The collapse of New York City was nigh. It was something everyone, the citizens and the government alike, were too afraid to admit. That the city was akin to a tattered stretch of cloth, ripping at the seams.

Mayor Gordon couldn't bring himself to acknowledge this either. He'd spent years clawing his way up, puckering and placing his lips on the right asses, lighting the right Cuban cigars with submissive fingers. When he wasn't gorging himself on steak and billing it back to the city, he was draining whiskey in gentlemen's clubs that charged by the ounce. At five-foot-eight and over two hundred pounds, Gordon didn't carry himself like a man of restraint, and, of course, his policies reflected it.

The Meyer Club was his most frequented haunt. It occupied one of Manhattan's earliest Greystone Gothic buildings, its arched windows staring down at the street like tired eyes. Behind the stone wall lay a private driveway, a rare luxury in the city. *IN* and *OUT* engraved in the gate columns directed limousines through the loop where tinted glass kept faces hidden from the street. The arrangement suited the members: politicians, businessmen, and wheeler dealers.

The building had other uses beyond that of the club, of course. It also housed various public and private offices from small to large. The entrance to the building acted like it was built for a king. Large wrought iron gates atop panes of glass arched doors stood permanently open (except for the closing hours) as security stood up front, ensuring whoever stepped out of a vehicle was meant to be there.

Inside, the hallway was well lit with swooping chandeliers that looked too heavy for any human to hang. A black and white checkered floor reflected the golden light from above. The Meyer Club stood immediately to the left of the hallway, its entrance dominated by a large red curtain that required two hands to peel apart.

Inside, a lavish hallway greeted its patrons. And lavish it was, for the room looked like it had been decorated by denizens of Hell itself—dark wood, more blood-red drapes, and a chandelier that outshone the opulence of the ones in the hallway. It was the ideal setting for the elite that wanted to pretend the outside world didn't exist.

Inside, Gordon held court. The club's second-floor lounge had become his true office, leather armchairs sunk deep with use, wood-paneled walls darkened by cigar smoke, and a round table polished by a thousand elbows. Dark figures struck darker deals in drab corridors, these deals sealed with damp handshakes and the quiet slide of envelopes across the table.

Gordon's descent started with small favors. A permit here, a fast-track there. Quid pro quo was the name of the game, coins under the table in exchange for a blind eye or a quick signature. Sometimes it meant ignoring a cop beating a gay man. Sometimes it meant greenlighting a mob-owned jazz club, and when the sanitation department begged for masks, Gordon handed the contract to a foreign campaign donor. When the masks arrived, they were brittle, moldy, and stinking from shipment rot. He fined small businesses over broken fixtures, yet spared mafia liquor stores and strip clubs. Everyone knew why.

But as Mayor Gordon would come to learn, greed comes to bite you in the ass, and it doesn't pucker as a courtesy.

The budget collapsed with the chaotic beauty of a controlled demolition. First it was the schools, then the sanitation department. Fire stations closed and the police response time slowed to a halt, not because they wanted to strike, but the resources available had dwindled. Whole blocks would burn for hours before a single siren echoed down the avenue.

The power grid was failing too. Blackouts weren't uncommon and neither were bodies in alleyways. Gordon jumped on television like he was hosting a game show, asking the public for handouts they didn't have, but eventually even the banks stopped responding, and suddenly the city was broke.

Manufacturing was one of the first industries to dry up, leaving a wake of unpaid rents that started to pile up. The middle class packed their things and fled to the suburbs, leaving behind the poor, the desperate, and the unlucky.

And all the while, the city was still pretending to function, still pretending to matter, but every subway ride, every street corner, every silent cop car told a different story.

And when President Ford turned his back, the *Daily*

News printed five words that echoed off every cracked window in the five boroughs:

FORD TO CITY: DROP DEAD

And so it did.

Some neighborhoods went dark entirely. Unlit, unpatrolled, and uncared for. In the East Village, a fire could burn for hours before anyone bothered to report it, and if anyone did, no one came to the rescue. And for a city built on power, pride, and noise, silence suddenly became its loudest feature.

But while the city crumbled from the top down, life clawed its way back up from the cracks. Artists, dancers, and the queer community sprouted across the Lower East Side like moss in an abandoned lot, wild, untamed, and impossible to ignore.

From the ashes of the Stonewall riots came something holy. A chorus of resistance, joy, and liberation. New York had been starving for camaraderie, and this was its rebellion.

Disco balls spun in sweat-drenched basements. LSD and marijuana blurred the nights. Behind shuttered windows and padlocked doors, the queer and Black communities threw kikis that spread like wildfire. What the daylight world tried to suppress, the underground baptized in glitter and bass.

And to Jerry and Billy, the belabored rise and fall of the city was nothing short of a camouflage.

BILLY'S JOURNAL.

Somewhere across the Atlantic.

I hate this ship. Cold, wet, stinking of rust and salt. It makes me sick, if that's even still possible. I keep telling myself this isn't me. Sitting here on a rotting freighter doesn't define me. I'm exhausted and tired, so do forgive me, journal, if I'm rambling.

I'm tired of running from humans. Every one of them should burn. But I know better. They're tools, stepping stones. They matter, even if I don't want to admit it. And once, I was the same.

When we get to the penthouse, I'll be fine. I tell myself that. I like the big places, the view. But the small ones, the little homes tucked away, they remind me of when I was young. Sometimes I miss that.

I'll survive. I always do. But Jerry... He hasn't said a word since Antwerp. That explosion in Amsterdam almost took him apart, and now it's like he's somewhere else entirely. I handled Moller, passed him the cash, and Jerry just...drifted. I like Moller. He's simple. Lost an eye, walks around like the docks own him. Looks like death, but he gets the job done. He's kept us moving for decades, and I should be thankful he was able to get us aboard this freighter. If not for him, I don't know what we'd have done.

Jerry though. My Jerry. His silence is worse than anything.

The ship just hit a wave that nearly threw me from my cot. I won't pray. Not to God, not to the Devil. I made my choice, or maybe it made me. Doesn't matter anymore.

I don't keep this journal like I should. It was Jerry's idea, he said it would be an amazing book one day, the things we've seen. I like reading back. Rome was my favorite place. The

Pantheon at night, still one of the most beautiful things I've ever seen. Strange, the things that stay with you.

AROUND WATER STREET, the skyline rose corporate and cold, grey towers pressed tight together in glass and stone. The Financial District always felt cut off from the rest of Manhattan, close to everything, but distant enough to feel like another city. On weekdays, the streets filled with sirens, uniforms, and men in suits chasing blood or money, sometimes both. By the weekend, the noise softened, and galleries opened their doors, the art crowd drifting in to pretend the place had culture.

The condo at 200 Water Street was easy, and buying it was even easier. Jerry had businesses, trusts, and offshore accounts set up across the entire planet, and the home in New York was purchased long before their arrival. Of course, given the suddenness of their arrival, they hadn't had a chance to see the apartment until now.

The building's lobby was sleek, with ebony panels lining the walls. Sconces cast warm light against the dark surface, fixtures shaped like antiques, but wired with new bulbs.

Glossed pillars rose on either side of the hall, their gold trim hiding every seam of construction. To the right, three elevator doors waited, brass arrows above them ticking to mark the cars as they moved between floors.

Leon, the manager, met them there at nine p.m. sharp, a clipboard under one arm. He didn't usually give tours that late, but when the buyers were stepping into a multi-million-dollar unit, rules bent.

"Thank you, Leon," Jerry paused his walk and spoke with a warm affection in his voice, "for showing us around so late at night. I truly appreciate it."

"Not a problem, sir. I had a couple other errands to run tonight, and, so, wouldn't you know, this whole thing worked out. Two birds, one stone," Leon said in his New Yorker accent, as he pushed the round plastic button with an arrow that pointed to the Gods.

"Alas, but, Leon, I wish I was a bird. I'd be a lot freer then," Jerry joked. Leon cackled in response.

The three of them stepped into the elevator, the brass doors closing with a heavy sigh. The car shot upward, faster than expected, and Billy glanced at Jerry with a smirk. Jerry didn't return it, but Billy's grin held. The speed of the ascent had always reminded him of how quickly Jerry could take to the air, a joke between them that needed no words.

The elevator opened up to a small hallway. It was the only apartment on this floor, but the undead were insistent on finding a building that did not allow the elevator to open immediately into the apartment. Security was everything to Jerry, and a building of this magnitude was no exception.

The entrance to the abode was luxurious. Large double doors dominated whoever stood before them; they felt like the entrance to a castle, not a penthouse. Leon opened the door for the duo, but stepped aside to let Jerry walk in first. He didn't say a word, and swanned in to the penthouse like a petulant child, like he'd seen the place before and was tired of it.

They stepped into the great room. The space opened wide, the black pillars from the lobby below rising here as well, anchoring the corners. Heavy red fabric covered the walls from floor to ceiling, flanking the one window that spanned the entire south wall of the apartment. Gold candelabras lined the walls in pairs, their stems polished to a mirror shine. Chairs with carved arms and brocade cushions ringed a low table of dark wood.

Jerry paused at the threshold. Candlelight on red fabric, gold gleaming against black stone—it was a sight that pulled him back across centuries. Romania had looked the same. Rooms dressed in shadow and firelight, wealth measured by the weight of wood and drapery. For a moment, he stood still, taking it in like he was home again.

"Now, if you gentlemen won't be needing anything else..." Leon said, looking from Jerry to Billy.

"Just one last thing, Leon, and then we're out of your hair," Billy Cole said, placing his hand candidly on Leon's shoulder.

"What would that be, sir?"

"Mr. Jerry follows a certain religion where he's required to rest and pray in isolation for long stretches of time. Meditation, if you will. Are there any locker rooms or storage sheds in the basement that we may convert into such quarters?"

"Would a bedroom not suffice for Mr. Jerry?" the manager responded, as Jerry threw himself on the fabric sofa.

"Well, he also needs complete darkness during his religious activities. Buddhism, you see. Sensory deprivation and mindfulness go hand in hand," Cole replied as he idly glanced at Jerry.

"We do have a space he could use, but between you and me, I'm not sure you'd want to go down there that much. Dark and damp, but it's quiet. I don't know that we'd need to charge you for it if he's just taking a mat or some candles down there."

"Well now, doesn't that sound...ideal," Cole spoke in a fine drawl.

"Very well then. I will show you the place."

THE MOVE to New York broke Jerry. The city gnawed at him, stripped what little soul he still clung to. Billy endured without a flicker, his contempt for humanity as steady as ever, his cruelty unsoftened. Jerry staggered under the weight of grief. The fire at the brownstone left his chosen family in ash, and with them went centuries of hard-won joy.

Their new home closed in around him. In the dark of his bedroom—never used for sleep—panic coiled and struck, leaving him breathless, chasing memories that returned sharper each night.

The curse pressed heavier than ever. Every lover, every companion burned away in time, leaving him a fugitive from permanence itself.

The only other release was death.

For weeks he barely spoke. His movements slowed to

a crawl, hours stretching until the clocks themselves seemed to mock him. He woke in bursts, a fleeting calm sometimes tricking him into believing life still held peace. But memory tore it away, quick and merciless, leaving him trapped in his own skull, sometimes wishing for the quiet of never waking again.

Still, every night at eight, he dragged himself into the shower. It was the only ritual left. As the sun slid behind the Hudson, washing the city in dying gold, Jerry rose and walked to the bathroom. The mirror above the walnut cabinet returned no reflection, but he lingered anyway, staring at the empty space where his face should be, as if daring the void to answer.

The shower felt like indulgence. Dark green tile sealed three walls, a glass pane made the fourth. The chrome head poured a violent rain. He turned the handle to scald. Heat bit his skin. It called back sun and mortality and the old memory of a body that burned. Steam hissed. Tile stung his feet. These small torments passed for life.

Billy stayed untouched. With a predator's patience he took the streets, moved through bars, watched alley mouths, leaned at lampposts until an opening came. Sometimes a dealer with quick hands, sometimes a woman with tired eyes and nowhere else to stand. He smiled, leaned close, bought a drink, offered warmth, and most came. They read him as company for the night, blind to the hunt.

He knew the corners. Alleys carried piss and frying oil and old beer sunk into cardboard. The forgotten pooled there, and Billy slipped among them unseen.

Tall and agile, he carried quiet strength. Weapons stayed put unless needed. He preferred his hands. Certainty lived there. A woman might laugh when he beckoned her deeper into the dark. She would keep talking, routine carrying her along, until his fingers closed at her throat. The voice quit. Eyes widened, white brightening as the air thinned. He kept the hold until the weight went slack. He held a beat longer, watching breath fail.

Men brought fight. Dealers carried knives or guns. He left no space for it. A hard twist of the neck, bone cracking against brick, or a blade pulled from his coat. No flurry. One sure stroke across the throat. They folded where they stood, blood striking the wall, steam lifting in the cold.

The blade had another use. It opened an artery, the flow guided into jars he kept in his coat. Glass clicked at his ribs while he worked in the dark. One jar, then another, each capped and slid back. By dawn, the satchel hung heavy, and Jerry's bedside table showed a neat row, enough to keep him fed for days.

Bodies stayed in shadow. A girl propped by a dumpster, eyes shut as if dozing. A man in the gutter, pockets already turned by whoever came first. Morning traffic rolled past. Sirens arrived late if they arrived at all. Billy kept walking, jars warm against his chest, pleased by the thought of Jerry waking to them like gifts.

Jerry did not reach for them. Jars sat untouched, their warmth fading to the room's chill. He slept through alarms, kept the curtains tight, skipped the shower some nights. Billy wore patience like an old coat, and even that patience thinned. He'd stopped sleeping in the makeshift coffin in the basement of the building, for the sheer hope that the sun would peer through the curtains in his bedroom and take him from this cruel eternity.

One night Billy brought a girl to the tower. She was in her early twenties, black hair cut blunt at the shoulders and a laugh that carried across the lobby. She giggled as the elevator doors closed, her body pressed to his, perfume mixing with the faint metal that never left his clothes. To the doorman, it looked like a couple going upstairs.

The sound reached Jerry first. The woman's heels clicked on the marble, as the keycard scraped in the lock. The door swung wide as the girl's voice rang bright at the size of the place, the sweep of glass and steel over the skyline.

"Christ," she said disdainfully, her smile wide. "You live here?"

Billy smirked, his hand at the small of her back. "I find the word 'live' to be quite subjective. Don't you think?"

Jerry sat in the half-light of the lounge, his body motionless, his eyes hollow. He didn't rise. He didn't greet her. But the scent reached him, warm, vital, cutting through the rot of grief in his chest. He clenched his hands, willing down his hunger, but it throbbed anyway.

The girl turned, finally noticing him. "Oh... Hi," she said, her voice softening in confusion. "I didn't realize..."

Billy leaned down and kissed her cheek, his eyes locked on Jerry as he did. "She's for you, Jerry," he stated, as if conducting a business transaction.

The girl blinked. Billy's choice of phrase unsettled her. She thought about asking what was going on, but Jerry was already standing. He crossed the room in silence, his shadow spilling over her. She tried to step back as her nervous laughter took over the room. Jerry stood close as he brushed her hair away from her neck. The girl accepted the situation, she had never had two men ogle over her in such a sexual and dominant way before.

For a moment he imagined turning away, telling Billy to take her, to let her live. But the heartbeat in her neck hammered against his fingertips, and that was enough. His lips parted, and his teeth slid in. She gasped, one sharp cry that echoed against glass and steel, then sagged in his arms.

Billy stood at the bar, watching, while he poured himself a drink.

Jerry drank until the heartbeat slowed, then paused. When he finally pulled away, the girl's head lolled against his shoulder, her eyes closed and the color drained from her skin. He stepped aside and let her limp body thud to the ground without any pretense.

Billy raised his glass. "Come now, Jerry. This has to be better than a jar, don't it?"

Jerry had snapped out of his funk. He wiped his mouth clean and smiled at Billy.

He was back.

∼

A few days later, Jerry stepped out of the shower, naked as he usually did. He walked into the great room, his hands on his hips in a masculine fashion and stared at his counterpart, who was reading a newspaper on the sofa.

"Billy, I feel like walking tonight."

For Billy, it was the jackpot. In equal measure a monster himself, the only thing keeping his mind alive were the ritualistic killings throughout the week.

As Jerry and Billy left the condo, they stood in the elevator without saying a word to each other. Both thinking their own thoughts, their own realities.

"Do you miss our old life?" Jerry asked Billy without even looking at him.

"Do I have a choice?"

"No, Billy. I don't think we've had the luxury of choice in the matter. Ironic, isn't it?"

Billy gave a half-amused chuckle.

As they exited the building, the streets around them were quiet, but not too quiet. Traders that had just left the office, people that had just left the bars were staggering around the Financial District looking for cabs or running to the subway. Others were drunken lovers kissing on street corners.

Jerry looked up to the sky, closed his eyes, and breathed in a deep breath. He held it for a while before exhaling, turning to Billy and smiling.

They walked in unison, slow with steps that seemed to mimic each other's. Jerry always had a habit of keeping his hands in his pockets, the high collar of his gray trench coat covering the back of his neck. Billy generally walked sloppy, his hands moving fast by his sides, head bobbing around everywhere looking for the next opportunity. But tonight, they were taking in their new surroundings.

They wandered south toward the docks. Past Fulton Market and past the rotting fish stalls and junkies curled like fallen leaves in doorway corners. The city was still wet from an earlier rain, and the gutters stank of old garbage and motor oil. Everything felt threatening; the buildings stood above the couple as if to tell them, *Don't fuck with this city*, but Jerry knew the city was already being fucked with.

Regardless, it was a city to be respected. Not everyone made it here, and you had to be built of good hard grit, something Billy and Jerry had established over the centuries. The two continued to walk for what felt like hours, hardly saying a word to each other. Yet both with the understanding of what they were looking for.

That's when he heard it.

Down a large alley off John Street, half hidden by a rusting fire escape and a crooked dumpster, three men were kicking another half to death. Jerry stopped first; he stood and watched. His body didn't turn, he simply moved his neck to observe what was happening, hands not leaving his pockets. Billy stood behind him, smirking like a homicidal maniac.

"Told you, Jerry," he said softly. "They're still the same as before. You just forgot who they are," Billy whispered, as Jerry moved his head slightly, and raised an eyebrow toward Billy.

The gang had been oblivious to the other monsters at

the mouth of the alley. One held a broken bottle, the other held the victim down, and the third was laughing. They were desperate, angry, and they wanted to hurt someone.

The crime rate in the city had soared since budget cuts were announced, and with half the police force laid off, crime was exponential. People could take advantage of everything and anything, and they did. Gang violence was increasingly on the rise, and muggings in broad daylight had become a common occurrence.

The victim screamed bloodcurdlingly, until one of the attackers landed a punch into his mouth that rendered him unable to scream any longer. That's when the three of them paused, realizing they might have killed yet another victim for a simple wallet grab.

Jerry's facial expression didn't waver. For a creature hundreds of years old, the bitter truth of man had always been obvious. But now, it was unavoidable. This was the species that made wars over borders. That built cages for children. That screamed cruelty to strangers on the street just to feel taller.

It wasn't Jerry who had changed. He was the same as he had always been, and he knew what he was, for better or worse. It was the world that had changed. And it had only gotten worse.

He took a step forward, then paused as if to change his mind. Then his hunger took over.

"Gentlemen," he said, his voice crisp and almost cheery. "I do hope I am not interrupting."

"And who the fuck are youse?" one of the men

shouted back in a thick New Yorker accent. The other two stopped beating the man on the ground.

The man on the ground skirted back in a panic, unsure if Jerry and Billy were also there to beat him to a pulp. Jerry stared down at him.

"I was just talking to my friend here about choices. So I'll give you something that hasn't been offered to me all that much. A choice. I suggest you take it and run with it," Jerry said casually, his hands still in his pockets.

The man took a second to regain his composure, and after a brief struggle with his legs, managed to find the strength to stand up and run toward the other end of the alleyway. The leader of the gang then walked toward Jerry, a knife in his hand with the blade pointed toward the vampire's face.

"Listen here, cocksucker, I'm gonna cut you the fuck up!" he said, but Billy struck fast, almost too fast to follow. Billy's punch dislocated the gang member's jaw so fast and so violently, the two other men were too shaken to move, their brains short-circuiting as they witnessed what real violence was.

The man dropped to his knees as he tried to understand what just happened, clutching to his jaw as it hung down to his chest. His tongue hung free, and the tendons on the side of his face stretched like a whale that was coming up to feed. He looked up to the other two in a desperate attempt for help, but it was no use, the shock of the blow and the pain sent the man into a coma.

Jerry didn't move nor blink. He simply smiled at the two remaining men and showed his fangs. Confusion continued to thrive in the alleyway, where the two remaining gang members tried to make sense of what was happening.

The knives clattered to the floor too late to matter. Jerry lunged at the second man, teeth tearing into his throat, his left hand locked in the hair to hold him steady. This wasn't the clean puncture of fangs; it was ungodly bloodlust. He tore and gnawed as his jaw worked like an animal's, shaking his head side to side while the man's body thrashed and spilled in his grip.

Jerry removed his mouth from the neck violently and half of the neck came with it. Tendons, veins, and bone shot up in the air as Jerry looked up to the sky. His eyes were yellow, most of his teeth had sharpened, and his skin had turned a dark gray, save for the red crimson blood that washed down his jaw and onto his coat.

He slammed the man against the dumpster like a dog breaking a rabbit's spine before howling toward the moon, the noise echoing up and across the alleyway buildings until it eventually faded at the top.

The third victim was breathing heavily. Knowing his actions had led to this, he ran his hands through his hair in disbelief, momentarily paralyzed before finding the energy to run. He turned and darted toward the other end of the alley and right into Billy Cole, who had moved his position during Jerry's attack. At six foot three, Billy was a tall man, and the third gang member's head ran straight into his chest.

"There, there," he taunted as he spun the victim around and held his arms behind his back. Billy held an enormous strength, one of ten men, and it took nothing to hold the five foot eight gang member in place as he thrashed and screamed knowing the terror that was coming for him.

JERRY LOOKED at the corpses on the floor, trying to decide whether this was the path he wanted to walk, as if he had other choices. And as he looked up, he saw the shadow of something at the end of the alleyway. A dark figure, watching and waiting.

"You know, Billy," Jerry said, brushing blood from his cuffs, "I think I want to explore more of this city. There's an energy here I can't quite put my finger on."

"There sure is," Billy responded.

A silence ensued.

"Do you see it?" Jerry nodded to the end of the alleyway toward the dark figure looking and waving at them.

"I do."

"And who do you say that might be?"

"First you drink something. Then we'll talk," he responded, and he stood watching the figure while Jerry consumed his first fresh meal in weeks.

CHAPTER 6
A DEMON CALLS

Outside the bar known to its few and far between yet religiously regular frequenters as Sanctuario, an uncharacteristic calm had descended over New York City.

The rat-infested garbage piles on street corners had vanished as if the sanitation strike had quietly ended in the night. No one asked where it disappeared to. The Hudson? Out to the Atlantic? That was fine, as long as it wasn't clogging the sidewalks or feeding the rats.

Fifth Avenue gleamed as if it had been scrubbed clean in the night, these nameless workers making use of the downpour to wipe away the filth that had formed layers on the sidewalks. And yet, there hadn't been any nameless workers. It was just the relentless downpour that had washed away grime and crime, and while it was at it, it even doused a few fires that the FDNY had stopped answering calls for.

To those who lived here, it felt like Manhattan had been resuscitated.

In Central Park, the rain made flora and verdant greenery sprout from the earth, creating a kaleidoscope of green that felt deeply pleasant to the eye of anyone who walked in there after the rain. Pigeons, regaining their confidence after the torrential weather, were perching on roofs and windowsills. Sparrows chirped in the branches that lined the walkways, and for the first time in weeks, the streets smelled like wet stone and spring instead of rotting grease and piss.

It was still New York, but today, it was the New York that New York wanted to be, not how it usually was.

Lucia Moreno tended the bar, staring through the glass she was cleaning as if it was not a vessel for whiskey but some mysterious magical artefact that might answer the questions clawing at her chest. The bar was empty, save for the black jukebox humming softly in the corner.

It had seen some better nights, for sure. Normally, the regulars would be filtering in by now—dockworkers off shift, young artists looking for a booth to sulk in, that one jazz musician who always brought some soul to the dull nights. And there was little she could do about inviting more customers to her bar than opening and closing at the regular time every day. She wasn't about that Happy Hour or Two-For-One-Tuesday life. Doing so would require overcoming her inertia, and that'd mean the bar would attract more people. She preferred it to be an ill-kept secret of the few rather than a popular watering hole for the bohemians who called this city home.

Tonight, given the pleasantness of the weather, the

customers stayed away from the bar. The retreating rain gave way for the citizens of the city to enjoy the streets, spend time sitting outside with bottles in brown bags, or get together on a rooftop, looking at the twilight sunset as it shimmered off each of the buildings across the skyline.

Lucia sighed with relief and exhaustion as she set the glass down on the bar. Behind her, a row of whiskey bottles stood dominantly above her, just shy of her arm's reach. She leaned back on the ebony bar and placed her hands on it as if to steady herself as she perused the delights of the liquor shelf.

But these violent delights dulled in comparison to what she had in mind; a blend of her own moonshine was hidden beneath the shelves in a cabinet that was usually under lock and key. Tonight she wanted (no, *needed*) to open it. Lucia pushed herself off the bar with a little pizzazz and bent down to open the cabinet. And there it was, glistening. In a tapered bottle that looked as if a soul could be trapped inside of it stood Lucia's home-made bourbon. A special blend of mash bill, maize, and, this being a family recipe, magic.

The drink would induce unknown effects depending on the user's temperament at the time. It could deliver secrets, or steal them from you, so needless to say, it was reserved for special occasions. She stood up firmly and grabbed a short cocktail glass from the top of the bar, before walking around to the row of bistro tables that adorned a long leather-clad bench.

The bench and tables sat under plantation-style shutters. Lucia had installed the shutters out of a necessity to see the outside world whenever she wanted to, and to shut it out when patrons were looking to escape it.

Tonight, she set the bottle down on one of the tables, knelt on the bench, and opened a shutter ever so slightly. The orange glow of a streetlamp immediately invaded the establishment, shining a warming tone on the glossy black fixtures within.

Lucia looked behind her, her chin tucked into her shoulder as if to say, *I built this.* But she didn't, her parents did, and the magic that kept it alive had been buried with Maria. She hadn't been the same since her mother died. She had desperately tried to cling to the rituals. But without the book, all of it felt performative, forced, hollow. She'd battled darkness on her own, fought it in many of its shapes and forms, but she craved the feeling that the book had given her that time in the tin shed.

For the life of her, she couldn't get rid of that feeling.

Lucia slid down from the bench with the kind of ceremony priests give to altars and poured herself a glass of magic. She didn't throw it back like a dockworker at closing time. No, she carried it with her, slow and deliberate, toward the jukebox crouched in the corner like some obsidian relic. An old Seeburg, skinned black to match the walls. She had painted it herself because she couldn't stand the carnival plastic it came wrapped in, that Times Square arcade look, all cheap thrills and sticky neon.

Her fingers danced slowly across the chalky white buttons before coming to a stop on L7. A mechanical whir kicked in and a black vinyl rose from its cradle—it turned and clicked into place. The needle dropped and Van Morrison's "Into the Mystic" began its soothing lullaby.

Lucia closed her eyes, tipped her head back, and smiled as if she'd waited her whole life for that chord to land. She drifted back to her table in a half-waltz, her glass lifted high as though making an unspoken toast to the shadows. Then she sipped. The drink hit her throat like warm, smoky, fire-laced rapture.

And then she moved again. A sway more than a dance, her arms weaving like branches in some wind only she could feel. The air thickened around her, made the hair stand on the back of her neck, put a few beads of sweat on her forehead. She might have been dancing. She might have been conjuring. Maybe the difference didn't matter.

THE S BAR didn't just exist above ground. Below, tucked beneath the brick bones of the building, a small cellar had been repurposed, lit only by candlelight. It served a more eclectic clientele—the kind that didn't care for daylight, or for being seen. It was Lucia's *pièce de résistance*, something she'd fashioned herself on long, lonely Mondays when the bar didn't open until five.

The entrance to the stairwell was tucked behind the bar, hidden in plain sight. Most patrons assumed it was just storage for booze and barbacks—after all, a New York basement wasn't exactly rare. But tonight as she danced, the bourbon humming in her blood and the record looping its familiar spell, Lucia noticed something different.

A flicker of light from the stairwell—but she hadn't lit any candles. At first she brushed it off, buzzed and nostalgic, chalking it up to the magic in the glass. Until it flickered again. And again.

She stopped mid-step. And as if in perfect sync, the jukebox stuttered. A faint crackle. "Into the Mystic" began to skip, the needle caught in a spiral of the same fading lyric, looping over in an annoying repetition.

She stepped slowly toward the back of the bar. Could it be that her mother Maria had decided to pay her first visit? Lucia had spent night after night attempting to conjure the spirit of her mother, to no avail. And when random spirits of the deceased had shown up instead, begging her to stop meddling with what they considered dark arts, she brushed it off. *What do they know?* she muttered to herself.

But tonight, another visitor had come to parlay, and it wasn't Maria.

Like fingers scratching a chalkboard, Lucia had come to her senses that the jukebox was skipping, and as she snapped out of her buzzed stupor, she trotted to shut it down and stop the constant skipping of Morrison, before looking back over to the stairwell. She was used to visitors in the night, things that made you second guess, but tonight felt different. Even her breath was on pause, and when it wasn't, she inhaled soft and slow.

She circled around the front of the bar and took a slow step toward the door to the establishment. Ever so quietly she unlocked it without taking her gaze off the stairwell. She imagined herself bolting out of it and never looking back. But that wasn't in Lucia's nature—she'd dealt with evil spirits in her short lifetime, and the things that went bump in the night piqued her curiosity more than curbing it.

She left the door unlocked and walked to the bar, caressing the brass rail that ran the perimeter, then followed on to the stairwell in the back.

"Hello?" she asked aloud.

"Lucia?" a voice asked back. It felt familiar. Feminine and welcoming.

She stopped in her tracks, bolting upright, her hand now clasping the rail instead of brushing it.

"Mama?" she responded. "Mama, is that you?"

"Lucia?" The voice repeated itself without changing its tone.

The light had not wavered from the basement, and continued to flicker as if more candles had been lit down there. She moved a little faster than she did before, taking a glance at the front door again to ensure it was still unlocked.

At the top of the staircase, Lucia grasped onto the limestone walls, steadying herself like an earthquake was about to occur. The chill of the wall sobered her up slightly; it wasn't just cold, it bit back. Frost-like crystals had formed on the wall like veins of something sinister was trying to escape the basement.

She took her first step. Then another.

The stairwell wasn't straight, it curved to the right, hiding whatever lived below. A welcoming space for the freaks above ground that wished for the exclusivity of the Sanctuario.

Lucia took another step.

"Mama?" she called out.

But a noise from above caught her off guard. The front door had opened, the bell above it swinging violently as it rang aloud—it caused Lucia to forget whatever was in the basement, and she promptly ran back upstairs.

"We're closed," Lucia said to the two men in front of her, her breath still shaky. "You'll have to come back another night." The men had caught her off guard, not just for disturbing her basement discovery, but the shorter of the men bore an uncanny resemblance to someone she thought she knew. Or someone the spirits had warned her about.

"Oh, well, if that is so, I guess we can come another night. We heard that the S bar was the place for people of a certain...persuasion," Jerry said.

"Is that so?" Lucia responded. "Well, you would be correct. I would love to know who gave you the 411 on Sanctuario, but alas, the section for the peculiar is off limits tonight. It's down there behind the bar where you see the candlelight."

"What candlelight?" Billy asked.

Lucia turned around and noticed that the blackness inside the stairwell had taken over any candlelight that had been there before. Just an old mop, a few boxes of empty whiskey containers, and the switches to the lights.

"Well, like I was saying, the S room is out of commission right now—however, since it's an extremely quiet evening, feel free to take a seat, anywhere you like."

Lucia walked around the back of the bar while Jerry and Billy cozied up to the other side, sitting on the stools that lined up against it.

"What will you be having?" she asked.

"It looks like you've been enjoying some solitude. What's in that bottle over there?" Jerry asked as he pointed toward the moonshine.

If an empty bar on a Friday night in Manhattan didn't give even the most vicious of vampires cause for concern, the sweaty, exasperated mess that was Lucia Moreno right now certainly did. She looked like she had been caught red-handed, either getting fucked in the bar when no one was watching, or that she'd stolen something that belonged to Jerry and Billy. Neither were true —yet. She took a breath, closed her eyes, and ran her hands back through her hair: and that was all it took to get her back on track.

The voice in the basement sounded different from the usual souls that occasionally reached out to her. This felt deeply sinister. And whatever it was had disguised itself as Lucia's mother.

"That…is not for sale." She chuckled as she walked around the bar briskly to pick up the bottle that she had forgotten about, still buzzed from the consumption moments earlier.

"Then pour us whatever you think would calm the nerves of two men who have just moved to New York and witnessed their first alleyway attack." Billy laughed.

"Oh, yikes! I mean…get used to it. This city is all but

fucked up right now, and that bastard mayor has done nothing to help things," Lucia said as she turned to grab a bottle of gin.

"Two cocktails comin' up. Trust me, you haven't tasted a gin martini like this before," she said as she looked up and winked at Jerry.

"Do you know where gin originated?" Jerry asked, tapping his fingers on the bar.

Lucia raised an eyebrow, already grabbing the sparkling martini glasses. "Please. Regale me."

The glasses caught the light from the sconces across the bar, sending soft reflections across the lacquered wood. As she ducked below to grab the vermouth, her eyes were level with the martini glasses situated atop the bar—but Lucia noticed something strange: the glasses reflected everything, including Billy. But not Jerry.

Too much moonshine, she thought, brushing it off with a smirk as she rose back up.

Three parts gin and half a part vermouth would perfect the drink. Gin martinis were to be shaken, not stirred—something she learned from watching old James Bond movies. *If it's clear, shake it up, if it's dark, stir that cup.* She made up the phrase herself and stood by it. The silver shaker cup was now full of ice and liquor. She held it over her right shoulder and shook it violently for exactly sixty seconds, another trick she'd learned from yonder ago.

Her gaze never left the two men, and the three of them stared at each other in silence, slight smirks on their faces as they all became hypnotized by the shaking. The icy shaker was sweating, a contradiction if ever there was one. The libation was poured through the strainer and into the two glasses, the liquid looked thick and inviting. Lucia grabbed a lemon from the fruit bowl and twisted it, running a peeler over the rind—the mist spritzing through the air. It danced briefly in the glow before fading and Billy flinched reflexively, like a man used to dodging far worse.

"Amsterdam," Jerry said, as if he hadn't noticed. "Well—technically, the Netherlands. Gin was originally called genever, after the juniper berry. Medicinal, at first. Then it became recreational."

"And here I was thinking you were just a well-dressed history nerd," she replied, slicing the peel into a twist.

"We're full of surprises," Billy added with a grin.

Lucia handed them the glasses, letting her fingers linger on the stem of Jerry's just a tad too long. "So, is that where you're both from? You don't exactly scream *tourists*."

"We have European roots," Billy said. "Spent some time in Boston, then went back to Amsterdam. Now we've found ourselves a nice place downtown. Great view. Super private."

Lucia nodded. "Sounds cozy. You two a thing?"

Billy nearly choked on his sip.

Jerry smiled. "You'd be surprised how often we get that. But no—he's not my lover. This is Billy, he's my right hand. My handler. My insurance policy." He clapped Billy on the back mid-swig, sending a splash of gin over the rim.

Billy coughed. "Glad we cleared that up."

Lucia smirked and leaned against the bar. "Well…I'm glad you found your way here. This place attracts all kinds—and all kinds are welcome."

"I'm Jerry."

"Pleasure," she said. "Lucia. And now that we've got the pleasantries out of the way, you're probably wondering how you just walked through that door without me inviting you in."

She stepped back, removing her hands from the bar, her eyes sharp on the men. Jerry's fangs emerged in a flash, and his eyes turned yellow and Billy rose from his stool violently, already pushing his martini aside.

Lucia didn't flinch. "It's cool," she said, raising up her hand. "But don't even think of pulling that shit on me."

She held their gaze as she stepped sideways to the cupboard near the bourbon shelf. "Listen, bloodsucker. Do whatever the hell you want out there. Manhattan's a buffet for people like you—rapists, mobsters, corrupt cops. You could feed for a thousand years and no one would blink. But try that shit with me…"

She opened the cupboard. Inside were crosses, wooden stakes, silver pistols, and a necklace of garlic strung like pearls.

"…and I'll end you before you finish your drink."

She closed the cupboard door, calm as ever. "You don't open a bar for the undead, the wicked, and the monstrous without a few precautions. After all—fore-warned is forearmed."

She glanced at Billy, then back at Jerry.

"Now you, sit your closet-case ass down. And you,

tuck those goddamn fangs away. I've seen bigger and better."

Jerry and Billy did what Lucia commanded. They looked at each other before looking back at Lucia, and Jerry held out his hand.

"My dear, I believe we got off on the wrong foot."

"You bet your undead ass we did." She responded, as she poured herself another glass of bourbon.

"So tell me, why are you really here?"

"Well, since you seem to have gathered what I am, how about you start with telling us a little more about you first?" Billy responded.

Lucia raised her glass but didn't drink. She let the bourbon catch the light, twirling the liquid like it might give her an answer.

"You ever inherit something you didn't ask for?" she said finally.

Jerry smirked, and Billy said nothing, he just swirled the last of his martini that hadn't spilled over onto the bar.

"My mother–she was a spiritualist. Espiritista. She talked to the dead and read dreams... People came to her for blessings, or curses, depending on the day. We lived in the Bronx for a long time after moving here from Puerto Rico."

Jerry nodded slowly. "And you took up the family business?"

Lucia gave a small, bitter laugh. "Not exactly. When she died, I inherited the bar and the apartment upstairs. That much was expected. What I didn't expect was the silence. She was the voice in the room I didn't realize I needed until she was gone."

Billy leaned in. "So what, you light a few candles now and then? Smudge the place with sage?"

Lucia turned to him. "She had a grimoire. It was bound in human skin. Man, it was old. Real old. One of those books that reads you more than you read it."

Jerry's expression flickered as he turned to look at Billy.

"She kept it hidden, said it wasn't mine to use until I was ready. But I wasn't patient and tried using it anyway."

Billy grinned. "And what happened? You summon a demon or just embarrass yourself?"

Lucia's smile was dry. "Both."

She set her glass down, as she pursed her lips.

"I tasted something that night. I'm not sure what it was, but it surged through me like electricity. But the book knew I wasn't ready. It shut me out, and took a piece of me in the process. After that, it went in the ground with her and I haven't felt whole since."

She looked back at Jerry, and for a second realized she'd let down her guard.

"So now, I run this place. S is for the weird and the damned. But the truth is, I'm just keeping the lights on until I find my way back to that feeling," She paused, then smiled again, pushing the moment away. "But enough about the dead. Let's talk about the undead."

She leaned forward, elbows on the bar, eyes fixed on Jerry. "You're older than you look. I'd wager you've crossed an ocean a few times or more."

Jerry smirked. "Guilty."

Lucia nodded. "So what brings a vampire and his handler to my doorstep in the middle of a city falling apart? You're not here for the weather."

Billy opened his mouth, but Jerry raised a hand.

"Let's just say we're in transition," Jerry said, tone calm but guarded. "We've had to leave some things behind and start over somewhat."

Lucia narrowed her eyes. "You make it sound like a breakup."

"No," Jerry said, sipping his drink. "Well, it was a death of sorts."

"Is that what happened in Amsterdam? A death?"

Billy shifted on his stool, fingers tapping his glass. "News travels fast."

"It does when the spirits whisper," she said, sipping her bourbon. "And they're very interested in you two."

"Amsterdam was complicated." Jerry exhaled.

For a moment the air between them felt like it was sucked out of the room. A group of barhoppers who'd had too much to drink stumbled past the shutters, flickering the orange light that was shining inside. They all turned to look for a second, and then back at each other.

Then Jerry raised his glass. "To new beginnings."

Lucia raised hers in turn. "To old debts."

The glasses clinked. And just like that, everything was fine again. This time, Lucia felt it in her bones. Something cold stirring in the stairwell, it felt like something was looking at her and snickering. But she kept her face still and smiled.

"Now drink up," she said. "Because when I'm done cleaning this place, I've got an old ghost to chase."

JERRY AND BILLY had left Sanctuario, still unsure how they'd even crossed the threshold. Vampires needed an invitation to enter a home, but bars, being public, carried no such protection. A subtle distinction, one the demons who made the first Vampyre had twisted long ago. They chalked it up to Lucia toying with them, her way of saying *I know what you are.*

Back inside, Lucia turned the key in the door and rested her forehead against the wood. The silence was unnatural. The kind that made her wonder if her old ghosts were watching, too afraid to show themselves. Even they, it seemed, were unsure what was coming. The air had grown cold again; Lucia glanced and noticed the sweat that beaded the martini glasses on the bar.

Gripping the bolt on the door, her eyes drifted toward the stairwell and saw the flickering light again.

"Lucia, help me," the voice hissed up from the dark. It was no longer smooth; it cracked, grainy and wet, the whisper of something half-formed and hungry.

She didn't hesitate. Shoving off the door, she stormed toward the stairwell, half-drunk, half-fueled by the thrill of putting a vampire and his handler in their place.

"Listen, whoever the fuck you are, you better..." But Lucia couldn't finish her sentence. She froze at the sight of it. A moving shadow sat at one of the bistro tables staring at her. Its eyes ever so small, but its jagged white teeth ever so real. She'd seen pictures of sharks in the ocean in newspapers and magazines, teeth that grow in whichever direction they pleased, and this presence, while smaller in stature, bore similar teeth.

"Do you know who I am?" the voice hissed at Lucia.

"I know you're not my mother." She didn't flinch. Her arms were steadfast against the stone walls, bracing herself.

"Clever child." The demonic being, a dizzying vision to behold, with its blackness making it phase in and out with the darkness around it, stood up from the chair without needing any assistance from its odd limbs that formed its shape. "Sit with me. I know things that you'll want to know." It chuckled to itself as it raised its arms to its face. Suddenly, claw-like digits formed on its hands as it tapped them together, attempting to hide the hideous smile that stretched across its face.

Lucia took one step toward the demon. "I'm fine just where I am, thank you."

"Very well," it hissed as it retreated, its smile and claw-fingers melting back into the formless blob that it was when it appeared.

"The monsters that you just entertained," the ghost drawled, "carry something that you have lost."

"Is that so? And who are you? Just another demon telling me lies and riddles?"

"Your mother is here with us." It laughed again. "She has a message for you."

"My mother hasn't had a message for me since I put her in the ground."

"You walk this Earth alone, you search for the one

thing that will make you complete. You don't know how to find it, but I do."

"What is your name?"

"Child, I have many names." The demon was moving in its seat constantly, its shape shifting into various blobs and shadows, moving as if it couldn't sit still.

"Pick one."

Instead of responding, the formless figure began to shrink, its shape bending in on itself as it began to shudder. The candlelight started to blow as if an arduous fan was hurling wind around the room. The subway train was audible as it ran parallel to the underground cavern.

The room began to shake, causing chairs to rattle and the bistro tables to dance on their tiny curled feet, and Lucia rushed to grab the liquor bottles that sat atop the small makeshift bar.

The horror was morphing into a new shape—first the shoulders formed, and a neckline began to take shape.

And then, the candles blew out. Blackness ensued, and a gasp escaped Lucia's mouth. For a mere moment, she was back in the tin shed. Terrified. She knew the basement like the back of her hand; it was easy to, the space was small and sat perhaps twenty people at most, the bar that sat immediately to the left of the stairwell was tiny, room for one server only, and only one of each liquor stacked up on a small gold tray.

"*La princesita*," a voice softly spoke.

The candles relit themselves; not all of them, but enough to light up the figure that now sat in place of the demon. The room had become cold once more, and the stone walls flickered with frost, sparkling like stars in the night sky, shimmering against the flames. The S room looked like a cave from prehistoric times, and for all intents and purposes, it might as well have been.

The figure had morphed into Maria Moreno, and Lucia rushed to it. To her.

"Mama, is that really you?"

Maria's death was quick, and Lucia had barely had time to grieve. The funeral was even quicker, and with money being tight, in a city that was already crumbling, she had deep regret in the way she had sent her mother into the ground.

A simple wooden box in a cheaper spot of the cemetery was hardly fitting for the voodoo queen of the Bronx. Nor fitting for a woman who carried her entire bloodline from Puerto Rico to the United States.

Lucia felt the pain every single day when she looked into the mirror; she longed for the day Maria would return to her to let her know everything was all right.

That the body was merely a vessel, transporting the soul to and from various realms, and that the burying of the grimoire wasn't a punishment to Lucia, nor was it taken due to mistrust. It was due to the power of a book bound in the skin of a dead man who parlayed with the Devil which, if it wanted to, could split the very planet in two.

Maria looked back at her, the same eyes Lucia remembered as a child. They glistened under the candle-light, the same color, the same sadness around the edges. She even smelled like Florida Water, the lemon-fresh smell that Maria would use, not only on her body, but in the tub, around the house, and on her clients for spiritual cleansing.

"*Mira cómo has crecido*," Maria said softly, reaching out. "You built this. You made it beautiful."

Lucia knelt down in front of Maria, her head resting on her lap as the tears ran down her face, like a dam that had finally been released.

"I have missed you so, so much," Lucia whispered, wiping the tears from her eyes as she looked up.

"The power you seek lies in the book of the one who drinks the blood," Maria said to her as she stroked her face, her smile now becoming sinister.

Lucia stood up slowly, removing her hands from Maria's knees.

"How do I know it's you? Tell me something only I would know."

Maria stared at Lucia for a moment, before laughter began to erupt. A croaky, old woman cackle escaped her lungs as if she'd already smoked fifty cigarettes that day. The candles in the room billowed and swayed once more.

"Mamá?" Lucia whimpered.

The demon's nails sank into its own cheeks, raking downward with a frenzy that peeled the flesh in strips. Skin tore like wet parchment, snapping open at the jaw. Sockets gaped raw, the eyes bulging wet and obscene, rolling back until nothing but white showed. The head lolled sideways, and the sight of it unstrung Lucia, sent her collapsing to the floor with her mother's name breaking from her throat.

She dropped to the ground and screamed, "Mama!" And while this wasn't really Maria, the apparition in front of her still presented so. The flesh dripped from the chin in thick drops, pooling at the demon's feet. It staggered forward like a creature begging for help, arms limp, shoulders hunched, yet still laughing. All the while, the raspy cackle continued.

Lucia pushed herself upright and stumbled back to the makeshift bar, her arm knocking the gold tray to one side as she reached for the bottle of vodka. With one arm stretched back, she gripped it hard and hurled it toward the evil spirit.

It missed, instead slamming into a stack of candles that stood adjacent to it. Glass shattered against the wall, and the clear liquid immediately erupted into flames, soaring across the row of wooden bistro tables and chairs.

The demon paused, standing still to regale in the horror that engulfed the room as Lucia stood motionless. With its menacing smile, it turned toward the fire and touched the flames with its melting hand, all the while its gaze fixated on Lucia. The fire immediately took to the blackness, climbing its way up whatever shape the ghoul had now become, engulfing it in red and yellow.

The menacing laughter continued to ring from the ruins, and from within her head.

Lucia unfroze and didn't hesitate to run out of the stairwell and across the bar. She wished that Billy and

Jerry were still with her, that anyone was here, even the spirits which had no qualms visiting her during more non-terrorizing moments.

As she fumbled with the key in the lock that was holding her prisoner, the fire had now taken hold of the stairwell, spreading as if it had a mission, as if it was clinging on to any remaining drops of alcohol to jump to the next flammable thing.

She burst into the street after ripping the doors open. The cold night air smacked her in the face, giving some relief to the intense heat she had felt in the basement. Around her, the city moved unencumbered and unperturbed; headlights flashed, voices called out, life continued, but all she could hear was the crackle of fire rising behind her.

Sanctuario was burning.

She kept her eyes forward, holding her breath. But the heat clawed at her back, and the crack of shattering glass forced her to look. Flames danced in the windows. Smoke pushed through the doorway, slow at first, then rising fast. The black paint on the exterior had started to melt, running in slick, uneven streaks that made the bar look polished and almost new. Then the windows blew out, sharp and sudden, like someone had thrown bricks from inside.

Lucia looked on; it had all happened so fast, all from a single bottle and a malevolent spirit. Nothing in her life had cut as deep as the thing wearing her mother's face, clawing its own eyes out while smiling. That would be the one memory she wouldn't be able to outrun.

A crowd had gathered, their screams muffled against

the ringing in her skull. Darkness pressed in at the edges of her vision. Then came the anger, crawling up her spine, steady and hotter than the fire eating her bar. Rage at the apparition. Rage at herself. Rage at the vampires who'd stalked her earlier, now perfect scapegoats for the ruin.

She didn't look back again. She didn't need to. The bar was gone, her mother's memory desecrated, and somewhere out there, the grimoire waited.

She would find it. And when she did, she wouldn't bury it this time.

CHAPTER 7
EVEN VAMPIRES GET SLOPPY

"You know, Billy boy, it's been a while, but I feel like dancing tonight!" Jerry chortled as the two of them stumbled down the street, riding the buzz from the martinis they had consumed in Lucia's bar. Neither noticed the fire trucks that hurled past them, howling and screaming, headed straight toward Sanctuario.

"I'm glad you've got your pep back. Dancing it is, and maybe later we can enjoy a...drink," Billy said, his signature devilish grin etched from ear to ear.

"I think we just enjoy our time tonight. Let us feed on the evil that thrives in this city. The vagabonds, criminals, people deserving of having their blood drained," Jerry replied, this shift in his sentiment occurring after meeting Lucia. "Come, let's ride the subway."

The nightlife buzzed on this busy yet cautious Friday night as Jerry and Billy were approaching Chambers Street Station. Drunk partiers clambered around them as they pushed their way through the dirty steps, holding onto the green rusted railings that were pinned against the stairs.

They looked around for a moment, observing the platform in front of them, the ticketing system to the left and a guard to their right. Jerry led the way, confidently striding toward the guard.

"Excuse me, my good fellow, how would one go about purchasing a ticket, and which train would one take to Studio 54?"

"Good fellow? Youse from England or Transylvania or somethin'?" The guard laughed back while writing down notes on his pad, his accent a thick mix of old-school New York and New Jersey.

"He gets that a lot." Billy laughed, always interjecting to correct the incorrect.

"Take the E train, uptown. Platform's down the stairs, hang left. Get off at Seventh Avenue. All right then, guvnor?"

Jerry paused, his smile momentarily turning into a grimace. He was a calculated vampire, cold, earnest, and pragmatic. But living for centuries with wealth that would surpass even the richest of the mortal didn't mean that he had completely foregone his ego, and occasionally, it would jump to his shoulder and push him to act in ways he normally wouldn't.

Yet with a slight squeeze on the shoulder from Billy, Jerry regained composure, and replied with great cheer, "Thank you, sir." They watched the guard walk away, shaking his head dismissively.

With their ticket tokens in hand, the two made their way toward the turnstiles, the smell of piss and cigarettes smacking their senses as they walked. It did little to bother Jerry, but Billy had a different view. He hated humans. And he hated the fact that it was this species Jerry had to rely on for his nourishment.

Lazy and chaotic, yet necessary, he would lament to Jerry, who had a more mature view on the world. Jerry knew that there would come a time when he would cease to exist, be it through his own choosing or another human, or something of equal measure ending him, and so he treated every day with the grave reality in mind that each day subtracted from his total life.

The platform was empty save for a handful of stragglers at the far end, partygoers on their nightly bar crawls. By eleven, most of the crowd had already moved on, leaving the station quieter than usual. Everyone knew the middle cars were where the chaos lived; the front and back stayed sparse, usually out of laziness of not wanting to walk the entire length of the platform. Jerry and Billy headed toward the front.

The guard they'd passed upstairs in the ticketing hall was here too, already on the platform, clipboard tucked under one arm as he prepared to ride along. "Count Dracula, you made it!" he called, his voice carrying down the tiled walls, ricocheting off the curved ceiling.

Jerry gave him a polite nod as he and Billy stepped into the empty carriage. Another wave of urine hit their noses, fresher this time, stinging in the stale heat.

The doors closed with a hydraulic hiss, and with no crowd to wait for, the train jolted forward, its wheels shrieking as it plunged into the tunnels.

"First time on the subway, prince of darkness?" the guard teased as he walked toward them.

"As is there for everything." Jerry nodded, as Billy sat back casually on the plastic seat, his arm stretched across Jerry's shoulder.

"And I suppose you're his first victim?" the guard continued.

"Something like that," Billy shot back, this time his eyes sharp and evil, as the guard gripped the silver pole that stood in the middle of the carriage for support.

"Whatever. Tickets, now." It wasn't a question, more so a demand, as the guard, who stood five foot eight with two hundred pounds of gristle, loomed over the men as they looked back up at him.

The fluorescent lights above flickered as the train continued its path into the darkness of the tunnels, momentarily blacking out the entire carriage before lighting it again, only for the ample graffiti to shock the senses; with every flash of static light from the rails outside, a new section of vandalism became apparent.

Jerry handed the tickets to the guard; his hand had already transformed into a claw, his fingers doubled in size and his nails extended from their cuticles, sharper and aged. The guard stared at his hand, then stared back at him.

"Looks like a manicure's in order, faggot." He laughed through a wince as he threw the ticket back at Jerry and began to walk in the other direction of the carriage.

The train was rocking side to side, reminding all who would even enter the box on wheels that the many scattered poles throughout would assist in steadying one's footing. And as the train jolted more aggressively this time, the lights went dark for a moment longer than they had before.

The guard fell onto one of the plastic seats, his hat falling off and his ticket notepad flying out in front of him. The blackness still interrupted by occasional electric static from the outside, the flashes giving small glimpses of hope as he reached underneath the seats for his items. Heaving himself up using the pole, he stood straight and adjusted his cap. The lights had not returned, but the static outside increased, illuminating the carriage in snaps of blue.

In one of those flashes, Jerry was now standing. His fangs gleamed white in the gloom, his eyes burning yellow.

"What the fuck?" the guard gasped, his voice breaking as he spun around, his fingers losing the notepad again. The book slapped the floor and slid away, but he barely noticed. Billy was behind him now, holding the railing with both hands, his arms outstretched, smirking.

The train jolted, throwing the guard sideways into another pole. His legs spread wide, his arms grasping for balance, the weight of his body tipping him into a clumsy crouch. He spun again, breath ragged, eyes darting between the two figures that closed in with each flicker of blue. Jerry's growl rolled out low and guttural, vibrating through the steel carriage, forcing the guard's head to snap back in his direction. His teeth glistened in the next flash, his smile widening.

"You know," Billy shouted over the scream of the tracks, his grin wide enough to split his face, "I *was* his first."

The words seemed to echo, bouncing down the hollowed car, but the guard couldn't answer. His mouth opened, a half-formed protest, and then he felt the sharp stabbing pain as claws bit into the flesh of his back.

He stiffened, eyes bulging, and in the strobing static light he realized there was nowhere left to turn. Jerry's gaze shifted past him, to the far end of the tunnel, where a faint glow was beginning to bleed against the dark. The next station was coming.

"Do it now," Billy ordered as he snapped his head back toward Jerry.

"No, no, please, I'm sorry, I'm a fag myself," the guard screamed back in pain and horror as he fell to the ground.

But it was no use; Jerry had already injured the guard, and even if he wanted to show remorse, it was too late. He struck at the speed of light, diving on top of him, clenching his mouth into his neck. Billy steadied himself with the poles and drove his boot into the side of the guard's face so he couldn't move, watching behind him for the approaching station.

Jerry came up for air for a second, his eyes a bright yellow, his mouth covered in blood. He heaved back and forth, breathing heavy as if he had just held his breath for a few minutes. Then he dove back in, this time sucking as hard as he could to remove as much blood as possible.

If this was going to be his meal for the night, he was

going to devour it. The guard was whimpering mini pleadings as his life flashed before him. Realizing that his girlfriend, his mom and pop, his sister, and all the boys he'd grown up with would never see him again.

"*Stop*, we need to go," Billy issued another order, and he reached down and grabbed Jerry by the scruff of his neck.

The lights had returned, and the guard was on the floor gurgling his last breaths as he clinched onto his throat, trying to make sense of what happened. His eyes stared wildly at Jerry as if to ask, *What the hell are you?*

The train entered the next platform and screeched as if it was holding onto the tracks by a thread, still jolting from left to right, sparks from the track jumping up and down, an announcement to the riders that it had arrived.

But this platform was much busier; crowds of people stood in its center, hollering and cheering that the train had arrived at all. As it continued to roll through the station, the scores of people began to diminish, and in true fashion, there was no one standing at the end of the platform.

The two men side-stepped the corpse that now lay before them. The blood had splattered and washed over the floor, blending in with the blacks, reds, and other colors that had been inked from vandalism. Jerry, returning himself to his usual poise, ripped out the tank top from underneath the guard's button-down and used it to wipe his face, the white ribbed shirt turning a dark moody red almost instantly.

The wheels had screeched to a halt, and Billy held

Jerry's bicep firmly in place, ready to usher him out of the carriage as he continued to wipe up the blood from his mouth and neck. And as the doors opened, the two vanished onto the platform and immediately up the stairs that led passengers to the exit.

JERRY CUPPED the water in the station restroom, splashing it against his face. Red water swirled in the basin before disappearing down the drain. Another patron of the restroom walked past, completely oblivious to the fact that Jerry bore no reflection in the mirror.

"You okay there, pal?" the drunken city boy asked, his tie loose, his shirt and jacket disheveled.

"He's fine. Got into a little bit of a fight. Thanks for asking. Enjoy your night, pal," Billy said, leaning against the chipped tile wall, watching the man leave the bathroom. Billy's reflection in the mirror was faint, warped by a crack that split down the center.

"Missed a spot," Billy said, nodding toward Jerry's collarbone.

Jerry remained silent. He just dragged a wet hand down his throat, then grabbed a wad of brown paper towels from the dispenser and scrubbed.

"You always get so fucking clean after," Billy continued, stepping closer. "Like a priest wiping the altar after communion."

Jerry finally met his eyes in the mirror, as if only Billy could see his reflection.

"Because it feels like a ritual," he said.

Billy smirked. "No, my friend. Because it feels like guilt."

The skin was clean, but the memory of the throat in his mouth—the heat, the thrum of fear—still lingered behind his eyes.

"You hesitated," Billy said suddenly. "Before you ripped him."

"I saw the station coming."

"Bullshit. You could've drained him in two seconds. You waited. Like you wanted him to beg."

Jerry looked at him again, this time not in the mirror.

"I did want him to beg."

Billy laughed with admiration.

"There he is," Billy said. "My little monster."

He stepped up behind Jerry and rested his neck on his shoulder, peering at the mirror as if he could see Jerry's reflection in it.

"This always gets me." He laughed.

Jerry turned off the faucet. His face, now dry, looked almost human again, except for the faint glimmer of yellow still clinging to his irises. "What, that you look like a puppet on a string in your reflection?" He smirked.

"Yeah, I just love our little life. Can't get enough of it. You ready to go out now?"

"For now."

They stood in silence for a second, the sound of dripping water echoing like a heartbeat through the filthy bathroom. Then Jerry reached for his shirt, bloodied and torn, and tossed it in the trash beside the paper towel.

"Let's find another one," Jerry said.

Billy grinned and pushed open the metal door. "Going shopping, are we?"

~

AFTER A BRIEF VISIT to a tourist store where scores of Statue of Liberty trophies and Big Apple paraphernalia stood in uniform across white plastic shelves, Jerry now had a clean shirt to wear. A white tee stamped with *I*  *NY* drew a smile to Jerry's face.

"Too campy?" He smiled as he turned to Billy.

"Eh, who cares?" Billy said, ever the loyal wingman to his undead compadre.

The store was brightly lit, part to allow tourists to check their wares in the many mirrors that adorned the shelves, and part to stop thieves from stealthily placing items in their pockets or book bags.

Jerry bought the shirt and immediately removed the price tag, asking the cashier if he could throw it in the trash for him. He removed his jacket, which revealed his bare muscular torso. The shirt slipped over his head with his brown surfer curled locks bouncing back into place as he poked his head through.

"There. I think I've nailed it," Jerry said to Billy as he tucked the white tee into his flared denim jeans.

"Jesus Christ. Let's get the fuck outta here." Billy chuckled, looking nervously around, noticing all the surfaces accentuating the light and the reflections. "Before these fucking mirrors give it away."

As they turned onto Broadway, Billy lit a cigarette,

his eyes scanning the sidewalk. "You think they'll ID the body?"

"Eventually," Jerry said. "Ours was the last ticket he checked off on that notepad, and neither one of us picked it up."

Billy blew out smoke through his nose, laughing at himself. "Amateurs."

Jerry adjusted his new shirt. "It's almost funny," he said.

"What is?"

"That people consider this the Mecca of the West. Look around, Billy. It's a city in ruins."

Billy smiled, but didn't respond. He knew that tone. Jerry was slipping inward again, reflective, almost as if he had regret for what just happened with the guard.

"So," Billy finally said, flicking ash onto the sidewalk. "Where to next, partner?"

Jerry tilted his head back and sniffed the air like an animal smelling the wind. "Here," he said, as the two arrived outside of Studio 54.

A LARGE GLOSSY awning jutted out from the art deco building on the corner of Eighth and Broadway, with a simple 54 etched in silver at the corner—nothing more needed. It was iconic long before it even opened its doors; the name Fifty-Four echoed in bathrooms and beauty salons alike.

To the right of the club, a low-slung parking garage sat tucked behind another building, its mouth open just wide enough to swallow limousines and spit out the elite. The walls of the club beat with bass so heavy it made the sidewalk thrum underfoot, the sound bleeding into the alleyways without a single neighbor bold enough or foolish enough to complain.

The energy outside was electric. Crowds pressed against the velvet rope, desperate for a chance to see a celebrity or artist escape their limo and swan through the ropes to the brass rimmed doors. They dropped names, offered bribes.

They waved, hoping for the off chance. Cameras flashed and glitter hung to the door as stage bulbs flashed intermittently along the perimeter of the awning. And standing by, the gatekeeper of the club, was the doorman. A heavy bouncer who stood at six foot five and was as broad as he was tall. If he didn't like you, you weren't getting in.

"Are we just gonna waltz in?" Billy laughed, already knowing the answer.

Jerry didn't even glance at Billy. He ran a hand through his thick brown hair and stepped off the curb, strutting toward the club. Billy threw his cigarette down and followed in tow.

In Bosnia, Jerry had once led soldiers across frozen ground. He kept them alive by talking, asking about their wives, their victories, the things that made them human. He was the kind of compassionate leader who listened more than he spoke, who negotiated before he drew blood. It was why men followed him and why his enemies faltered. He always preferred negotiation over fire.

That compassion never left him and would ulti-mately be the flaw that would one day make him immor-tal. Yet now, as he approached the club like a king returning to court, there was no ego in his step. Only a confidence that could have been forged on a battlefield.

As Jerry approached the bouncer, he tucked in his *I*  *NY* shirt a little tighter, his confidence swaying with each step as he locked eyes with the man. The bouncer stared back, unmoving, until his clipboard sagged to his side. Something was different about this man, and for the *no goods* on the sideline, the ones who would never see the inside of the club, it could have been the perfect moment to slide by unnoticed.

The bouncer immediately stepped forward and unlocked the velvet rope from its gold counterpart before nodding in agreement with the vampire, his resolve loos-ening under Jerry's gaze as he submitted to the spell that had been placed on him. Billy followed close behind, amused, one hand adjusting the lapel of his jacket as he donned the $2 shades he had just purchased in the tourist store.

❧

THE HALLWAY WAS NARROW, almost claustrophobic by design. Light spilled in strange angles, golds and reds layered like oil and water, bouncing off the glossy black walls. Mirrors angled at odd slants fractured Billy's reflection as they moved forward, stretching his grin. Jerry's reflection wasn't returned, but no one noticed yet. They were far too entranced on the doorway ahead, the doorway that would lead them into a whole new world.

"We are family..." the voice of Sister Sledge wrapped itself around them like velvet, the piano intro bursting just as they entered into the main room.

Lights roamed in columns across the ceiling as all eyes in the club turned to stare in their direction. The DJ booth stood like a pulpit at the far end of the floor, spinning vinyl under a rotating disco ball that sprayed stars onto every surface.

A fog machine let out a low hiss near the stage, rolling mist across the platform where a pair of dancers moved like gods in synthetic light.

The club's Moon Man hovered slowly above the dance floor, silver and wide-eyed, suspended from the ceiling in theatrical glory. Its mechanical arm held a gleaming spoon that caught the strobe lights just right, sending flashes across the crowd like a blessing or a warning. Every few minutes, it glided across the club like a celestial mascot, arms outstretched, watching the chaos below like some disco deity. Each time it passed overhead, the crowd erupted, reaching for it, screaming its name, as if worshiping something holy and hollow all at once.

Jerry and Billy stepped into the mezzanine and walked over to the bar. The atmosphere above was thick with cigarette smoke and money, crowded with the elite, their champagne glasses catching the lights. Some straddled the original velvet-backed theater seats that still clung to the floor like relics of a forgotten theater. A long balcony with a brass railing spanned the mezzanine from end to end, and down below, the dance floor heaved with bodies.

The crowd was a constellation of the city's most uninhibited souls desperate for a way to see out the decade. Artists straddled each other, coating each other in lipstick and glitter. Drag queens in floor-length fur coats towered over Wall Street boys stripped to mesh and leather. Queer couples danced chest-to-chest, unafraid and unapologetic.

Models lounged like sculpture on mirrored platforms while punks in torn denim poured champagne into their mouths from the bottle. Everyone stared, no one judged. Inside Studio 54, every form of expression held court.

Jerry was swaying his hips as Billy looked onto the crowd down below, the two of them sucking down another martini; gin, one of the few alcoholic drinks they could tolerate.

Behind them, what looked like a pair of models sat as if they owned the place. A tall, slender-looking black woman with a luminous afro hairstyle sat with her legs crossed. The mini skirt barely covered her genitals, but she didn't care. Her legs looked as if she was ten feet tall, glossy and moisturized, shimmering and commanding. Her counterpart, a smaller white female with ashy blonde hair, was pouting around the room as if she were looking for a neck to bite, and wildly unimpressed at the caliber of veins that surrounded her.

The two women, however, weren't looking for fresh blood, but for a semi discreet moment, as they pulled out two compact mirrors from their clutch purses in the sea of partygoers. The blonde woman promptly reached inside the black tuxedo-style jacket she was wearing and pulled out a small metal tube. She effortlessly removed the lid with her thumb and index finger as she continued looking around the room, her friend leaning in, smiling and kissing her on the cheek.

The tube was tipped to its side and out sprinkled white powder onto the mirror. Cocaine had never looked more glamorous. The women both reached down, holding one nostril as they inhaled the contents, wiping any residue with their middle fingers and subtly rubbing it inside their gums. Their eyes never left the crowd, and their smiles never left their faces.

Jerry and Billy looked down at them and back up to each other.

"That's a slippery slope if ever I saw one," a voice called out from behind.

Jerry turned and nearly lost his balance over the mezzanine.

The woman staring back at him stood nearly eye to eye, five foot nine in heels, her permed blonde mane gathered in one hand as she fluffed it over her shoulders, giving it extra bounce. Blue glitter shadow swept across her eyelids, shimmering beneath the lights, and her lips gleamed with a glossy rose finish. A martini in her right hand, she plucked olives from the toothpick with her left, slipping one between her lips with confidence.

She reminded Jerry of Maria, his long-lost love.

"And who might you be?" he asked, a smile curling at the edge of his mouth. Their exchange ever so slightly elevated to cut through the noise of the music.

"Lilly," she said. "Lilly Thurman."

"Ms. Thurman," Jerry said, offering a slight bow, "the pleasure is all mine."

Lilly's eyes drifted down, clocking the shirt with one arched brow.

"You know," she said, sipping her martini. "Wearing an *I* ♥ *NY* shirt here. Bold. Either you're brave or hopelessly foreign."

Jerry looked down at himself, then back at her with a faint grin. "Is it that offensive?"

"Only if you're trying to seduce someone who lives here."

He chuckled, already disarmed. "And if I were?"

"Then it's going to take more than a tourist tee and high cheekbones," she said, tugging playfully on his thick luscious curls.

Jerry inclined his head, amused. "Noted."

She leaned a hip against the railing; her shimmering blue mini dress matched the eyes that were still scanning the crowd as if impressed by all of it.

"And what about you?" he asked. "What do you do, when you're not cutting down strangers in novelty shirts?"

She turned back to him. "I do a little bit of this, that, and the other. But these days, I'm thinking about going into publishing. Wrangling authors, herding editors, pitching to publishers. Seems a hoot and a half, and they say publishing is an evergreen industry."

Jerry smiled. "A lover of stories."

"The dangerous ones," she added, giving him a grin. "Stories that end well are so over and done with. It's the ones that leave you in emotional tatters that I want to chase."

He held her gaze a moment longer. "And are you in one now?"

Lilly downed the last of her drink and placed it casually on an empty tray a passing server was carrying. "That depends. Are you about to ask me to dance?"

As Jerry held out his hand to Lilly, she paused for a moment, looking down at his hand, back up, and then across to Billy, who was leaning against the railing. She offered her hand over to him and allowed him to lead the way to the dance floor downstairs.

Billy rolled his eyes and looked away.

They walked the short distance to the stairwell, its walls clad in red suede, plush and strangely warm to the touch, like the inside of a jewelry box or a padded confession booth. Jerry led the way, one hand curled around Lilly's fingers, parting the crowd with the same ease he used at the rope outside.

She followed without hesitation, her heels clicking softly against the mirrored steps, her posture radiating the same effortless confidence that had first drawn his eye.

The stairwell twisted downward in a wide arc, and the deeper they went, the more the air changed—thicker, more perfumed, laced with sweat, smoke, and something sweeter underneath. The music grew louder, before pausing for a moment. And as Jerry and Lilly took to the dance floor, the Moon Man above began to move toward them, as "Voulez-Vous" by Abba began to entrance the crowd.

~

"You know," Billy said, turning to Lilly, "you should really come hang out with us."

The sidewalk outside the club had become a melting pot of sweat, glitter, and perfume. It was two a.m., and Studio 54 had exhaled its last breath for the night, spilling the beautiful and the wrecked onto 54th Street. The glamorous were in search of taxis, afterparties, and anything that might make the night last a little longer. No one wanted it to end.

"I could get down with that," she responded, as she tugged on a cigarette.

"You know they're called cancer sticks for a reason," Jerry said, nodding at her cigarette.

"Trust me," Lilly replied as she exhaled, her response coated in the smoke, "it'd take a lot more than this to kill me. And you know what they say, I'm here for a good time, not a long time." She followed this with another wink and an exhale. Jerry wasn't sure what she meant, but he was nonetheless intrigued.

Billy and Jerry smiled at Lilly, as they stepped down from the curb and hollered at a cab.

The three of them sat snugly in the back of the yellow taxi. With no one wearing a seatbelt, the bouncing of the cab felt like any one of them could be launched out of the window at any moment, save for the plastic sheet that separated the driver from the passenger.

Lilly reached for the window lever and rolled it down, allowing the city air to course through the cab like a howling wind on a thunderous night.

She leaned into it, closing her eyes and smiling while extending her arm outside and allowing her hand to dance with the flow of the air that fought against her, pretending it was an airplane.

Up front, beads of sweat could be seen dripping down the side of the cab driver's face as he nervously looked back toward his three passengers.

In the rearview mirror, he noticed Billy staring out of the window while Lilly enjoyed her love affair with the city via her dancing hand, but in the middle of them, no one. He glanced back and noticed Jerry staring back at him, his face motionless, his expression nonexistent.

The driver's throat clicked as he swallowed.

He knew.

And Jerry knew that he knew.

CHAPTER 8
HUMBLE PIE

The taxi driver put his foot on the pedal as soon as the three had exited his cab. He'd tried not to instill panic in himself or his three patrons and, in his defense, he'd only intended to tap his foot ever so slightly on the pedal, sending a clear signal, *I'm not here to cause any trouble.* But fear got ahold of him faster than his rationale could, and it was his entire foot on the pedal, zooming through the late-night traffic.

As he drove off, he caught sight of the two passengers fading from view in his rearview mirror. The third wasn't visible, setting the panic deeper into the driver's psyche. The steering wheel had now turned damp from the sweat, the driver's flat cap soaked as he ripped it off his head, revealing a bald moist dome that had been collecting heat under the woolen tweed accessory.

He'd try to forget that this ever happened, and maybe, somewhere down the line, in a few days, months, or even years, he'd not remember the reflectionless man and his two strange acquaintances. Yes. That was a good plan. He'd go home, warm himself some Campbell's soup, maybe open a can of beans or fry some bacon, chase it all down with a beer, and that'd be the end of it.

Lilly and Billy rode the elevator to the penthouse alone. Jerry had, as he liked to call it, gone to fetch the mail.

Just a couple of blocks ahead, the traffic light turned red, and for a moment, the driver thought of flooring it once more. *Go through the light, go through the light,* he told himself. On that same note, he also tried to make himself accept that his business is his business, and theirs is theirs.

He continued to drive as the light turned green, and as curiosity got the better of him, he turned around to see if Jerry was still standing there. He wasn't.

A moment of relief washed over the driver as he turned back forward, only to see Jerry standing twenty feet in front of him.

He slammed his foot on the brake. Though for a moment he toyed with doing the same on the accelerator pedal, killing the thing in front of him, but he knew better. If Jerry was able to transport himself in a flash of light and suddenly stand in front of the taxi, the driver knew that there was no escape.

Jerry's expression was a mix of disappointment and regret. He stepped to the side, signaling to the driver he could move forward, but not leave. The driver pulled up beside him and Jerry walked to the window.

The driver just stared forward, fear coursing through

his blood. He noticed Jerry's waistline at the window. His long fingers with the equally long fingernails. Jerry slowly tapped on the glass, demanding the driver to roll down the window.

"What is your name?" Jerry asked the driver, as he bent down to lean on the window.

"J...J...John. I swear I don't want any trouble."

"Well, John" Jerry continued with a smirk, "I'm going to give you a choice, the choice I never had."

"Please don't kill me," the driver pleaded.

"I'm going to give you this," Jerry said slowly, as he handed the driver a wad of stacked hundred-dollar bills. "You're going to drive home right now, and forget you saw anything tonight. Do we have a deal?"

"Uh-huh. You bet, mister. You bet," the driver said, his voice high and broken, tears spilling down his face. "I have a family, a wife, and we just had our first..."

"Spare me the sympathy porn. I don't need your life's story. I've given you a choice. And you chose well."

Jerry leaned back and stood tall. John began to blubber further, sobbing like a child that had his favorite toy taken from him.

Tonight, he was in the wrong place at the wrong time, his first and only child born a month ago flashing before his eyes, as the terror of whatever had jumped into his taxi threatened to take everything away from him.

He stared forward, unsure if he was still in danger, unsure if he was allowed to drive off. That was until Jerry tapped the top of the taxi, giving him the signal that he could pull away.

THE FINANCIAL DISTRICT was desolate at this late hour. It amazed Jerry how a city that apparently never slept did, in fact, sleep on the weekends. Even during the day on a weekend, the smaller pocket of Manhattan resembled still life, clean, quiet, and empty. Jerry watched the taxi drive off, taking a beat before walking back to the apartment. The breeze washed over him and his brown surfer hair as it flapped in the wind.

But something shifted behind him. His hands in his pockets, he turned his head and perused the thing again. The same shape that was in the alleyway. The black, almost formless demon stood a hundred feet away, waving at Jerry as if to remind him who it was.

The only time he had encountered a similar figure was centuries ago when he lost the love of his life, Maria. But this demon looked different. Its shape was pliable, its teeth jagged and smiley, and its eyes, its eyes pierced the dark night like two headlights.

Jerry began to walk, then run slowly, jogging toward the creature. Instead of disappearing, it just continued to wave at him, slowly lowering its arm as he got closer. The ground below his feet was dewy from the rain that had poured down on the island. His loafers, a sharp black contrast to the flared denim he was wearing, smacked against the asphalt with each step. They were uncomfortable and large. Jerry didn't care; he wanted to get to the demon and ask what the hell it was doing following him.

He could, of course, teleport to the creature if he so

wished, but simple earthly pleasures were now part of his daily routine, and his first instinct was always to use his limbs, not to tap into whatever unearthly power he had deep inside his blood.

He ran straight into the road, oblivious of the car that was coming in the opposite direction, slamming on its brakes. Jerry heard the screech of the tires before the horn, stopping him dead in his tracks. He stared at the driver, then looked back toward the apparition.

There was nothing to see except for an empty street.

"Sorry about that," Jerry announced as he walked into the penthouse from another room. "Expecting something important from Europe."

"Is there another entrance to this place?" Lilly asked, accepting a bourbon from Billy.

"Emergency exit. Since we're the only apartment with a private elevator, there's an emergency staircase down the hall."

The truth was, there was no emergency staircase within the penthouse. Instead, it stood in the hallway adjacent to the elevator, and Lilly knew it. The blatant green EXIT sign was hardly subtle; in a building built out of blackness and art deco styling, anything lit up shone off every surface like a reflection in water.

"Lilly, tell me, what kind of music do you like?" Billy asked, strolling over to the record player.

"While I like to think of myself as a disco queen, I do love a little Morrison."

"How about this?" He pulled a Chuck Berry record from its sleeve and placed it on the turntable. Picking up his bourbon again, he lowered the needle and, after a few hissing pops of static, "You Never Can Tell" kicked to life, the guitar shimmying through its entrance as the unforgettable voice began to sing. Billy, somewhat inebriated, began to do the Hustle, a dance he noticed people a few hours ago performing in Studio 54.

The music was filling the room, the acoustics echoing each chord off the high vaulted ceiling, dampened by the large red drapes that adorned the entire width of the large windowpane that blessed such a penthouse. The red curtains measured twenty feet in length and, with the push of a button, they would begin a dance of slowly closing, dragging themselves before meeting in the middle.

The windows were also tinted from the outside, a request from Jerry to the owners if they were wanting to sell the five-million-dollar property at asking without contingencies, to ensure that even if they were accidentally opened during the day, only minimal sunlight would filter through.

The music continued to pound the room. Jerry grabbed Lilly by the hand again and spun her around, her deep blue shimmering dress catching every ounce of light as she let the vampire take control of her, dipping her down to the floor as her hair brushed the stone. Pulling her back up, she grabbed hold of her forehead as she slightly smiled, the alcohol reigniting.

"Okay, okay, I'm sitting this next one out." Lilly stated, whimsy all over her face.

"I'll join you," Jerry said, as Billy continued to cut a rug on his own. "Let's sit down."

The two slumped themselves down on the deep blue velvet couch, a coincidental nod to Lily's blue dress. If it wasn't for the shiny sparkling beads, she'd have camouflaged into it a lot easier. The pair looked into each other's eyes as Billy poured himself another glass of bourbon, his back turned toward the vampire, intentional almost, as he knew what was coming next.

"You know..." Jerry said, as he stared into Lilly's eyes, "you have the most remarkable blue eyes."

"Well...y'know..." She gave him a sly smile, her eyes half-closed. "This brown bouffant you have going on is just adorable." She ran her fingers slowly through his mane.

Jerry leaned in, and without taking his eyes off Lilly, he passionately kissed her lips. He pulled back playfully, letting his teeth slowly tug at her bottom lip before pushing forward and kissing her again.

In the background, Billy stood, his arms crossed as he leaned against the record player with the crystal glass still in his hand.

If Jerry had learned anything over millennia, it was how to touch a woman, how to caress her, and how to make her feel like she was the only person on the planet.

Lilly twirled a lock of Jerry's hair between her fingers, her dress shifting higher as she moved against the sofa. Jerry brushed her curls back from her face, tucking them behind her ear to expose the line of her neck. The skin there glowed pale in the low light, the vein beneath pulsing like a current.

He pulled back long enough to meet her eyes. They lingered, then fell into another kiss, mouths parting, tongues sliding against one another with passion. Jerry leaned over her, pressing closer, and she moaned into him. Whether it was approval or warning, he couldn't be sure, but her hand tangled in his hair and pulled him down harder.

Their movements grew rougher, Lilly's hips grinding against him, the friction sending shudders through them both. Jerry's hand found the neckline of her dress and tugged, but she caught his wrist, halting him. She had played with temptation before. She'd let him take her in front of Billy, but not tonight. Jerry eased his grip and let the fabric slip back into place, instead tracing her hair aside again, lowering his lips to the line of her neck.

He kissed her there, soft at first, from the ear down to the hollow where the vein throbbed. Jerry's fangs extended silently. His left arm locked her against the cushions, his right hand buried in her hair, steady and waiting for the inevitable flinch that always came.

His fangs slid out with a soft, wet click. His left arm curled tighter around her waist while his right hand threaded deeper into her hair, bracing her for the fights he'd weathered before. He kissed her there once, then twice, before a third time. Then he opened his mouth. His fangs brushed her skin.

And in an instant, he was airborne. He was flying backward, his body thrown like a ragdoll across the living room. Crashing through the air, past Billy, who dropped his glass just before Jerry slammed into the far wall with a sickening crack.

The lights blew out and total darkness ensued, flickering and buzzing, as if a malevolent entity had surged the energy in the room.

Silence.

Then, another flickering occurred before the lights came back on, illuminating the room and Lilly, who was standing in front of the velvet sofa, her hair wild, her eyes lit with something ancient. Her right arm was stretched forward with her palm clenched open, her fingers jagged as if she was ready to claw Jerry's dead heart out of his chest. She was holding Jerry in place against the wall with nothing but will.

Billy stood frozen, back against the bar, as his breath was caught in his chest. For the first time ever, a witch had put them in their place.

"Try that again," Lilly said, voice calm and clear, "and I'll show you what a real predator looks like."

Jerry attempted to transform into the bat. A common allowance for vampires that was usually reserved for moments in small towns or cities where dark alleyways and empty subway trains didn't offer easier prey.

Swooping in on your prey before flying out again was an easy way to target. His body began to shake, vibrating in place. Muscles clenched. Limbs twitched. The change refused him. The frustration was etched across his face, sharp and humiliated.

Billy stood by, unsure whether to intervene or run. He reached into his back pocket and pulled a knife. He already had the strength of ten men, but it gave him something to hold as he lunged toward her.

Lilly looked at him once and that was all it took. With a flick of her hand, Billy was lifted and flung through the air. His body hit the same wall Jerry had crumpled against moments earlier, only harder, the stone cracking on impact.

"There, there," Lilly said, floating forward slowly, her voice coiled in venom.

Neither responded. Jerry's body still trembled under her hold, vibrating like he was being shaken loose from the inside.

"Enough," he growled through clenched teeth. "A truce."

"I'll tell you," she thrust both arms forward, a pulse of energy exploding from her hands, a shockwave of invisible force that struck both men at once, "when *I've* had enough."

She lowered her arms, and the two men dropped to the ground like bricks falling from the sky. Turning her back, she strutted back to the sofa, walking on her tiptoes as if she was wearing heels. The bourbon from earlier still sat in the crystal glass, enough left for one last swallow. She swung down and grabbed the glass cockily as she lifted one leg up to curl up in the corner of the velvet sofa.

Jerry and Billy were slowly recovering. The blast that Lilly delivered was enough to render them useless for a few minutes. Sweating, they slowly stood up, their chests puffed, arms braced and shoulders back.

"I'll see to it that we end you," Billy growled. But Lilly didn't flinch; she stared down the two as she washed the last of the bourbon down her throat, enjoying the burn that coated it at the same time. And without the movement of her hand and without any nod, she willed the large red drapes to open automatically, revealing a light blue twinge in the sky's horizon. It was after four a.m. and the sky was turning a mix of gold and purple.

"Not if I get there first," she said.

"What are you?" Jerry asked, heaving in his chest and coughing up at the same time.

Lilly didn't move from the couch and she didn't respond. She leaned back and stretched her neck as if she was already bored of the encounter.

"You should be grateful," she said, toying with the empty bourbon glass. "If your teeth had broken my skin tonight, Jerry, you'd be the one begging for your life."

He didn't respond. By now, the intrigue had a hold of both of them. They hadn't encountered anything like this before.

"I *am* what I *am*," she sang to herself. "Someone should make a song out of that." She laughed to herself.

She glanced out toward the skyline; the city was glowing as the first sunlight touched the tallest spires.

"I've seen things," Lilly said calmly, her voice like silk pulled tight. "Been places neither of you could survive. I've walked through fire with witches older than your bloodline. I've palavered with the Devil. I've bargained with the same being that made you."

Billy shifted, casting a glance at Jerry. But Jerry stayed still. He watched her, his chest still rising and falling, his pride smoldering. Lilly turned her gaze from the window, the city beyond now glowing with the slow bloom of dawn.

She lifted herself from the sofa and walked toward the door.

"Next time," she added, brushing imaginary dust from her dress, "think twice before you put your mouth on a witch."

And with the final words of warning, she willed the curtains closed once more, allowing Jerry a reprieve from the slight burning he could feel on the back of his neck. She grabbed her stilettos and walked toward the elevator of the penthouse. She turned her back to the two men as she bent down to slip on each of the heels, leaning on the frame of the elevator as she did so, her long, bouncy curly waves draping down the side of her face.

Jerry and Billy stood up and stared at each other in defeat. They had acknowledged that the woman in front of them was far more powerful than they ever could have imagined or dreamed up. And so they let her go without a fight.

"What now?" Billy asked, still breathing heavy, his arms still clenched.

"Now?" Jerry growled. "Now? Now, bring me the book. I need to know how to destroy this witch."

LUCIA KICKED a curled piece of grey paper across the floor, not sure if it had once been wallpaper, a receipt, or part of the building itself. It didn't matter. Whatever it had been, it turned to ash beneath her toe and vanished. The apartment looked as if it had been melted from the inside out.

The blackened walls had grown darker still, shot through with veins of smoke-stained gray. Wooden window frames had reduced to carbon, their shape still visible but hollowed out, as if they'd been sketched in charcoal and then smudged away.

The furniture stood intact, fused to the floor like wax sculptures, frozen in their final moments. She crossed the living room to a sideboard she barely recognized, its lacquer bubbled, the once-glossy surface now pitted and ashen. On top, the remnants of framed photographs curled in on themselves. Family, childhood, Maria.

The glass had melted after shattering, the images behind it warped beyond recognition. She reached for one, hoping for anything that might've survived, but it crumbled in her fingers. The fragments slipped through her hands like beach sand, soft and silent, leaving her palms smeared in soot.

Tears welled before she could stop them. They cut down her face in quiet streaks, mixing with the ash already clinging to her skin. There was no way to wipe them. Her hands were black, her home was gone, and there was nothing left to touch that wouldn't turn to dust.

She walked deeper into the apartment, stepping over fallen beams and blackened fabric as she made her way to what was once the bedroom. The air was still heavy with the scent of smoke and scorched wiring, a chemical bitterness that clung to her lungs with every breath. The bed frame had collapsed inward, coils and wood splintered beneath a mattress that had partially dissolved in the heat. On the wall, a mirror had melted in slow drips.

At the edge of the dresser, something glinted faintly beneath a crust of soot. Lucia reached for it, brushing away the char with the back of her sleeve. She held it in her palm and stared down at the ruin of it. It was her mother's amulet, the one she used to protect her from evil.

With a scream building from somewhere deep inside her, she hurled it across the room. The chain snapped in the air, clinking against the wall before vanishing behind a scorched chair. Lucia stood there for a moment, her chest rising fast, arms rigid at her sides. Then the weight of everything hit her at once. Her knees buckled, and she dropped to the floor, both hands catching her as the scream tore loose from her throat.

THE OUTSIDE AIR felt foreign to Lucia after absorbing the blackness that had once been her home. Even the breeze against her skin felt different. The news of the fire had spread fast. *Long standing queer bar burned to the ground,* they printed, completely mislabeling the establishment. The next day, the papers were reporting on something else, like the fire never even happened, and Lucia, left to endure, felt like the world had abandoned her.

With her family's apartment in the Bronx long gone, sold after her parents passed, she had nowhere to go.

A friend from the neighborhood offered her a sofa for the week, but the cushions were stiff, and the kindness was wearing thin by day three. The apartment was small at best, surrounded by plants in an effort to disguise the dinginess, a red cotton sofa that was five feet in length stood in the middle of the already cramped room, and by day four, Lucia left of her own accord.

Sanctuario had never paid her enough to save money. The rent had taken what little she earned. Insurance? Nonexistent. Contingency plans? A fantasy. Now she was just another ghost on the street.

She walked to the Fox & Hound, a dark dive bar that a friend of hers bartended at. He occasionally picked up some shifts at Sanctuario when the basement needed an extra hand, and today, Lucia found herself sitting at the bar toward the back.

"I'm so sorry, Luce. Is there nowhere you can go?" Oliver asked, cleaning glasses. Oliver had been a good reliable friend to Lucia. Any chance to earn money in a city that was bankrupt was welcome, and he spent most of his waking hours working behind any bar that would take him.

"Seems like there isn't. I wasn't really close with the regulars; I was just their vessel to a sanctuary I guess," she responded, sinking her second glass of bourbon.

"Well, listen, I'm not gonna tell you what to do, and I wish I could help. I'm still staying in my parents' basement, and you know what they're like," he lamented as he put the last of the clean glasses on the shelf. "Hang out here as much as you need. Just don't get too wasted. It won't help the situation."

Lucia didn't respond. She just tucked her head into her chin as if to acknowledge what Oliver was saying was correct. And when she looked up again, he was gone.

The restroom was just as dingy as the bar, one stall and one cracked dirty sink, with a makeshift metal mirror that looked like it was recovered from a prison cell.

Lucia walked into the stall and peered down at the toilet. It was scratched, names etched into the black plastic toilet seat, and a small roll of paper sat atop the dysfunctional metal roll holder.

If she'd hit rock bottom, then this was it. Usually, taking a piss in this type of dirt box wouldn't have even registered with Lucia, but on days like today, when she realized she had nothing, this dirt box felt like home, like the only place she unjustly belonged.

Her denim jeans were tight, clinging to her ample frame. She pulled them down just far enough past her knees where her behind wouldn't need to touch the seat. She hated squatting. She'd held this piss in long enough where it would be a long one, and even twenty seconds of squatting had her legs burning.

She pondered her half-drunken self as she stared at the door in front of her, resting her elbow on the wall beside her and using her right hand to push down on her urethra to ensure the pee went straight into the bowl.

A shuffle outside the stall made her look up.

She finished off her stream and jiggled the top of her vagina a little to let any last remaining pee escape. Her underwear would have to do in absorbing any remaining liquid. Heaving her jeans up and taking a deep breath, she walked out of the stall with her head still down.

"All yours," she muttered to whoever was in the bathroom with her, but when she looked up, there was no one there, just the flickering of the overhead light.

She looked into the mirror once more and turned on the faucet—a sprinkling of water relieved itself, splattering down onto the bowl below. She held her cupped palms underneath, gathering as much water as she could, and splashed it onto her face. There were no paper towels to dry her hands, so she wiped them down her black tank top and grabbed the metal handle to the rickety door.

"Luciaaaaa..." a whisper beckoned from within the stall.

"Ugh..." she grunted. "Eat shit."

She ripped open the door and walked back into the bar.

The bar was a dive indeed. The only real light pouring into the place was from the sunlight at the entrance and a few neon signs displaying the variety of beer that was stocked, or not. Across from the bar sat a few booths, which accommodated small groups on busier nights or those that wanted alone time with a larger space.

"The thing in the basement wasn't wrong," a voice said.

She stopped, blinking into the haze.

A man sat alone at the far booth. He had dark skin with wide shoulders and a black fedora pulled low. He tapped a silver coin against the wood, a pint of Guinness in his other hand.

"What?" she asked, wiping her face with the back of her wrist.

"The demon that told you about the book," he said. "If you want to right what was wronged, or become what you were meant to be, you'll need it."

Lucia walked toward him slowly, looking around. Oliver was gone and so was everyone else.

"And who are you?" she asked.

He smacked the coin down on the table.

"Someone who wants the same thing you do."

He took a breath and picked up his pint of Guinness.

Lucia sat down across from him. Her tears had dried, and a sudden wave of soberness had washed over her. For the first time in a while she felt like she had hope. Many patrons of the Sanctuario would come to her and offer advice, some would offer gifts, paths to other realms, witchcraft, but something different stood out about this man.

"Who..." she paused before leaning in, "are you?"

"You can call me...Mr. Tambourine Man." He smiled, before pausing and giving another sinister smile. Shadows flocked to this man from all over the dive bar, bathing him in black, leaving only the glint of his eyes and the shine of his teeth as distinct, discernible features.

"What are you selling me, Mr. Tambourine Man?"

"A lightning rod," he said, tapping the coin once. "A way out of this godforsaken city. The vampire and his familiar are holding one of the last surviving grimoires on this earth. Your mother had one too. Though I doubt it's still down there with her."

Lucia's eyes snapped. Her body leaned forward instinctively, hand balled into a fist.

"Don't you dare speak about my mother." She grimaced.

"Touched a nerve," he said, his white-toothed smile growing wider in the dark. "That's good. Pain makes a better key."

He picked up the silver coin again, letting it roll idly between his fingers. It never slipped.

"I didn't come to talk about the dead. I came to talk about the book."

Lucia folded her arms. "You know where it is?"

"You already know who has it. The vampire and his familiar. You saw it in their eyes. They're guarding something they don't understand."

He leaned in, matching Lucia's stance and energy, his face a whisper away from hers.

"The grimoire doesn't want them."

She whispered back as if the bar was full of patrons, "The fuck does that mean?"

"It wants you, Lucia."

Lucia stared.

"And you want me to what? Use it for you?"

"Not for me," he said, finishing his Guinness. "For yourself. You've got something inside you, Lucia. The grimoire will see it and multiply it. You want revenge? It'll give you more than vengeance. You want power? It'll burn down the world just to crown you."

He slid the coin across the table.

"But it can't act unless someone opens the door.

That's what I'm offering. A key. You just have to say when."

"Luce, you okay?" Oliver called from behind the bar, his hand resting on a beer pump.

She shot around and stared at Oliver, before looking over to the others sitting at the bar, just as she remembered.

But when she turned back to the Tambourine Man, it was as if he'd never even been there.

CHAPTER 9

THE BECOMING

It wasn't until she was robbed of her own home that Lucia thought about the plight of the homeless and what led them to this ill fate.

Bad decisions, drugs, and general irresponsibility always made her believe people ended up this way by choice. But now, as she trod down Orchard Street on the Lower East Side, sleep-deprived and stiff from concrete, she understood how quickly the world could take everything. When the sun went down and you had nowhere to go but an alleyway, survival stopped being a choice.

The Lower East Side still felt somewhat like home. Red brick buildings stood humble and weathered. They rarely climbed past seven stories. Oak trees rose between them like guardians, rooted into the ground as if they had been here first. In some places, their roots pushed the sidewalks up and over, showing people the sheer strength and magnitude of what the oak giants could do.

As she walked past them, black, brown, and white

faces blurred together in the flow of the city. Each block carried a new identity. Bangladeshi takeout nestled beside vintage record stores. British tailoring faced tattoo parlors. Everything tried to matter and make the American Dream happen.

Here, Lucia could walk the streets and look unremarkable. She could fade into the background, and that was exactly what she needed.

On the corner of Orchard and Grand stood a narrow gym, its entrance painted chrome with bold lettering meant to evoke strength and iron. Large windows stretched across the front, letting the world peer inside at runners on treadmills and bodies pushing limits under the clang of metal plates. The gym didn't look fancy, but most here weren't. They served as places of hard work and getting things done.

She still had a few weeks left on her membership. Maybe longer if they failed to check the billing system right away. Mornings passed easily enough. She woke up from whatever corner she had collapsed into, dusted grit off her clothes, and walked inside like she belonged. If she showered every morning and evening, at least she didn't smell.

Oliver had returned the many favors from Sanctuario and handed her a few of his shifts at his bar. Fifty bucks a week stretched far when she didn't have rent to pay, and it bought her a second set of clothes, a small book bag, and the luxury of sitting in a laundromat for an hour every two days while she cycled through her clothing.

But as the sun closed on the day, the reality of where she would lay her head became clear. In a city laden with crime and murder, she often wondered if she would wake up the next morning.

A few blocks down from Orchard Street, Stewart Park spread small and green. A newly constructed housing development loomed over it and cast shadows across the park most of the day. More oak trees dominated the concrete, larger, thicker, and taller than the ones that lined the sidewalks. The sun struggled to penetrate any part of this park, and that made it attractive to Lucia and others.

THE OCCASIONAL CRASHING for the night on one of Oliver's bar booths had stayed its course, and tonight, on a colder night, Lucia left the bar at two a.m., an hour after the last customers departed and cleaning was complete. Outside, the streetlamps looked like orange halos as they cast their illumination onto the street below, overflowing black trash bags littering the street.

The walk to Stewart Park gave occasional glimpses of the Manhattan Bridge and the lights that trailed up its structure, giving Lucia the feeling of ambition and that, whilst temporarily homeless, she was in a city of people that didn't quit, that didn't give up. And each night as she made her way to the bush she momentarily called home, the bridge was her reminder that she was still strong.

The colder air had settled in more. Lucia took her blanket out from her book bag and laid it on the floor. She kept two, one for lying on the ground, and the other for covering her body. It ensured that her clothes didn't accidentally fall into some dog shit, or get too covered in mud if it was a rainy night, which was common for the city.

The book bag was large enough to accommodate the two blankets, along with two tops, one sweater, two sets of underwear, and pants. In the side pocket, a deodorant stick, toothbrush, and mouthwash.

The bush looked like a large igloo with a small opening, as if someone had carved out an entrance just for her. Creeping through it, she immediately felt a sense of safety. If someone was going to come inside, she'd hear it, for there was no other option other than the opening on the south side of the bush.

She would lay down and witness the sparkle of the Manhattan Bridge once more, as the steam from the city danced in front of it, twinkling the lights on the railing like stars in the sky. The humming of the cars and trucks driving sending her into a deep slumber.

But tonight was not going to be so peaceful.

She'd passed out for all of thirty minutes when the first blow came. A sharp kick to her stomach, knocking the air clean out of her. Opening her eyes fast, she only saw the large black workman-type boot, the one you'd expect a dock worker or sanitation worker to wear.

A kick struck her stomach so hard, she gasped before she could even open her eyes. Her body folded in half, the air inside her expelled. The blur of a black work boot hovered in her vision, retreating only to be replaced by the next blow, a fist to the back of the skull that sent her crashing into the dirt. For a moment, she wasn't sure if she'd lost consciousness or if the pain had simply collapsed the night around her.

She came to on her back. Pinned down by a heavy man, thick arms, a bloated gut, and a greasy gray shirt too short to cover him. He'd straddled her chest. His knees pressed into her biceps as his weight cut off her breath again, slowly and cruelly. Another man gripped her legs as she thrashed, trying to twist free.

A third, just out of view, rummaged through her bag, finding nothing but a few small bills and her clean clothes.

"She's got shit and Shinola," he grunted.

The third brute heaved and pulled at her skin-tight pants. Her voice was buried under the man's palm as he pushed down on her lips harder. She was trapped, reduced to nothing but heat and rage in a body too shocked to act.

"Ain't got time for this shit. Just rough her the fuck up," a hovering, deep voice boomed.

The one above her smiled, then pressed harder, twisting her nipple beneath his hand with a vicious pinch before punching her across the jaw.

Another blow to her ribs and a kick to her thigh left her howling. The three of them unleashed violence like they were owed it. As if her existence had offended them.

"What the fuck do you think you're doing?" a voice came from the distance. Two men, also homeless and sleeping in the park, had heard the screams. That was all it took for them to run over and attempt to help.

Lucia didn't see who shouted. She only heard the shuffle of panic, the way the men's bodies lifted from hers, cursing and scrambling. One of them stomped on her leg on the way out. Then they were gone.

She lay there quivering, crying and confused. She turned her head and looked at the bridge, the lights blinking at her before slowly fading out to black.

And as she closed her eyes, something else inside her was stirring.

HER HANDS WERE SHAKING as she rattled in her pocket, trying to fetch the one key to Oliver's bar. It was the only place she knew to retreat.

Inside, the bar was as black as night. After unlocking it and rushing through, she slammed the door behind her, convinced that the three men had been following her on the way back. She locked the door frantically and rested her body against it, slowly falling to the ground as she sobbed. Her eyes swollen, the back of her head bruised and bloody.

No one is coming to save you, she remembered her mother, Maria, used to say to her. *Get up off your knees and keep going.*

She breathed in heavily through her nose, the snot and tears making a noisy sniffling sound, before wiping her eyes and nose with her forearm. Lucia put one leg up first and rested on her knee, heaving herself up from the floor. She switched the lights on as she walked toward the bar, slowly, for her legs, breast, and head were in agony from the beating.

She grabbed some whiskey from the shelf and put

the bottle to her lips, swigging two gulps like it was water. The liquor immediately hit, burning her throat and distracting her from the pain that was coursing through her body. It felt good. Even holding the bottle felt like a reprieve from the past few weeks.

The bathroom would be the next station she would go to. Opening the rickety door, she walked in and turned on the faucet, watching the water drip through. She ran her hands under the tap and splashed it on her face, a reminder of the last time she was in there. Placing her head into the bowl, she splashed more water on her face before looking back up to the mirror.

And there it was.

The living, breathing horror from the basement looking at her from over her shoulder. Its teeth wide and jagged, claws for hands, as it reached for Lucia through the mirror. Gasping, she ran out of the bathroom and back into the bar, trying to convince herself that it was just her taxed mind playing hallucinatory games with her.

And as she looked to her right, Mr. Tambourine Man was waiting for her again, as if he'd never left.

"What do you want me to do?" Lucia snapped, grabbing the whiskey from behind the bar and stumbling into the booth beside him.

The menacing man said nothing at first, just rolled the silver coin between his fingers, slowly, before slipping it into his inside pocket. From the other, he pulled a cigar and lit it with a snap of his fingers, inhaling deeply, holding it, savoring it like it held ancient Cuban wisdom. Then he exhaled, watching slow, thick ribbons of smoke reaching toward the ceiling.

"I don't want you to do anything. Let's be clear about that. It's what you want to do for yourself. And what you want to do," he said while following the smoke, "is kidnap the vampire's familiar. An easy enough target. And you will not be alone. My men will help you subdue him. You've already gotten a taste of what they can do."

She stared at him. Then, with no hesitation, she screamed and hurled the whiskey bottle across the bar. It shattered against the wall, a spray of glass and amber exploding into the dark.

"Are you..." she choked, rising from the booth, eyes wild with fresh tears, "fucking kidding me?"

Her voice broke. "You mean to tell m-m-me... The men who just tried to kill me after—" She couldn't say the word. "Those were your men?"

He merely looked at her with quiet amusement.

"Sit down."

"Fuck you."

"Now you know what they're capable of."

She stood, heaving her chest and clenching her fists as she trembled.

"A small price to pay," he continued, lighting the cigar again with a second flick, "for dominion over the planet. And maybe one day, the universe."

Lucia didn't sit back down. She stood as her breath still raged. Running her hands through her hair, she backed up from the table and turned toward the bar.

"You think I'd work with them?" she spat, looking back at him. "After what they did to me? After what you let happen?"

Mr. Tambourine Man shrugged with a slowness before saying, "You wanted a reminder of what the world takes from you. Now you know the price of mercy."

She reached behind the bar, grabbing the first bottle her fingers touched, a thick, brown bottle of rye, and flung it toward his head. It shattered inches from his ear, glass exploding across the floor. He didn't blink or move, he just continued to smoke.

"Try again," he said; this time he didn't smile. "Break every bottle in the place. I won't stop you."

"You're not untouchable!" she yelled, eyes red, lips quivering, face flushed.

"I am to you."

"If you think I'm going to be your weapon, you've got the wrong bitch."

Now he laughed. It rolled out like thunder echoing through empty streets.

"Oh, Lucia. You are your own weapon, and you're already ready to launch. You just need the match."

"I'll light the match! You better know it. I'll light the fucking match!" she roared.

"I don't doubt it," he said.

Lucia stopped and took a breath. Something inside her told her to scream, to rage, to curse the man in front of her. But that wasn't who she needed to be now. Not anymore. She needed to be pragmatic.

She needed to be the kind of woman who didn't blink in the face of horror.

"What now?" she asked.

"Now," Mr. Tambourine Man said, "let the smoke perfuse through you. Let it consume you. Let it guide you to the grimoire. You will become stronger than you are now. Strong enough to take on the vampire's familiar. And then you take the book for yourself."

"What smoke?"

He smiled and rolled the cigar between his fingers, watching the smoke curl from his lips in perfect spirals. It moved unnaturally, like a dancer with invisible limbs.

Slowly, the smoke thickened between them. It climbed upward as it coiled and stretched. A face began to form inside it, eyes wide, a mouth that stretched ear to ear, smiling at her. It was the same demon she'd seen in the basement. The same one that had whispered her name when no one else did.

Mr. Tambourine Man held his cigar low, watching the form in the mist with cautious reverence and excitement. Even he wasn't sure if it would obey him.

"Lucia..." he whispered, not taking his eyes off the smoke. "Are you ready?"

"Give it to me," she said.

The smoke recoiled, as if bracing itself, then it swelled. The face grinning wider as the mist expanded with a rush of force, it launched forward like a bullet from a gun, straight into her. It slammed into her face and forced its way up her nostrils and down her throat. Her body convulsed, shaking violently as her arms flailed. Her spine bowed backward, and she shot out of her seat screaming, and Mr. Tambourine Man jumped back in the booth, watching with evil delight, with wide eyes and a crooked grin, as Lucia turned her back on mortality.

The smoke continued as if it went on forever, like it had been waiting centuries. Her fingers curled into claws as the demon poured into her, clawing for space in her chest and her mind.

Thrashing on the floor, her body twisted even more, her legs snapping behind her, her fingers working independently as they scratched and searched for something that wasn't there. As the Tambourine Man watched on, throwing pork rinds into his mouth, chewing incessantly, Lucia's veins turned black, so black they were visible through her skin.

She screamed in an animalistic, unnatural primal pitch.

And then... Silence.

She opened her eyes, and the blackness had taken over. And at the door of the bar stood the three men that just hours before had tried to kill her.

CHAPTER 10

RETURN OF THE WITCH

"Mr. Cole," the doorman spoke through the intercom, "there's a woman down here in the lobby to see you."

"A woman?" he asked, looking over to Jerry, who was chomping on an apple, watching the sky fade to black as the sun had set on the city.

"Yes, sir. Lillian Thurman. Said you'd be expecting her," Leon replied.

"Ah, yes," Billy replied. "Lilly. Send her up."

There were few earthly pleasures greater than a human entering the home of a known vampire and his familiar willingly. The centuries had afforded Jerry and Billy a life of wealth, experience, and decadence, a kingdom built on blood and hiding in the shadows, but immortality had its own kind of hunger. It reminded them constantly of what they'd lost: friendship, love, connection.

And on rare occasions, what they could no longer have was all they craved. Life could be cruel like that, sending, every so often, a beautiful woman in Jerry's direction who looked just enough like Maria to make him ache.

Lilly was that reminder. Not in looks, for those were sparing. Maria had olive-toned skin, dark curls, and warm, doe-like brown eyes. Lilly, with her wavy blonde hair, piercing blue eyes, and slender pale frame, was in almost every way the opposite.

But it wasn't the surface that stirred Jerry. It was her energy. The way she moved with quiet control, the confidence that made a room lean toward her, the stare she gave when she was serious or passionate; those moments mirrored Maria with unnerving precision. And that was enough.

Enough to haunt him and enough to make him wonder what could be.

The doors to the penthouse opened swiftly with a hushed whoosh, and there in the great room stood Jerry, eating his apple, as Billy stood next to him, his arms crossed with a sarcastic smile upon his face.

"My dear," Jerry announced, waving the apple in his right hand, "I am glad that you have graced us with your presence once more."

A more casual Lilly stood in the doorway of the elevator, white hot pants, knee-high socks, with simple white Converse, and a tight black sweater. She had one arm raised, resting high on the frame, a cocky show of force. Her posture said she was in control, but her energy shifted with the quiet dread of knowing she might need to make another deal with the Devil.

"We need to talk," Lilly announced, striding into the room and straight to the mini bar.

The two men looked amused as they watched this new character stride with confidence. Ripping the head off the decanter, she stared back. She now knew them, and they knew her. Lilly cared not for whatever the black liquid was inside the crystal bottle, only that she knew it would help calm her nerves. They watched her pause as she took a long sip, Jerry's eyes amusingly staring at her throat as he watched the liquid gulp down her neck.

"Sit down," she commanded as she slowly placed the glass down on the bar cart. "I insist."

Neither Jerry nor Billy had encountered a woman like this before. Lucia's garlic threats at the S bar were laughable by comparison, but this was different. There was something oddly enjoyable about being told what to do, especially by another ethereal being.

Jerry embraced it first, crossing the room with a smirk. Billy followed, slower, warier, still carrying the memory of their last encounter. They sat like men summoned to a reckoning, unsure whether they were on trial or already convicted. Lilly moved to the sideboard and leaned back against it with her arms folded as she began her epiphany.

"The woman you met a few weeks ago at that bar," she said, making Jerry and Billy look at each other before looking back at Lilly. "What happened in the bar?"

Jerry raised one leg over the arm of the armchair and leaned back, tossing his eaten apple onto the coffee table.

"Nothing happened," Billy shot back, prompting a chuckle from Jerry.

"Well, it wasn't as if nothing happened," Jerry responded.

"Did you try to attack her?"

"Not really. She revealed that she knew who we were, so a natural response was to armor ourselves, but she beat us to it. It was a misunderstanding of sorts."

"Did she mention anything about a demon?"

"I don't think so," Billy responded.

"Wait, she did say something. Almost chased us out of the bar, before saying she had an old ghost she had a bone with, or something."

"Where's the book?" she asked.

Jerry didn't move. His eyes flicked toward Billy, who had done the same.

"How about you start telling us a little more about you, Miss Thurman?" Billy cut in. "After our last encounter, my interest is piqued, but so is my danger."

"What the fuck's that supposed to mean, jackass?" she snapped back, lowering her head in disbelief, her eyes wide with sarcastic amazement.

"Let's be civil, please," Jerry said sharply, waving his hand to the armchair. "Miss Thurman, please. I earnestly want to know more about you."

She moved to the armchair opposite them and sank into it with a calmer demeanor.

"Fine," she sighed. "Before I was called Lilly Thurman, I was Lilly Frost. And there was a time when I had just the one L in my name. But then, so did other women who were named Lily. I changed that, not that that's either here or there. I've toyed with my name over the centuries, and yes, that's not an exaggeration. I was born in Salem. I was one of the first women in the country to be tried for witchcraft, and when I hung on the pyre, a spirit came to me. Call it a demon, a guardian, or whatever else you will. It offered me a choice. I'm sure you can relate with that as well."

Jerry's gaze sharpened. He could relate. Deeply. And she knew it.

"Anyway," she said with a dismissive casualness that hurt Jerry as he heard her words, "when you're alive for as long as I have been, you climb your way to the apex of the pyramid. I am one of the most powerful beings that walk this planet. Not just physically, but spiritually. I've crossed realms you won't understand until someone finally puts an arrow through your chest. I've met the Devil head-on in Bridgewater. The list goes on."

"What?" Billy blinked.

"Small town not far from here," she said nonchalantly as she turned from the window with her arms crossed. "It's where I ended up...after escaping Salem."

"What do you want?" Jerry asked again, his voice a touch more urgent now.

Lilly walked back toward them, her tone matching Jerry's.

"A war is coming, Jerry. And you can't stop it."

"A war?" Billy chuckled, as he got up and walked to the bar. "Do you hear yourself?"

She turned to him, her eyes glowing with old rage.

"Oh, you think that you're not going to be affected?" she retorted. "You stand there, William, still clinging to your atheistic view of the world, pretending that what's happening isn't real. You refuse to acknowledge the Devil made you. You ignore the fact that you've walked this Earth for centuries, helping a monster survive by draining the blood of human beings. And you think, because you can walk in the daylight and eat a Big Mac, it makes you...human?"

She looked back at Jerry. His face held a multitude of expressions. Impressed, annoyed, yet excited.

"It doesn't. You're undead. So don't act like what I'm saying is a fairytale. And don't...laugh at me," she lectured from the armchair, her fingers tapping its armrest. "Because if you do, I won't just throw you against that wall. I'll wedge you into it. For a decade. Maybe two."

"All right." Billy raised his hands in surrender. "Go on."

"When I touched you that night, in the club, I knew instantly what you were. I got a vision of how you came to be, how it all started. I'm sorry you had to live through that. But sympathies won't resolve the dispute that's on the horizon."

Now Lilly leaned forward, staring intently at Jerry. "And there is conflict on the horizon. A demonic presence has been haunting your steps. You've seen it down dark alleyways, in random moments in the street. It waves at you, smiles almost. It's showing itself to you."

When Jerry nodded in recognition, Lilly continued. "It can't latch onto people who are strong, which is why it's posturing to you from afar, letting you know that it's around, trying to throw you off your game, cause confusion and cause you both to ask each other questions. I dare to think you haven't encountered something like this since the origin of your...Vampirehood?"

"No, we haven't. We have ways of communicating when we need it. Through fire, things like that," Jerry replied.

"The woman in the bar, Lucia, came from a long lineage of witches; well, half-bloods. She lost her parents, and has been struggling to keep her bar afloat. I don't know if you've heard, but the bar burned down the same night we met at Studio 54."

"That's the night we went there," Jerry surmised.

"There's no connection, but regardless, this isn't Lucia's fault. The demon attached to her is called Surgat. I've heard of it before, but never encountered it. It wants chaos. It's been whispering to her for years, hiding in plain sight, wearing her mother's face. She hasn't realized it yet. She thinks she's in control, but she's not.

It feeds on her weaknesses, and the Tambourine Man has surfaced to sway her mind."

"Seriously? The Tambourine Man?" Billy chortled.

"Yes, the Tambourine Man," she snapped. "It's what the Devil calls himself occasionally when he comes up here himself to fuck around. You know. He's got personas for days. Nicholas Scratch. Mephisto. Lord of Flies. And I don't take it lightly. He only adopts that persona when there's an opportunity for him, something big."

"Why did you ask about the book earlier?"

"Your book is what it wants. Well, the demon at least. Surgat attached itself to Lucia as a child. Her mother had a grimoire and the demon tried to possess

Lucia then. When her mother died, she had the book buried with her, and usually, when a grimoire is buried with someone, you won't see it again."

"Why does it want the book?" Jerry asked, concerned now, serious.

"Your grimoire, believe it or not, has the power to open the gates of Hell. And that's exactly what the demon wants."

She cooled her tone, as she realized that she needed the two men as much as they needed her. She walked back over to the bar to pour her and Jerry a drink.

"Now, hold onto yourselves."

She paused her speech to let the silky amber liquid flow slowly into the two glasses. The glow from the sconces around the room bounced off each inflection in the carved crystal decanter. She raised the glass to her lips and let the sharp, bitter taste smack her tongue before turning around.

"Surgat is a nasty piece of work. If you remember back to the 10th century when that black shadow talked to you, dial this up by one hundred, sprinkle in all the evil you've acted out over the centuries, and you still won't come close."

She walked slowly back to the sofas. Now she had their attention. Billy had curled back the last of his quips; he knew when to act serious around Jerry. He could read him like a book.

"It's possessed Lucia. I felt it last night... And now, she wants the book." Jerry took the drink from her. "And if she gets it, Surgat will use it to open a crack in the earth." She paused. "So now she's more than just a half-blood with a grudge. She's a conduit."

"How do you know about the book?" Billy asked.

"Errr, hello?" Lilly replied, conjuring a spark in her fingers.

"Woman... I've destroyed armies, I've fed on thousands of men over the millennia. I'm not scared of Lucia. I'll simply tear her apart," Jerry snapped.

"You can't stop Surgat. Not with what you have. Not with force. The only thing standing between Lucia and the end of this world..." she looked at both of the men intensely, "...is me."

"What do we need to do?" Jerry asked.

"I don't know yet. Is the book safe?"

"It's safe," Billy chimed in, his tone much more friendly now. "Well, it's in the basement of this building."

"That's not safe," she said, matching Billy's energy. "I can place a cloaking spell on it for now. It'll buy us some time, but the demon knows where you live. Let's go."

"Now?" Jerry asked, surprised.

"Yup, then get your dancing shoes on, I'm taking you both out."

"Your wish is my command," Jerry said, bowing to Lilly, kissing her hand.

"There it is." Billy pointed, as the elevator doors opened to the basement.

Behind a row of rented storage cages fashioned from

chain-link fencing stood a single door, half-hidden in the shadows. Leon had told them it led to an unused storage room. It was perfect. Forgotten, unmarked, and easy to miss. Billy made sure of that.

Each time they came, he dragged a rolled-up rug across the front of it, leaning it just so, the way a careless renter might abandon junk. To anyone passing through, it looked like nothing more than clutter. To them, it was an entrance, and a disguise no one thought to question.

They squeezed through the fence and Billy pushed the rug aside. The door didn't have a key, and it simply opened with the turn of the knob.

Inside, the smell of raw dirt and damp hit their senses. The room was large enough, at least ten by ten feet. A wooden box that Jerry had built into a makeshift coffin lay dead center. A small lightbulb hung from the ceiling by a wire that looked like it could snap at any moment. Above that, a small plastic air vent hugged the ceiling, rattling quietly as it pumped oxygen into the room.

"Don't tell me that's where you sleep," Lilly probed as they stepped inside.

"You should've seen the dumps I've slept in. This is the Ritz Carlton by comparison," Jerry responded, flicking on the light.

"Why?" she replied, stepping farther into the room, steadying herself in the high heels she was wearing. "Guy such as yourself, you should be indulging in some creature comforts."

"I agree. But there are some habits that I can't shake. This being one of them."

"What's the dirt for?"

Jerry had walked to the back of the room. He was focused and concentrating on a heavy iron grate that likely led to a sewer beneath the basement. He rubbed his hands together before responding to Lilly, heaving the grate up and shifting it to one side.

"What was it some poet said? Dust thou art, to dust returnest?" he said, sliding the grate to one side and reaching inside the hole with one arm. "It rebirths you. Especially if you've been injured or sick."

He pulled out a large book that looked like it belonged in the profane chamber of a forgotten archive. Dusting it off, he held it in both hands before offering it to Lilly.

"No, no, don't hand it to me yet. Put it on the floor," she said, stepping away in fearful reverence of the grimoire.

"Very well then," he said, placing the book down on the floor in front of Lilly. Billy stood with his hands on his hips, wondering what was coming next. He hadn't dabbled too much with the book, and always considered it a mystery as to why Jerry had one in the first place.

"When did it call to you last?" Lilly looked up as she asked Jerry.

"It's been a few decades. I don't really touch it. One gets bored of reading the same book time and time again." He laughed.

"This isn't your mother's grimoire," Lilly said. "You don't read it, Jerry. It reads you." She continued without taking her eyes off it, "This isn't human skin. It's something much older."

Lilly pushed the coffin to the side of the room; it was surprisingly light. She then reached into her pocket and pulled out a small black hair band, placing it between her teeth. She bunched her hair back and tied it into a ponytail, wrapping the black band around her hair twice.

"Please step back and keep your distance. I'm going to try something," Lilly said, pulling her sleeves up to her elbows.

"What?" Billy quipped.

"I'm going to try to communicate with it. Grimoires like these, they're sentient."

Both Jerry and Billy were entranced; not by the book, but by the witch. And not due to any magic, but due to the sheer confidence and power that this woman had over them.

She waved her hands over the book; it shimmered back at her before vibrating, its skin pulsing in the orange glow of the light bulb up above.

"What is it doing?" Jerry asked.

"Shh," Lilly said. "It speaks."

The grimoire shifted again before it snapped open and what looked like centuries of parchment paper flickered back and forth, some pages blank, some with inscriptions and ancient texts. It stopped on one page, then shifted again as if it needed something better, all the while sending gusts of wind through the room.

The page it landed on didn't shimmer like before. It vibrated faintly like a heartbeat that was buried deep in the paper. Lilly's hand hovered above it, and as her fingertips lowered, a warmth spread through her skin.

Her vision blurred, not in the way magic normally

distorted reality, but more like memory softening at the edges. The room around them faded, the walls, the coffin, all of it disappeared as a new image began to take shape. Jerry was standing alone in front of a large stained-glass window that rested at the top of a wooden staircase, the sun behind him slowly rising.

She then saw him walking through a cloud of dust, looking over his shoulder, being hunted. And then came the men. Two of them. One older, almost weathered into stone. The other was younger, maybe twenty, he was afraid, but sharp. Lilly didn't hear the name at first. It appeared to her on a page that only she could see, the way one knows a dream is really long after waking, but she felt the gravity of its message: the boy wouldn't just be a threat. He'd be the end of Jerry and Billy.

Charlie.

Jerry and Billy peered over to the book's page, trying to see what Lilly was looking at.

"Do you see that?" she asked, not looking up.

"Nothing," Jerry responded.

"Do you know anyone called Charlie?"

"Presently, no. But I've come across my fair of Charlies over the years. There was a time when it wasn't Charlie. It was Charlemagne, Carolus, and even Ceorl," Jerry muttered, his gaze inquisitive.

The book didn't explain further. It didn't need to. Jerry's fate was sealed, and not by anything Lilly would do. He would be chased from New York. He would fall back into monstrosity. In a final act of cruel symmetry, he would die at the hands of someone too young to understand the history he was ending.

The grimoire's pages resisted closure.

Even as the vision of Jerry's end faded, the paper beneath her palm continued to vibrate, slower now, darker, like the sound of a storm gathering far out to sea. She saw Lucia next. Not the woman they'd met in the bar. This woman felt dangerous; it looked like Lucia, but amplified, angry, vengeful, and full of rage. Her eyes were black and shining. A crown of bones sat atop her head, and Lilly could see the demon Surgat wrapped around her like smoke, wearing her like skin. The woman was gone.

What remained was purely a vessel.

Then came the message. Carved into Lilly's mind. As if the book had opened a door inside her rather than outside. It came in the form of a voice she hadn't heard in centuries. Bridget Bishop. The one who had first dared to teach her, who had opened Lilly's eyes behind the ale house in Salem, where candlelight flickered against stone walls and the scent of herbs clung to their skin.

Bridget had taught her how to call her power by name, how to shape it with intention, and how to stand tall when the world demanded women be seen and not heard. It had been those nights of shared breath and incantations that had given Lilly her first taste of who she truly was.

But it was those same nights that would ultimately lead to their ruin. Bridget was hanged, her body swaying beneath a gray sky as townspeople looked on, convinced they'd killed part of the storm. Lilly had nearly followed, the rope already taut around her neck when the demon came. She'd met this demon long before her battle cry. It had nurtured her through her childhood years, kept her safe when danger was afoot, and taught her how to talk to the trees.

But in this final moment, full of rage and breathless resolve, she accepted the demon's invitation to become something so powerful, not even the town of Salem could escape her wrath. Bridget hadn't been so fortunate.

She left behind her gold, her ale house, and her grimoire tucked into a hidden alcove that only Lilly knew existed. And when Lilly rose again, she burned the entire town of Salem to the ground. When she was done, she returned for what was left. She took the book, the memories, and the gold too.

She must be broken from within.

Lilly's breath caught. The page glowed faintly, and more writing appeared beneath the first line.

Fall into the wall, I will catch you.

The text faded, and silence fell upon the room.

A chill swept through the room and caused momentary whimpers even from Jerry. For him, the supernatural in appearance wasn't a common theme. He had been left with the curse of immortality and feeding on the living, but that was all. He was never visited by the Devil or a demon again. His curse was never explained to him, and he never received a response in the darkness of his despair. He simply came to be the vampire he was.

Lilly sat frozen. The knowledge had shifted something in her. Jerry would fall. That much was written. Fate had already wrapped its fingers around his end. But Lucia... Lucia was still a choice.

She looked down at the grimoire one last time. It had nothing more to say. Nothing more to show. It had given her the future, and in doing so, had demanded a reckoning.

Then, without warning, the book lifted off the ground. Lilly stood up fast. The grimoire hovered chest-high, its cover slowly rotating in the air, as if acknowledging every soul in the room. Jerry, Billy, and her.

It paused, then began to shake violently. The edges of its pages flared with white light, brilliant and searing, brighter than the sun. Yet, not deadly.

All three of them raised their arms to shield their eyes. Then came the whoosh, a deep exhale from the book's center, like something being expelled. A gust of wind rolled outward, scattering dust, dirt, ash, and anything small enough to be caught in its wake. Jerry's coffin behind them rattled and the cage outside the walls creaked.

The book dropped, landing at Jerry's feet with a loud thud.

Manhattan was a living, breathing city, guttural growls of bass booming from nightclubs, the dull roar of the reveling populace mixed with the machinic sound of vehicles chugging away in a line, exhaust fumes rattling and pouring smoke into an already clog-aired island.

Jerry, Lilly, and Billy sat crammed in the back of a cab, heading north through Sixth Avenue, toward Washington Street.

Jerry wasn't overly nervous about another driver not seeing him in his rearview mirror. Over the centuries it had become exhausting to consider killing yet another victim who had dared to challenge what they had seen with their own eyes. Lilly, on the other hand, had just the spell; the same cloaking mechanism she used to hide the book had been cast over the driver. As far as he was concerned, there were three people in the back and that was that.

"Oh God, we're finally here!" Lilly exclaimed, glee plastered all over her face, clapping her hands together and pulling on the door handle to exit the cab.

Across the way from a small strip of park that broke the street in two stood the Stonewall Inn—a public house draped in red brick and influence. People from all walks of life spilled into the street, drinking and dancing outside a bar that started a revolution. This was a liberty parade, freedom ensued both inside and out, and the Devil would have to raise Hell himself to break it apart.

"What is this place?" Billy asked warily.

"This," Lilly replied, "is one of the best goddamn bars in the city. Make you wanna forget that 54 crap. And you better know that this city just sparked a new generation thanks to the men and women behind that door."

Lilly grabbed Jerry by the hand and led him to the entrance of the bar, her hips confidently swaying as she strutted to the queen at the door. The doorman—a larger than life black man who measured at least six foot eight even when sat down—donned a large blonde wig, impeccable makeup, and a peachy white dress that looked like it belonged in the Baroque era.

"Now, honey, I know these two ain't your boyyyyyfriends...?" The words were a mix of a statement and a question as he leaned in to Lilly.

"Baby boy, did you miss me?" Lilly flirted as she leaned in, rested her elbow on his shoulder, and planted a kiss on the drag queen's cheek.

"Girl, you ain't brought that nasty ass down here in a long long time. Now where the hell you been?" he shot back, clapping a fan from behind his chair and flapping it in Lilly's direction before looking away in dramatic fashion.

"Hell and back, baby, and this time I brought two devils with me," she replied, looking at Billy and Jerry and twirling the drag queen's baroque wig.

"Jerry," the vampire proclaimed as he reached his hand out to shake the doorman's.

"Jerry? Jerry h-what?" he returned, pronouncing the h in the *what*, prompting a chuckle from Lilly and a stutter from Jerry. "Girl, you don't know yo last name? Errryone up in here got a last name..."

"He's a shy queen." Lilly laughed, as Jerry looked on in amusement.

"Okay, hag, take your fags and get inside," the queen responded, not caring to know who Billy was, before patting Lilly on the ass to allow entry.

The bar was packed as it could be without being claustrophobic. The trio couldn't walk without squeezing up against someone. To the right, brown wood cladding adorned the entire side of the room across from a long bar where four or five bartenders were busy busting out drinks and shots. Drag queens, queer folk, and men clad in leather donned the joint, watching around the room with an awareness in case another riot was afoot.

"Drink of choice?" Lilly shouted at them both over the thudding music.

Jerry raised his eyebrows at Lilly.

"Never mind," she replied. "Billy, why so uncomfortable?" she continued, prompting a laugh from Jerry.

He didn't respond, he just continued to look around the room as Lilly ordered three rum and Cokes from the bar.

"Here, try these," she said, handing the drinks to each of them. Billy stared at the cherry in the glass. "Have you two never been to a gay bar?"

"Why would we?" Billy snapped back, prompting Lilly to raise her eyebrows at him.

"It's not like they're commonplace," Jerry responded, looking around the room.

"You two have walked the earth together for how long, a thousand years, and you're telling me you've remained just good friends all this time?"

"Yeah, that's right," Billy responded nonchalantly, not giving in to Lilly's humor and sarcasm.

She started to shake her hips, dancing on the spot and feeling the energy in the room, while Jerry watched Billy struggling to maintain composure. The two bourbons he'd had at the penthouse earlier had left him feeling inebriated, and his defenses were up. His unbridled disdain for the world and its dominant denizens made him see them as pathetic yet necessary. He walked off to the restroom, knowing that all he needed was one person to bump into him to give him the reason he needed to start another riot.

"What's her problem?" Lilly teased as she glanced over Jerry's shoulder, noticing a small table that had just opened up. "Quick, let's sit down."

The two of them moved fast to the high top that seated four. Jerry and Lilly sat opposite each other against the wall. "So, what's his deal?"

"Eh," Jerry said, his gaze drifting toward the bar as he rubbed the side of his neck. "He's always hated being reminded that we were once human. It is not a pleasant feeling. Imagine never being able to taste an apple ever again, and then walking into an apple orchard. I bite into them regardless, but to my palate, they are crunchy and bland. I do it for the memory. And at this point, I don't have any memory. All I have is a memory of a memory of a memory. And that memory is painful. And when we come here, places like this, see people with their limited lives indulging in pleasure and vices like there's no tomorrow, like *they're* the ones who are immortal, it brings out all sorts of envy and bitterness in us. We might not be humans, but we're not above emotions, Billy and I."

She leaned forward a little, tracing the rim of her glass with one finger. "You know, you're easier to talk to when he isn't around."

Jerry smirked. "I could say the same about you."

For a moment, they just sat there, the bass of the bar vibrating through the soles of their shoes, the warmth of the room clashing with the quiet between them, and they both forgot that they were no longer human.

Lilly looked at him intently and felt the gravity of what the grimoire had shown her. She saw not the vampire in front of her, but the one he would become. The one who would fall. The one who would die in a basement in a small dwelling in California.

"You ever feel like fate is something you're walking toward," she said, "even when you're trying to run?"

Jerry raised an eyebrow. "A book teach you that turn of phrase?"

Lilly smiled, taking a sip of her rum and Coke. "I came up with it all on my own."

Billy returned from the restroom with a scowl carved into his face. He didn't say anything at first, he just stood beside the table, looking out at the crowd like they were insects swarming too close to his skin.

"This place reeks of performative desperation," he muttered. "It's like they're all pretending they're not dying just to make the night feel worth it."

Jerry raised an eyebrow. "Come now, Billy, don't be a sourpuss."

Billy didn't answer. He looked at Lilly, then back at Jerry, and whatever storm had been brewing inside him cracked.

"What's the matter, Billy boy? Someone grab your dick the restroom?" Lilly smirked.

"I can't stand it," he snapped. "I'm leaving." Chugging his rum and Coke in one go, he added, "You two can stay here and enjoy the land of the living, and when you're ready to face what you are again, you know where I am."

Billy disappeared into the crowd with rude urgency,

pushing through a pair of drag queens mid-spin without so much as a glance back.

Lilly watched him go, then turned to Jerry. "He always this charming?"

Jerry shrugged.

They finished their drinks slowly, letting the music press into their bones one last time. Then, without much discussion, they left the bar and wandered into the warm Manhattan night.

THE STREETS HAD THINNED and the heat was wearing off. It was around midnight, and the energy of the night still remained, albeit a little less so than before. Lilly and Jerry found a small coffee shop on a corner just a few blocks away. It was an inviting coffee house with a cream exterior and a large window.

Inside, the shop was dim, its olive-green walls catching what little light the fixtures gave off. The décor felt like something out of a grandmother's kitchen: plates hung neatly along the walls, a strip of tartan wallpaper behind them, cream-colored cloths spread across the tables. Hard red leather booths lined the room, stiff and unsympathetic, as if they were designed less for comfort than to hurry drunks through their midnight coffee.

Lilly and Jerry slipped into one of the smaller booths near the back, the vinyl sighing under their weight as they settled in.

A waitress came up to greet them almost immediately with a fresh pot of coffee in her hand. "Coffee?"

"Thank you," Lilly said, as the waitress poured the black gold into two old diner-style mugs that were already out, waiting for their next addict.

"You two hungry?"

"Oh, I could crack a neck and put a straw in the carotid," Jerry quipped, his sinister eyes narrowing.

"Too much acid tonight, young man?" she replied in a vexed voice. "I'll just set these down here, holla if you need somethin'."

"Humor really isn't your strong point, is it?" Lilly said to Jerry, as he took a sip on the coffee.

"So," she blurted, unable to help herself, "why'd you try to bite my neck, ya cunt?"

Jerry almost spat up.

"Are we going to be real with each other?" Jerry asked. Lilly frowned at him sardonically.

"You remind me of someone I knew a long time ago," he continued.

"Maria," Lilly replied, taking a sip of her coffee too and not looking up at Jerry.

"She died," Jerry said again, quieter this time. "I was two days away from being home. Just two."

He didn't look back. His eyes stayed on the swirling black coffee in his mug, like if he stared hard enough it would give him a different ending.

"Vlad's men came through the valley while my forces were still in Bosnia," he said. "They wanted it all, power and money, and they tore down anything to get it. I'd fortified my home; I thought she'd be safe."

Lilly said nothing.

"She didn't die in battle. She died hiding. With an axe in her hand trying to defend herself. When I found her, I stopped being human."

Lilly blinked. That was the first time she'd heard Jerry say something that didn't sound like sarcasm or carefully buried grief.

"I was devastated. You hear or read about these things. It was more common then too; men would go to battle and rarely came home. But the pain, when I returned home and saw her there, dead. Disbelief ran through my veins. It's a weird feeling. It's numbing. Then panic, when reality hits you, it's the panic that gets you, the loss of control. And then... Well, then you question everything."

He stopped for a moment as if he was about to shed a tear. "I read everything," he continued. "Every cursed page I could get my hands on. I bled into rituals, summoned things I didn't understand. I was willing to trade anything. And I guess eventually something heard me. Back in those days, monsters and Devils were real, not like today."

"Trust me, the Devil is still around today," Lilly brooded.

"Well, whatever it was, it gave me what I wanted. No man would ever hurt me again. I'd be able to defeat the monster that killed my family. But there was a catch. There's always a catch."

"The Devil's in the details," Lilly said, grimly staring at Jerry.

Jerry nodded. "I'd spend eternity chasing what I lost.

I'd see it. Feel it brushing my fingers. But I'd never hold it again. I'd never love. The feeling would stay right there, just out of reach. I'd find someone I could love once more, and then just as things are about to click, she'd be ripped from me."

He finally looked up.

"You remind me of her, you know. Not in the way you look. In the way you feel. But I don't get to hold it anymore."

Lilly's expression softened with recognition.

"Maybe you don't need to hold it," she said. "Maybe it's enough to know you can still feel it."

Instead of responding right away, Jerry looked out the window, mulling over what she'd said, watching the city being alive and unreachable.

"Was it...Vlad...the Impaler?" Lilly asked. This time, she had shrunk the sarcasm and the cockiness—she allowed her motherly instinct to kick in and empathize with the monster sitting in front of her. If it weren't for the fact she was at least two hundred years old, the words Vlad the Impaler leaving her mouth would have sounded silly.

"Yup." Jerry's eyes had turned yellow, his rage returning, his fangs pointing ever so slightly.

"Yikes," Lilly said, and then said ever so slowly, "I know how you feel."

"How could you possibly know how it feels?" Jerry snapped, slamming his fist onto the table. It prompted a look from the other coffee goers, the waitress looking on concerned as Jerry hid his face by staring at the wall next to them. Lilly mouthed *It's okay* to her.

"Well," Lilly said softly, "after I became a witch, sometime later I met someone. David. We had a beautiful baby boy; he was the most beautiful thing ever. They were stolen from me. To this day, I do not know what became of them."

Jerry's eyes softened, his fangs retracted, and his skin returned to its smooth glossy appearance.

"If I hadn't said yes to the demon that turned me, I would never have had the child and put my family through whatever they went through. And yet, if I'd never become a witch, I never would have known him or my husband."

"How long ago was this?" Jerry asked.

"Oh, hundreds of years ago, mid 1800s. But let me tell ya, it still stings like it happened yesterday." She wiped a solitary tear from her cheek.

"So I guess you do know how it feels," Jerry said, his head sunk low, taking in the wafting aroma of the coffee.

"I do. And it must suck."

"What must?"

"Having to feed on humans to stay alive. How does it feel to be...you?" she replied, changing the topic.

Jerry didn't answer at first. He just stared into his cup, watching the last swirl of coffee settle like sediment in a riverbed. His voice, when it came, was quieter and human.

"It *feels*," he elongated the word, "like being stuck."

Lilly leaned back, letting him speak.

"Everything slows down. Not time. Time keeps racing. People die, cities change, empires fall. But you slow down. You stop reacting. You stop reaching. You just exist. You wonder what's next, like, *What am I going to do for the next thousand years?* And then, of course, you think of eternity."

He lifted the mug, swirled what was left. "And the hunger—it's always there. It's not pain or anything like that, it just lingers. Lustful almost. Like a buzz in your ear or a shadow on your heels. You learn to manage it. You choose who to feed on, and you justify it. Even when it's wrong. But deep down, you're always asking yourself if you're still worth saving."

"And are you?" she asked.

Jerry looked at her, his expression unreadable.

"I haven't decided yet."

She smiled faintly. "Fair enough."

They sat in silence for a minute, the air between them thick with shared grief, mutual recognition, and something else—something not quite trust, but not far off.

"What's the *best* thing about it?" she asked, smiling.

"The sheer knowledge. There isn't anything you can ask me I wouldn't know the answer to."

"Yeah, I feel that..." Lilly said, looking out to the other patrons. "Most people don't get it. They think becoming something powerful makes everything better."

Jerry snorted. "It just makes everything louder."

She laughed, a quiet, tired sound. "Amen to that. But tell me, is Jerry your real name?"

Jerry chuckled. "It is now. My original name was Gellert, so Jerry felt like an easy transition. Something less medieval."

"And you chose Manhattan?"

"We ended up here, yes. Billy and I had been bouncing between Boston and the Netherlands, setting up shell companies and trusts—it's part of the routine. We build safety nets. New names, new money, new exit strategies. I try not to go back to the same place twice, but Amsterdam I did. Twice, actually."

"Why?"

"We got chased out the first time. By a professor." He smiled dryly. "Thought he was close to figuring out what I was. And, ironically, we're here now because of another one. Different century, same damn pattern. And they say lightning doesn't strike twice."

Then Jerry exhaled, as if deciding to say something he hadn't said out loud in a long, long time.

"You know," he said, "I wasn't always like this."

Lilly raised an eyebrow.

"After the turning, I was the vilest thing on the planet. Centuries of rage and grief. And the hunger, it twisted me. I wasn't hunting out of necessity. I was enjoying it. Some days I still do."

He looked up at her now. "War criminals. Rapists. Dictators. Europe was full of them. A few decades ago, I thought about taking down Hitler, just to see if I could."

Lilly smirked. "Ambitious."

He shrugged. "He did it himself before I ever got a chance. Say what you will about Hitler, but he'll forever be the guy who killed Hitler."

The smile faded quickly from his face. "But time... Time does something to you. Civilizations advance. Things change. They've just released all these new cameras," he said, swaying his coffee cup around, "they're calling CCTV in office buildings and alleyways. Being like this twenty-four seven, three-sixty-five gets exhausting."

"You mellowed?" she asked, more curious than judgmental.

"I adapted. I started choosing my moments. Pretending. Wearing the skin of civility. I learned to walk amongst men instead of through them. I found that a lot of the rage inside me is still ego, and that if I simply move on from that, it reminds me that I'm something powerful, and that power isn't always necessary. Kind of like having a sports car. When you know you can beat someone in a race, you care less about proving your point!"

He paused, leaning forward slightly, his voice lowering.

"But it never leaves you. Billy doesn't get tired of it. He thinks like it's the old days. But me? I've ebbed and flowed. I go through periods of empathy. I convince myself there's something worth saving in humanity...and then humanity reminds me there isn't."

"Yeah," Lilly said softly. "They have a way of doing that."

Jerry gave her a long look. "Have you ever gone through that? The rise and fall?"

Lilly nodded, the memory of Bridget, of David, of her son passing over her face like a shadow.

"More than you know."

"So how did you survive all this time?" Jerry continued.

"Mentally?"

"No, no, financially."

"The woman that helped me blossom into the person I am now was a good friend. Humans ripped her from me too. She had left behind a small fortune, whether she conjured it or not I had no clue, but..." She paused as if an old long-forgotten memory had come back to her. "I took it. I took her grimoire, her money, and anything I could, after...after I burned Salem to the ground."

"Ambitious, yourself." Jerry smirked back.

"Then, I bought the town of Bridgewater from a small group of men who went on to do something with railroads. I facilitated the introduction of iron works; I could foretell what would become successful and what wouldn't. I worked with a few companies that went on to have huge contracts. I gave them free land in exchange for a percentage in the company. And that..." she cheered her mug toward Jerry, "made me very, very rich. Still around to this day, they are!"

"Impressive," he replied.

"What about you?"

"I had wealth from my days in Bosnia," Jerry said, settling deeper into the red booth. "I led armies into battle, and was paid handsomely by the king. Land, gold, loyalty, all the things men with swords thought would last forever."

He paused to sip his coffee, then gave her a tired smile.

"Then everything changed. The gold meant nothing once I couldn't stay in one place. I'd never grow old and I'd never die. I had to start thinking differently. So I did."

Lilly listened, her fingers wrapped around the warmth of her mug.

"I started with gemstones. Easy to transport and even easier to sell. Bearer bonds were my real friend for a while, but knowing what I know about humans and how they operate, there's always a bad actor that ruins it for everyone else. So I can imagine they'll be gone soon enough."

He took a deep breath before continuing. "Precious metals and the like. Then I got interested in the Dutch. Their banks. Their obsession with trade and debt. I followed the rise of capitalism like it was a new religion. Compound interest, dividend payouts, long-term equity positions, all the boring shit that makes the world run now? I understood it early. And I learned how to hide in it."

He looked up at her, more amused than proud.

"I have vaults. And the rest, that's all the compound interest ever asked for. I started trusts. Shell companies. Bought up land in places no one cared about—Nairobi, Mumbai, Singapore—then waited."

Lilly gave him a long, impressed look. "You're telling me you were playing emerging markets before they had names?"

"I've had centuries, naturally," he replied. "Eventually, I figured out what not to touch. Oil was too volatile. Gold too obvious. But housing? Infrastructure? Things people couldn't stop needing?"

He tapped his temple once, saying, "That's where the blood's at now."

Lilly raised her mug in response.

"To long games," she said.

"To not dying in poverty," Jerry replied wryly.

"Okay, I'm gonna head out. I'll reach out to you tomorrow or the next day," Lilly said, wiping the coffee stain on the table with a napkin.

"I have a feeling Lucia is going to attempt to find you in the next few days. Right now, her body is adapting and resetting itself to its new host." She said the words like they meant nothing at all.

She pushed herself up to leave, then paused. "Listen, if you do ever come across a man named Charlie, promise me one thing."

Jerry looked up. "And what's that?"

"Give him a choice before you rip his head off of his neck."

Jerry was perplexed for a moment there, knowing that Lilly knew something he didn't. But then he raised his cup and said with dry panache, "You got it."

CHAPTER 11

WHAT MONSTERS DO

Billy loved Jerry. For all intents and purposes, he considered Jerry his brother in arms. With a mind hardwired to handle catastrophes, this cognitive behavior several centuries in the making, Billy knew his job well. Keep Jerry alive.

So he spent his days predicting every scenario in which Jerry could be killed. As with everything, it had its pros, but it also had its cons. For one, Billy knew he would do anything for Jerry, and as would Jerry. Jerry took good care of Billy. But here was the kicker of it. What was Billy's identity? Who was he, other than Jerry's living shadow? He had spent lifetimes upon lifetimes following someone else's lead.

Watching his back and cleaning up his messes.

Sleeping down the hall from a man he would die for.

Living solely to serve.

And strangely, he liked it that way. Because service, at least, gave him a purpose.

And in return, he got to stay close enough to feel

Jerry's heat. To hear the rise and fall of his breath during the day. To see the rare, fleeting moments when Jerry let his guard down, when something soft flickered behind his dead eyes. That was Billy's favorite version of him. The one no one else got to see.

The pair had it all. Wealth, immortality, strength, and a vast knowledge of the world that only the Gods above could match. But living your best life every day for all eternity came with drawbacks. Billy struggled to grapple with the constant upheaval that would inevitably behest them.

They would move to a new city, settle down, explore the arts scene, the nightlife, and everything a place had to offer, but eventually, the authorities or a vampire hunter would find them and drive them into hiding again, forcing them to move to a new territory that, luckily, they'd already planned for.

But if there was one thing Billy had carried with him from his mortal life, it was his craving for stability. Even with a demon's mind, part of him, the worst part, still remained human. That conflict would haunt him forever. Just as Jerry, cursed with eternity, would never love again—and know it.

The role, whether it was practical or emotional, also had its perks. Billy never had to visit a doctor. He would never grow old and he'd never die. He didn't worry about money, housing, or survival. Jerry handled all of it. He always had. Billy helped, of course. But occasionally, loyalty came with friction. When Billy's frustration boiled over, he'd go out alone and kill for the sake of killing, just to remind himself he was powerful.

They both harked from a time when everything was driven by ego, land, family, wars. Jerry would wax philosophical every few decades, pull out some fragment of humanity buried deep in his chest, and start seeing the world through the lens of compassion.

Billy hated it, seeing it as weakness, and worried Jerry would grow soft enough to get himself killed, or worse, decide to end it all himself.

And that's what truly terrified Billy. Because deep down, he didn't know what would happen to him if Jerry died. He suspected, as most would, that a familiar can't survive without their vampire. That when Jerry goes, he goes too.

But the fear was more than just death, it was about being left behind, alone.

THE WALK from Greenwich to Midtown had sobered Billy just enough to make the ache worse. His head still buzzed from the rum and Coke, but it was dulled now, replaced by a quiet throb just beneath his skull, this throbbing reverberating under his sternum as well.

He didn't know why he walked north. He just followed the glow of Manhattan like a moth, undecided on which altar of fire to offer himself to burn.

Despite all his lamenting, he liked it here. He always took a short while to adapt to new pastures. And tonight, he wanted to explore more of a city that felt like it was crumbling from the outside, when inside, a quiet revolution had begun. Was this the place he could call home forever? It certainly felt like it.

El Corso sat like a temple on East 86th, tucked behind an unassuming black door framed by chipped red brick. There was no sign and no lines outside, just a small plaque etched in brass and a guy leaning against the wall, smoking a Lucky Strike, pretending he wasn't clocking every single person who walked by.

Billy gave him a nod, but the guy didn't return it. He just opened the door, and inside, the world changed. The air was thick with cologne, sweat, and cigarette smoke. Soul and salsa warred on opposite sides of the room, the music bouncing off the low ceiling like it was trying to escape into the apartments upstairs.

A soft orange haze coated everything; the light fixtures were old chandeliers, stained amber from years of tobacco. The walls were painted a warm, almost rusty maroon, and most of the furniture was wood, heavy and scarred from the memories of a harsher time.

And then there were the men.

Latino boys in tight jeans and sleeveless mesh tops, or just plain white tees. Older men with pencil mustaches and leather waistcoats. A few queens with glitter shadow and deep voices. But mostly, beautiful, wary men. Men who held themselves like they were used to looking over their shoulder, and could very well throw someone over it should the need arise. These men had been built to show the world that they didn't care what people thought. At least not inside the club. Here, they could be themselves.

Outside was a different story. Most kept to themselves, sticking to neighborhoods around Chelsea or the meat packing district. They offered safer spaces so they could live their lives without fear. Street smarts was the name of the game; they knew how to evade the watchful eye of the common straight man who might just be looking for a reason to beat someone's ass.

Billy stepped inside like he'd been there a thousand times before. He had been to gay bars; sometimes he'd walk toward the door and just keep walking, hoping that the door would open just as he walked past so he could get a glimpse of the world within.

But he always remained on the outside. Always afraid that someone would see through him, not just the vampire part, but the other part. The part that stared a little too long at the bartender. The part that envied the boys with their heads on each other's shoulders in the corner booth. But in reality, Billy was more afraid of what he'd do to them. His victims would become Jerry's.

He walked to the bar and ordered a neat bourbon, because it felt like the kind of drink a man would order when he didn't want to be noticed. But, of course, he was. A few men glanced his way. Maybe it was the broadness of his shoulders, his height, the thousand-yard stare, or maybe they just smelled the grief on him.

One of them approached. The man was in his early thirties with light brown skin, black hair in a short, tight wave, and a cross on a silver chain.

"You by yourself?" he asked.

Billy didn't look at him, for even the cross around his neck gave him some discomfort. "Sometimes."

"First time here?"

"No." A lie Billy told with conviction.

The man smiled. "It's my favorite place. Nowhere else in the city lets you be loud and quiet at the same time, you know?"

Billy finally turned to look at him.

"Name's Ramón," the man said, offering his hand.

Billy took it, slowly, and didn't say his own.

"You don't have to talk," Ramón added. "Some people just come here to get their dick sucked."

Billy let out something close to a laugh, more exhale than joy. He didn't let go of Ramón's hand right away. And for a moment, just a moment, the familiar conceded.

"Is that so?" Billy quipped, laughing, letting his guard down.

Ramón was leaning against the bar, his head cocked to one side as if to rest on his shoulder. "Why? You want your dick sucked?" he said, making light of the situation.

"Not tonight. Well, at least not here," Billy said, then shot down a gulp of his bourbon.

"That's a stiff drink."

Billy glared quietly at him and raised one eyebrow in a *Really?* motion.

"Aight aight, I'm done, I'm done. I'm jus' fucken witchu, man," Ramón replied.

"So what do you do, Ramón?"

"I'm a dancer."

"No shit," Billy said, giving the guy a once over. Taking another sip, he nodded to the bartender to bring him another. "Drink?" he asked Ramón.

"Wallbanger," Ramón replied, looking at the

bartender. "Thanks, bubba... Yep, sometimes I'm up there shakin' my ass for the dudes in here."

"How quaint," Billy remarked.

"You wanna go sit down in that booth?" Ramón asked, and Billy looked around to the small booth in the corner. He didn't say anything to Ramón, he just got up and walked over to it.

"Guessssss so," Ramón said as he rolled his eyes, grabbed his drink, and followed the behemoth of a man to the booth.

They slid into it, Billy first and Ramón second. The table was narrow, the kind that forced knees to touch if either of them leaned in even slightly, and Ramón did. He sipped his Wallbanger, watching Billy as if he were studying a work of art hung in a museum gallery.

"So," Ramón said, reclining, "you always come into a place like this looking like a fucking mob boss?"

Billy looked down at his shirt, then back up with a deadpan face. "Is that what I look like?"

"No," Ramón said. "That's what you feel like."

Ramón leaned forward again, elbows on the table. "You ever dance?"

Billy scoffed. "No."

"That a vampire thing?" Ramón said with a smirk.

Billy's eyes flashed up. Ramón blinked. "Kidding. Jesus."

"Maybe."

"You're not from here."

"No."

"You from Europe?"

"Kinda."

"God, you really like giving the least amount of information possible, huh?" Ramón laughed.

"You're like a hot guy at a funeral. You show up, you look good, you say nothing, and everybody walks away wondering if they should've been nicer to you."

Billy smirked. "What makes you think I've ever been nice?"

"You sat down, didn't you?"

Billy didn't answer, but something in his stare softened for a split second.

"I don't know what your deal is," Ramón said. "But I've seen that look before. I know what a closeted man looks like. I know what it's like to want someone and be scared of them at the same time."

Billy said nothing. He just smiled back.

"You've got all this heaviness on you, like you're waiting for someone to tell you it's okay to let it go."

Ramón leaned back. "Or maybe you just like feeling dangerous. That it?"

Billy's eyes were darker now. "You don't know me, punk. But I bet you want to."

Ramón smiled. "Yeah, I think I would."

Then Billy leaned in, slow, close enough for their knees to touch. "I bet you do wanna suck my dick here, huh?"

Ramón's voice was quieter now. "I can take a lot. I'm not afraid of men like you."

Billy let the silence stretch. "You should be."

❧

THE HALLWAY to the bathroom was narrow and dimly lit, more shadow than light. Ramón led the way, glancing back only once to make sure Billy was following. He stepped into a side stairwell that led into the basement.

Downstairs, another hallway of darkness was lit only by the occasional red sconce illuminating the doorways to each private bathroom stall. The single-occupant bathroom was grimy but private. A chipped white sink sat beneath a scratched mirror that had seen better decades. The smell of whiskey, cheap soap, and cologne lingered in the air. Ramón clicked the lock behind them, and for a moment they just stood there, facing each other.

Then Billy grabbed him.

It wasn't tender; it wasn't meant to be. His hand was around the back of Ramón's neck, pulling him into a kiss that was all hunger and frustration. Ramón responded instantly, arms sliding inside Billy's jeans, pulling him closer. Their bodies slammed against each other, the kiss turning aggressive. Ramón moaned into it, wrapping a leg around Billy's thigh.

Billy spun him around and pushed him against the sink. He stared for a moment at Ramon's ass before clenching his tank top with his left hand in a holding pattern, using his right hand to rip down his jeans with the uttermost ease, exposing his firm toned brown behind. A light dusting of black hair coated the cheeks, and Billy used the same hand to squeeze one of them, lifting the cheek with his thumb so he could get a glance of the inside.

"Just gonna look?" Ramon whispered.

But Billy ignored his question, instead spinning him back around and lifting him onto the sink like he weighed nothing.

"Fuck," Ramón gasped, half-laughing, half-breathless. "You're strong."

Billy didn't answer. His mouth was on Ramón's neck, his hands gripping under his thighs. The mirror behind Ramón creaked under the pressure.

"Easy," Ramón said, his tone still playful, but his voice slightly unsure now.

Billy's breath was heavy. He wasn't listening. His grip tightened, and with one thrust, he slammed Ramón's back into the mirror. It cracked behind his head, sharp, immediate. Not shattered, but fractured like ice.

"Hey—" Ramón shoved at Billy's chest. "What the fuck, dude?"

Billy froze.

Ramón's chest was heaving now. "You tryin' to kill me?"

Billy stepped back, hands still slightly raised, as if unsure whether to fight or freeze.

"I—I didn't mean—"

But Ramón was already off the sink, brushing glass from his shoulder, readjusting his shirt, eyes furious.

"Get the fuck off me," he snapped. "Fucking psycho."

He unlocked the door and stormed out, upstairs and into the bar.

The hallway downstairs no longer echoed the drum and bass from the bar upstairs, it was quiet for a moment. Then came the shift and the sound of murmuring from above. The sense of eyes turning toward the stairwell opening. A drag queen near the jukebox had stopped mid-song. The bartender, now at the end of the bar, was staring.

Someone muttered, "What happened?"

Billy stepped out from the stairs and into the main room, and every face turned toward him. The bartender grabbed a bat from under the bar.

"You need to go."

Billy stood still, chest rising and falling, but he didn't protest. It took every ounce of his being not to rip through the bar and turn it into a bloodbath. But instead, he just looked at an upset Ramon, then turned and walked out into the night, alone again.

THE WALK back down Sixth Avenue was long. It took Billy at least a couple of hours to reach 200 Water Street where his bed was waiting. He loved his rest and couldn't wait to climb into the California King bed with its hard mattress, silk sheets, and Egyptian cotton pillowcases.

The doors to the building swung open and Billy walked right in. The doorman, Leon, wasn't there. Billy assumed he was likely attending to the mail room, or using the bathroom. He paid it no mind and continued on to the elevator.

For the most part, he enjoyed Leon. The older Jewish man gave him a fatherly comfort that he hadn't felt in a long time, waving at him each time he walked through the door. Normally, he would have given Leon's absence another thought, but tonight, he was too ashamed and beaten down to give a fuck.

"How comes I never sees that Jerry with you durin' the day?" Leon would ask with a huge smile on his face, his balding head shining from the spotlights above, his eyes squinty from the heavy eyelids that were encroaching on his eyeballs. Billy wondered if he could really see anything at all. "He averse to the sun or something?" He would chuckle.

"You know Jerry. Always on the graveyard shift."

The alcohol and encounter at El Corso had taken its toll tonight. Billy Cole, after all, was part human, part monster, turned by Jerry as a willing participant. And whilst sickness was never an option, the effects of alcohol or drugs could still render him inebriated.

The fireplace was roaring, crackling low in its stone hearth. A perk of the penthouse, and a satanic comfort the two of them lusted over. Their nights were often spent in the twin red Buster chairs that flanked the fire, angled inward like old war generals waiting for battle or death.

Jerry would sit for hours just staring into the flame, and sometimes, the flame spoke back. They would talk all evening about times gone by; they had, after all, centuries of stories to keep each other entertained.

Only one lamp in the far corner was switched on, casting just enough glow to define the room's edges and nothing more. Shadows moved thick along the floor, creeping over the Persian rug.

"We got the dirt from your fucking coffin downstairs,

you loser," the first brute snarled as he walked out from the kitchen to Billy's left.

"See, Leon, I told you your precious vampires would come back soon. Although, where...where is the vampire?" the second brute asked as he walked in from the hallway to the right, laughing with the evilest grin slapped across his face.

Billy didn't react.

He walked over to Leon and stopped short of the pentagram that was etched into the floor from the dirt in Jerry's coffin. He stared down, at first holding no expression. Then, as if he'd reminded himself of who he was, he let out a little smirk before looking back at the gang. "A sacrifice?"

Behind him appeared the third brute, who walked slowly toward Billy, cracking his knuckles.

"Hey, big boy," he sneered.

The three men started to close in on him in a triangle motion. This wasn't the first time Billy had encountered a standoff, and it sure wouldn't have been his last. He rolled his sleeves up and smirked at the men as his eyes danced between each of them. Then suddenly, his eyes flicked up. Not because he heard her, but because something in the air changed.

Like a membrane had torn in the corner of the room. Lucia's body hung from the ceiling like a spider, twisted, holding on like there was zero effort, her limbs bent at unnatural angles, her face still human from a distance, but to Billy, that wasn't her anymore.

It was the beast.

Surgat.

Its eyes like bottomless pits locked onto Billy's face as the demon grinned with jagged, bone-white teeth. The brutes didn't even look up; they couldn't see it. To them, she was just Lucia, suspended like a possessed saint waiting to descend. But to Billy, the illusion had long peeled back.

Billy didn't speak, but Leon moaned in front of him, the chair rattling softly as one of the brutes tightened his restraints. Another pulled a hot poker from the fireplace.

"Tell us where the book is," brute two demanded, grinding the poker into the ash.

"You want this to stop? Tell us." He ripped the tape off Leon's mouth.

Billy's eyes never left the ceiling.

"You're wasting your time," he said coldly as his gaze followed the demon. "I'm the one you need to fear."

Leon interrupted the conversation, blurting, "I survived the Holocaust, you pieces of shit. You think I sit here scared? You should be ashamed of yourself." He cried as blood dripped down his lips, causing his words to be half-muffled as he screamed at the three men.

Brute one crouched beside Leon with the red-hot poker in his hand. He grabbed a fistful of his hair and yanked his head back. "One more chance, freak."

Billy didn't flinch. He knew what was coming. He knew they'd kill Leon no matter what he said. That's what monsters did, and right now, Billy couldn't tell if that meant the ones on the ground or the one grinning from the ceiling. Hell, he felt like killing Leon himself, just for the fun of it.

"I think you forget I'm a monster too," he laughed,

and his eyes glittered with the grin that slid across his face, feral and satisfied. The brutes paused, glancing at each other, unsure if this was bravado or a promise. Then brute two struck Leon across the face, a hard, backhanded blow that sent a tooth skittering across the floor.

The first brute, a sizeable henchman, taller than his fellow, hesitated, the poker still glowing red in his grip.

"He's bluffing," he muttered, as he drove the poker into the doorman's neck. It pierced the skin, causing blood to gush out, yet cauterizing the wound at the same time. The air filled with the smell of burned flesh. The scream from Leon echoed throughout the great room, causing the demon to dance on the ceiling and scream in unison, a mix of laughter and something else demonic.

"I don't bluff," Billy replied, his voice low and steady. "If you're trying to break me, you picked the wrong immortal. I've killed priests, children, kings, and I've enjoyed every second of it. You think dangling a bleeding doorman in front of me is gonna make me beg?"

He took a step forward, and the brutes got caught off guard, one of them stepping back. Billy knew how to display arrogance, and whilst he'd walked the earth for centuries with Jerry, it was on a rare occasion that he would be cornered by a group of men larger than him, not to mention a demon from Hell. Keeping up a tough act in such scenarios was essential for survival.

"It won't," Billy continued, almost thoughtfully. "But it does make me wonder...how many bones I can break before one of *you* talks."

It took mere seconds for the brutes to look at one

another, before Billy struck. It felt for everyone in the room, including the demon, that time had slowed down. The skin on Billy's hand had turned a pale white as his fingers slowly curled into a tight fist, his knuckles bulbous and battle worn.

The air around him was unable to keep up as he sped through it faster than a bullet would leave a gun, his fist striking one of them in the chest. But before the brute could react, a red wave of blood splattered outward, and the look of shock on his face started to become apparent. He realized something was very wrong.

Billy's arm had vanished, leaving the men to wonder for a mere moment where it had gone. He had punched a hole so violent, so bloody, that his arm had penetrated straight through the man's chest and out his back.

He held the beating heart in his fist, blood dripping from his fingers, vascular tubes still opening and closing as if they, too, were stalled in understanding they no longer connected to other vital pathways in the brute's body. He was face to face, almost chest to chest with his victim, locking eyes with him as the brute began to realize what happened.

"How's that feel, buddy?" Billy whispered as he clenched his heart even tighter, causing it to burst in his firm, rocklike hand.

The demon above screamed in anger as Billy's arm was caught in the rib cage. It shook violently, hissing and thrashing as if it wasn't able to move from its spot. Billy looked behind, preparing his next attack, but before he could remove his arm from the chest of his victim, the larger of the vigilantes fired a dart directly into his neck.

Billy ripped his arm out of his assailant and pulled the chrome bullet from his neck, a red feather attached to the end.

"Appropriate," he muttered as he looked at the dart.

He took a step forward toward the larger brute, but this time didn't move at the speed of sound, instead, stumbling a little, trying with all his might to keep his focus and balance. He grabbed onto the shoulder of Leon, whose head hung low. A creak emanated from the wooden chair, and Billy, with all his weight, collapsed the wood, sending a hogtied beaten old Jewish man to the ground, his body falling with no life, no struggle, just peace that he wasn't being tortured any longer.

Billy, now on his knees, crawled to the brute. The dart that had been fired into his neck was enough to tranquilize an elephant, which is just the amount of strength that Billy had coursing through his veins. And as he reached the brute's large black work boots, he grabbed onto his shin with one hand, almost breaking the bones. His grunting face looked up at him, as if trying to muster the very last bit of energy and strength, but it was no use, the dart had taken its toll. Billy gave up, and his head slammed to the ground with a thud that could be heard throughout the room.

And as he lay there, slowly losing consciousness, he saw the demon through blurred vision crawl down the side of the apartment wall in a spider-like motion, and toward him. Then he blacked out.

❧

Jerry thought it odd that Leon wasn't at the front entrance. He always was. But Jerry, for all his intelligence and centuries of learned caution, didn't sweat the small stuff. He wasn't wired for catastrophe like Billy. Leon was probably using the restroom, or out on rounds. Entertaining any other theory would only spiral into distraction—and Jerry loathed distractions.

Bliss, in his experience, lived in the margins of ignorance. Like a politician with a handler, Jerry had Billy. There had been countless times across centuries where Billy had *handled* things. Bribes, cover-ups, disposals. Jerry never asked. Billy would just offer his trademark one-liner: "It's been handled."

The doors to the penthouse were open, and Leon was the first thing Jerry saw as he walked into the apartment. The wooden chair acting like the cross of Christ, pinned to Leon's back via a thick brown rope that kept his arms by his sides and his legs suspended off the floor.

Pools of red crimson swam around the chair, ever so slowly leaking into the etched pentagram, and creeping toward the many rugs that commanded the space.

Jerry could hear his heart beating from across the room, a slow beat, slowly letting go of mortality. The fire was still roaring, the lamp still on, and the curtains still drawn tight. Yet unlike any other mortal would do, Jerry did not rush to Leon's aid.

His eyes darted from left to right before stepping into the room. Was it a trap? Or an ambush? Tossing the mail he'd picked up downstairs, he breathed in the room and knew that he was alone. He walked slowly to Leon, his face stern, irritated by the distraction that this event had now bestowed upon him.

"Leon, who did this to you?" Jerry asked, as he bent down to him and lifted up his bloodied face.

But Leon couldn't speak, the poker had made sure of that. Tucked into the lapel of Leon's suit was a folded-up piece of paper, a note etched in pencil across the academic blue lines.

"Ah, the pedestrian ransom note. Let's take a look," Jerry said to himself as he unfolded it.

Bring the book to us.

That is all the note said.

Jerry pondered for a moment. Below him, gurgling and whimpering, lay Leon, half-dead and trying to generate a simple request from his scarred throat.

Jerry merely looked at him in pity. He hadn't prepared for a battle so quickly. He knew the day would come when he would need to leave Manhattan, he'd be chased out like he was in other cities, before returning once a generation had died out. The same way he had from Antwerp to Boston, twice. But he'd been in New York for just over a month, and was still recovering mentally from the attack in Amsterdam. It did nothing for the empathetic side of him that wanted to believe that not all humans were bad.

He could smell the iron in Leon's blood, and could hear the slow beating of his dying heart. He could feed on him now, drain the entire body of blood and be satisfied for days, if not a week or more, without having to feed again. Leon looked up at him with doleful brown eyes. He didn't have to say anything, his eyes told Jerry everything he needed to know. A request, a dire request, to end his suffering, and use the lifeforce within his blood to get revenge on his attackers.

Jerry pushed back the grey and white strands from Leon's face. This man had taken care of them, given Jerry a resting place when he didn't have to, allowed Jerry to store his coffin in a place that he shouldn't have. He knew deep down what they were. But he didn't care to be involved. He played the game, and now, he had been caught in the crosshairs, losing his life cruelly.

Jerry shed a tear, the drop of clear liquid falling onto Leon's cheek. But it didn't draw any empathy from the man, who managed to mouth back, "Do it."

Before Jerry administered the final act in Leon's long life, he noticed the brute behind him with the hole through his chest, a signature move from his brother, Billy, if ever there was one. The blood from his body nearly drained completely as it spilled out across the penthouse floor.

Jerry's eyes returned to their jewel yellow, and his teeth grew larger. His fangs extended first, then the rest of his mouth opened up. His jaw began to extend longer and wider, taking on the form of a jackal. His jagged teeth grew larger from his gums in any direction they could, forcing his lips and mouth to extend open, as if they were trying to escape his mouth.

The bones in his face shifted beneath the skin, hidden ridges sliding into place until his cheekbones jutted sharp and high. His brow thickened, heavy, casting his eyes into shadow, and his eyebrows sprouted coarse hairs that had never been visible in his human guise.

The changes came quick, a mask of flesh reforged for flight and for war. He snapped his head back, throat opening, and a howl ripped out of him, vicious, unrestrained, a sound that clawed its way down the hallway and rattled through every corner of the building.

Heaving and catching his breath in his beast form, he looked down at Leon once more before ripping into his throat and swallowing every part of him.

CHAPTER 12
I DON'T CARE FOR DISTRACTIONS

A few days later, the afternoon breeze threaded its way between Manhattan's skyscrapers, carrying with it the city's noise and heat. Sunlight slid in and out of shadow as clouds drifted overhead, the glass towers flashing bright one moment, dim the next.

New York was slowly clawing its way back to normal. Its markets steadier, its streets restless with movement.

Lilly Thurman kept a ritual. After lunch she gave herself a few hours, then rolled out her mat at Yoga Box, her favorite yoga studio. When class ended, she drifted through the city for another hour, walking without purpose and letting Manhattan soak into her bones. She called it her power hour. Here, life roared at full volume. Not in her home town Bridgewater, not in Salem, but here.

On Eighth Avenue, the suits came in waves, briefcases swinging, faces blurred into sameness. It felt, to her, like a simulation where the background characters had all been copied and pasted.

She stopped short when she passed Eric's Electrics, a squat technology store on the corner of East 28th St. and Madison. In the wide display window, a row of wood-paneled television sets glowed with the same grainy Channel 5 broadcast. Antennas jutted upward like insect feelers.

Inside the screen, a young anchorwoman with a bouffant and a shoulder-padded suit stared into the camera, her expression grave. In the upper left corner, a photo filled a box, yellow police tape and a smear of blood across the grimy tile of Chambers Street Station.

The headline beneath made Lilly's stomach clench.

VAMPIRE KILLER?

She pressed her palms to the glass. Her eyes tracked each line of text as it scrolled across the bottom of the screens.

"...Police are still investigating the murder of a man found late Friday evening in Chambers Street Station. Witnesses say the victim's throat had been, quote, 'torn open,' though no weapon has been recovered. Investigators believe the killing may be connected to an earlier attack in the Financial District, where two young men were found in an alleyway bearing similar puncture wounds. Both men were pronounced dead at the scene, their bodies completely drained of blood.

"Authorities are also looking into a string of other homicides across the city in the past month. In those cases, the victims were also drained of blood, though no puncture marks were found. Detectives say there is, at present, no evidence linking these murders to the so-called 'torso killings,' a series of dismemberment cases currently under separate investigation, but they are not ruling out the possibility of a wider pattern."

The camera cut to a wide shot of the station entrance with uniformed officers standing stiff behind yellow tape. Then the screen split: on the right, the grainy still of a subway platform, two men walking toward the exit. One taller, broad-shouldered. The other leaner, his head turned as if speaking. Both dressed in dark clothing, their backs to the camera. The caption read: *Persons of interest in Chambers Station homicide.*

In the corner of the frame, barely noticeable, was a smear of red on the taller man's sleeve. The image had been captured by a woman who had just bought a new camera, coincidentally taking pictures of the station, when she noticed two men arm in arm hobbling out of the train cart, one of them seeming to be injured.

The anchor's lips kept moving as the subtitles chased her voice.

"The torso case, dating back to 1967, involves dismembered remains found along the Hudson and East Rivers. While the city has suffered an average of six homicides per day in recent years, authorities say

the Torso Murders and the Vampire Killer each present their own distinct, serial patterns. The most recent torso discovery was made just last week, when a fisherman found a pair of severed legs wrapped in burlap.

"Police stress there is no evidence linking the two series, but investigators admit both have stirred public fear. Forensic experts say the lack of weapon marks, combined with the precision of the exsanguination in the so-called Vampire Killer case, is highly unusual. Tonight, the NYPD is seeking two men described as tall, well-built, and last seen exiting a southbound train at Chambers Street shortly before the latest killing…"

B-roll flickered on the screen and showed police hauling a black body bag from the water.

The screen then cut back to the anchor.

"Investigators urge anyone with information on either case to contact the NYPD. They remind the public not to approach the individuals in the photograph, as they may be armed and extremely dangerous."

The news had spread through the city like wildfire, stoking a paranoia that even the most hardened criminals couldn't shake. Whispers of two homicidal maniacs, dubbed the Vampire Killer and the Torso Killer, rippled through subway cars, pool halls, and late-night diners. It was said they were painting the town red in the most literal sense.

Muggers who once prowled the parks after dark now stuck to daylight hours. Dealers in Washington Square cut their business short at sundown. Even the pimps along Times Square walked their girls home early, their usual swagger replaced with watchful glances at the shadows.

Daylight robberies still plagued the streets, but once night fell, the city's underbelly stayed indoors. Too many friends, too many co-criminals, had been found in dumpsters, headless, or pale as marble with every drop of blood gone. It was as if Jerry and Billy had solved Manhattan's crime problem.

THE AIR inside the precinct was a soup of cigarette smoke, stale coffee, and the faint tang of wet wool from a dozen coats drying on hooks by the door. Typewriters clacked, interrupted by the squawk of police radios and the occasional bark of a sergeant dressing down a patrolman.

Outside, Jacob Stein hesitated to walk in, clutching a shopping bag from his store like a lifeline. He hadn't planned to come here. He'd walked past the precinct twice already that morning, the Vampire Killer headline still rattling around in his skull like a loose screw.

The closer he'd come to the building, the heavier his legs had felt. His brain kept saying you're wasting your time, they'll laugh you out of here. But every time he tried to go home, the image of those two men in his store, the taller one's ice-water eyes, the shorter one's shirtless torso and insistence on wearing that *I* ♥ *New York* tee, immediately yanked him back toward the station.

He told himself it was civic duty, but the truth was darker. Jacob was afraid. Afraid because the news anchor's grainy crime scene photo had stirred up something he'd been trying to bury since that night. That strange hum in the air when they left the store. The way the taller one had smiled, like he knew something Jacob didn't, and wouldn't like once he found out. But more importantly, the way the smaller one didn't cast a reflection in any of the store's mirrors.

Jacob's bag had the *I* ♥ *New York* logo printed across it, looking suddenly absurd in a place like this. It was cheerful, cringy, and prompted a few laughs from the officers behind the desk.

A drunk slouched on the bench to his left, mumbling about his goddamn constitutional rights, while two uniforms hauled a cuffed man toward the holding cells in back.

The desk officer glanced up, his expression somewhere between curiosity and irritation.

"Help you with something, fella?"

Jacob stepped forward, his voice low. "I think I saw those guys. From the news. The Vampire Killer thing."

That was enough to make heads turn. The officer up front told him to wait for a second as he picked up his phone and dialed the detective who sat in a room to the left of the waiting area.

Jacob peered through the square window in the door.

The detective lifted his head, spotted him, then turned toward the officer who had made the call.

DETECTIVE LEONARD CALLOWAY had seen whack jobs wander into the precinct before, many with tall tales, some even confessing to murders they didn't commit just to feel important for a day.

Twenty years on the force meant there was very little left in the human condition that could surprise him, and the last decade in Manhattan alone had been enough to season him with a cynicism that stuck to his bones. Bank robberies gone wrong, mob hits disguised as accidents, the occasional domestic turned slaughterhouse. If it bled, Leonard had stepped in it.

He'd started as a beat cop in the Bronx in the late 50s and learned fast that the badge didn't make you invincible, it just made you a more visible target. But Leonard wasn't built like the others. He earned his stripes by walking into the kinds of crime scenes that made rookies puke and quit.

He could smell the body of a deceased without needing any nose balm to hide the smell. He could stare at a throat that had been ripped from its neck without flinching.

And while he didn't believe in ghosts, or anything that couldn't be explained by a switchblade or a bad decision, Leonard had been around long enough to know there were gaps. Gaps in cases, in human behavior, in the moments between one heartbeat and the next, where something happened that you couldn't put on paper.

It was those gaps that kept him awake.

Yet, at the end of the day, he would go home, kiss his daughters on the forehead, and make love to his wife with ease. And while the images stuck, he remained true to form. He had zero emotional sentiment about it; he knew this job wasn't about saving the world, it was about keeping the wolves from devouring the whole damn flock in one night. And if he had a knack for anything, it was smelling when trouble was more than it seemed.

❦

STEIN SAT in one of the molded blue plastic chairs bolted to the floor, facing the front desk like a student waiting outside the principal's office. He looked like he'd been lifted straight out of a high school yearbook, the kind of math club kid who spent lunch in the library.

His beige polyester pants were ironed into submission, the center seam sharp enough to cut paper. The cuffs were neatly turned up, revealing stark white socks above scuffed brown loafers, and between his knees, held tight as if it were a life preserver, sat the *I*  *NY* bag —the cheap kind with stiff handles and glossy plastic that crackled when it moved.

He kept one hand clamped over the top, not because anything valuable was inside, but because the act of holding it grounded him.

Every so often, his eyes flicked toward the heavy

glass entrance to the precinct, half-expecting, half-dreading that one of them might walk through. He told himself over and over that coming here had been the right decision. That the unease in his stomach was just nerves, not a warning. But the truth was, a sliver of him wished he'd kept his mouth shut and stayed behind his counter, selling souvenirs to tourists who'd never hurt him.

The detective in a wrinkled gray suit pushed back from his desk, stood upright, and pulled up his baggy pants by the brown leather belt around his waist. His tie was loose, and his shirt was yellowed at the collar from too many days on the job, but his eyes were sharp. He didn't say a word, other than motioning Jacob through the window and over to him.

The officer at the front desk walked around slowly toward the double doors, beckoning Stein over as he unlocked the door.

"Okay, you're up. Head down to that desk there," he grunted, cocking a thumb, letting Jacob wander through.

He walked slowly as he glanced around the room. The chaos of other officers, smoking and talking loudly. Some grouped together at one desk shooting the shit about the night before or some "broad" that happened to come across one of their paths.

They looked at Jacob as if he was a serial killer, his demeanor giving off a similar type of energy. It was this energy that Leonard knew to look for; it was the energy that separated a whack job from the saner of citizens, an energy that said, *I don't want to be here, but I am choosing to be.*

"Take a seat, Mister...?"

"Stein... Stein, Jacob Stein."

"Very good, Mr. Stein. Whaddaya know about the murders?"

Jacob told him about the two men who'd come into his store. "Mustache, the taller one had a mustache... I never trust men with mustaches, screams crazy to me," he said as he bent forward toward the desk, his bag still at his chest.

"They were after a shirt, something touristy. Ended up with the *I* 🩶 *NY* tee, same as on my bag here, see? Normally..." he stumbled, "normally people haggle with me. Everyone does. But not those two. They paid without a word and started talking about hitting a club uptown, like nothing in the world could touch them."

The detective cut in. "So two guys buy a t-shirt in your shop? Fascinating." Leonard's tone was dry enough to crack. "They give names? Say anything useful about that night?"

Jacob shook his head, then leaned forward. "They said they'd just moved to town. Something about a penthouse downtown. Had accents, but you could tell they were forcing the American sound." He hesitated. "And one of 'em didn't even have a shirt under his coat. He acted like it was life-or-death to get a new one. Asked me to dump the tag right there."

The detective's pen moved faster. "All right, thanks for coming in. If you think of anything else, give me a call." To Leonard, it sounded more like loneliness than evidence. Two men buying a tee didn't scream homicide.

"Wait. There's more." Jacob's voice sharpened.

Leonard dragged the word out. "Go onnnn."

"I saw blood. On the short one's skin. Mouth. Neck. Hard to explain, but I've had blood on my hands before. Tried to wash it off. It never comes clean. That's what it looked like."

This perked Leonard up and suddenly the dots came together. Two men, needing a new shirt, with blood stains on their skin. That changed everything.

"Would you recognize these guys again?"

"In my sleep." Jacob sat up rapt.

"I'd like you to meet with our sketch artist. Would you be available for that?"

"Yes, yes, of course. But listen, Detective, there's one other thing. And I want ya to know I'm not crazy, okay?" Jacob stuttered more, and he looked around, before leaning forward again.

"And what's this other thing?" the detective asked, raising an eyebrow.

"This guy, he didn't cast a reflection in any of my store mirrors. I thought it was odd at first and that I was tired, it was late after all, but the taller man, he was just fine. It was the shorter one. I pretended not to notice, but..."

Leonard's breath paused, as if the wind had been taken out from him.

"Okay, thank you, Mr. Stein. Listen, do you have time to hang around and I'll see if our sketch artist is available now?"

"Yes...yes, of course, whatever you need."

∼

It FELT like hours before Leonard returned with the sketch artist, but in reality it was a mere twenty minutes.

"Can I get you any coffee, Mr. Stein?"

"No, no, I'm quite all right, thank you."

"Mr. Stein, this is Paul, our sketch artist. He'll take notes, put a face together, and you just tell us if it matches what you saw. Sound good?"

Paul was a quiet man, thin as a broom handle, with a face as neutral as the blank sheet on his clipboard. Sketch artists, Jacob realized, were part detective and part confessor. They didn't just draw what you said; they coaxed it out of you, shaping the memory until it matched the ghost in your head.

Every stroke of his pencil was fast and focused, as if Paul had done this a hundred times before. Of course, he had. The first scribbles drew curiosity from Jacob, and he tilted his head, leaning over the desk subtly as he was trying to see what Paul was drawing.

"Mr. Stein, it will be much faster if you just sit back, relax, and let the artist do his work. Just answer briefly when questioned," Leonard interrupted.

First came the outline, a jaw that could have been carved from marble, the high cheekbones, the straight Roman nose.

Then the eyes. Paul lingered there, glancing up at Jacob as if measuring how much cold could be packed into an iris before it stopped looking human. Shadows deepened under the brow, a slight narrowing of the gaze, until the page itself seemed too tense.

The hair came next, thick and styled like someone out of a Californian beach commercial. The mouth was last, drawn with a kind of patience that felt unnerving; a subtle curl to the lips, the faintest hint of a smirk that made the whole face look like it knew something you didn't.

By the time Paul leaned back and set down the pencil, the man in the sketch wasn't just a picture. He was sitting there on the desk, staring at Jacob with those same unblinking eyes.

He slid the sketch toward Jacob. The noise of the paper shifting across the wooden desk made him feel uneasy, as if the secrets he'd been hiding from the store had finally come to fruition.

He stared at it for a long moment. It was him. Not "close enough" him, not "looks sort of like" him.

It was him.

Those eyes, so exact they might as well have been cut from his own memory and pasted to the page, stared back at him with that faint, knowing smirk.

Jacob's gaze drifted toward the precinct window, if only to break the spell. And that's when he saw him. Standing across the street, on the sidewalk, staring at Jacob. The denim flared jeans and black platforms, with the *I* ♥ *NY* tee tucked tightly. His gaze didn't waver as people walked behind, in front, and all around him. For half a heartbeat, the world went silent. Just the static hum of his own thoughts.

Then, as a truck roared past, Jerry was gone.

Jacob blinked, hard, and looked down at the sketch again. Those same eyes met his; he was looking at the vampire.

"Man... A vampire, a witch, the audacity of this bitch," Lilly said, her tone a mix of disbelief and humor as she read the ransom note Jerry handed her. She pursed her lips to one side, eyes scanning the lined paper like she could will some secret to surface. "I can't sense anything from this at all. And usually I can."

Jerry's voice was ice. "When I find her, I'll rip her fucking throat out."

"Yeah, I'm not gonna disagree with you on this one." Lilly's gaze didn't leave the note. "She was here."

Jerry's head snapped up. "What do you mean?"

"I mean exactly that. She was here. In this room. She's already transformed. I didn't think it would be this quick."

They stood in the penthouse's great room, the view behind them a glittering panorama of Manhattan at dusk. Ferries cut across the river, their wakes catching the last blush of daylight. Skyscrapers lit up in staggered patterns, a thousand watchful eyes peering down at 200 Water Street.

The fire in the hearth roared like it knew a storm was coming. There was no trace of Leon, the brute, or the pentagram. Jerry had cleaned it all away with the precision of a man who'd erased scenes like this for centuries.

"You saw the news," she continued. "They're going to come here. Maybe tonight. Maybe tomorrow. But they will."

"Let them come," Jerry said with a sharp smile. "I've handled this before."

"And where did that land you?" Lilly shot back.

Jerry's jaw tightened as a siren wailed in the distance. Not unusual for Manhattan, but Lilly noticed Jerry's eyes flick toward the window anyway. It was instinct. Predator's caution. The sound twisted through the streets, echoing up the side of the building until it bled into the crackle of the fire.

Lilly walked over to comfort him before delivering an additional piece of news that she knew Jerry wouldn't like. His arm was raised on the window for support as he looked down into the streets below, watching cars zoom by.

"I'm tired of this," Jerry whispered, his voice cracking.

"Listen, when I tell you I understand, you know it's the truth. But right now, I need to tell you something."

"Lilly, please, not now. I'm trying to figure out how to get my Billy back."

"This has to do with Billy. There's something you need to know. There's a reason Lucia needs Billy," she said quietly. "And it's not just for the book."

Jerry's eyes shifted as they found hers over his shoulder. "Why would she need him?"

"She can't do it alone." Lilly let her fingers trail along the heavy velvet curtain. "Spells like this don't come from one set of hands. They need alignment."

Jerry turned slightly, the city lights glinting in his yellowing eyes. "Alignment?"

She stepped closer to the glass. "Surgat needs three things to open the gates of Hell." She held up a finger. "A grimoire strong enough. Like yours."

"A second thing," she went on, raising another finger, "the blood of a half-breed."

"And the third..." Lilly let the pause linger, her eyes steady on his. "A human with even the faintest trace of magic."

She was now standing next to Jerry, looking out the window with him at the blurred city lights. "It's like a key that only works when it's in the right lock. The grimoire provides the lock, the half-breed's blood turns it, and the human...the human makes sure the door blows wide enough to swallow everything on the other side."

Instead of replying, Jerry walked away from the window and sat down in the buster chair by the fire.

The worn red leather that now looked almost black creaked under his weight as it adjusted to his figure. The fire was heavy, the flames dancing up into the chimney above in an effort to communicate with him. He gripped the arms of the seat, sinking his claws into the leather as it crushed and crinkled the seams, ripping them slightly.

"You've never encountered this before, huh?" Lilly asked, crossing the rug and lowering herself into the opposite buster chair. The firelight caught her cheek-bones, painting them in flickers of gold and shadow.

"It doesn't make any sense to me."

"I don't think it's meant to. At least not yet," she said, swirling the bourbon that had appeared in her hand as if it had always been there. "It makes more sense to me, I guess."

Jerry's eyes flicked toward her. "What do you mean?"

She took her time answering, letting the fire crackle

in the space between them. "I've spent my life in this arena. Spells, witches, the Devil. The strange and the terrible are my bread and butter. This," she gestured with her glass, "is my normal. You, though, you were touched by that demon once, long ago, and then left to drift. You've been existing. Not living in the mystique, not embracing it. You've grown used to the idea that you are what you are, and in that comfort, you've forgotten the deeper truth."

Jerry leaned back, the leather of his chair groaning. "And what truth is that?"

"That you're part of something bigger. Something that doesn't give a damn about your comfortable penthouse or the centuries you've survived. You feed because you have to, and you brood into that fire knowing damn well that the Devil is looking back. But you've let yourself think you're beyond it. You're not."

Her tone was sympathetic, but it cut like glass.

"Clever witch, aren't you?" Jerry said, but there was no real bite in it.

The call buzzer shattered the quiet like a gunshot. The harsh, metallic ring ricocheted off the high ceilings, bounced across the marble foyer, and hummed through the floor under their feet. Lilly's head snapped toward the wall-mounted intercom as if it had just spoken her name.

Jerry's eyes followed, slow but sharp, his jaw tightening again.

Neither of them moved at first.

The buzzer droned again, longer this time. Whoever was downstairs wasn't leaving. Lilly rose from her chair and Jerry mirrored her. They padded across the living room, bare feet whispering over the rug.

At the intercom they paused, trading a look that said, *You first.* Then Jerry pressed the black button.

"This is PH1," he said, voice frosty.

"NYPD. Sir, we need a word."

CHAPTER 13
BEWITCHED, BEWILDERED & BOTHERED

Leonard stayed on his feet the way he always did, moving his eyes across the opulent space, undoubtedly impressed by the penthouse, but not expressing it. People like Jerry needed no fluffing, and the less impressed Leonard acted, the easier it was to coax out information. He thumbed his notepad open, pen scratching a line or two of nothing, just for show.

The two uniforms stood either side of him. Doyle was young, broad through the chest, his hands shifting in and out of his pockets. He couldn't keep his eyes off the room and the many treasures that lay in open sight. Vasquez turned her cap in one hand, thumb working the strap. She'd been watching the fire since they came in.

"Tea, coffee, water, Officers? Or perhaps something stronger?" Jerry said, the corner of his mouth smirking.

"I'm on the clock." Leonard smirked back. "So look, Mr. Gellert, I believe?" he said. His voice carried that Bronx gravel that never washed off. "We're investigating a couple of incidents that seem to link back to this building, so I just wanted to ask a few questions, if I may? Last Friday of last month, around ten p.m. Where were you?"

"He was with me," Lilly said, her tone carrying the droll of boredom. She stood up and walked to Jerry's side. "All night, at that."

Leonard let the seconds stretch out a little longer. "And you are?"

"Lilly Thurman." She gave him a smile. "Though he makes it a point to call me his disco queen."

Doyle coughed something like a laugh and then remembered where he was. Vasquez's eyes flicked, once, toward a series of framed abstracts on the wall, then back to Leonard's notepad. She smirked knowing there was nothing on the notepad but a scribble.

"Ah, the alibi, huh?"

"Detective," Jerry said, gentle as a teacher about to correct a child's arithmetic, "you arrived in my home at night, unannounced, asking if I'm a murderer. Surely there's more to it?"

"There is," Leonard said, and finally reached into his coat. The paper he pulled out was already creased in quarters, soft from being folded and unfolded a dozen times.

He flattened it on the glass entry table between them. "An eyewitness put someone on a platform at Chambers Street that night. Two men. This ring any bells?"

A grainy photo showed two men walking arm-in-arm toward the exit. The taller one stood upright, broad and confident; he seemed to be holding up the smaller of the two.

Jerry warily watched Leonard watching him instead, a small game, then dipped his eyes to the image as if indulging him. "Those could be any two fellows in this city," he said. "Aren't we all just lovers in the dark from a certain angle?"

"Cute," Leonard said. He slid a second paper from his pocket. Paul's hand had been steady that afternoon and the sketch looked like an accusation. Wavy hair. Carved cheekbones. The mouth, a little cruel, a little charming. Eyes that didn't mirror light. He turned it so the face stared up at the man it pretended to be.

Lilly's wrist tightened around her glass. Vasquez shifted herself, biting her lip as she removed her hands from her pockets. In the hearth, the flames climbed a fraction higher, a nod to the Devil that could be in the room any given moment.

"Do you know how many men in this city have this hair style, Detective?" Jerry asked, his tone both curt and soft. "God bless American vanity."

"I'm not in the blessing business," Leonard said. He didn't blink. "Apparently you were seen in a store on Canal with an *I* ♥ *NY* shirt. Another customer saw you changing, slipping the tee over a naked torso. Now, why would you change in a store?"

Lilly cut in, saying, "I told you, he was with me all night. What's so hard to understand?"

Leonard allowed the briefest smirk. "What about your doorman, Mr. Leon Singer?"

"What about him?"

"Your doorman, Mr. Gellert, hasn't been seen since

two nights ago. Wife called him in missing. You notice anything unusual?"

Jerry drew a fingertip along the glass table, a small idle stroke. "Leon…is a creature of habit. I assumed vacation, or illness? Hardly a murder. The man is always about doing some kind of business in the building. This place has more than one doorman. And besides, I'm usually a man of the night. I work European hours, shall we say."

"Vacation," Leonard repeated, tasting the word. "And how would you know that, given you keep European hours?"

"Because I'm fond of people who hold doors," Jerry said. "It's an ancient art in decline."

Vasquez's radio crackled, prompting her to jump a little, startled almost, as she fumbled to turn the volume down.

Leonard finally wrote something down. A single word the others couldn't see. It wasn't *vacation*.

"Here's what's going to happen," he said, folding the sketch and the photograph back into his coat. "We're going to talk to a few other people. We're going to ask the other doormen what they've seen. We're going to pull every scrap of film this building owns, if any, and every shopfront on the block. And if I find that it was you who stepped off that train, I'll bring cuffs next time instead of questions."

"You misunderstand me," Jerry said, the smile returning, thinner now. "I have no fear of questions."

"That right?" Leonard asked. He stepped closer, into the warmth of the room. Close enough to smell something expensive under Jerry's cologne. Close enough to see that the man's pupils didn't quite behave like other men's pupils in low light. "Then riddle me one. How'd you know Leon Singer's case is a murder?"

"Detective," Jerry murmured, "everything in this city is a murder. Look around. Blaming an immigrant is hardly welcoming, now, is it?" he finished as he shot him a smile.

"Time to go," Leonard said to his officers without looking away. Doyle moved first, grateful to be told what to do. Vasquez lingered, her eyes doing the same lap they'd done since they arrived, the fire, the sketch's ghost on the table, the man who wasn't sweating under their heat.

Lilly stepped forward. "Detective," she said brightly, "if you decide to return with handcuffs, do bring the courtesy of a warrant. I'd hate to see you thrown out of this building."

Doyle again barked a laugh he regretted immediately, but Leonard didn't. The two officers walked out of the penthouse and into the hallway, calling for the elevator.

Back in the room, Leonard reached into his coat and produced a card. Plain white, black letters.

"If you remember anything," he said, "or decide to grow a conscience, you call. I might need to have you down the station tomorrow for a line up."

"I wouldn't expect my call," Jerry said.

"Very well. I guess the same as not expecting a reflection in that window then," Leonard answered as he nodded to the glass plates behind Jerry and Lilly. Then he turned on his heel, half-petrified and half-patting himself on the back for the bravado he'd just shown himself.

As the elevator doors slid shut on the penthouse, Leonard watched the seam of them narrow and pretended he didn't feel his stomach in his throat.

He told himself it was just the light. He didn't believe himself.

THE ELEVATOR WHINED as it sank. Leonard hated elevators in towers like this. The building was new, but the elevator was too clean and fast. Doyle adjusted his belt for the fifth time, the clink of his radio spritzing in murmurs that weren't meant for him. Vasquez stood stiff, staring into her reflection, wondering how she would be able to one day afford a penthouse like the one she'd just witnessed.

Leonard didn't speak right away. He let the hum of the machinery fill the silence.

Sure enough, Doyle shifted himself and said, "Guy's a creep. There's something really off about him. Talks like one of those snooty-ass college professors. Dresses like he's full of himself."

Leonard's jaw flexed, but his eyes stayed on the floor numbers. They glowed red as the car descended, like a countdown to Hell.

"I don't like it," Vasquez muttered. Her voice was softer, meant for herself, but in the mirror Leonard saw her eyes dart. "I'm tellin' ya, the Devil lives in that apartment. That fire was nothing if not evil."

Doyle snorted, eager to dismiss. "It's a fire. All fires are evil. It's incumbent on something that burns to be so."

"Incumbent, Doyle? Where'd you go and learn five-dollar words?" Vasquez smirked.

"Crossword today," Doyle said, his face darkening.

The car jolted as it hit the thirteenth floor, then continued. Leonard leaned back against the wall, his hands loose at his sides. "Men like him don't sweat, Doyle. They don't flinch. You know why?"

"Because they're guilty?" Doyle asked.

"Because they've had centuries to practice."

Doyle laughed, short and awkward, as if trying to shake the words off. He wasn't quite sure what Leonard meant. Vasquez didn't. She put two and two together and came up with four. She knew what the detective meant.

The detective pulled the folded sketch from his pocket. He let his thumb trace the pencil lines as if trying to assure himself he was right. He breathed a heavy sigh. The resemblance had been too sharp to ignore. And Jerry had smiled at it, like the damn thing was an inside joke.

"You know what smug bastards hate most?" Leonard asked, still staring at the sketch.

"What?" Vasquez said.

"Evidence." He slid it back into his coat. "They think they're untouchable. Then you find one nail sticking out the coffin lid, and you pry until the whole box comes open."

The elevator slowed again. They were almost at the lobby.

"Tomorrow," Leonard said, his tone clipped now, businesslike. "We start with Stein. Walk him through every angle of that lineup. If Jerry so much as breathes sideways, Stein's memory will put him on the hook."

Doyle nodded, eager. "And surveillance?"

"It's all so new. Street cams. Building cams. Anything with a lens in a two-block radius." Leonard snapped his fingers. "I want film that shows what our witness saw. You get me that, we walk into court with a hammer."

The night air rushed them when the lobby doors opened. It bit Leonard's face like a slap and cleared the last of Jerry's cologne from his lungs. He welcomed it. The city outside was alive in its usual diseased way, sirens in the distance, a cab horn bleeding down the avenue, two drunks shouting at each other in a language Leonard didn't recognize. All of it felt normal, and it comforted him. It was the silence that scared him.

Vasquez caught up with him, her voice low. "Boss... If Stein locks up tomorrow, if he can't do it—"

Leonard cut her off with a glance. "He'll do it."

As the doors closed behind them, Doyle asked, "So what's the next move after Stein?"

Leonard didn't stop walking. He pulled his coat tighter against the wind. "After Stein, we put in for a warrant. And then we go back up to that palace in the sky and walk that bastard straight through Stein's memory. Step for step. Word for word. He won't grin then."

That bastard's smile was still in his head. Like a song you loved and couldn't erase from your memory. Leonard had seen mob bosses grin like that before the knives came out. But this one wasn't the mob. This one was worse.

～

THE PENTHOUSE WAS QUIETER once the elevator doors sealed.

"I just want to be perfectly clear," Lilly said, her voice low but hard, "I don't condone any of this."

Jerry turned his head slowly in an almost reptilian motion. His brow creased faintly, more amusement than surprise. "Any of what?"

She gave a humorless laugh and ran a hand through her hair, shaking her head. "Don't play coy. I saw the sketch. I saw the photo. And I just helped you lie your way out of a murder investigation."

The firelight caught his royally high cheekbones. He didn't reply. Which was worse than if he had denied it.

"I have made a lot of deals," she said, walking the room, arms folded. Her nails tapped the fabric of her sleeve like a metronome. "This is the first time I have covered a cold-blooded killing because I did not want someone I like to end up in cuffs."

She let the sentence sit, then pushed it further with a laugh that had no humor. "Okay, the second. Vampires make more trouble than they are worth." She said it as if trouble was an old friend, as if she knew the shape of it up close.

Jerry rose and closed the short distance between them.

"Not now," Lilly said. Her voice broke once and then found its edge. "You lost control, Jerry. Do not give me that feeding or survival sermon. Leon was someone you knew. If you expect me to smile and be your alibi every time you snap, you are wrong."

"I did not ask you to. You know what I am."

"No, you did not. But you let me do it anyway." She shook her head. "And the man on the subway, his partner. Do not pretend that was not you."

Lilly exhaled, hands smoothing her blouse until the fabric lay flat. She turned to the windows. Moonlight poured across the buildings.

"Just tell me you will not make it worse," she murmured.

Across town, in a cluttered back room stacked with boxes and tomorrow's inventory, a man who had made it worse watched the city through a cracked window. He sat very still and waited.

He would not last the night.

THE CLOCK HIT two a.m. as Jacob Stein sat in the back room of his tourist store.

In the back office, he kept his accounting books, a small television, and a little fridge tightly stacked around one another.

The room was small, around six by six feet, and allowed for a small desk amongst the other items that kept Stein comfortable during quiet times in the store, or after hours, when he simply wanted to get his accounting done while chewing on a sandwich and watching Henry Winkler on *Happy Days*.

The fluorescent light above him illuminated the wooden walls that surrounded the room, it ticked and flickered occasionally when the subway train underneath ran through.

Nothing to be concerned about. But tonight, it flickered even when the train didn't move. And that was cause for concern for a man that was already on edge.

Stein didn't plan on sleeping much tonight. He was already regretting the moment he'd stepped into the precinct, the moment he saw a phantasm of Jerry stood in the daylight outside of the window, as the sketch artist scribbled his replica on a piece of white paper. He also regretted agreeing to witness a line up the next afternoon.

Instead of locking himself away in his closet of an office, it would have been easier to keep the shop open all night and stand behind the cashier's desk.

But the potential for nodding off into a deep slumber, only to wake with half of his products stolen was too much to bear. He barely made enough cash as it was. Rents were high and his products were cheap.

He couldn't charge more than $5 for a small replica of the Statue of Liberty, and could hardly charge more than $15 for a crappy *I* ♥ *NY* tee. The rent for his store and his cramped studio apartment set him back around $1,000 per month, and he had to sell four t-shirts a day just to break even.

On top of that, rising costs in Manhattan meant money was sparse.

He brewed another pot of coffee until a noise from outside interrupted him. A mist of fine brown powder sprayed across the desk instead of into the filter it was meant for. *Dammit.*

He laid the coffee scoop down and perused the peephole, trying to normalize the noise that emanated from outside.

Nothing.

He turned back toward the room, eyes darting, sweat sliding from his brow as he attempted to retrieve some of the fine coffee powder that had sprayed across the desk.

A noise.

He spun again, stooping toward the peephole.

And there he was. Jerry, standing outside the store in the shirt Stein remembered selling. Only the metal shutters stood between them.

A whimper caught in Stein's throat as he lunged for the telephone. He ripped the receiver from the base, his wet palm slipping, dropping it against the desk. The cord tangled and jerked uselessly as he scrambled to catch it. He pressed the switch hook again and again.

Click, click, click.

But no dial tone came. Only silence.

The walls seemed to close in. The office shrank around him. He glanced at the ceiling as his mind was racing. Could he climb through? Squeeze into the ducts? Find some impossible way out? His legs trembled as he bent back toward the peephole.

Jerry was gone from the shutters. He now stood by the cash register inside, watching the office door.

Stein looked again and lowered his head against the

wood, his arms braced against it, as though pressing hard enough might actually keep it closed. Tears blurred his eyes as he pleaded into the grain.

Slowly, with his hand shaking, he turned to reach the dialer again, but it was no use; the cold plastic of the telephone pressed to his ear returned nothing but palpable silence.

There was no lifeline out of the small room. The cord had been cut from somewhere on the other side, and Stein was realizing the cold hard reality that this night could be the end of him.

"You've caused me a great deal of trouble, Mr. Stein."

The voice traveled throughout the store and into Jacob's back office as if transmitted by a virtual Tannoy.

He didn't answer back. The mouse was now fully cornered, the cat outside. He panicked, ruffling through the papers on his desk, searching for nothing but anything at the same time. His older fingers plagued by arthritis, he began to breathe heavily, his chest rising deep as he gasped for air.

"Please, please, I'll tell them I was mistaken," he pleaded at Jerry, who was now on the other side of the door, rattling the knob with his claws.

"Jacob. Open the door."

The demand came soft and slow. Jerry didn't want to kill the old man. He wanted to get on with his life. The death of the witness would cause more problems for him, should he suddenly vanish.

But Jacob had given too much away, and that cut deep for the vampire.

The rattling had stopped, but Stein knew it wasn't

over. On the other side of the door, Jerry had already come apart, his body started to break down into a dark vapor that pressed against the seams. It wasn't smoke the way Stein knew it.

Smoke drifted and scattered. It moved with intent, sliding low then upward, filling every gap as though it already knew the map of the room.

Stein pressed himself into the door, holding fast. And then he saw it: thick threads pushing under the frame, gray and writhing, like fingers feeling their way in.

More of it followed, rolling into the office in slow waves, pooling across the floorboards, lifting into the stale air. It looked like the store was on fire, and the smoke was breaking through into the room.

His throat went tight. He wanted to scream, but couldn't find the breath. The room felt smaller with every inch the vapor claimed.

It now bellowed into the room, brushed against the legs of the desk, spread beneath the chair he had just stumbled from. It was alive. It was looking for him, and it was regaining shape.

Jacob began rummaging for anything else that would help him—a weapon, a Bible, anything. He tore through receipts, bottle caps, a bent letter opener, until his hand landed on cool metal.

A crucifix.

His grandmother's. He had mocked it for years, but now it felt like a lifeline. He clutched it with both hands like a drowning man to driftwood, whispering whatever fragment of prayer he could remember from his childhood, and held it toward the mist.

The smoke that had slowly started reforming began to shake, expand and contract. Dancing around the room like it was confused.

Eyes that belonged in Hell formed in the smoke as it hissed at the old man.

Stein shot up, getting to his feet without his hands leaving the crucifix. He turned the lock to the metal door and ripped it open, bolting out of the back office and out through the emergency exit to the street.

A feral Jacob Stein flew out the exit, gasping for air as the Manhattan night slapped him in the face, the door clanking hard as it smashed against the wall that held its hinges. The cold concrete on the ground hit him even harder as he tripped on trash that hadn't been cleared, his glasses skittering across the wet sidewalk.

He scrambled blind for his lenses, murmurs and tears leaving the orifices of his face as he panicked to find the delicate metal of his circular frames.

Salvation. He touched the familiar frame with his thumb and immediately pulled them to his face, shoving the smeared lenses over his ears with his trembling hands. The world returned—blurry, wet, refracted by tears, but it was the world nonetheless.

Now, he had nothing else to do but run.

STEIN WAS BORN IN MANHATTAN. He knew every avenue, every street, every alleyway shortcut that taxis would brag about. But tonight, the city was a stranger. It had twisted on him—buildings leaned differently, signs glowed like spells, and the sidewalks stretched too long between streetlights. It wasn't just disorientation; it was a maze. And he was the rat.

He jogged for three blocks as his lungs were giving out. He wasn't built for this anymore, if he ever had been.

The night air clawed at his throat as he stumbled to a halt beneath a blinking streetlight and bent over, wheezing with his hands on his knees. The crucifix still dangled in one of them, slick with sweat.

Then the ground hissed. From the nearest subway grate, a jet of smoke burst into the air, and within it, Jerry emerged.

No longer the smug man in the tourist tee. This was something older. His face was shadowed. His fangs caught the light, long and sharp, as his eyes shone like two lanterns, glowing with fury and hunger.

Stein let out a dry, hopeless yelp as his knees almost buckled. And then, to his right, a potential port of hope. A loading dock. The kind truckers used to back into with crates of dead animal meat. It had been left wide open. The plastic flaps trembling in the wind. The back-light inside the warehouse buzzing weakly, casting just enough of a glow to make the entrance feel like a portal to safety.

He ran toward it. The plastic strips slapped him in the face as he pushed through, the cold interior air smacking into him like a freezer blast. His shoes squeaked on the concrete slick with water and old blood.

Metal hooks dangled from overhead rails, still faintly

swinging as if they, too, were nervous. The room was bleak, dark, and cold. And Stein didn't know where to run first.

He ducked low and bolted deeper into the factory, weaving between swinging carcasses of pigs and cows, their bodies glazed in frost, their hollow eye sockets staring at him. The smell of cold death filled his nostrils.

He ran to the end of the room, whatever room it was, and dropped to his knees, crawling behind a piece of rusted machinery, curling into himself like a child hiding under blankets. His crucifix trembled in his grip.

The sound of Jerry's steps echoed throughout the warehouse. He walked slow. One step, then another, then silence.

"Jacob, Jacob, come out, come out, wherever you are," the vampire teased.

Stein looked into the opening of the warehouse, far beyond his reach right now. The blackness blanketed the room save for the large lamp in the alleyway that shone a small glow of hope throughout the hall.

He now regretted running into the meat packing factory. *If I make a run for it, I might just be able to get out.*

One of the pigs started to sway in the distance. The hooks above Stein then trembled as though some invisible wind had set them swaying. One clinked against another with a hollow ring. Then another. The sound built slowly like a devilish choir had come for him.

Stein pressed himself tighter against the rusted machine, his breath fogging the cold air. He tried to silence it, but every wheeze of his lungs came out louder than he intended.

The warm fog of his breath acted like a lighthouse to the vampire that was closing in. His hand clenched the crucifix until the edges cut his palm.

"Jacob…" Jerry's voice echoed through the room, carrying effortlessly over the racks of hanging flesh. "You know running won't save you. It never saves anyone, and yet everyone thinks it does."

He bit his tongue to keep from sobbing, and covered his ears with his hands, as he saw the shadow of the vampire along the far wall. His fangs were even visible; elongated by the angle of the shadow, Jerry's teeth looked a foot long.

Stein tried to crawl sideways, pushing himself deeper into the machine's shadow. His knees slipped in something wet. He glanced down. A pool of thawed blood, black in the dim light.

The hooks clinked again.

And then one dropped.

The carcass of a pig, half-thawed and stinking, hit the floor with a wet thud a few feet away. Stein jerked back with a strangled yelp, and crawled into the open to a waiting Jerry.

He stood at the other end of the machine. The vampire's eyes glowed faintly; his fangs bared.

"You gave them my name," Jerry said, stepping forward. "You painted my face onto paper. Do you know what that means?"

Stein's crucifix shot up between them, his arm trembling but unyielding. "Stay back!"

Jerry paused. The light caught his smile. "Faith." He

almost sounded pleased. "You have to have faith for that to work on me."

Jerry unleashed menacing laughter in the quiet place.

Stein's lips quivered, words spilling out ragged and fast. "I am a Roman Catholic, and believe me, I have faith."

The vampire hissed and recoiled, just slightly. He covered his glowing yellow eyes with his claw-like hands before dropping them and laughing at Stein once more.

Stein's hope flared as the crucifix glowed ever so slightly. He surged forward, pressing the cross out like a weapon. "The Lord is my shepherd; I shall not want..."

But Jerry disappeared. One moment he stood across the warehouse, the next his breath ghosted hot against Stein's ear. Fingers like iron clamped around Stein's wrist, forcing it down. The crucifix burned against Jerry's palm, smoke curling between them, but the vampire didn't let go.

"You almost believed," Jerry raged, burning eyes aglow, spreading malevolent light from his face onto Stein's.

Stein screamed as his wrist snapped, the crucifix clattering to the concrete. It skittered beneath the hooks, sliding out of reach, and Jerry shoved him backward, his frail body cracking against the machine.

Stein gasped, tears streaking his face. "Please, please, I have only one child left..."

Jerry's eyes blazed, the yellow burning brighter. "I don't want your begging." He leaned close, lips brushing Stein's ear. "I wanted your silence."

Jerry's claw slashed at Stein's torso, a long strip of crimson red spilling out almost immediately. Stein screeched and tried to scoot back away from Jerry, his palms working overtime as he crawled backward like a spider.

Then, from nowhere, Jerry appeared again fast, striking Stein across his face, spilling more crimson onto the ground.

The vampire was taunting the old man. Punishing him for what would now be a never-ending circle of accusations from the NYPD.

It was clear that Leonard couldn't be bought, and whether Stein stopped short of giving evidence, or whether he was dead, it wouldn't matter. He had now set in motion the eventual downfall of Jerry the vampire via a detective who wasn't going to stop.

Stein managed to get on all fours, drag himself up to his knees, and hobble toward the entrance of the warehouse.

He bashed into the two-hundred-pound pigs that hung from the hooks above, knocking them any which way he could to get out. His glasses had already fallen from his face again, and now all he could do is run toward the blurry light at the entrance and grip his lacerated torso as tight as he could.

The pigs gave him an advantage; Jerry couldn't see beyond them either.

The blurry light was getting closer, and Stein felt a sense of victory about to kick in. Outside, police lights blurred and wailed, a nod from Detective Leonard, who assumed someone might try to take the life of the shopman before the night was through.

Stein reached the entrance to the warehouse and called out to the officers who were a hundred feet away on the main street off the alleyway.

But it was too late. Jerry's hand wrapped around his face, each finger 10 inches in length, the fingernails like silver blades attached to the limbs.

A murmur from Stein, and then silence, as the claws dug deep into the man's face, piercing anything in its way. One finger dug into his eye socket so deep that it vanished.

The other crept into his mouth, piercing the tonsils and back of his throat. Jerry's other hand dug into Stein's back, cutting into the flesh like a hot knife through butter. Until Stein stopped screaming.

His body jerked once, twice, then slumped as Jerry dragged him back into the warehouse and fed.

The sound was obscene, wet, desperate gulps echoing through the factory. The hooks above swung harder, clinking as if to reflect the gutturalness of the vampire's hunger.

When Jerry finally lifted his head, Stein's face was pale, eyes rolled back, mouth frozen mid-plea. The crucifix still lay glinting beneath the carcasses, smeared with blood and useless now.

Jerry wiped his mouth with the back of his hand. He stood for a moment, listening to the cops walk down the alleyway, flashing their lights into the opening.

"There's blood down there. Ya see it?" one cop said in his heavy New Yorker accent.

"Dude, it's a fucken pig factory. You dumb or some-thin'? Prolly someone forgot to shut the door is all," the comrade replied, and he leapt up to grab the rope that would close the door to the warehouse. He pulled it tight, and the door slammed shut with a loud metal thud that would be heard a block away.

And when Jerry had drained the shopkeeper of all the blood he had, he picked him up and hung him upon a pig hook before vanquishing into smoke once more, and returning back to his abode.

AT THE PENTHOUSE, the fire had gone out. Only embers glowed faintly in the grate. Lilly stood at the window, her arms folded tight, watching the city breathe beneath her. Her jaw worked silently, her eyes fixed on the lights below.

Jerry stepped inside without any sound, his coat still damp with blood. He didn't announce himself.

"You killed him," she said.

Jerry's silence was answer enough. Lilly turned, her eyes hard. "Every time you do this, you make it harder for me to stand by you. Do you understand that?"

Jerry met her stare as he poured himself a drink, the clink of glass on glass filling the quiet. "The city won't miss one old man."

Lilly stood stiff as she turned her gaze back to the glass, her reflection layered over the skyline. For a heartbeat, she looked like one of the city's statues, immovable, cold, backlit by lights that flickered as if afraid of her. She didn't turn when Jerry crossed the room.

"Say something," he said, setting his glass down on the bar.

"What's left to say?" Her voice sounded exhausted. "You're still a monster. And I'm still the fool who thought I could make you something else."

Jerry's jaw tightened, but no rebuttal came. He knew she was right. Monsters didn't get cleaned up by love, or by clever alibis talking in detectives' ears.

The embers cracked faintly in the fireplace. Smoke drifted lazily toward the ceiling, stretching as if it wanted to take shape. Lilly's gaze flicked upward and for a second, she saw a face in the smoke.

"I'm leaving," she said suddenly. "This city's getting louder with everybody that drops. Louder with you. If you want to drown in it, fine. But I won't go down with you."

Jerry stepped closer. "And yet..." His voice was low, almost a growl. "You're still here."

That silenced her more effectively than a hand around her throat. Because he was right. For all her threats, she was still tethered to him by something deeper than sense or survival.

Something older and darker. And deep down, Lilly knew what it was.

FAR FROM THE PRECINCT, far from the penthouse, in a

house on a dead-end street in Red Bank, New Jersey, something else stirred.

The demon, Surgat, lay coiled in formless smoke, bathed in all of Hell's acridity, waiting.

CHAPTER 14
I'LL RAISE HELL

The house in Red Bank had been dead long before Surgat moved in.

A modest three-up, two-down with peeling white shiplap and newspaper-covered windows, it had been foreclosed years ago, left to rot in the salt air. The stark furniture that remained hadn't been sold at auction. Splintered chairs, a sofa with its stuffing clawing out from the seams, and an old grandfather clock that stopped in some other decade.

At the end of the narrow hallway, wedged between the kitchen and the staircase, stood the door to the basement. The wood swelled with damp, hinges rusted orange, the knob coated with the grease of a hundred long-forgotten hands. Inside, the stairwell leaned down into blackness.

Each plank of step groaned with damp fatigue, threatening snapping.

It was the kind of staircase that dared you to

descend, promising that once you did, the house would snap its jaws shut and keep you forever.

Light didn't belong down there. The high basement windows, too narrow for escape, let in only moon-silver slivers, a mockery of illumination.

And somewhere inside this decrepit mausoleum of haunt and rotting memory was Billy Cole.

Bait.

And those for whom he was bait, they were beckoned in the dead of the night.

Given the time of the night, the two drove to New Jersey fast, the witch and the vampire. Two ethereal beings in a car made for humans on the way to destroy a demon. What could go wrong?

The car's deluxe interior relaxed Jerry. Its amber leather, mixed with subtle strip lighting that cast a golden hue on the shadows of the night, gave way for a pleasant ride to Hell.

When the pair arrived in Red Bank, they parked at the end of the street to the house, slowly and quiet as they could. The air around them was quiet, and the sky was the perfect mix of black and midnight blue, with the stars above twinkling back at them. From the end of the street, they could see the demons circling above the possessed house.

"There," Lilly said, nodding at the desolate ruin of a house. "The demon is in there. I can feel its presence."

"I can feel Billy's," Jerry said.

"What's our plan?" Lilly asked.

"Isn't this your territory?" Jerry asked, breaking his gaze and turning to her. "Having danced with demons and Devils before, one would think you'd know a thing or two more than me."

"I have. And I would know a thing or two. But there's a powerful cloaking spell at play here. I can only pierce it enough to sense Surgat's presence, not more. We might as well be going in blind."

"Trust me, darling. Cats and vampires, we never go in blind."

Jerry let the house arrest his attention once more. He opened the door to the Range Rover slowly as he climbed down onto the road.

It took Lilly a second to join him, her hands still on the wheel. She tapped them on it, more inquisitively than nervously. She'd seen this house before. In apocryphal visions showing her the end of days, when Lucifer himself would walk the earth. A time when the antichrist would be born. A future not so distant.

Jerry didn't wait around for her, he slowly started walking toward the house, forcing Lilly out of the vehicle to join him. She closed the door as softly as she could before trotting over to his side.

"Listen," Lilly whispered as she jogged to catch up to him. "You have to be very careful once we're inside, this thing already knows we're here, and will do anything to get what it wants."

Jerry ignored her as they reached the front of it. They both paused.

"You see this?" Lilly whispered.

"Of course I do."

The place was alive. Not in the way mortals would see it, just a rotting shell slouched on a fog-choked street, but in the way only those tied to the underworld could perceive. To Jerry and Lilly, the air itself burned with a cold light.

A glow of sickly blue and white clung to the house, rising hundreds of feet into the night, tethering it to the heaving storm clouds above. Within that glow writhed shapes and faces that stretched out of the clouds.

Spirits of the dead that looked like vampires, werewolves, and other creatures of the night smiled as they danced above the structure. Their shapes trailed behind them like smoke, circling the roofline, diving and clawing upward, holding for the signal to cross into flesh.

Hellions from the pit, they gathered, snarling silently at the promise of release. They were guarding the house. They were waiting, hungry gazes glazing over every surface, looking for anything that moved.

"I'm just trying to wrap my head around it being this easy. And fast," Jerry growled.

"It wasn't easy, or fast. This demon has been watching you for centuries. You thrived in a world it expected you to die in. It doesn't want you to succeed."

Jerry took a step forward as Lilly grabbed his arm. "Careful."

The front door creaked for a moment. For both Lilly and Jerry, their immortal hearts began to beat faster. This was a scenario that neither of them had experienced before.

Jerry stood firm. He had fought battles blindly with no knowledge of what waited on the other side of hills and mountains. He had been visited by a demon when he had turned. He had talked to the Devil through fire when he needed to prove his mortality to humans in order to escape death. But they faced a sobering realization, that this evening could be the end of them.

The door continued to creak, then slowly opened, exposing the blackness within. The demons above still flying up and around the house, ignoring the two immortals that stood before it.

But the witch and the vampire had bigger things to be concerned about. Lilly grabbed Jerry's hand, and he looked at her, surprised almost, like he didn't need her support but wanted it anyway.

They walked up the path and into the house. The doorway was dark, and neither of them could see inside, except for the moonlight above casting a scant amount of light onto various fixtures.

They stepped inside. Any concern of closing the door behind them fell short; they didn't need it, as it closed for them the moment they stepped inside.

They could hear each other's breaths. Standing in silence for a moment, they looked around the dilapidated home, taking stock of whatever the moonlight would allow them to see.

And in the corner of the living room, a living darkness sat in an old fabric armchair. Its arms and hands were planted firmly on each armrest as the broad-looking figure sat in the shadows, not moving.

A grandfather clock slowly ticked in the room.

"Do you know who I am?" it cough-croaked at them.

"I have an idea," Lilly responded. She held her arm out, fully slamming it into Jerry's chest to stop him launching forward toward the figure, pushing him back as she stepped forward.

"Do you know who I am?" she asked back.

"You smell it, don't you?" the voice said, still croaky, almost sickly. "It's in the walls. On the ceiling. In the fibers of the carpet. What I've done."

Lilly said nothing.

"I don't speak of Babylon now," it continued, "though I could. I speak of now. This city. Your city. The one you think you've protected with little charms and half-channeled invocations in circles of salt. Does your comrade know what you are, Miss Frost?"

Its voice deepened and gained more gravel and shape. If this thing had smoked a hundred cigarettes that very day, it wouldn't have been a surprise.

"I've walked your streets in shoes bought for men long dead. I've sat beside women on subways while they cried into their coats. I've followed them home under scaffolding. Listened to their lives. Learned their habits."

It leaned forward into the moonlight, revealing for a breath of time not a face, but the suggestion of many, stacked like tissue. It was the body of the larger brute. Mario.

"I take only what I can cherish," it said, heaving as if to take a breath, like it was learning the vocal chords of the man it possessed. "The young ones. Those who hum to themselves without realizing. Who pray each evening to their God."

The demon paused and took a satisfying breath before letting out a cackle of laughter fit only for a lunatic.

"They scream, Lilly. Oh, do they scream. I enjoy their screams; it helps blur out the noises in my head."

She stepped closer.

"You're the Torso Killer," she said.

It chuckled back at them, a chuckle that came from the pits of Hell, evil and vile.

"Ahhh... I've been given many names," it said, savoring the line like wine. "That one is new. It fits. I like it. Before this city had rats in its subways and halos on its towers, they called me Kudurru in Akkad. 'Boundary stone.' But not of land. Of body. Of soul. I divided them, you see. I still do."

Jerry's fangs showed slightly now, unconsciously.

"You chopped them up," Jerry said.

"Like you, I liberated them." The demon cackled. "I turned body into artifact. I removed identity. Mysteries, Mr. Catura. Isn't that what art is?"

Neither of them answered.

"The mother found the torso two blocks from the laundromat. Her daughter's head, later, in a plastic bag. Do you know what I wrapped it in?"

"Does it matter?" Jerry said.

"I wrapped it in Christmas paper. Isn't that poetic? And last week, the waitress. She wore a yellow dress. I kept her coat. I like yellow."

Lilly's voice came in sharp.

"You're lying."

The figure stiffened slightly.

"I lie not."

"You're not the Torso Killer," she said, arms crossed. "You read about him. You wanted a name, so you took one."

The demon shook and pulsed the room, a wave of vibrations bolting out and slamming into Jerry and Lilly, disorientating them both.

"Careful," it said as it lifted its demonic fingers and flicked them up and down.

"No," Lilly said, stepping forward. "I've heard demons like you a thousand times. Always with the ancient names. Always with the riddles. But you're all just scavengers. Bottom-feeders for attention. You can't do anything unless someone gives you credit. You're not powerful, you crave attention, otherwise what's the point?"

Its voice dropped to a near whisper.

"I have turned this city into my cathedral, witch."

"No," she said. "You're squatting in a burned-out home, wearing dead skin and trying to sound important. The real Torso Killer, he was never caught. Maybe you saw his work and decided it was yours. Or maybe you're nothing but shadow and story, like the rest."

The temperature dropped in the room to a chill.

"What you seek is down below," it whispered.

The demon shifted abruptly, but not toward them. It vanished backward, folding into its own silhouette, getting smaller and smaller until it disappeared from view. Lilly and Jerry turned. A faint flicker came from beneath the basement door at the end of the hallway. The metronome, wherever it was, had begun again.

Tick.

Tick.

Tick.

Without speaking, they walked toward the basement.

～

Below, the blackness was unlike anything they'd seen before, viscous, even, except for a glowing red ember coming from somewhere else in the basement. The deeper they descended, the more it thickened, as if the dark were no longer an absence of light but something physical.

The lightbulb hanging from the ceiling swung gently on a length of brittle cord, its glow stuttering with every sway. Lilly lifted her hand and snapped her fingers. The bulb flared once, then settled into a weak amber glow that revealed the room for what it truly was.

The smell came next, metallic and sulfuric.

Both Jerry and Lilly's eyes darted everywhere they could to familiarize themselves with the potential monsters below, avoiding the horror that Billy Cole lay dead and cold at the bottom of the stairwell.

Jerry noticed first and gasped.

Not a sound of surprise, but a sound pulled from somewhere deeper. Lilly barely registered the motion before Jerry shoved her aside on the stairwell, his feet hitting the concrete hard as he lunged forward and dropped to his knees beside Billy's body.

His half-breed blood had poured from his ears, his

nose, and mouth, congealed now into black stains that traced down his throat and pooled into his collar and onto the concrete. But it was his open eyes that held Jerry in place, still staring into the low-hanging bulb above them.

He touched his face, gently at first, then urgently. His fingers searched for warmth, a pulse, any sign of resistance in the flesh. But there was nothing; the skin was cold and the breath was gone.

Then Jerry's breath became heavier and angry as his face and body began to morph into his full vampiric state. His eyes yellow once more, his teeth congested as each one of them grew into sharp daggers. His face was pale from the realization that the bond he'd carried for centuries was gone.

Behind him, Lilly didn't move. Her focus was elsewhere. Her eyes lifted from Billy's body to the wall on the other side of the room. The smaller brute lay dead in the wall as if he'd been absorbed. Half of his torso was fused with the cracked concrete, as if the wall had liquefied and swallowed him slowly.

His skin was gray where it stretched thin like latex. From the shoulder down, his arm disappeared completely into the structure, lost somewhere inside the architecture.

She stepped aside Jerry and walked toward it.

The wall convulsed, just once, and a jagged crack split down its center as the wound split open from pressure within. A thin stream of smoke hissed outward. It smelled like scorched meat and rotten eggs. Beneath the surface, faces began to push forward; one, then another, their features warped. They had been melted in the fiery furnace of Hell and now they oozed through the fractures.

Hands came next, long black fingers stretching from within the seams, tapping along the inner frame of the wall like spiders climbing their webs.

And then came the sound. Cries of agony and despair echoed throughout the basement, wailing and crying as the creatures within were inches from their escape. Jerry joined Lilly's side as the pair looked on in amazement at the scene in front of them.

"What is it?" he asked quietly, still watching the wall as the surface began to blister and stretch.

"Katabasis. A gateway to Hell," Lilly said, her breath rattling, her fingers trembling.

Jerry took a step back, eyes growing wider with shock and the ferality of the spectacle. "They are alive."

"They once were," Lilly said, harrow and sorrow the baritones of her voice.

For a moment, neither of them moved. They stared at the wall as it expanded and contracted, a boundary held together by threads. Each pull of breath from the thing on the other side stretched the drywall thinner. Something bigger was waiting. Something watching through the cracks.

Then, behind them, Billy Cole rose.

His body lifted behind them like he had been pulled up by strings. The blackness had taken over his eyes completely, and his sinister grin had returned, permanently fixed onto his face; even if he wanted to scowl, it wasn't an option.

He blinked once, adjusted his shoulders, and walked forward.

The knife had been in his back pocket the whole time, sealed in the grip of death. Now it came out clean. He opened it without a sound, the silver catching a breath of moonlight filtering through the basement windows and the orange glow of Hell.

Lilly and Jerry didn't hear him approach. They were frozen before the wall, entranced by the grotesque expansion of what lay beyond.

The grimoire at Lilly's feet began to vibrate faintly; it, too, sensed what was coming. She looked down and reached toward it—but it was too late. Billy stepped behind her and, without a noise, drove the blade into her back.

And then the wall howled.

Lilly screamed, a raw sound that tore through the basement. Jerry stumbled back, crashing to the floor, eyes locked on Billy, who was staring right back. The knife came free from Lilly's back in one sharp jerk, only to be buried deeper this time.

She staggered toward Jerry as she stretched out her hand, blood pouring between her fingers. But he didn't reach back for her. He just watched as she crumpled.

"What is happening?" Jerry screamed at Billy.

Inside, the room was loud, the demons in the wall celebrating their catch, screaming and rejoicing as they dragged her magical body into the wall.

Into the pits of Hell.

A howling wind swooshed around the room as the portal began to expand and open even more.

"Where is Lucia?" Jerry demanded Billy to answer.

"Lucia never was. She died in the fire at Sanctuario," he replied in a monotonous drawl, the speech of the dead.

"You're not Billy," Jerry stated, his fangs still protruding from his mouth, his eyes still a yellow diamond glow.

"You've known me too long, sir," Billy continued. "I am Surgat, and I was never interested in this fiend you called a friend, nor was I interested in some whore with her magic tricks in a rundown bar. I needed the witch all along, and you brought her directly to me."

Jerry didn't wait to mourn the loss of his friend, his familiar. Surgat had barely finished speaking before Jerry crossed the distance between them, launching himself into the possessed body of his oldest friend with all the violence centuries of repression could summon.

They hit the concrete hard, the floor beneath them cracking outward like a ripple of shattering glass. Jerry's fists were no longer fists—they were hammers, claws, and ancient tools of execution. Each strike came faster than thought, bone smashing into meat, skin tearing under nails.

Billy's head snapped to the side, then back, then to the other, but the grin never left him. His jaw hung unnaturally, unhinged, teeth bared like a machine forced to mimic laughter.

"You thought it was the book," the thing inside him said, blood leaking from its mouth with each syllable. "That's why this is all so beautiful."

Jerry grabbed the front of his shirt and slammed him

against the floor again and again until teeth skittered across the ground like broken tiles.

"It was never just the book," Surgat rasped through broken lips. "It was the witch and the book."

The wall behind them convulsed.

It began with a moan, but deepened into something far worse. A pressure shift and a psychic siren.

The air folded inward, then exploded out in a howling roar as the wall finally tore itself apart, cracking down the middle, split in half, and giving way to a rupture that seemed endless, a wound in space that bled creatures.

They escaped after being locked up for eons, bursting into the basement.

One after another they surged through the gap: gaunt shadows stitched together by pain, things with wings made of bone and lungs that hissed smoke. Their mouths stretched wide, not for biting, but for screaming.

Long limbs slapped the ground and launched them skyward through the floor above. Gravity was alien to them as they soared through the house, shattering wood, insulation, and beams as they went. Some raced up the staircase and others simply broke through the roof.

Jerry stumbled back, staring upward through the hole in the sky. The house had been torn open as he saw the demons above. Car alarms began firing off one by one. Lights flickered in neighboring houses. The sky, once dim, now churned with ghostly shapes twisting in smoke, some tiny, some gargantuan, all of them wailing.

They were free.

Surgat rose, slowly and methodically. Billy's body

was ruined; his right arm hung useless at his side, his jaw split, and one eye socket caved in. But still, he moved. The demon was burning the body down to its final ember.

"You never understood," Surgat's deep voice boomed heavy in the air. "You came for salvation. You thought the book would close the gate. You thought the girl would stop the end. But she was the end. I've been waiting for the witch for centuries."

The basement trembled as a fresh vibration of energy shuddered through the floor. Cracks spiderwebbed through the foundation. Ash blew from the open wall like a volcanic eruption, for something else was trying to come through now, something larger.

Jerry crouched, looking at the wall once more. His fangs were still extended; all he had to do was turn. A bat, a wolf, the smoke. Anything. He could free himself from the basement right now and take off into another land. But this was Gellert cel Catura. The man who fought wars. He reached into the very depth of his soul, if there was one left, and realized that if he didn't stop this now, he'd have no land to fly to.

"You used my friend," he snarled. "You took her. You lied."

Surgat just roared with laughter. Then he struck. The pair collided like beasts in a cage. With a twist of his shoulder, Surgat hurled Jerry into the support beam, cracking it clean in half. The ceiling above groaned as more debris fell.

Jerry barely held himself upright. His back screamed as his chest heaved. Blood trickled from a gash at his side where Surgat's blade had slipped beneath the ribs. The grimoire lay open where it had fallen, splayed across fractured stone, its spine glowing from within.

Its pages flipped fast. A language Jerry couldn't read bled across the parchment, sigils that squirmed and reformed, shifting from shape to shape, whispering in languages he'd never heard before. And then the movement stopped. The page froze, and one word glowed brighter than the rest.

He staggered forward. Each step felt like dragging a heavy corpse. His fingers trembled as he reached for the book as Surgat pulled at his feet, dragging him back. The second his fingertips brushed the parchment, the words leapt from the page and burned into his thoughts.

Destroy it.

He saw it, not in letters, but in vision. He picked up the grimoire and hurled it into the wall, the demons clawing at it, dragging it in, not knowing what it was.

Then the house began to shake violently, rumbling as the pages in the book began to tear apart in the chasm that was bleeding in the basement.

Surgat screamed, the air shattering as it tore through the basement like thunder. The space buckled, and the demons swirling above them stopped in midair and looked down toward Jerry in anger, screeching.

The wall behind him twisted in on itself, folding like paper doused in flame, the breathing wound sealing in a flash of sulfur and light. And then the wind shifted. A weightless pressure filled the room, followed by a scent. Her scent.

Lucia materialized from the wall from smoke, amorphous smoke and liquid, bilious fluids, taking the shape of the sassy Latina bartender who used to swill magical moonshine in life.

She raised her hand, and the air grew impossibly still. Chains formed from nothing, lightless gold, slick and fluid, sped through the air.

They struck Surgat without warning, wrapping his limbs and binding his chest. He screamed through Billy's throat, the sound sharp and dissonant, a noise that was more vibration than voice as he tried to retreat.

The room convulsed as she pulled Surgat forward, inch by inch, without any resistance. The demon's soul detached from Billy's body, leaving him laid there in his original form. His jaw intact, his arm not broken. The golden chains wrapped around Surgat, pulling the demon back into Hell.

He thrashed as the demons above fell back to the basement, each of them pulled by an invisible force, a gravity from which there was no escape. He called out their names, not curses, but divine syllables meant to unmake what was happening, divine words meant to command. But they had no power here, for he was already unravelling.

Lucia stepped toward him, her voice calm and steady. "This is not your time, demon."

The final word she spoke, no one could understand. But it made the air ring, shattering any window that remained standing in its frame. The chains pulled taut, and with one smooth motion, she dragged Surgat back through the crack, into the dark, into whatever still waited for balance on the other side.

The wall sealed shut and the silence returned. Billy's body lay on the floor like a discarded coat, the blade clattering from his hand. Leaving only the stillness of a house that had once held the dead and had now given some of them back.

EPILOGUE

The streets of Red Bank had begun to stir by the time the two men disappeared into the Range Rover. Sirens were louder now, closer, echoing through the dark like mechanical banshees. Flashing lights painted the treetops in dashes of red and blue.

Neighbors were gathering in the cold, their robes pulled tight as their arms were folded across their chests, their faces turned toward the house with the missing roof. Smoke still drifted up from the open wound in its bones, and even the curious knew better than to get close to something that had just spat a piece of Hell back into the sky.

Jerry kept his head low as he guided Billy toward the car. Billy said nothing, he just limped as Jerry held him upright, staring blankly at the ground beneath his feet.

The Range Rover was right where Lilly had left it, parked with the door slightly ajar. The keys still sat in the dash, as if she knew she wouldn't be driving it again.

Jerry got Billy into the passenger seat and pushed the

door shut. The vehicle's interior smelled faintly of her, leather and cloves. He sat in the driver's seat for a moment without starting the engine, staring at the madness at the end of the street.

The silence between them was thick, and neither companion was ready to break it.

Billy looked worse under the soft dome light, his blood crusted at his ear and temple. His pupils were uneven as the black tar slowly was removing itself from the whites of his eyes. He rubbed at his face, pausing; even the shape of his own jaw felt foreign. After a long moment, he turned to Jerry.

"I'm trying to remember, Jerry. I can't remember."

"What do you mean, Billy?"

"I remember *something*. My body wasn't mine, and I remember that that wasn't a pleasant feeling. I tried to stop it, but it felt like I was under...well, not underwater, because water is lighter. It felt like I was buried under layers of molten tar. I couldn't move, even if I wanted to." He closed his eyes. "Was I the one who caused all that?"

Jerry stared out the windshield at the road ahead. "No," he lied as he turned the key, the engine humming to life.

The drive back to Manhattan was long and silent, broken only by the low murmur of the radio as it picked up The Mamas & the Papas. Billy drifted in and out of sleep as Jerry drove like he was on autopilot, the city skyline eventually blooming in the distance. He hadn't thought about what came next.

He never had that luxury.

Lilly was the one who saw the moves ahead in this

city, who pulled the strings behind the scenes. Now she was gone. And Jerry was just left with the silence she left behind in their short time of knowing each other. But this was what he was used to. The curse that was bestowed upon him.

It never got easier.

When they arrived at the penthouse, the sky was beginning to bruise at the edges. They had made it home just in time. Jerry helped Billy up the elevator, one arm slung around his shoulders as the city beyond the glass moved on, oblivious to what had happened in Red Bank.

And for a split second, Jerry hesitated walking through the elevator doors to the penthouse. He thought he might find her there, half-drunk, leaning on the window with that smirk she wore when she knew something no one else did. But the space inside was still.

It was a gripping reminder of losing someone. The moment when you walk back into a house after a breakup, the moment when you wake up in the morning after experiencing a death in the family.

He helped Billy to the sofa, laid him down, and turned on a single lamp. The light was soft, yellow, and too warm for how cold the world felt now, and for the first time in centuries, the caretaker was being taken care of. Billy curled into the cushions as his body still tried to recalibrate—his mind still somewhere else entirely.

Jerry paused for a moment before closing the large red curtains that shielded the daylight from his skin. He walked slowly into the kitchen. He was hungry and thirsty at the same time. His mind exhausted.

And there it was.

A note resting on top of Jerry's grimoire on the marble countertop, held down by her gold ring. He stared at it for a long time before picking it up.

I believe this belongs to you, and I think it's time we part ways.

Don't worry about me. I've died before, Jerry.

Consequences of being an immortal witch.

I am sure you suffer from your fair share of consequences.

I suggest you leave town, go far. Lay low. Buy a house. A small one so as not to attract attention. We both know you've attracted enough of it already.

And as for me, maybe I'll see you soon, maybe I won't.

–L

He read it thrice.

The second time slower as he formed a small smile.

The third time with a kind of stillness he hadn't felt in centuries as he took a deep breath. There was no message of love and no vengeance for Jerry letting her fall into the wall. There was no promise that she'd come back.

Just instructions on how a vampire and his familiar would survive the next stage of their lives. It gave him pleasure to know that somehow she survived. That perhaps there was a caveat to his curse.

Maybe she knew all along.

In the other room, Billy breathed unevenly. He would heal, eventually. But they were marked now.

And if they stayed, more doors would open and more things would crawl through.

THE NEXT EVENING, Billy had regained most of his normalcy. He showered as Jerry finished packing up a few boxes. His clothing, his grimoire, and his coffin. He walked into the shower as Billy was still cleansing.

"How you doin', champ?" Jerry asked.

"Fine as can be, given the circumstances," Billy said. Then, looking at Jerry with uncertainty, and the slightest betrayal of fear in his eyes, he asked, "What's the plan?"

"Well, I think, my friend, that city life is not for us. We've clearly overstayed our welcome here. I'll talk to you on the ride about the details. But we've got a long way to go and a lot of work to do."

"Where are we going?" Billy shouted through the shower glass.

"A little town called Rancho Corvalis."